SHADOW TIER

2ND EDITION

BOOK 1 - SHADOW TIER SERIES

STEVEN STRATTON

PRAISE FOR SHADOW TIER

"Steve Stratton has created a unique and interesting protagonist that reminds me of a young Painter Crowe. Thriller fans will want to pick this one up ASAP." Todd Wilkins - Best Thriller Books

"A fast-paced, anything-goes revenge thriller with non- stop action that transports the reader back to the brutal drug wars of the late '90s." Steve Netter - Best Thriller Books

"A vicious journey of gut-wrenching loss and action- packed retribution with a new take on the war on drugs!" Kashif Hussain - Best Thriller Books

"From the opening rounds of a restaurant firefight to the death knell of a notorious Mexican cartel, Steve Stratton's 'Shadow Tier' is one hell of an adventure barely on the side of legal. It's a movie script made to order with every warrior's fantasy target—the takedown of El Chapo himself!" Julie Watson - Julie Watson Reviews

Published in the United States of America by Pratton Media

Trade paperback – Feb 2024 ISBN-13 978-1-963298-01-7
eBook edition – Feb 2024 ISBN-13 978-1-963298-00-0

❀ Created with Vellum

The best revenge is not to be like your enemy.

—Marcus Aurelius

For Elle, who lit the fire.

1

Mexican Army Special Forces Command, Mexico
We're going hot," Master Sergeant Lance Bear Wolf said to his assembled special forces team. What had been planned as a training mission with Mexico's new Fuerza Especial de Reacción special forces unit had turned operational.

Providence...coincidence, I don't care. I'm not going to let any more families suffer at the hands of the drug cartels like mine has.

Recent operations against the cartel by the regular Mexican Army had resulted in twenty-three soldiers lost in three ambushes. The cartel had shot down two helicopters and badly damaged another. They needed help and the United States had offer Wolf's in country team from 3rd Battalion 20th Special Forces Florida National Guard.

Wolf and his team had used the advanced capabilities of American satellite technology to find a suitable target. Only a short walk from a clandestine runway, the level of activity at the target was frenetic. Only one problem, the target was secured by a multi-layered combination of sophisticated technical devices and patrols.

Wolf and Staff Sergeant Oleus LeBlanc, his senior weapons sergeant, had built a hide site on an earlier recon and spent four cramped days inside. They took shifts doing surveillance and found and reported the technical measures and patrols surrounding the target.

Major Carlos Gonzalez commander of the Reaccion unit and American team leader, Captain Alonzo Franks, planned an up-close look. Wolf would lead the officers in with LeBlanc providing security.

They would chopper into an offset position eight kilometers and two ridge lines away to minimize the risk of detection, then patrol the rest of the way to the hide.

As they had flown in, the wheels of the Black Hawk smacked the top of the canopy as the pilot danced along the mountainous terrain. Wolf smiled, he like fast and dangerous. Sitting back in his seat he had closed his eyes and sung his death song.

As a Crow Indian warrior, it was a traditional way to prepare for battle, asking the spirits to help him be brave and die with honor if it was his time. Prior to infiltration, Gonzalez had questioned him about the practice and his growing up on the Crow Reservation.

Wolf told the major the abbreviated version of growing up on the reservation and learning how to survive and hunt in the woods at an early age. He told the story of his vision quest and how a wolf turned maiden had spoken to him. He left out the part about his father over-dosing on heroin supplied by a Mexican drug cartel.

The helicopter flared to a hover, and they repelled through the thick jungle canopy. When Wolf's boots hit the loamy soil, he shifted his mindset from planner to hunter.

He became his namesake and took his time smelling, listening, and picking their way through the outer layers of the site's security.

They belly-crawled the last fifty meters to the hide, where Franks gagged at the stench left by the rotting jungle combined with odorous remains of Wolf and LeBlanc stay.

The combination sweat, urine, and decay assaulted the uninitiated.

Franks was first in and stuffed his head into his arm to stifle his coughing. He shrugged and gave Wolf a look. Sorry, amigo. Wolf shook his head as Gonzalez crammed in and made it three men in hide built for two and gear.

Wolf pointed some of the marijuana growing areas around the twenty-five-hundred-meter-long valley. "Look to your right along the runway and you'll see the lab and processing operations, Wolf whispered.

"Our target. The Marines can deal with the marijuana," Gonzalez said.

"Agreed," Franks said.

"Our options are forced insertion via parachute or by helicopter assault. I like the aircraft and paratrooper option. Fast and hard," Wolf said.

The officers whispered among themselves. "It's a company-sized operation at a minimum," Franks said.

They were broken from their thoughts by barking dogs. "Dog handlers headed our way," LeBlanc radioed. Gonzalez and Franks turned to go, but Wolf held them back.

"Hold on. Let me figure out where they are," he said then crawled out of the hide next to LeBlanc. A beat later he radioed. "They'll be on us in five, we have to bug out right now."

After the officers climbed out, Wolf pulled on a log and the entrance to the hide collapsed making it look like another pile of jungle debris. He headed north across the face of the mountain toward a waterfall he had memorized from their planning.

The dogs and their handlers were closing fast, not worried about tripping alarms or booby-traps.

Wolf went as fast as he dared while scanning ahead, the echoes of the dogs lessening as the roar of the waterfall overwhelmed his hearing.

He worked his way along the wet, rocky edge, looking for a place to cross. Under a ledge, he found a cavern, damp and passable. He crept into the void and was joined by Gonzalez and Franks. LeBlanc stayed at the entrance, rifle at the ready.

"You guys go. I'll hold them off and catch up with you later," he said.

"No! We stay and fight as a team," the captain yelled over the rushing water.

"This space is too small to fight from. One good burst and we are all dead," Gonzalez said.

"He's right, Wolf said.

"Roger that," Franks said. "Let's go."

LeBlanc swapped positions and took point, leading Franks and Gonzalez out of the cavern then around an outcropping and up the wet rock face. Wolf watched them for a second, then spun and dropped his ruck.

He took off his boots, stuffing them inside. Now barefoot and feeling more secure on damp rock, he slung his M4 around his back and drew his Randall fighting knife while he waited for the dogs.

This battle would be one-on-one.

Two minutes after the others had left, Wolf tensed as the dogs stopped at the entrance to cavern. Between the roar of the water and the dogs barking and snarling he couldn't tell what the handlers were saying or planning.

They were playing it smart and fired through the waterfall into the cavern. Bullets ricocheted in every direction, and one ripped a stinging groove into Wolf's right thigh.

He glanced at the groove in his leg. It will have to wait.

Then someone jumped into the space followed by another man. They stood bunched up their heads swiveling back and forth as they tried to peer into the darkness.

Wolf charged out of the darkness pushing the men into each other. They slipped on the damp rock and He was on top of them slashing and stabbing. Taking them in order of closeness he dispatched the first man then was on the second when the guard got a shot off.

It missed Wolf's head, but muzzle flash blinded him for a beat. They wrestled for their lives. Wolf holding the guard's rifle barrel in one hand while they fought over control the knife. Wolf grunted and the guard cursed as they moved, and counter moved.

Wolf found himself on the bottom as they rolled. The guard moved to his side, which freed Wolf's legs. He snaked his legs around the guard's head and neck.

He curled up bring the guard closer and twisted his wrist to free the knife. The guard attempted to stand but Wolf buried the seven-inch blade in his rib cage and sawed.

The guard's scream turned into a gurgle. Wide eyed he stared at his opponent. Wolf had seen the look before. Shock, despair then nothing.

Wolf pushed him away and stood breathing deep and ragged. He make out someone yelling. He sheathed his knife, adjusted his rifle and heaved on his pack. Then he rolled the dead and their weapons into the rushing water.

He stopped at the opposite side and popped a CS grenade rolling across the cavern. Then he scooted around the side of an outcropping of rock and out of sight from the dog handlers. Looking up he could see LeBlanc and the officers making their way up the chunky rock face.

He followed and joined them at the summit. On the other side of the crest, they drank water and called for exfil.

Gonzalez scowled. "Now that we're busted, we need to accelerate our timeline or there won't be anything left on site," he said.

2

Sinaloa State, Mexico

The task force commander, a Mexican Army lieutenant colonel named Miguel Segura, had a Ranger mindset. After reviewing the surveillance and reconnaissance data, Segura and his staff had come to the same conclusion as Gonzalez and Franks

This would be the Lion Squadron's first operation in Mexico's new war on drugs. An airborne insertion from a C-130J Super Hercules aircraft filled with sixty-four Mexican special forces paratroopers. To include eight Lions, which Gonzalez would lead.

Four Mexican Army medium transport helicopters with twelve troopers each would serve as a backup and quick reaction force, staging in a landing zone seven kilometers away to await orders.

Wolf's team was assigned the role of providing pre-drop intelligence for the coordinated assault. Wolf and Franks, with their split teams inserted first.

WOLF and his team were in place two hundred meters from the end of the runway, their elevation giving them a clear line of sight down

its length. Franks and the other half of the split team were in place to their south as a blocking force.

He took note of the time, 0630 local, as teammate Sergeant First Class Stewart Portes used a Nikon E3 to capture photos of a Beechcraft King Air 300 on final approach in the pre-dawn light.

The big turboprop aircraft touched down, braked, and turned around at a wide spot near their end of runway, then taxied back to a loading area.

Wolf watched through their spotting scope as three armed gunmen walked off the airplane first, weapons at the ready, and two more formed a small perimeter at the nose and tail of the aircraft.

Another armed man exited and turned to extend a steadying hand to a woman who shrugged it off and strode down the stairs like she owned the place. In the weak light from the lab buildings, she moved like a cat. Dressed in tan cargo pants, a tight white shirt with a pistol at her side she looked like a cat who could kill you for profit and or pleasure.

When she turned and scanned the horizon, it was as if she was looking right at him. And he knew the face. He'd seen during the pre-mission briefing.

He glanced down to a laminated set of headshots he liked to call his "post office wall." She was the only woman on the page. Eliana Cortes, sister of Alejandro Cortés, El Chapo Guzman's lieutenant for west coast operations.

Wolf whispered to Portes. "You on this, brother?" He looked at his watch. The main body should airdrop in minutes.

"Oh, yeah, I'm gettin' all of it."

A Jeep sped up to the plane, and the woman turned to acknowledge someone rushing to meet her.

"Any later and they would have seen the—"

Portes was interrupted by Sergeant First Class Henry Harris, the senior comms operator on the team channel.

"Assault force is one mike out."

Wolf waited for Franks to radio his understanding, then he and his element advanced down the mountain.

As he led the men out of the jungle, he was fired upon by a security patrol from across the runway. He dropped, rolled, and returned fire, killing one gunman with a three-round burst before the rest of the team overwhelmed the other two shooters.

Standing, he turned back in time to see the C-130J at eight hundred feet above the deck with the last of the paratroopers exiting the ramp via static line. The more experienced men slipped air from their parachutes to get to the ground faster, and many were already shooting down from under their canopies.

In the growing firefight, more cartel soldiers had been alerted and spilled from a barracks to engage the paratroopers. One of Gonzalez's black-clad team members hung limp in his harnesses and hit the ground without rising to the fight.

Wolf wanted to scream at the paratroopers to slip air. His stomach churned as he remembered being fired on during his low-level jump into Grenada. Wolf scanned the fight, looking for anywhere to help. The aircraft had restarted it's engines.

He turned and yelled, "The King Air, follow me!" He sprinted off down the runway, It will only need half of the distance.

LeBlanc sprinted to his side. "Half mile, let's go loser."

As the team pounded down the tarmac, they had to stop twice to engage gunmen who fired at them from the wood line. Wolf realized they weren't going to make it in time to stop the plane.

He halted the team and had everyone stand abreast on the east side. If they could concentrate their gunfire into the cockpit and engines of the King Air, they might have a chance. He took two deep breaths and settled himself, watching it roar closer.

"Remember to lead out in front of the nose and let them fly through our fire," Wolf said. The pilot broke contact with the ground and raised the landing gear.

The plane's speed increased and just before reaching the team position the pilot turned it onto a knife edge for a high-g banking climb, the wing tip just feet from the ground.

As the aircraft flashed by he unleashed his own rifle barrage. He saw Eliana Cortes flash by in a window, eyes on fire, presenting him a middle finger.

He heard rounds impact the skin of the aircraft before it climbed away, rising just over the trees then disappearing over the crest of the mountain into the dawn.

Franks his element called from the wood line and joined them on the runway. "Who the heck was on the aircraft?" Franks asked.

"She's Eliana Cortes, sister of El Chapo's right-hand guy for the west coast."

THE OPERATION WAS CONSIDERED the Mexican Army's best result to date, and it was trumpeted in the media. Many millions of dollars of drugs taken out of circulation. Dozens of weapons, RPGs and, interesting enough, Israeli-sourced encrypted communications equipment.

The president of Mexico held a jubilant news conference touting the mission's success. Experienced journalists thought was perhaps a bit over the top in its assertion of turning a corner in the war on Mexican drug cartels.

The nation mourned the loss of three Mexican Army Special Forces troopers and two of Gonzalez's special operators, all unnamed to protect their families from cartel reprisals. Their flag-draped coffins lay in state in the Palacio Nacional for three days and their full-dress military funerals were carried on national television.

At the combined wake held for the two Lions, Wolf told those assembled he was honored to serve with such brave men. It wasn't the first time, nor the last Wolf would see courage in battle or have to bring his own to a fight in Mexico.

3

Puerto Vallarta, Mexico

On leave after the mission, Wolf joined his mother Alma and stepfather Andy in the resort town. They were in Mexico at the request of an old friend of Andy's from Vietnam.

At the beach he sipped tequila with them and watched the sunset over the Pacific. The last of the sunbathers had left as the sun disappeared.

Now was his favorite time of the day, when the steep angle of the sunset provided deep reds, oranges, and dark blues. He relaxed his eyes to widen his gaze.

He turned and clinked glasses with his mother, Alma Bear Wolf-Anderson. Enjoying a drink with her had felt odd earlier in his life, but now it felt perfectly normal.

It had been twelve years since he had an opportunity to join his mother and stepfather for anything more than a hasty dinner. All three of the Bear Wolf - Anderson children had joined the U.S. Army, and family gatherings were few.

"It's been a year of big changes for you. Are you are missing your old life?" she asked.

His mother was the most intuitive and insightful person he knew.

Her questions had always gone right to the heart of a matter, connecting the unconnected, but allowing him to see his path and make his own choices.

He sighed. "Yes, I suppose so."

"But you're still serving our country," Wolf's stepfather Andy said. "When I left Vietnam alive, I felt like I was cheating my dead teammates."

Wolf hung his head and closed his eyes remembering his lost friends and teammates. "It took me a while to figure it out, but I understand the feeling. It's why I joined the guard. To continue to serve and honor them," Wolf said raising up and locking eyes with Andy.

The next morning, Wolf ran down the beach and worked his kinks out. The fresh scab on his thigh was tight as he picked up speed. A reminder of how close life and death are. Inches, minutes, a blink apart.

He wasn't used to having multiple days off in a row, and he thanked his spirit guide for putting him in this place and time.

Odd. Why in Mexico and why now?

After breakfast, he would help his parents make the drive from Puerto Vallarta back to Tucson. The three of them would take turns driving and continue to get caught up on what little Wolf could tell them about his life and exploits.

On their second day working their way along the coast to the U.S.-Mexico border crossing, Wolf suggested they stop at a restaurant Gonzalez said served excellent seafood. The owner was his brother, Hector. He would take good care of them.

The El Gran Pez restaurant northwest of Culiacan in Sinaloa stood like an island in an ocean of debris, the hint of a bygone fishing industry still wafting around on the afternoon breeze from the Pacific.

The Sinaloa drug cartel's breathtaking affluence was on display. Bright colored cigarette boats under covered berths in the marina and expensive cars in parking lot stood in stark contrast among rusty, less well-maintained boats and vehicles.

Wolf and his parents emerged from the pickup after the five-hour drive. The area had a strange odor of dead fish and rusty decay. Why does it have to be in Sinaloa?

As they stretched, three blacked-out Range Rovers raced into the parking lot nose-to-tail and skidded to a stop in front of the entrance. A security detail leaped out and several men with submachine guns faced outward in a perimeter.

Three more escorted a slender woman inside. She was tall, with a lean, athletic build, long black hair, and perfect skin under extra dark sunglasses. She had the look of a predator.

"Eliana Cortes," Wolf whispered to his stepfather, turning away. "Sinaloa."

"None of our business," Andy said, shrugging.

"The cartels have been my business since I my first trip to Colombia," he said.

"Well, now your mother is excited about eating here, let's be alert, have a nice lunch, and be on our way." Andy said and led their small group to the restaurant's front door. When he pulled it open, a rush of cool air spilled out.

Crap, head on a swivel, Wolf.

A handsome young man met them just inside the restaurant. "Good afternoon," he said. "I am Hector Gonzalez. Are you Mr. Wolf?"

"Yes." he gestured to Andy and Alma. "These are my parents."

Hector Gonzalez smiled with genuine warmth. "My brother said you might be stopping by on your way home. Please let me show you to your table."

The restaurant was busy at midday, and Hector led them to a large booth at the windows overlooking the harbor.

He took note of escape routes and choke points as was his customary process, and the bizarre island of elegance in its rundown seaside setting.

Muted tones on the walls framed what looked to be original Joaquin Sorolla and Francisco Goya prints of fishing and life on the water. A sign at the far end of the dining area read VIP. Two men from the Cortes security team guarded the door.

"I apologize for seating you next to the kitchen," Hector said, reaching to a nearby cart for a bottle. "But this booth gives the best view of the ocean. Please accept this gift of wine for your inconvenience. I think you will find it pairs well with our fish entrees."

Wolf's parents ordered the chef's specialty, Colorado Snapper with a lemon-butter caper sauce. He ordered Goliath grouper, wanting to compare it with the grouper back in Florida.

What was to be a pleasant family lunch had turned chilly with the presence of the drug princess and her security team. Wolf attempted to send a message, raising his glass of wine in a toast.

"Here's to a safe trip home."

His parents raised their glasses. Andy's suppressed scowl his response. After a few minutes, he and his parents were talking and laughing. Another forty minutes and be back on the road.

The waitress appeared with their food. The air was filled with the aroma of grilled fish and exotic spices. Wolf was savoring a bite of grouper when he noticed Hector being escorted toward the kitchen with a scowl on his face.

His escort was a goon with a Heckler and Koch MP5 who was steering Hector with a hand on his shoulder. A sudden crash of plates and a burst of automatic gunfire sent people screaming and running.

Threat identified, and in his response flow Wolf rushed toward the scene Browning High Power pistol in hand. He glanced behind to see Andy following with his Colt .45 at the ready. He crept to the edge of a wall and peered around the corner.

The large man who had been steering Hector held his still smoking MP5 at the ready as he stood over a lifeless waitress. Hector was on the floor, his hands in a don't shoot me position. Was it an accident?

From his semi-concealed position, Wolf yelled in Spanish for the thug to drop his weapon. Surprised again, the goon swung his MP5 in Wolf's direction.

He didn't hesitate and put two rounds into the gunman's chest. As the man dropped, spraying more rounds, another burst of automatic gunfire cracked past him, a round striking Andy in the right arm.

"I'm hit!" Andy said. Wolf pushed him back behind the wall and snatched a cloth napkin from a nearby cart. He wrapped it tightly around his stepfather's wound. It filled the white cloth with crimson blood.

"Get Mom! See you at the truck."

As Andy left, he crawled behind a column and knelt. The room was in chaos, with bodies slumped across tables and littering the floor from the gunman's random spray.

A security detail surrounded Eliana Cortes as they rushed her out of the VIP room. As they moved toward the front door, he locked eyes with her. Was there a moment of recognition? "Kill Hector and the Americans!" she shouted.

Bullets cracked against the column, splintering the wood veneer. The gunman was shooting from the middle of the dining area. Need to stop the threat so more innocent people don't get hurt.

He moved around the left side of the column and shot three times in rapid succession to put the man down.

Wolf holstered his pistol and retrieved the MP5 and extra magazines. In his peripheral vision, he saw his parents running toward the kitchen and he hoped was a rear exit to the parking lot and safety.

Headed for the service door. Good.

MP5 raised, Wolf worked his way to the front door, where he saw a cartel security man in the shadows, his weapon pointed outside. No, you don't!

He put two rounds into his upper back, and the gunman toppled out of the door, causing more screams from those who had fled outside.

He kicked away the man's weapon and scanned the scene. Wounded staff and diners littered the parking lot. Tires screeched as two of the three black Range Rovers roared away.

From his viewpoint in the doorway, Wolf thought he should have seen his parents getting into the truck by now. He performed a combat reload, inserting a fresh magazine in the machine pistol. He slapped the charging handle to ready the weapon, then stopped cold.

Over the clamor, he could just hear his mother's voice. She was singing.

Oh, Mom...no!

Rushing back into the restaurant, Wolf heard his mother finish her death song and scream a war cry. Andy's .45 barked twice and seconds later the sound of an MP5 on full auto erupted from the kitchen area.

He blasted through the waiter's door and found two dead gunmen. To his right, another gunman who stood over bodies was turning to shoot.

He killed him with a three-round burst and shot him twice more as he stepped over the man.

At the open the service door, he found Andy facing back in and draped over his mother.

No, no, no!

He checked Andy for a pulse, nothing. A concentrated circle of wounds in his back confirmed his fate.

You saved her.

A lump formed in Wolf's throat as he slid the man he looked up to off his mother. He checked her for injuries, two entrance wounds in her back, no exits.

Putting his fingers on her carotid he found a pulse, weak but steady. A few feet away, Hector lay dead, his arms around a woman Wolf suspected was his wife.

Alma was alive, and Wolf's combat medical training would ensure she lived. As he tended to her wounds, the rising wail of sirens brought hope.

He stood and disassembled his handgun. Then he threw the parts and holster into the kitchen trash, pulling wet food garbage up over his deposit. Next, he slid Andy's .45 and the MP5 across the floor to the lifeless cartel soldier.

Wolf cradled his mother. Don't give up on me, Alma Nighthawk, I need you.

The restaurant swarmed with Mexican law enforcement and medics.

He handed over his mother to some medics and stood as they loaded her onto a stretcher. Blood dripping from his hands he spun to find a towel and found a police officer with his pistol drawn. He was ordered to the ground.

"I'm her son, not cartel. I need to go with my mother," he said his hands out palms up.

Another officer appeared pistol drawn and screamed. "Last chance. Down or dead."

He said nothing and complied, laying prostrate on the gritty asphalt with his arms held away from his body. The first officer held him at gunpoint while the second officer grabbed his arms and handcuffed them behind his back.

"Come on guys, please? I'm her son, let me go with her. Please, I'm not a threat."

Face down and handcuffed, he twisted and watched the ambulance drive out of sight, lights flashing and siren wailing. Wolf squeezed his eyes shut, tears streaming he visualized the coming war and sang his death song.

4

Los Mochis, Sinaloa

The thirty-minute drive in the back of the police car gave him time to think. He had been fourteen when his stepfather Andy came into their lives, a kind man who treated he and his mother well. He became the father Wolf wanted.

The Army had taught him to push his emotion aside under duress and work the problem in front of him with cold precision. The training wasn't working. This was different, the problems many and proliferating.

He struggled to contain a growl. His hands were balled into fists he drummed on his thighs. His thoughts flashed back and forth between the need to care for his wounded mother and the white-hot desire to retaliate for his father's death.

He just had to get through this nonsense with the Mexican police. Even though he was well connected to the Mexican military through Major Gonzalez, it was only beneficial if he got a phone call.

He'd learned it wasn't uncommon for prisoners to disappear into the Mexican prison sub-culture for a long time. Sometimes forever. Wolf understood why he was being treated this way. It had been ordered, and he thought he knew who. Eliana Cortes.

Wolf sat at a table in a windowless cinder block room. His handcuffs had been removed. The interrogation room had been excluded from recent police station renovations. Exhausted best described the building, mood, and activity level of the police officers and administrators.

A younger, fit-looking man with a thick black mustache and shaggy eyebrows entered the room. He rolled in an old TV and a bulky VCR. His well-tailored blue suit and effortless movement set him apart from the other cops.

He set a battered Panasonic audio cassette recorder on the table and sat down across from him. They stared at one another for a moment, then the man spoke in English.

"Mr. Wolf, I'm Lieutenant Victor Cárdenas. I would like your statement about today's events at El Gran Pez." Without waiting for an answer, the lieutenant turned on the cassette recorder. "Tell me what happened."

He knew how these things usually went. He had conducted interrogations. He expected a multi-hour visit, given the carnage at the restaurant, but hoped the lieutenant would get to the point.

"How long is this going to take? I need to get to the hospital for my mother," he snapped, clutching his hands together in his lap.

The lieutenant smiled and nodded. "Indeed, I understand. I will make this as quick as possible."

Wolf told his version of events at the restaurant and noticed the detective wasn't taking notes.

Why am I wasting my time? They won't do anything against the cartel.

He noticed Cárdenas bristle at the mention of Eliana Cortes and her security detail.

He spoke for eight minutes, and the cop thanked him for his story. "Your ability to remember details is impressive."

If you only knew. The Army had sent him to an Agency training facility where experts had honed his good memory to just short of perfect.

The sound of Cárdenas sliding a video into the VCR broke him from his reverie. The playback of restaurant surveillance video confirmed Wolf's account of cartel soldiers shooting up the place.

When the video showed Andy and Alma entering the kitchen to escape, the detective stopped the dining room video and replaced it with another video cassette. He fast-forwarded for a few seconds and then hit pause. The view this time was from the kitchen.

"Are these people your parents?"

Wolf nodded, and Cárdenas restarted the video. With a lump in his throat, he watched his stepdad work to get Alma to safety. He sighed as Andy ignored his own safety to get the service door open. Watching him get hit again and fall backward was harder than he expected.

He forced himself not to show emotion in front of the officer when his mother appeared in the frame, leaning over her husband and fussing at his wounds. She sat him up and ran her hands over his torso. They came away drenched in blood. He was still alive but dying.

The voices were hard to discern over the gunfire.

But his mother's voice got louder and louder.

"What is she saying here?" Cárdenas asked as he stopped the playback.

"She's singing her death song."

Wolf had only heard his mother sing her song a few times in his life, and he remembered the way her voice carried on the wind.

Cárdenas raised an eyebrow. "I was raised in the U.S., and I have never heard of this before."

He stared at his mother's image and nodded. "They don't teach Crow Indian culture in American schools. We sing it before battle when we believe it's our time to die."

The lieutenant restarted the video. Wolf's mother stood tall, screamed a war cry, and fired a pistol at targets off-screen. It had been her suppressing fire with Andy's pistol he had heard.

Then she turned to help another woman toward the door when they both were shot from off-screen, bullets slamming hard into them from behind and blood spattering everywhere as they collapsed.

Wolf's heart swelled with admiration and desolation as a wounded Andy rose to fling himself over Alma. Then a second gunman appeared in the kitchen video and fired into the prone bodies until his MP5 was empty. Wolf entered the video and killed the gunman before blocking the camera to dispose of his weapon.

"Azul's shooting of the waitress was an unmistakable accidental. You and your parents turned an accident into a massacre," Cárdenas said, looking at him. Not angry or accusing, as cops will do. Just a statement.

This suggested to Wolf the lieutenant wasn't convinced his statement was true, but rather an attempt to get an uncontrolled response from him.

"Accidental or not, you know the guy who started the gunfight," he said.

"Yes, he's a mean one, from Eliana's security detail. We know of him. But you could have run away like the rest."

"Would you have?" he countered. "We had no choice. People were dying."

"And your firearm, Mr. Wolf? The one you used with such great proficiency?"

"I picked up a discarded handgun from the floor. I couldn't just stand by and wait to be killed any more than you would."

"Yes," the lieutenant admitted, then was silent for a moment. Then he pushed a manila envelope containing Wolf's wallet, passport, truck keys, and cellphone across the table.

Wolf nodded and stood, focused on controlling his frustration. "Lieutenant, what is the chance you can find these killers and bring them to justice?"

He shrugged and shook his head.

"Finding them is simple, my friend, but I am sorry to admit it is unlikely they will be brought to justice. It's a situational thing in my country. But you are free to go for now. We will give you a ride back to your vehicle. Your mother is at Medical Center hospital." Cárdenas extended his hand and Wolf shook it. "I will pray for her speedy recovery."

"Thank you, L-T," Wolf said, using the military shorthand reserved for lieutenants who garner respect from their troops.

"Gracias," Cárdenas said.

Wolf wasn't two steps out of the interrogation room and his mind was one hundred percent focused on his mother. He sent a quick request to her spirit guide, the nighthawk, for her strength to recover.

5

El Rancho Cortes, Sinaloa, Mexico

Eliana Cortes sat across from her older brother, Alejandro, and gritted her teeth. He was on the phone with a source at the Los Mochis police department about the shooting investigation.

As usual, he was shouting at the informant who was certain to be quivering in his boots and fearing for his life. Alejandro had many such compensations for his shortfalls.

Unfortunately, he was not the inspirational leader his father had been, and this was troublesome. Despite Alejandro's somewhat cartoonish portrayal of a gangster, he was a very dangerous man.

Most people found his lack of emotion terrifying. If asked, Alejandro would say their father, Romulo, had beaten it out of him. He saw himself as the future cartel boss of bosses, challenged by no one.

Eliana thought back to their early years. He had always made sure she knew her place in the organization. She could be wealthy, but she could never be in charge.

The Cortes family roots as simple farmers belied their current profession. The switch from growing Mexican staples to marijuana had in the early 1980s brought them into an alliance with Miguel Ángel Félix Gallardo, known by his alias, El Padrino, the Godfather.

Alejandro's family had stayed on the production side of the business. Until Romulo gave the Federal Police what they needed to capture El Padrino.

Since then, his business had continued to expand its operational footprint and stamp out competition until it become the leading supplier in Sinaloa.

Romulo had been the first to aligned himself with El Chapo. The pivot from supplier to the head of west coast operations and distribution was Alejandro's idea.

Change accelerated after Romulo's passing in December 1990. But the Cortes base of operations continued to be the family ranch outside of Los Mochis. Eliana thought it had lost its old-world charm and begun to take on the air of a military base.

Her brother ended the call to the police department and glared at her, not speaking or moving. Eliana went on the offensive.

"Alejandro, we are in this situation because Hector was stealing cocaine from our shipments." She tried hard to sound calm and convincing, but no one knew better how mercurial her brother could be when provoked.

"Sister, I am confused. What did Hector do to start a war in his restaurant?"

"It wasn't Hector. It was an American."

"I send you to get our cocaine back and your guard dog Azul kills a waitress because she dropped a tray. Then an American kills Azul and all hell breaks loose? Why is that?"

She drew an angry breath to reply, but he cut her off.

"Don't speak...I'll tell you." He struck his forehead with an index finger several times. "You didn't use your brain."

"But I was smart. I did not order any shooting."

"You were smart?" he scoffed. "Your 'smarts' have elevated our status in the news as killers of innocent Mexicans and Americans. The Americans will push our government to act against us."

Eliana sat unmoving. There would never be a positive spin on the lost cocaine, or the political capital they would spend fixing her mess. In all her thirty-four years, Alejandro had never respected her. He wouldn't start now.

It had been her idea to establish the El Gran Pez restaurant as a trans-shipment facility. It had been successful because no one batted an eye at the old fishing village.

Since then, Eliana had worked hard to prove she could operate on her own. With El Chapo as her guide, she had transformed from Romulo's little girl to a feared member of the cartel and one prone to violence.

Alejandro was angry over the restaurant shootout. It had burned the site as a viable trans-shipment location. The police would be watching it for weeks, if not months.

"Tell me about the meddling Americans?" he asked.

"We don't know who they are, but they may have been ex-military or police. Whatever their training it was not enough for my men." she said, with a smug smile.

Alejandro turned and stared out the bay window at the garden.

"Not enough? Are you stupid? The three Americans killed seven of your men." He shook his head in disgust. "Work with Joaquin to find out everything on them you can. The police interrogated the surviving American. He must have fed them some great story, because he was released."

"Yes, Alejandro."

"One more thing, Eliana. How are you going to pay me back for the lost product while fixing this problem?"

She had been waiting for the question. She froze, mouth open eyes blinking. Her brother was ruthless in business and her status as his sister changed none of that. She'd seen what he did to men who caused problems, and who knew what he would do to his own flesh and blood.

"Pay you back? The loss was to us both." She growled. "I'll give you twenty percent of my take until I pay it off."

With a wave of his hand, he cut her off. "Taking money from you is not a lesson in responsibility. Nor in respect. You must learn violence is not always the best option." He took her elbow. "Come with me into the courtyard."

Eliana stiffened but followed him into the courtyard. Large palm trees and colorful flowers lined the high-walled perimeter. In the center was a large stone fountain. Eliana's blood ran cold at the sight of two bodyguards and Tomas, the ranch blacksmith. Tomas wouldn't look at her.

"Tomas is a master at this sort of thing," Alejandro said with a smirk.

He was waving fire from a propane torch back and forth across a red-hot plate bearing raised letters. Eliana's heart raced. Before she could say anything, the two bodyguards grabbed her and held her arm down on the wide ledge of the fountain.

She struggled and kicked trying to escape their grasp, but it was useless. She glared at her brother with eyes filled with rage and tears.

"What do you think you're doing, Alejandro?" She said and turned to the bodyguards. "Release me!" she screamed. Their lack of compliance and blank stares frightened her even more.

He nodded to the blacksmith. He picked up the plate with tongs and pressed the red-hot brand onto her forearm, the flesh sizzling under the intense heat. Hot tears burned her eyes, and she grunted through clenched teeth, but she didn't cry out. She wouldn't give him the satisfaction, and she was much tougher than he knew.

But her pain was incalculable.

Tomas lifted the brand. She stared at the angry red flesh still smoking on her forearm. The raised welt said PENSAR—THINK.

You bastards, it will be my turn one day. Eliana snapped out of her thoughts. She glared daggers at him. You are no longer my brother!

"Let go of me, you apes!" she screamed.

A nod from Alejandro, and the bodyguards stepped back. She plunged her arm into the fountain and the combination of relief and pain was staggering, but she willed the bile to stay down and to not faint. Still glaring at him, she brought it out.

He grabbed Eliana by the wrist and held her. "Think! I will not tell you again."

She nodded and snatched her arm away before reaching to her ankle holster.

"Tomas, I also have something for you."

The guards jumped too late to intervene. The single gunshot from her Walther PPK brought additional security streaming into the yard, only to be waved off by Alejandro.

Eliana stood over Tomas, staring into his eyes as they slowly glazed over, the wound to his neck spurting blood through his fingers. Then he was dead. She put two more shots into his head, anyway.

Eliana returned the gun to its holster and stood as tall as she could manage. She shot a hateful glance at her brother and marched out holding the injured arm.

6

Fuerza Especial de Reacción base southeast of Mexico City

Carlos Gonzalez watched from the instructor's deck as the sergeant major led Alpha team through room-clearing training. It had taken two years to build the special counter-narcotics assault squadron inside of Fuerza Especial de Reacción.

Gonzalez and a cadre had trained the hand-picked team to a level on par with its American counterparts at Fort Bragg. He'd been so competent and popular he soon rose to squadron command, which was how he came to know Lance Bear Wolf and to collaborate on the marijuana site takedown.

Gonzalez realized his well train squadron was the public face of a once-in-a-lifetime opportunity for what amounted in Mexico to an operational command. It had become so fabled in popular culture it was often used on army recruiting posters.

Operational command suited him. His original strategy to become the Mexican Army Chief of Staff had fallen away for his disdain of politics. His wife had given birth to their third child. Their location close to his mother and his retired father, a former Mexican army colonel, had eased his wife's burden. The feeling of right place-right time was about to be proved out.

Gonzalez had been at their secret Lion headquarters compound for ten days, drilling and refining assault methods. He jotted a few notes about the squadron's training performance and walked down to the training floor to confer with his sergeant major.

The soldiers rallied around him. Just then, a young corporal trotted up and stood at attention, waiting to be recognized before speaking.

"Take five," the major said to his troops, and the team relaxed but didn't move away. He turned to the young man. "Corporal, what is it?"

The anxious boy saluted. "Sir, you have a call from the police in Los Mochis."

He turned back to his men. "Sergeant Major, take the men back through scenarios Bravo and Charlie. I want it tight this time."

"Yes, sir!" the sergeant major barked.

He followed the corporal back to the Operations office, where he picked up the holding call.

"Major Gonzalez here. Who am I speaking to?"

"Sir, this is Lieutenant Victor Cárdenas of the Los Mochis police. I am sorry, I have some bad news for you."

Magdalena? The baby? The kids? Gonzalez's mind raced. "Yes, what is it?"

"Sir, I must be direct. I am sorry to tell you your brother Hector and his wife are dead. Killed by the Sinaloa Cartel in their restaurant."

Gonzalez's brain shifted into operational mode, calculating time, speed, distance, and options. His blood ran hot with controlled rage. As a Mexican Army Tier 1 Squadron commander, he was accustomed to being decisive.

He had assets at his disposal, and he decided to deploy them all on his brother's killers. "Thank you, lieutenant. I will be there in four hours," Gonzalez said before hanging up.

Their father didn't know who Hector's investor was, but Carlos did. He had quarreled with Hector about taking tainted drug money many times. It would surely come out now. Some smart but wary reporter would discover and print the connection to the Sinaloa cartel and their blood money, which had supported Hector's dream. The news would devastate his parents if it became public knowledge.

Gonzalez pulled a handset from his web utility belt and radioed his deputy, aviation Captain Jorge Juárez, advising him to ready the troops and the squadron's new helicopters. Two MH-60G Pave Hawk helicopters.

He would provide the mission brief to Juárez and his pilots en route to Los Mochis. Gonzalez's justification for using government equipment to investigate the death of his brother and wife would be recorded in the unit log as a no-notice training mission, thus requiring no advance advisories up the less-than-secure chain of command.

Gonzalez assembled his team and gave them a warning order. Exchange training ammunition for 5.56mm M855 steel-tipped penetrator rounds and prep to move out in two hours. Full combat load. He would use the time to plan.

This mission was different and possibly career ending. Sinaloa had killed his brother- and sister-in-law. With official approval or not, he was going for retribution.

He reflected for a moment on this turning point. He had often hoped his old military prep school friend Alejandro Cortes would leave his family business, at least once he had become wealthy.

Instead, he had taken his father's place in a leadership position of the Sinaloa cartel and became responsible for the Gonzalez family murders. He always believed it was inevitable he and Cortes would meet as adversaries one day. Today would be the day.

TWO LION SQUADRON helicopters came in low and fast at tree-top height and flared at a steep angle to arrest their momentum, settling in the large El Gran Pez parking lot to offload. The Alpha team assaulters dismounted and ran to set a security perimeter.

After just seconds to deploy the team, the helicopters roared back into the sky in great hurricanes of rotor wash. They headed to a staging and refueling point at the nearby Los Mochis International Airport.

Gonzalez advanced the team toward El Gran Pez, their M4 carbines up. The restaurant was believed to be empty, but the Lion'swere cautious. Death had already visited here.

Gonzalez signaled to hold in place and tore through the crime scene tape at the front door with both hands. Dressed in black battle gear and wearing his Kevlar and ballistic goggles, he was an imposing figure.

Upon seeing him, a middle-aged cleaning woman screamed and dropped a box of water glasses, which shattered across the floor.

"Who is in charge here?" Gonzalez demanded. The woman pointed across the dining room to a balding, middle-aged man who had come out from the kitchen. Weapons had swiveled in his direction when he appeared, but he seemed oblivious to them, and unafraid.

"I am in charge. I am Ernesto."

"Ernesto, who do you work for and what are you doing here?"

"We are from Limpieza Comercial. We are contracted to clean up the building before they reopen the restaurant."

Gonzalez considered for a moment. "Are there any police here?"

"No, sir. A police officer was here to open the restaurant for us and then he left."

"Your people should stop what they're doing and follow this soldier," Gonzalez said. He gestured to a commando behind him.

"Yes, sir. We will comply."

The sergeant behind Gonzalez slung his weapon. Then escorted the workers out of the restaurant with the kind of sing-song happy talk a mother uses at a child's birthday party.

Gonzalez keyed his throat mic. "Lightning Nine, Lightning Actual. Choose four men to come inside with us. Have the rest pull security."

Sergeant Major Dominguez clicked his mic twice. A few moments later, he and four of his soldiers entered the restaurant.

"I want you to help me find any evidence of Cortes's involvement. Grab any security tapes if they are still here. Search the entire building, understand?" The sergeant major nodded. "Assemble back here in forty minutes ready to report," Gonzalez ordered.

"Yes, sir," they replied in unison.

The smell of death still permeated the air, and pools of dried blood were everywhere in the large dining room. Several had the appearance of lurid red swirls where the cleaning crew had started to clean them up with pungent cleaning fluid and shaggy absorbent mops.

The body count had to have been more than a dozen. He shook his head. His gaze taking in blood evidence at many tables. The indiscriminate machine gun fire must have been devastating.

He removed his eye protection and helmet. Then stepped outside to call Lieutenant Cárdenas. Now he didn't care about the affect his brother's relationship with the cartel might have on his career. It was time for the cartel to pay. He would make sure of that.

Thirty-five minutes later the four men led by Dominguez gave their report. The sergeant major held an empty MP5 magazine in one hand and in the other a handful of 9mm brass.

"Sir, the MP5 mag and German 9mm ammo suggest Cortes shooters."

He raised the other hand filled with expended brass. "We also found American-made 9mm and .45 ACP shell casings. The security tapes are missing."

Gonzalez looked at the German magazine and shell casings with disgust. It was well known Israeli and German military contractors had trained the Cortes security detail. They bought only the latest Heckler and Koch machine pistols and rifles. Their handguns, the best from Sig Sauer.

Who knew what other, more dynamic weapons the cartel could deploy?

I have a few surprises of my own. This is going to be a bloody fight.

Cárdenas showed up thirty minutes later in an unmarked white

Chevrolet police car. He shook Gonzalez's hand, and they walked toward the dining area.

"Lieutenant, what can you tell me?" he asked.

Cárdenas crossed his arms over a broad chest. "Security tapes show a cartel security guard known as Azul escorting your brother to what we believe was his office when the incident started. Azul was a large man, a clumsy one, and he collided with a waitress. She dropped a tray of food and I can see in the video the sudden crash startled Azul. He spun and opened fire, killing her. One of the Americans in the restaurant, a man named Lance Bear Wolf, responded to the unprovoked murder, killing Azul."

Wolf? Gonzalez focused on his feet to hide his surprise.

"That is when the Cortes security detail started shooting up the restaurant. The gunfight continued until Wolf stopped the last shooter. The kitchen tape shows a cartel gunmen killed Hector as he tried to open the service door. We found him and his wife with fatal wounds in their backs." Cardenas paused.

"The cartel soldiers also killed Wolf's father, and seriously wounded his mother."

Gonzalez stood silent as he absorbed this information. I told Wolf to stop here, and now I'm responsible for his father's death.

His brother Hector had made a deal with the Devil and it had it cost had him and his wife their lives. And the innocents in the restaurant only seeking lunch.

Wolf's parents!

"The Americans were here in Mexico helping a friend and I met them in Puerto Vallarta. I told them they must eat here on their way home." Gonzalez said and focused on not shedding a tear.

"I told them to come for the, ah ... for the, you know, ah ... the seafood."

"Major, please. You did not make Wolf's choice to run toward the gunfire. Unfortunate as it is, they played their parts in this, too."

"Lieutenant let's not forget my brother's part. His choice to partner with the cartel ended in death."

Cárdenas nodded without speaking. Hector's rumored connection to the cartel, now confirmed, excited him, but he kept it to himself. "Yes, of course."

"How well do you know Alejandro and Eliana Cortes?" Gonzalez asked.

"Well enough. I grew up here with your brother's wife. We were best friends in school. The Cortes family are devils, but they are also seen in many barrios as saints. The locals do not object the drug trade when they see it as an American problem."

Gonzalez knew how easily people were corrupted, especially low-paid police. Even Army soldiers went AWOL or deserted outright and became cartel soldiers, bringing along their training, methods, and often even their weapons.

"How did you become a police lieutenant instead of working for the cartel?" Gonzalez asked.

Cárdenas's eyes darkened. "It was a simple choice for me. When I was twelve, the cartel killed my little brother and sister, and they hurt several more children in a drive-by shooting. My parents sent me to Texas to live with an uncle. I got American schooling and police training before coming back. I thought I could make a difference." he sighed.

The lieutenant's story matched the intel Gonzalez had reviewed and the cop's reputation was clean. Gonzalez could work with this guy without fear of a dagger in the back. Cárdenas's radio cracked to life. "Lieutenant, the surveillance team is asking for assistance."

"Okay, standby." Cárdenas turned his attention to Gonzalez. "Major, can we get your help to raid a suspected cartel trans-shipment operation?"

Gonzalez didn't have to be asked twice. Energized by the opportunity to hit a cartel operation, he responded by keying his throat mic.

"Lightning Actual." "Lightning Nine."

"Nine, rally the Lions outside the restaurant's front entrance. We have a mission."

"Roger," Dominguez radioed.

"Thank you, sir!" Cárdenas said.

Changing frequencies on his radio, Gonzalez called Juárez.

"Lightning Two, Actual."

"Actual, go for Two."

"Two, strike mission Los Mochis. Pick up in fifteen, my pos."

"Roger that, sir!" the captain said.

7

E l Rancho Cortes, Sinaloa, Mexico
Alejandro sat in his office, facing the oversize oil
painting of his father. Romulo Cortes's portrait rested on an
ornate, high-back leather chair adorned with inlaid gold medallions
topped by the family crest.

It was a stately painting, except for the fact it was fake. The Cortes
family was not from one drop of royal blood.

El Rancho Cortes, located a few kilometers outside of Los Mochis,
was just forty minutes from the Gulf of California. Its proximity to
the cartel's water, overland, and aviation shipping routes made it an
ideal location.

The old ranch house, barns, and pens were still in use and
housed Alejandro's prize bulls and Eliana's dressage horses. From the
road and the air, it looked like a working ranch but for a cluster of
new buildings.

Cartel operations, intelligence, and communications functioned
in separate climate-controlled buildings. An expansive new ranch
house served as home, headquarters, and Alejandro's office.

Alejandro leaned back in his chair and sighed. His father had drilled "think like a man" into his sister from the day she was born, and she'd made his life complicated by complying.

He did not regret having her arm branded, he just doubted it would teach her a lesson.

Alejandro's phone rang. It was Joaquin Zapana, his intelligence lieutenant.

"Boss, contacts tell me the Lion Squadron is headed our way."

He gritted his teeth. "Find out how soon and why."

"Yes, sir. One more thing. Two Americans survived the shooting. The woman is in intensive care at Los Mochis Medical Center. Her son is with her."

"What have they told the police?"

"Nothing useful."

"Good. We have time to prepare."

He hung up and took a deep breath. What happened at the restaurant was a major screwup. According to his sources, there were three gringos present, a young man and his parents. The report he'd gotten indicated the younger man seemed experienced and composed as he killed Azul. The old man had obvious combat experience and even the woman showed impressive calmness under fire. She'd stood up and ran toward one of Eliana's men, firing her pistol, and shot him dead.

Who are these Americans?

"You called?" Martin Amaro said as he entered the room. He did not look the part of a cartel lieutenant, more like a banker or accountant on a business casual Friday. His operations team managed marijuana, crack, and cocaine production with the manufacturing professionalism of General Motors.

Amaro had been a revolutionary in his youth, part of Sendero Luminoso, the communist Shining Path party in Peru. The switch from poor guerrilla living off the land to buttoned-down operations lead for the cartel was Alejandro's idea. He'd seen what Martin was capable of when his people provided protection for cocaine shipments, and Alejandro needed help to grow his business.

"Lion Squadron is on the way," Alejandro said.

"No" Amaro said. It was unlike Mexican authorities to challenge the cartel. Something had changed.

"Yes. I want you and Joaquin to keep a close watch on this mess. There are two Americans at the medical center that must go away. I instructed Joaquin to prepare a plan," Alejandro said.

After Amaro left, Alejandro mulled over his options. His cousin, El Chapo was given to violence. His preference was to deal with an issue right away versus waiting to see if it warranted escalation.

Both styles had their pluses and minuses, but the key to Alejandro's style was to maintain independence of action while keeping his commitments to the cartel and its distributors. Handle problems, but ship the agreed amount of product on time, all the time.

And now this Army intervention was coming. He picked up a phone and called his boss. El Chapo picked up on the first ring.

"Alejandro, why are you causing trouble? The Americans are pushing our president to send the military after us."

"I will fix it."

"What about Fuerza Especial de Reacción?" El Chapo's voice rose with each word. "You leave us open to attack!"

"It will not affect our business. I will deal with them."

"What about Eliana?"

He relayed his lesson for Eliana.

"Send her to Los Angeles," El Chapo said. "Yes, boss!"

8

Los Mochis Medical Center, Mexico

The Los Mochis Medical Center smelled clean and fresh. The walls and floors were painted a light blue, no doubt to ease the worries of people clamoring for information about loved ones. Wolf weaved his way to the information desk.

"Where can I find Alma Anderson?" he said in Spanish.

The young receptionist tapped on her computer keyboard. "CCU, third floor."

"Gracias," he said and bounded up the stairwell. He strode through the critical care unit doors as if he owned the place. A nurse stepped into his path.

"Who are you?"

"Lance Wolf. My mother, Alma Anderson, is here."

The nurse raised a brow, then scanned some paperwork on her clipboard. "She is down the hall and to the left." She pushed the clipboard toward him. "Please sign in and I will take you there."

A quick scribble and they were on their way. They turned left and then another. A police officer stood outside the room.

When he spotted Wolf, he put his hand on his pistol and further blocked the door. Wolf raised both hands to his sides to show he was not a threat.

The charge nurse turned to the police guard. "It's good, the patient is his mother."

The officer nodded at him, then yielded and walked to the nurse's station across the hall. The charge nurse asked for Miss Anderson's status.

"She is stable, but continues in a coma," another nurse said.

Wolf's stomach churned at the dump of adrenalin. He needed more answers. A man walked up and introduced himself as Dr. Mateo Munoz, offering his hand. He guided Wolf into his mother's hospital room.

"When we received your mother, she had head trauma and two gunshot wounds in the lower back. The surgeon extracted the bullets, and we treated her with medication to limit the brain swelling. She is out of immediate danger, but remains in a comatose condition," Munoz said.

The room reminded him of a mad scientist's lab, with all its equipment, cables, electrodes, and tubes running to and around his mother. She was intubated, her face ashen and tense as if she was fighting. He sensed her pain.

He had spent years relying on his intuition. Against his better judgment he had put aside his inner alarm bells and remained at lunch after the cartel showed up. His stepfather had paid the ultimate price. Now his alarm bells were clanging again and there was nothing he could do about it.

He'd been taught from an early age to be a protector for his family. It had developed into watching out for anyone being bullied or mistreated. Sitting on the sidelines was not an option. It frustrated him to sit idle while his mother recovered, though clearly there was no other option for him.

Wolf planned to get his mother back to the States and a Tucson hospital as soon as possible. He would stay through her recovery. Then he would get revenge for Andy's death and for the other innocents killed who had no one to act on their behalf.

Looking across the hospital bed, he remembered how his mother had drilled into him education was the path to freedom. She was the one who taught him to love and respect the land and animals.

With is biological father often high or drunk, it was his mother and uncles who taught him to see with all his senses. How to run swift and quiet, flowing with the land. What it meant to be a Crow warrior. She had sung her death song, but he needed more time with her.

If his mother recovered, it would be due to the selflessness and bravery of his stepfather. Andrew Anderson was a good man. A former Army Ranger in Vietnam, he was a man of action, of honor.

I'm not waiting until mom recovers. Let's see how they like my version of guerilla warfare.

The machines beeped and moaned. He squeezed his mother's hand again and then went across the hall to the nurses' station.

"Excuse me," he said in Spanish, "May I make a quick phone call?"

The nurse smiled and handed him the phone.

"Gracias," Wolf said. He called his stepbrother Bjorn and gave him the rundown of what had happened. He tried his stepsister, but she didn't pick up.

When he got back in the room, he sat in the chair and sighed. His stomach growled, and he realized he hadn't eaten since the few bites he'd gotten at the restaurant before the shooting started. He relaxed into a combat nap to restore his body while ensuring his other senses protected them both.

The rustling woke him. He sat up, his mother was shaking, then relaxed.

Wolf flung open the door. "Nurse, get the doctor!" he said.

He stroked his mother's hair. "Mom, wake up. Alma Anderson, wake up." He repeated in his command voice, "Alma Anderson, wake up!" Her eyes stayed closed, but there was rapid movement under the lids.

Dr. Munoz rushed into the room with a nurse.

"Doctor, my mother had a seizure of sorts. Look at her eyes."

"Yes, I see. Step back, please."

Dr. Munoz tapped a tongue depressor on Alma's moist forehead. Nothing. He opened her left eye first and shone his penlight into her iris and got a very slow response. He did the same on the right and got the same result. Then he slowly rotated her head.

"Good oculocephalic reflex is present, Mr. Wolf. Your mother's brain swelling has reduced."

Wolf exhaled the breath he was holding.

"I want you to continue to talk to her. She suffered serious trauma, but she is in good overall health, and her body and brain are working hard to recover. It may take time, okay." Munoz said.

"Yes. Thank you, Doctor," Wolf said as he gazed down at his mother. He was proud of her for being such a fighter. He wasn't sure she'd approve of what he was about to do, but the fire in him said it and more was okay.

Hello darkness my old friend.

9

Los Mochis, Sinaloa

Gonzalez and his sergeant major had devised a quick and simple assault plan using Cárdenas' knowledge of the target. With the team looking on, Gonzalez used his notebook as the house and mapped out the rest of the area with rocks and sticks.

"Our mission is a suspected cartel stash house in Los Mochis. The police say we can identify the house from the air by a white paint mark on the corner of the roof. We fast rope onto the objective to avoid the power lines here and here." He pointed.

"Sergeant Major and Lightning Three Six will provide air- borne over watch. I will lead the Alpha team breach. We have no intel on the interior, so we flow. Lighting One will lead his team to blocking positions here and here."

Heads nodded affirmation all around. They heard the Black Hawks approaching in the distance.

"Cárdenas, I will see you on-site," Gonzalez said.

Once boarded, they closed the doors to give the flight an administrative guise. The flight time from Topolobampo was only sixteen minutes. Fast ropes were readied, and weapons checked.

Gonzalez leaned back in the canvas seat and let his emotions go.

He visualized his brother and wife shot down in their restaurant, murdered in cold blood, and he got a surge of adrenalin as he thought of what was to happen.

Retribution was a descriptive but often under-used word, and it would govern the next hours. A small start, but I'll take it.

The left-side door gunner spotted the house. He clicked his intercom button twice. "Sir, we have the target. Three hundred meters off our port side."

Gonzalez moved forward in his seat. "Roger that."

The helicopters dropped to fifty feet, banking hard. Juárez flew in hot over the stash house, slewing the helicopter sideways like a runner sliding into third base. He stopped the helo right over the street.

Two fast ropes dropped out and men streamed down the forty-foot descent. The Bravo team helicopter followed closely behind. As the Black Hawks roared away, Alpha moved forward, their M4s up and scanning the area as they looked for movement from the windows.

Gonzalez signaled for the breacher to place his explosive charge. When it detonated, the ornate wooden door disintegrated inward in a cloud of splinters and dust. The team flowed in just as they had in countless hours of rehearsal, moving in pairs to clear the house.

They cleared the front room and kitchen. Gonzalez led as they advanced down the hallway. He hated hallways because they could be bullet funnels.

He stopped at the first closed door on the right. Two men stacked up behind him. A third stood ready to open the door. A squeeze on his left shoulder told him the team was ready to go.

Gonzalez nodded, and the door was pushed open. He was moving froward when someone on the other side slammed the door back into him, pinning him against the frame. A hand reached out, grabbing the barrel of his M4.

He was wrestling the weapon back when two rounds blasted through the door next to his shoulder, killing his attacker. When he looked back, he saw Alpha Three's smoking rifle barrel.

Pushing open the door and stepping over the body, they cleared the bedroom. They cleared a second room without resistance and headed for the master. Gonzalez was more wary than ever. Where are the cartel soldiers?

The squad was ten feet from the master when a cartel soldier jumped out, spraying AK-47 rounds down the hallway. Luck was on their side. The gunman was either on drugs or had never shot an AK before, as the rounds climbed the walls and struck the ceiling before he was killed in a hail of M4 rounds.

Gonzalez threw a flash-bang grenade into the room and the men surged in to find three dazed and confused older drug mules hiding in a closet. They had been loading their backpacks with kilo-sized bricks of cocaine.

While they brought the flex-cuffed mules out, he gave the all clear and ordered comms to signal Cárdenas it was okay to send in his police.

Gonzalez watched from the bedroom window as Bravo searched the backyard for hidden caches of cash, drugs, or weapons.

"Anything, Bravo One?" he radioed. The radio crackled. "Negative."

He led Alpha back to area between the house and garage where a young Bravo sergeant approached him.

"Sir, there is a very bad smell in the garage."

Gonzalez followed him into the large, detached building. The smell hit him as he entered, taking his breath away. Sickly sweet, and pungent enough to make him gag. He ordered a corporal to open all the doors and windows, and to break windows that wouldn't open.

He radioed. "Alpha Five, garage."

Cárdenas covered his mouth with a handkerchief.

"Mother of God, what is that?"

Just then a tall, broad-shouldered sergeant entered the garage with a fireman's Halligan tool, a combination ax and pry bar.

"Open the wall here." Gonzalez said, holding the drive-on rag knotted around his neck to his face as he pointed at a stain leaching from a crack in the surface.

He opened the wall with a few hits and pulls on the bar. In doing so, though, he penetrated a plastic bag enclosing a bloated and decomposing woman hidden behind the wall. A tsunami of odors hit their senses like a hammer.

Gonzalez blinked. He could find words for the horror.

10

Los Mochis Medical Center, Mexico

Bjorn Anderson was in a zone, processing what his brother had relayed about the gunfight. Andy's death at the restaurant and his stepmother's condition. He grabbed the phone and asked his teaching assistant to cover for him. As the dean of the USC Brovard College School of Criminology, he set his own schedule.

He called a friend at his old DEA aviation unit and was able to secure two seats on a plane headed south to Mexico in a few hours.

Like his stepbrother, Bjorn had joined the Ranger regiment. The same year that Wolf entered special forces, Bjorn passed the Army's helicopter pilot course. After graduation, in an unprecedented move by the 160th Special Aviation Regiment, he was selected for the unit straight from training.

Bjorn excelled as a combat pilot. He had a sixth sense about flying. Commanders sought him out for their missions because they believed he would always get them home safe.

It was a nighttime raid on a Syrian compound that resulted a wounded helicopter he wrangled to a hard but survivable crash landing. He sustained a debilitating back injury. A medical board decided he could no longer fly.

After a year of intensive rehab, he began his second career as a pilot for the Drug Enforcement Administration. It had been interesting enough, but he didn't get the same satisfaction as military combat flying. After resigning from the DEA, he finished a doctorate in Criminology and began teaching at USC.

He called his sister, Sierra, and briefed her on what their brother had reported. After a quick call to his wife, he jumped into his SUV and headed for the DEA aviation unit in Long Beach. An hour and twenty minutes after his call to his sister, Sierra walked from the private aviation area to the DEA hangar, and they boarded a Gulfstream GV for their hop headed south.

The two-hour and thirty-minute flight, with two stops before Los Mochis, was a grind. Sierra an OB/GYN sat silent reading a medical journal.

At Los Mochis International Airport, Bjorn's DEA contact had a rental car waiting for them. The tension in the car was palpable as they drove in silence to the hospital.

He wasn't sure what to expect. The hospital reception area was a crowded mess. The receptionist told them where to go, and they made their way to the third floor. Nerves danced in his stomach. He didn't like aid stations or hospitals, as he had been in too many with wounded friends over the years.

Wolf had told him their mother was awake, so there was some good news and something positive to look forward to.

When they approached the room, the police guard, who had been told to expect family members, stood and open the door. "You and your family are in my prayers." he said.

Bjorn saw his brother sitting in a chair next to his mother's bed. He looked fatigued but alert, on guard. His stepmother seemed to be sleeping.

"Hey guys," Wolf said with a half-smile. He stood and group-hugged them both. "Glad you're here."

His sister grabbed the bedside chart and scanned. Her look soured as she dropped the chart back in its slot.

"I'd like to see the doctor supervising Mom's recovery."

"Okay, I'll get him."

Just then the doctor walked in, and Wolf introduced them. "Dr. Munoz, this is my brother, Bjorn, and my sister, Dr. Sierra Morton."

"Sorry to meet you this way," the doctor said.

"Thank you, doctor," she said. "I appreciate all you have done for our mother."

"You are welcome, but we hope for more, do we not? We will continue to make her as comfortable as we can during her recovery."

Munoz filled them in on the tests and the prognosis. Their mother was expected to make a full recovery, but it would be a long road. Her brain was functioning and getting closer to cognitive awareness every day, but more time was needed. He said his goodbyes and left the room.

"I'm going to check in at the hotel," Sierra said. "Lance, you look like you need a break, so why don't you come with me? Bjorn can stay with Mom for a while."

"You got this, bro?" Wolf said. "I can stay if—"

"I got it. Get some rest. I'll stay with Mom."

After his siblings left, Bjorn took a seat in the chair next to his mother, holding her hand and talking about his childhood for an hour, just fun stories to lighten his mood.

Bam, bam, bang.

Bjorn jumped to a defensive posture and placed himself in front of his mother's bed, shielding it from the door. The adrenalin dump took him straight to fight mode. He knew what gunshots sounded like and they shouldn't be coming from a hospital hallway.

He moved to the door and saw the police officer run to the stairwell, then an emergency alarm sounded. A pre-recorded voice in Spanish and English directed everyone to leave the building, then repeated it.

Nurses and aides scurried around the floor prepping patients to leave, some on foot, some still in their beds.

More gunshots then, a different weapon. A nurse came in and disconnected Alma's EKG leads and switched her oxygen from the wall outlet to a backup canister attached to her bed.

Bjorn assessed the situation and concluded he could get his mother out faster if he carried her down the stairs in his arms. "I will take care of her, go help other patients."

Less than a minute later, shouting echoed throughout the hallway. Someone was yelling. "Where is the American woman?"

There was no time, so Bjorn wrapped his mother and her oxygen canister in her blankets and carried her in his powerful arms as far as the door, where he stopped and waiting. When he saw two gunmen enter a room down the hallway, he crossed the hallway and placed his unconscious mother in a storage room. He did a quick search of the darkened space for anything to use as a weapon. There was nothing.

He dashed back into his mother's room and thought he was out of options until he spied the monophasic defibrillator cart.

He cranked the defibrillator up to its maximum output of three hundred and sixty joules. He readied himself with a certain smug confidence, a defibrillator paddle ready in each hand.

When the gunman opened the door and strode through, Bjorn stepped behind him and pressed the paddles to both sides of the man's head, depressing the triggers. The gunman's hands spasmed and his grip tightened. A full automatic burst tore up the room and blew out the windows.

Well, there goes my element of surprise.

The assassin dropped his MP5 and collapsed, falling back into Bjorn and tripping him into the hallway. Out of the corner of his right eye he sensed movement to his left and covered himself with his dead gunman's body.

It took the brunt of a full-auto burst. When the shooting stopped, he looked up to see the other gunman fumbling his reload.

Bjorn flipped over on his back Jiu Jitsu style and propelled himself back into the room. He grabbed the dead guy's gun and reloaded the weapon with a magazine dropped when the gunman fell dead.

The seconds seemed like minutes as he worked to control his fear. The assassin's barrel broke the sightline of the door frame. He fired two three-round bursts, the first two feet up from the floor and the second higher. The gunman fell across the doorway, blood pooling, his eyes opened and frozen wide in disbelief.

Covered in blood, Bjorn self-assessed and found a grazing wound across his left shoulder. It could wait. He cleared the hallway and, with no threats in sight, he slung the machine pistol and rushed to the storage room where he'd left his mother.

He said a quick thanks to Thor. His mother was unharmed. He bent to pick her up when from behind intense pain shot though his body. It felt like he was being electrocuted.

He let out a grunt as his body convulsed and he collapsed to the ground. He tried to push through the haze, but his body wouldn't respond. There were muffled sounds, his arms were pulled behind him, and he blacked out.

∼

"BJORN," a voice said. "Wake up."

He peeled his eyes open. His body ached terrible, and the light was too bright for his eyes. What happened?

He tried to sit up and groaned, the pain radiating down his back. Wolf and Sierra helped him to his unsteady feet. His wrists were bound in front of him.

"Lieutenant, please take the cuffs off my brother."

Cárdenas nodded to a uniform and the officer uncuffed Bjorn's wrists. His hands were asleep due to the tight restraints, and he flexed them to get the blood flowing.

Then he remembered. "Mom!" he said, and he took off down the hall with brother and sister behind him. When they got back to the CCU her room was empty. Bjorn looked in the storage room where he'd left his mother, but it too was empty.

"She was right here. I left her right here!"

"It's okay brother. Retrace your steps."

"There were killers searching the floor, yelling for Mom. So, I rushed her into this storage room. And then—"

Dr. Munoz appeared, interrupting their conversation. He had a forlorn look on his face. "I was looking for you."

"Doctor, where is our mother?" Wolf asked.

Dr. Munoz sighed. "I am sorry to say she did not survive."

"Jesus," Sierra said, tears welling up.

"What?" Bjorn growled. "She was alive when I was tasered."

"I am sorry," the doctor said. "When we found your mother, she did not have a pulse. We tried several times to resuscitate her, of course, but we were not successful. I suspect an aneurysm due to her head trauma."

Bjorn looked at what was left of his family. In a fit of rage, he punched a hole in the wall. "It's my fault."

Wolf placed a hand on his shoulder. "It's not your fault." His brother pulled away and punched the wall again.

"You didn't kill Mom," Sierra said. "I'm sure of it."

"You think it was a cartel thing?" Cárdenas asked.

"Sierra and Bjorn, this is Lieutenant Cárdenas of the Los Mochis police. This is my sister and brother," Wolf said.

"I do think she was murdered," Sierra said. "I'm going to order an autopsy and tox screen...Those bastards killed our mother!"

11

L os Mochis Medical Center, Mexico
Carlos Gonzalez and his Lion Squadron had taken over an old maintenance hangar at the airport after the raid. He had reported up his chain he had supported the local police as an extension of his training.

The Alpha team comms sergeant rolled a cart with a small television over to their commander so he could watch the local TV news report on the stash house raid. The breathless bulletin was well-informed. It was so fast in being reported, he was certain Alejandro was seeding information to friendly media.

The announcer said a federal drug unit was being hailed as heroes for freeing men forced to mule. The report showed video of the gruesome find of dead bodies in the walls of the garage.

They called out Gonzalez as the team leader who had supported the police. Mass murder by the cartel at the El Gran Pez restaurant was no longer a lead story. He pondered how his name in the news would madden his chain of command.

As the Mexican Army's Tier I counter-terror, counter-drug unit, they had access to classified files on the Cortes family.

They were rich with information but of little value when it came to prosecution. The politicians, wary of an all-out war with Sinaloa, were loath to have the Mexican Secretary of National Defense authorize direct action.

Cárdenas called and briefed Gonzalez about the attack at Medical Center. It was clear Alma Anderson had been the target. She was the only witness who could corroborate Wolf's story and help build the case against Eliana Cortes.

They agreed it would take a different approach to find justice for the wounded and dead. Maybe the Americans could be the answer they needed.

The Santa Ana Hotel got its look from the 1930s, with ornate ironwork and an expansive circular drive to the front door rimmed by flowers. The bellman acknowledged Cárdenas by name and the manager let them know Mr. Wolf was in room 2031. He escorted them to the second floor and Wolf's room, where he knocked on the door for them before departing.

"Come on in," he said, swinging open the hotel room door. "Major Carlos Gonzalez, please meet my sister, Dr. Sierra Morton, and my brother, Bjorn Anderson." They shook hands.

"Pleased to meet you, Dr. Morton," Carlos said. "And we know your brother, of course—they teach our pilots his daring and heroism during Operation Gothic Serpent."

"Thank you, Major," Bjorn said.

"Lieutenant," Wolf said, "Anything new to report?"

"Yes. The prosecutor will not move forward without a witness to corroborate your story."

"I'm the only one left alive who can place Eliana Cortes at El Gran Pez, correct?" he asked.

"Yes."

"I called work to ask for intel on the Cortes family. It's classified, so they can't send it in the clear and I have no SCIF access in Mexico to receive it." Wolf said as he paced the room. He turned to Gonzalez. "Carlos, who leads Sinaloa intelligence and operations?"

"Two of Alejandro's top lieutenants, both former Sendero Luminoso. Martin Amaro runs operations and Joaquin Zapana heads the intelligence group. They brought their guerrilla training, doctrine, and experience to the drug trade. They have combined the security of a guerrilla warfare cell organization with Amazon-grade distribution capabilities."

"The cartel has become so well-run that if it sold widgets, it would be on the cover of Forbes," Gonzalez crossed his arms and continued.

"It has raised Alejandro Cortes's status in the cartel. It doesn't hurt he's El Chapo's cousin. The Cortes family owns what would have been called a franchise back in the Eighties. They own all the drug production and distribution through the Western states and up into Canada. The only consistent thorn in Alejandro's business is the Tijuana Cartel. They control Baja to Los Angeles. They are also trying to break into other Cortes-owned cities, such as Phoenix and Las Vegas."

"Major Gonzalez is correct," Cárdenas said.

"Is Alejandro violent like El Chapo?" asked Wolf. Carlos waved his hand.

"He's had moments. He's unpredictable and bi-polar. Very calculating, operating in the shadows."

He turned to Cárdenas. "Lieutenant, what about the video showing Eliana at El Gran Pez?"

Cárdenas nodded. "What we have only shows her running from the shooting. Not her shouting the kill order. We know she has her own crew. She is rash, and she doesn't shy away from violence."

"We can exploit her," he said. "Where is she now?"

Gonzalez shook his head. "We have no leads and no one inside the cartel to help us."

Wolf scanned the group, finding various combinations of frustration, anger, and resignation. And he could identify with those feelings, except for the resignation. He could see it in Bjorn's eyes, too. We've only lost if we give up.

"I have an idea," he said. "Aside from those of us in this room, how many people know Mom is dead?"

"One of my officers and Dr. Munoz.," Cárdenas replied. Sierra said, "The morgue assistant and the coroner."

Wolf closed his eyes, his hands flowing left and right. He used visualization to stitch together his thoughts. Then it hit him. "Lieutenant, any chance we can change the name on mom's paperwork and charts to Jane Doe for the time being?"

Bjorn furrowed his brow. "What?"

"This is going to sound strange, but I think if we can trick the Corteses into believing Mom is still alive, they will have to make another try. We have been reacting to cartel moves until now. So, let's go on the offensive. Let's set a trap and catch someone we can leverage."

The room was quiet as everyone mulled over the idea. It was so outlandish] Wolf wasn't sure Cárdenas and Gonzalez would lend their support. In the moment, he had bypassed justice and told himself what he wanted by name. Revenge.

"Count me in," Gonzalez said.

"Me, too," Cárdenas said.

"What's you plan?" Bjorn asked.

Wolf moved to face the group. "We'll go back to the hospital, and I'll play the distraught son who has been told his mother is dead only to find out it was a mistake. Dr. Munoz will direct me to a room on the third floor. I'll make a scene. Once the cartel figures out Mom is still alive, they will send someone else to complete the job."

Gonzalez chimed in. "I like the plan, but we cannot include you. You cannot operate in Mexico without permission from my government as well as yours."

"You're right, but I can aid local law enforcement," Wolf said.

"I'll be the bait," Sierra said, and everyone turned to look at her.

Bjorn let out a growl. "No! You have a family, kids to take care of. We can't put you at risk."

He thought of his nephew and niece, and a pang of guilt hit him. Wolf didn't enjoy using his sister as bait, but it made sense. If they wanted to seek justice for their parents' deaths, this might be their only shot.

"She won't be in the room when the attack happens," Wolf said. "She will impersonate mom long enough to bait the trap and Bjorn will be providing protection. Cárdenas and Gonzalez's men will be in an adjoining room, protected from detection by a contagious-disease protocol. Gonzalez's team will use their surveillance cameras to keep an eye on the hallway, the nurses' station, and the room.

"Once the scene is set and seen by various hospital staff, one of them will inform the cartel. I'll trade places with Sierra, and she and Bjorn will go back to the hotel to give the appearance of needing rest. An officer will pretend to stand guard at the door. Lieutenant, do you have someone we can trust?" Wolf said.

Cárdenas smiled. "Yes."

"What if the hitman uses a pistol?" Gonzalez said.

"I'll wear body armor and hope the gunman doesn't prefer head shots,"

"Hope is a poor strategy," Bjorn said.

"It's a risk I will take. How soon can we make this happen?"

"I can have men at the hospital in forty minutes," Gonzalez said.

"Okay, come in the loading dock," Wolf said. "Sierra, can we trust Dr. Munoz?"

"Yes, I believe so."

"Good, let's read him in on the plan. Have him meet Gonzalez's team and set up in cleaning and nurse scrubs, whatever you can find. They will transport you to the room on the third floor. The lieutenant and I will take care of the paperwork and chart changes. Sierra, call me when you are ready. I'll make a scene in the lobby where a cartel source can report the news. And then we wait."

They were silent for a moment, the plan's danger making itself felt. They were about to put Wolf in the Cortes line of fire. If they didn't control the space, it would be a one-act play with death having the last say.

12

E l Rancho Cortes, Sinaloa, Mexico
The Lion Squadron raid on the stash house moved the El Gran Pez murders off the front page, replacing it with a positive story.

It was a story TV channels and newspapers dreamed of. The Mexican outlets might have come to this happy reporting concept later than their U.S. counterparts, but they were quick to grab the next new thing.

Now they left investigative reporting to the newspapers. Not that there were a lot of investigations given the life span of reporters who dove into the workings of the cartel.

Joaquin Zapana sighed. El Chapo and most of his leadership underestimated the value of how well his intelligence network and advanced methods protected the cartel.

His Russian contacts had told him the next frontier for influence and manipulation would be in the digital realm, and Zapana embraced it. He wrote himself a note to read the RAND Corporation report and U.S. Army War College articles on the subject.

He was walking to Alejandro's office when his cellphone rang. "Is she dead?" he asked.

"Yes, boss. I gave her the full dose myself."

"Did you see the sicarios?" Joaquin asked.

"Yes. They were Eliana's men."

He ended their call, then squatted, picked up a stone, and threw it at the fence before entering the main house. What was she thinking? Alejandro had told her to stay out of it.

Zapana entered Alejandro's office to find him watching TV coverage of the shooting at Medical Center hospital. No patients or visitors were hurt but for the heroic efforts of an American who'd stopped two gunmen.

He eyed his intelligence chief. "Joaquin, what happened to a quiet plan?"

"The woman is dead. My source says the sicarios were Eliana's."

He turned his back, but he wasn't hiding the anger he felt about his sister's betrayal. Zapana stood there in silence. He turned back around, his face placid.

"Have her come here, now. I have had enough. I'm sending her to Los Angeles. El Chapo said send her and I agree."

"Yes, sir." Joaquin called her number. She didn't answer, so he left a message. "Alejandro, I do not think your sister gave the order."

"What do you mean?"

"She would not betray you. So, who else could it be? I suspect her number two, Jorge. His is very ambitious, always looking for a way to please Eliana, and to move up in the organization. It makes sense he would try to fix the problem for her."

"Joaquin, if you are right, I want him gone. Regardless of who ordered the hit, she must go. It came from her team, and El Chapo has had enough. It's done, she goes."

"I understand, Alejandro. I will go find her," Zapana said and headed for the horse barn.

Four minutes later, she arrived on her black stallion. Her tight pants accentuated long legs and slim hips. The starched white shirt strained against her black lace bra. Zapana realized he was not breathing as she dismounted and walked to him.

"Joaquin, what's this about?" she asked.

"There was an attack at Medical Center hospital. Two of your men are dead."

"Not possible. I did not order such an operation."

She's a skilled liar. I almost believe her. "Eliana, if it's true, then someone went behind your back. Alejandro is furious. El Chapo is furious. We need to give them someone to blame this on. I suggest Jorge."

Her eyes widened. "No, Joaquin. He's my best. I can't."

"Please, stop for a minute. I know he is a trusted soldier, but who makes more sense? Jorge would do anything for you, correct?"

"Yes."

"So, it ties into a story he ordered the attack to try to clean up El Gran Pez loose ends for you. He needs to go. If you do it now, it will look better for you with Alejandro."

She thought for only a moment. "Damit. Yes, yes, it's the right choice." She dialed her head of security and gave the order.

A few minutes later, a single gunshot rang out from across the ranch. She placed her hand on Zapana's forearm.

"It's done. Gracias, Joaquin. You look out for me in all things, and I appreciate it." Together, they walked into Alejandro's office. She wore an air of confidence as she strode into the room. Alejandro looked up from his paperwork with a blank expression.

"Alejandro," she began. "I was out riding when I received news about the attack at the hospital. I did not give the order. It was Jorge. I have taken care of the problem."

He walked around the front of his desk. "Thank you, Eliana. I hoped this was not a betrayal. But it was your crew, yes?"

"Yes, it was."

"El Chapo thinks you are a problem."

"What? El Chapo says I'm a problem?"

"Yes, he does, sister. He wants you sent to Los Angeles. We want your attention on the Tijuana Cartel. But more later." He waved and huffed. "Now, I need to talk to Joaquin."

She looked as if she had the wind knocked out of her, but she recovered. "I will wait for your instructions," she said in a rigid chop, then she left the room with her head held high.

Just when Zapana thought he couldn't love her more, she displayed irresistible strength. Alejandro was El Chapo's boy, and he'd just sent away his own sister because he couldn't figure out how to put her talents to good use.

"Joaquin, put a local gang spin on this hospital thing. Donate to Medical Center from the family foundation."

"Consider it done, Alejandro."

"What have you found out about the gringo Wolf?"

"It's not just him. He has a brother and a sister. I am still collecting information, but as of now, I know the father was a Vietnam veteran. The mother was a schoolteacher. The younger brother was a DEA pilot. We are looking into Wolf and his sister."

"I need to understand if they are leaving, or if they will remain to be an issue," Alejandro said.

"The other matter we need to discuss is the house we let them raid."

"Yes. It looks like it worked."

"Partially," Joaquin said. "It redirected the police, but the garage had also been used to hide bodies. Not the best choice. Now they have requested the army to support them until they complete the investigation."

"The army can harm us. Keep an eye on them, Joaquin."

Zapana nodded and walked back to his intel center, immersed in thought. *How do I expand Alejandro's thinking? His arrogance blinds him to other possibilities.*

He thinks he has the locals on his payroll, but Cárdenas is clean and wants us all in prison. And this guy Wolf, he is different. He acts more like a professional soldier than a tourist caught in the wrong place at the wrong time.

What am I missing?

13

L os Mochis Medical Center, Mexico
Gonzalez's commandos assembled at the hospital and changed into hospital clothing provided by Dr. Munoz. They took their time infiltrating the CCU, using different times and routes to access the third floor. Cárdenas made sure they saw him bringing his officer into the hospital and up to the CCU to guard the American woman's door.

Two men dressed in scrubs and wearing temporary workers badges brought Sierra to her third-floor room. She appeared unconscious. The disguised commandos took their position at the nurses' station.

Dr. Munoz logged onto the computer, showing them a few key screens to open should there be questions about the American woman. A very large and imposing soldier, dressed as a police sergeant sat at the door.

Men dressed as maintenance made like they were working on the air conditioning system. They were installing surveillance cameras. The best U.S. military aid could buy.

They provided an unobstructed view and would record the three critical areas. The hallway to the elevators on the left, and past the room to the right facing where there was an emergency stair-well, and the room where Sierra lay.

Gonzalez and his three-man quick-reaction team sat across the room from the recording system operator, checking their body armor before reaching into a Pelican case to add suppressors to their 9mm Beretta M92 pistols.

Their backup weapon a Colt M4 carbine. Considering Cortes's gunmen carried 9mm pistols and Heckler and Koch MP5s, it would make pinpointing the bad guys easier should the situation go sideways.

In a delivery every bit reminiscent of a high school drama class, Wolf played it loud, arguing with Dr. Munoz in the hallway, then announcing he was going upstairs to be with his mother.

Sierra turned to the opening door to see her smiling brother enter the room. "Next stop, Shakespeare's Globe Theatre," he said.

Sierra pointed a finger at him. "Not funny. This is serious."

"You know me, sis. Always trying to break the tension."

Sierra worked quickly to bandage Wolf and place him in the bed, positioned to look like a woman in a coma. Turning the lights down completed the scene. She walked outside to find Bjorn, who was speaking with the police officer as if they were old friends.

Bjorn's language skills had been exceptional since childhood. Interrupting them, she signaled it was time to head downstairs.

As they walked by nurses and administrative staff, they made sure they could hear their conversation about their mother and meeting their brother at the hotel. They left through the front door and walked to the hotel.

Back in the shadows of the dim lit room, Wolf slowed his breathing and expanded his senses. The mechanical noise of the medical equipment corrupted the silence. He tested his ability to move. He might have just one shot to do it right or be dead.

This is a first. Come on death, come find me.

14

E l Rancho Cortes, Sinaloa, Mexico
"The Anderson woman is not dead." Alejandro stopped in his tracks and wrapped the phone cord around his hand as the words sank in.

How can it be? Zapana's men never failed. This had to be a mistake. An epic one.

"What? Are you sure?" he growled.

"Yes, boss. There is a police guard at the door, and she is in the bed. Her family is just leaving now for their hotel. She is in a critical care room on the third floor."

He hung up the phone in haste. He clenched his fists in anger. "Marta!" he screamed for his assistant. "Tell Joaquin and Martin to come to my office right now."

Alejandro paced his office, his neck veins bulging as he clenched the whole of his body and screamed at the sky just as he had since childhood when frustrated or denied. He gulped a large breath to calm himself before sitting at his desk and pulling his 1911 .45 pistol from the top drawer.

He sat down and was wiping the pistol when Martin Amaro and Zapana walked in.

He stared at them for several seconds.

"Joaquin, your plan failed—you failed. The American woman is still alive," he said.

"But my source told me he gave her the full dose!" Joaquin protested. "There is no way she is alive."

"And yet she is not dead," he snapped.

"I will send my people again," Zapana said.

"Your people didn't do the job the first time. Why should I trust them now? No, this time you complete the work. You make sure it's done properly."

Zapana's eyes widened. He looked afraid, and Alejandro liked that. He should be afraid.

"But the risk—"

"It shouldn't be a problem for a man with your military background," he said. "Such things are like riding a bike. And I need you to show your commitment to this family. It stops now." Alejandro slammed his palm on the desk and gestured with the pistol.

"I want us us back on track. Or I find someone who can." "Yes, boss!" Joaquin said and hurried from the room.

Zapana sat alone in his office. The last time he'd been part of an actual operation was in the '80s in Peru. His focus since then had been intelligence and data harvesting, not trigger pulling. He had created the sophisticated network which kept the Cortes family in business.

Now Alejandro questions my loyalty, my commitment?

Zapana's man at the hospital had the doctor's scrubs and white lab coat ready for him. The nametag read Dr. Félix Marques, Neurosurgery. The lab coat hid his suppressed .22 caliber Walther PPK.

It was against his guerrilla training to not bring a knife for backup, but the woman was a soft target. Access to the room would be simple, his task easy.

Zapana waited until visiting hours were over to approach the floor. At the nurses' station, he inquired about Miss Anderson's recovery. As the nurse handed him the chart, Zapana's hand slipped inside his lab coat to his pistol.

"Nurse Péna," Joaquin said with a friendly, collegial tone. "I see from your tattoo you were in the Army."

"Si, medico," he replied with a smile. "I was a combat medic in Brigada de Fusileros Paracaidistas, an army paratrooper, five years ago. This is job pays much better, and no one shoots at you."

"Yes," Joaquin said and smiled, lowering his hand.

The police officer stood and announced he was going for coffee. "Does anyone else want anything?"

Joaquin smiled his best smile. "Gracias, sergeant." He handed the officer three hundred pesos. "Coffee with milk for me please, and two for the nurses. If there is any change, spend it all on donuts or something."

"Gracias, doctor!" the officer said, nodding, and he headed to the first-floor café. Zapana read the Alma Anderson chart, making affirmative noises. He understood little of the medical jargon, but the gist of it was the woman had been dead and extraordinary measures had brought her back.

Now he intended to return her to a state of death that wouldn't respond to extraordinary measures.

Joaquin looked up from the clipboard and glanced at his watch. "I must check in on Señora Anderson. My dinner awaits." Nurse Pena just smiled and went back to his computer keyboard.

His gun hand sweated as Zapana entered the room and closed the door behind him.

Shallow breathing and rapid heartbeat threatened his vision and stability.

His pistol pulled from under the lab coat, he held it with both hands and tiptoed forward, aiming for the sleeping woman's bandaged head.

A loud gunshot erupted from beneath the hospital sheets and struck Zapana's vest in the center chest.

The force knocked the breath from him and flung him back against the door as if a mule had kicked him.

Stunned, he fired too late. And now a man was on top of him and punching his face.

They tumbled to the floor in a jumble of arms and legs. Zapana tried using his legs to flip his attacker, but the man had wrapped them up.

The attacker was using Zapana's suppressor as leverage to rip the handgun from his grip.

His strength was fading fast, the result of his cushy cartel executive life, and he struggled to fight back.

Zapana let go of the pistol to protect his face and strike back, landing a glancing, ineffective blow.

He recognized the mistake and screamed when his knee exploded in agony, splashing lurid red blood splatters across the pristine white lab coat.

More people surged into the room, they switched the lights on, and Zapana felt hands restraining him.

They gagged him, zip- tied his hands and feet, and they slipped a black sack over his head and cinched under his chin.

Dr. Munoz and Nurse Péna cleaned and field dressed Zapana's shattered knee, immobilizing it as best they could in the short time they had with this patient.

Péna raised a hypodermic filled with a clear liquid. Without preamble, he pushed it into Joaquin's upper arm and pressed the plunger. "Go to sleep."

Head spinning, chest hurting, and devastated knee on fire, Joaquin embraced the darkness.

15

Airport interrogation site

"I still find it hard to believe, but as you say it, we have struck gold," Gonzalez said. "You have captured Joaquin Zapana, Alejandro's head of intelligence!"

Wolf smiled. His wrist ached from the fight, but it had been a small price to pay for the capture of his prize.

After the scuffle, a soldier in nurse's clothes brought a gurney to the room. They covered the limp Zapana with sheets and headed to the loading dock where they loaded him into an unmarked van and driven away.

"Where are we headed?" he asked as they piled into Cardenas's police car.

"We are not going to my office."

"Why not?" he asked.

"Too many cartel eyes and ears in the police building. We have a place prepared to interview him somewhere else."

The van driver headed to a nondescript airport maintenance hangar with no signage or identification. Gonzalez radioed ahead to Sergeant Major Dominguez the team was on its way.

Wolf didn't care where they went. All that mattered was getting information he could use against Alejandro and Eliana Cortes.

He leaned back and closed his eyes, allowing himself a moment of respite. Earlier, Sierra had told him the results of their mother's autopsy had returned. The tox screens had come back positive for an unexplained lethal dose of morphine and propofol.

His brother and sister were taking their parents back home to the reservation for burial, but he was staying behind to help with the Zapana interrogation. And likely more.

On the ride to the hangar, he processed everything, from the conversation about stopping for lunch in the heartland of the Sinaloa cartel to the capture of Zapana.

The cartel had attacked his family and the time for subtlety was long gone. Wolf smiled at the thought, not with pleasure but resolution.

The sergeant major had displayed amazing creativity in readying the interrogation space given the lack of resources, classic senior NCO magic. The room was in the office with its windows blacked out and soundproofing in the form of mover's blankets hung on its walls.

If you sat stock still, the lack of noise created a ringing in your ears as your brain struggled to hear. There was no air conditioning or air movement. The only furniture was an old metal office chair and a conical floor lamp on an adjustable stand.

The van pulled up at the hangar's man door and stopped. No one moved or spoke. The hot engine ticked as it cooled. Zapana's sedated breathing in the back was the only sound.

Before moving his prisoner into the hangar, Gonzalez gathered the team together inside the building to set the standard operating procedure for the interrogation.

"First and most important, we always keep our faces and any tattoos covered up. We do not want this guy identifying us. Second, we always have two people in the room with the prisoner. Three, we follow army rules for interrogation of a terrorist."

Lion Squadron teammates dragged the still unconscious Zapana from the van and into the makeshift interrogation cell. He was propped upright in the chair and flex-cuffed at his legs and arms.

A team medic checked his pulse and then emptied a bottle of water across his face. Zapana choked and spit as he came out of his sedation and struggled against his bindings.

He shook his head and water flew from the bag on his head like a dog shaking off a dip in a pool. Wolf moved in front of the drug boss and laughed, pulling tight the balaclava over his face and yanking the black bag off Zapana's head.

The cartel man took a heavy breath and assessed his surroundings, taking in the men standing before him and grasping his plight.

"You are all dead men." He nodded toward Wolf. "Especially this stupid American."

Wolf removed his mask. "Not today, Joaquin," he said, laughing. "You will answer our questions. If you do, we will treat you well and you may yet live out the rest of your pitiful life in witness protection. If not, we will treat you like a terrorist."

"What do you know about terrorists? I was a freedom fighter... Sendero Luminoso."

He leaned a menacing grin just below his flaming eyes. "Ancient history, amigo. What you were, what you think you are, it's all gone. We own you now," he said, circling the prisoner.

"I know your training. You will talk to us. It's just a matter of time." Wolf drew a knife from behind his back and gouged it into Zapana's wounded knee, turning the blade so it scraped the bone. Zapana screamed once and passed out.

"Enough!" Gonzalez said as he bear-hugged him from behind and pulled him away. "Sergeant Major, put two men with the prisoner and bring the medic to bandage his knee." He turned to to his friend. "Let's get some air." He motioned to Cárdenas, and the three left the building.

They stepped outside. Wolf was seething. He wasn't ashamed he'd enjoyed Zapana's pain. He was ready to deliver a lot more before the day would end.

Cárdenas pointed at him. "Too much too soon, and he shuts

down! What the do you think you're doing? Where does all this anger and violence come from?"

"My mother is dead!" he shouted.

But even through his darkness and despair, he knew he'd been wrong. "I'm sorry, I lost control. But we need actionable intel right now."

"Agreed, but we have to be humane for our own sanity. Let's go back in there and play the good cop-bad cop routine. Cárdenas can observe via video. It should be operational now," Gonzalez said.

They went back inside and didn't speak to Zapana for a full ten minutes.

"Joaquin," Carlos said. "I am sorry for my friend's behavior. He thinks we should kill you very slowly. You help me, I help you. I can put you into the American witness protection program. You can live a good life in the U.S., drive a pickup, shop at Walmart."

Zapana remained silent, but he looked up.

"Tell us what you know about the murders at El Gran Pez and the hospital, and I will make the call," he urged. "You will be eating breakfast in America in forty-eight hours."

Joaquin laughed. "Alejandro will have me killed if I tell you the time of day."

"Not if you are in the U.S.," he countered. "He will never find you if you aren't stupid. We can protect you from him."

"You are Fuerza Especial de Reacción," Joaquin said. "You cannot protect anyone."

Zapana was getting his swagger back, so Gonzalez cinched the hood back on and turned out the lights. Wolf clenched a fist, then connected with a right hook to Zapana's face. He went limp.

"Hmm. Glass jaw," he said.

Carlos huffed. "This piece of dirt seems ready to die before he talks. Lieutenant, what are your thoughts?"

"I don't think so," Cárdenas said "I don't sense he is ready to give up his life, we must break him now. We do not have much time."

"Let me wake him up this time," Wolf said.

Then he asked the team medic for a syringe filled with cold water. He took off the bag and held Joaquin's head up by his hair.

He jammed the syringe into his ear and pushed hard, tearing the eardrum membrane. Zapana screamed, his head snapping up and eyes wide open.

Wolf whispered in Zapana's good ear. "I've only read about water boarding. I hope it doesn't kill you."

He placed the black bag back over Zapana's twisting head and pushed the chair backward. Zapana let out a groan as his head smacked against the dirty concrete floor.

It came fast and did not stop. Zapana held his breath for as long as he could, but it wasn't long enough. drowned him, and he passed out.

He slipped the bag from Zapana's head and slapped his face. "Joaquin, Joaquin, wake up, amigo." He was slow in coming around.

"I didn't give the order," Zapana whispered. He coughed up watery vomit, and it dribbled from his mouth when he turned his head.

Gonzalez leaned in. "What order is that, Joaquin?"

"To kill the Americans at El Gran Pez."

Gonzalez frowned. "Joaquin, you are not a stupid man. Please don't act like we are. We know you didn't order the murders. It could only come from one of two people, Alejandro or Eliana. Alejandro understands there is nothing to gain from a mass murder. But Eliana is a cold and angry bitch who uses violence first. And she was at El Gran Pez."

Zapana shook his head and strained against his restraints. "No, it was Martin who ordered the hit on Hector Gonzalez. Hector was skimming the drug shipments, and we found out about it. Martin acted without telling Alejandro."

Wolf came from behind, tilting the chair halfway back off the floor where it was held by two commandos. He slopped the wet sack, reeking of vomit, back over Zapana's head.

"You're lying to us," he said.

The water came again, hard and continuous. Zapana held his breath, but he punched him in the stomach, forcing him to breathe.

Gasping for air, Zapana found water, then blackness.

To be safe, Gonzalez pulled the sloppy wet bag off Zapana's head.

They left their prisoner on the floor and walked to the next space where the video surveillance was setup. Cárdenas looked up as they entered.

"Lieutenant, what did you see?" Wolf asked.

"Not much, though when Carlos called Eliana an angry bitch, he tensed. There is something between the two. Why else would he give up his longtime friend Martin?"

"Do we keep up with this line of questioning," he asked, "Or do we move on to the murder of my mother?"

"I suggest we tell him we have DNA proof it was Eliana," Cárdenas said. "Make it clear it's useless to lie to us. He needs to say it was Eliana if the interrogation is to stop."

Zapana had awakened by the time his interrogators returned and he looked bad. Wolf could imagine every nerve ending in the man's body was screaming for relief. His eyes were bulging and bloodshot, his knee was bloody and swollen, his face contorted with pain.

Gonzalez towered over the man secured to the chair. The odor of vomit, piss, and desperation rose from him.

"Joaquin. Eliana was at El Gran Pez. We have DNA proof she was there. She ordered the murders, yes?"

Zapana nodded.

"I need you to speak the words, Joaquin."

Zapana lifted his head and looked Carlos in his face.

"Eliana gave the order to kill Hector and the Americans."

Gonzalez patted Joaquin on the shoulder. "See, you are a smart man." Wolf stood beside Carlos with his arms crossed, better to not strike out.

Zapana turned to Wolf. "You are Wolf, right? I reviewed the restaurant video. Your mother was singing before she killed one of our men. Who sings before killing?"

Wolf froze. At times he hated his perfect memory as it replayed his mother's death song and the odors of burning seafood and gunpowder.

Wolf was stunned for a second. "Who ordered the murder of the Anderson woman in the hospital?"

Zapana looked away. "The hospital attack was Eliana."

"Did Alejandro order the second try?" Wolf asked.

Zapana nodded his head and muttered a weak laugh. "Your ruse worked, and he blamed me."

"Well, here you are, Joaquin. Alejandro has given up on you," Wolf said. "You are expendable to him. Do good leaders throw away their most loyal men? You remember this from your Marxist training," Wolf added. "Trotsky, I think. 'Go where you belong from now on, into the dustbin of history!' Alejandro has thrown you into the dustbin."

Wolf walked out of the hangar, leaving Zapana there to fester in his own guilt and failure. Torture wasn't Wolf's thing, but in the moment, he had stopped caring and reveled in the power of revenge he would wreak on Sinaloa.

They have no idea what I'm capable of.

16

El Rancho Cortes, Sinaloa, Mexico

Alejandro hated waiting, and it was all he seemed to do these days other than the occasional meal with his family. He stopped and glared at Amaro standing in the doorway. Alejandro left the table to guide him into the kitchen. A quick nod to the cook cleared the room.

"Why hasn't Joaquin called? Is the American woman dead?"

"I do not know. Shall I send one of my men?"

"Yes, Martin. Make sure they do it quietly. No more shooting."

Amaro left and Alejandro rejoined his family for lunch. He asked each of his three children about school and reminded them of the need to do well.

He clutched his wife's hand and asked if the pediatrician's medicine had helped with the baby's allergies. To an outsider, it might have looked rather normal if you didn't know the family business.

In the back of his mind, all Alejandro could think about were the very serious problems if Zapana was dead or arrested. He was once again left to do nothing but wait and waiting made him angry.

Twenty minutes later, Amaro returned. His boss kissed the kids and told his wife he would see her for dinner.

"Vaya con Dios," she said with gravity. Go with God. She always said it with serious intent because there was never a guarantee her husband would be alive the next time, she saw him.

He motioned for Amaro to follow him to his office. Once inside, Amaro closed the doors.

"I have news," he said, turning toward his boss. "Joaquin's contact gave him the doctor's coat and name tag. She saw him take the elevator up to the CCU floor, but no one has seen him leave. The security video shows male nurses putting a body in an unmarked van. No one knows those nurses, and we can see one of them has a paratrooper tattoo on the back of his neck." He looked down. "There was blood in the room."

"What does all this mean?" Alejandro demanded. Amaro hesitated. He feared angering his boss.

"Someone changed the paperwork on the American woman to deceive us. She was dead yesterday."

He bit the inside of his lip and lingered in the metallic taste of his blood. He responded in even tones, which Amaro knew represented him at his most dangerous. His even tone often preceded an apocalypse.

"So, tell me, Martin. Why did our people report her still alive?"

"The doctors deceived us by changing the paperwork and Wolf staged a drama in the lobby for our sources to report."

"So, the woman is dead, and Joaquin is missing." he slammed a fist into his table and pulled his pistol from the top drawer. Without thinking, he checked to see if it was ready to fire.

"We believe the army has him," Amaro said.

"Why not the police?"

"Because we would know if he was being held at police headquarters," Amaro said.

"We would also know if he was in custody with the regular army. Those sources are solid. I know who has him. The Lions," Alejandro looked out the large windows of his office. The garden flowers are especially colorful today. "Will Joaquin talk, Martin?"

"He had resistance training in Peru, but has never been operational. We must plan as if he will break. The Lions will do whatever it takes to make him talk."

Alejandro's mind raced through many possible unacceptable outcomes. As the Cortes intelligence chief, Zapana had in his brain everyone on the payroll of the Cortes portion of the cartel and the leadership around El Chapo.

He also had a working understanding of the Cortes distribution network. It might lead to the interdiction of drugs, cash, or the shutdown of a productive trade route.

If it was a Columbian cocaine route, it could be deadly.

"Martin, I have three tasks for you. First, I'm directing you to take over our intelligence network. I will call the team and let them know you are in charge. Second, tell our friend at the federal police to arrest and deport the gringos."

"Yes, sir!" Amaro said. He was thrilled. He'd only been a captain during his Peruvian Army time. This was like getting a field promotion to general.

"Good. Third, put everyone in our network on finding our friend. He is too valuable to our organization. Either you find him and bring him back, or he dies with his secrets."

17

Airport interrogation site

Gonzalez's words were stuck in Wolf's head. Maybe he'd gone too far, but now he didn't regret any of it.

They'd gotten answers, and now they were one step closer to giving the prosecutor what he needed to bring Eliana Cortes to justice. But would it hold up in a Mexican court? As the police lieutenant said, Mexican justice was often situational on its most judicious day.

Joaquin slumped in the chair. He looked terrible.

"I suggest we let him rest," Cárdenas said, "We need to feed him and clean him up. He cannot go back to the cartel now. Once they realize he has disappeared, they will suspect the army and reach out to their informants. We must assume we will not have him much longer. Maybe another day or two, at most."

"You both know the Sinaloa leadership," Wolf said, "But what about the production sites and the distribution network? They are high-value targets. If we identify and execute operations against HVTs at those sites, we will recover intelligence leading us to more targets."

Gonzalez raised a flat hand. "That's our job, brother, not yours. Remember, you are not even here."

Wolf half smiled. "You're right. But when I'm back at my civilian job, I'll try to help you as much as I can."

Wolf glimpsed Cárdenas staring with curiosity and not following the gist of the conversation.

"L-T, in my day job I work for the U.S. Special Operations Command in the intelligence staff. I'm also a Florida Army National Guard Special Forces team sergeant. Major Gonzalez's Lions and my team trained together."

Cárdenas just nodded. This explained a lot.

Over the next hour, the commandos gave Zapana food and water. Once he had become almost human again, they placed him on a cot set back against the wall. They still flex-cuffed his hands in front and secured his ankles so he couldn't just up and run away. His eyes were soon closed and every so often he would let out a moan or a snore as he slept.

Wolf sat a dozen feet away and stared at Zapana.

Cárdenas walked over, pulling him from his thoughts. "Bad news. There is an arrest warrant out for you and your family."

He furrowed his brow. "Where did the order come from?"

"I suspect the cartel is using their influence. The federal police based the warrant on your supposed interference with a police investigation."

"What a joke," he scoffed.

"This is no joke. If the federal police arrest you then you will stay arrested, and there's nothing I can do for you. We must send you home tomorrow," Cárdenas said.

"Can I have twenty-four hours? I can pull more from Joaquin."

"No, I'm sorry," Cárdenas said. "This is a rule I must follow."

Wolf let out an aggravated growl. He wasn't ready to give up.

Gonzalez, who had been standing nearby, put a hand to his earpiece and raised his head. "Gentlemen, the cartel is planning a visit." He directed his men to take up defensive positions. Then he radioed Juárez to take Sergeant Major Dominguez and three men with the helicopters to the far end of the aircraft parking area to await follow-on orders.

"Will Alejandro attack us here where everyone can see them?" Wolf asked.

"Yes, he will," Gonzalez said. "He is calculating, but not afraid to use violence. And in this area, people have conditioned themselves not to call authorities when gunfire erupts, but flee for their own safety. We're on our own here. Now, we need to prepare"

A commando gave Wolf a chest rig with plates, an M4 rifle and six loaded magazines, a 9mm Smith & Wesson 5906 pistol with three mags, and a team radio. As he donned the gear he said, "They will try to force us to leave the hangar, so we are easier to attack."

Gonzalez turned to Cárdenas. "Lieutenant, you can help us. We can draw away some gunmen by putting a Zapana decoy in your car and then drive with lights and siren back to your police station."

Wolf chimed in. "Grab your car and pull around to the hangar door. I'll work with the team to build the dummy."

Gonzalez's cellphone rang, and he turned away to take the call.

He had a grimace on his face when he turned back.

"Gentlemen, we've encountered a bit of a problem," he said. "I just got off the phone with my commander. Someone called the secretary of defense and told him we are holding a prisoner."

Wolf's eyes widened. "How did they find out?"

Cárdenas shook his head in frustration. "Cartel spies and informants are everywhere, like bacteria. Now you see why it's so hard to fight them."

Gonzalez smirked. "I told the colonel the police have detained a suspect, not us."

Interrupted by a radio call, Gonzalez's eyes narrowed as he listened to his rooftop sniper report. "Alpha Actual, Alpha Eight, tangos inbound, seven vehicles in convoy at the outer marker."

Gonzalez clicked his radio microphone twice, acknowledging. "We've got less than ten minutes before our visitors arrive," he said. "Lieutenant, go now. Wolf, prepare the dummy. The lieutenant must be on his way before they cross the airport entrance."

Cárdenas ran from the building and headed toward his unmarked police car. Wolf grabbed a soldier, an old set of coveralls and got to work. The soldier brought a tire inner tube, which they inflated and bent in the shape of a head. To finish the illusion, the sergeant major handed them a black sack, like the one Zapana had over his head.

Cárdenas pulled up close to the hangar doors as they finished stuffing the coveralls. Wolf kept low, acting like he was protecting the dummy as he placed it in the backseat of the car and secured with the seatbelt. The lieutenant raced out of the airport with emergency lights flashing and the siren wailing as he screamed past the incoming cartel convoy. One Range Rover from the convoy turned around to give chase.

Back inside the hangar, the commandos readied their weapons and adjusted their positions. Wolf put Zapana in an office between an overturned metal desk and an interior cinder-block wall. He checked to make sure the flex-cuffs around Joaquin's wrists and ankles were snug. Gonzalez assigned two of his men to guard the prisoner and radioed the sergeant major.

"Cut the power to this building if you can find the box."

"Yes, Major!" Dominguez said. The sergeant major pointed to a commando. "Go to the junction box and pull every fuse or control lever you find to chop the power."

Wolf picked up an old-school break-action M79 grenade launcher and pointed to a corporal. "Toss me a bandoleer of HE rounds." He climbed the interior ladder to the roof taking a position next to the sniper.

From his position, he could see the cartel Range Rovers as they parked nose-to-tail in two tight columns of three, one hundred meters in front of the hangar doors. Not tactical brilliant, but whatever.

The gunmen appeared leaderless, milling about talking and lighting cigarettes, seeming to wait for orders. Wolf wasn't waiting. He loaded a high-explosive round into the shotgun style launcher and snapped it shut.

The small soda-can-sized grenades made a distinctive thump when fired. The first 40mm grenade struck between the lead Range Rovers and they both exploded into a mammoth fireball, flinging cartel soldiers across the ground and into the air.

In quick succession, Wolf launched two antipersonnel grenades thump-thump at the largest throng of enemy, cutting them down.

Two more high-explosive rounds detonated through the windshields of the trail vehicles. They too exploded, and men on fire spilled out of the SUV's doors to flop around on the tarmac, screaming. The second trail Range Rover fuel tank exploded, dropping it onto the two middle SUVs in the column.

The anti-personnel canisters had annihilated the cartel soldiers who had been smokin' and jokin', thinking they were safe in the dark. They weren't.

Now there were four destroyed and two damaged SUVs plus a dozen or more dead or mutilated cartel sicarios.

Wolf did the math. Six vehicles with five gunmen each. Thirty soldiers minus maybe twelve dead, say, and subtracting perhaps a half-dozen more still alive but out of the fight. Most of those would die soon without medical attention, which they were not going to recieve. So, about twelve cartel tangos against eight of Mexico's fiercest Tier 1 operators.

They're going to need more bad guys, he thought with a malevolent grin.

18

Airport interrogation site

Wolf spied the sniper shaking his head before turning back to his scope. Wolf was singing his death song, just in case. Either way, he would make his ancestors proud today.

He radioed Gonzalez and recommended everyone hold fire until the cartel moved toward them. Gonzalez radioed. "Are you crazy? You want them to attack?"

He smirked. "Just helping them make up their minds," he said, as he watched the sniper shoot two gunmen trying to retrieve something from one of the destroyed vehicles. Then he changed positions for a better sightline on several other enemies.

Wolf rushed down the ladder to Joaquin.

"Alpha Three, any movement?" Gonzalez asked.

"Negative."

Just as Gonzalez was about to move his men, one of the Alpha team soldiers defending the hangar door radioed. "RPG! RPG!"

From the roof, the sniper dropped the shooter when he saw the rocket flash but the cartel soldier had fired first. His aim was a little right of center and the rocket-propelled grenade warhead connected with the larger hangar doorframe, creating a hole the size of a truck.

Wolf felt the fiery blast as he stood in the office doorway. The molten slug formed by the rocket shaped charge struck near two Alpha team members who had taken cover behind some wall lockers.

Gonzalez said, "Alpha Three, Alpha Actual, report."

"Alpha Three is up, Alpha Four is down," a sergeant radioed back.

Seconds after the blast in the hangar, another rocket hit the office's front door. The explosion destroyed the reception area and office across the hall.

Zapana screamed as supersonic blast waves slammed into his injured ear, and hot metal fragments strafed the walls with shrapnel.

Wolf checked to make sure his high-value prisoner wasn't leaking and, staying low, he risked a glance down the dark hallway. He fired a three-round burst from his M4, and his bullets found the abdomen of the lead gunman, who dropped to the floor like a sandbag.

The other three gunmen with him jumped sideways into an office for cover and to reconsider their life choices.

"Ha, there you go, hide!" he yelled in Spanish. Then he pulled the pins from two M67 fragmentation grenades and rolled them along the wall. "Hide from this!"

He ducked back behind the overturned desk and covered Zapana with his body. About three seconds later the grenades exploded in series. They peppered where they hid with hot splinters of metal as piercing as dental needles.

Wolf and Gonzalez moved silently through the hallway with M4s at the ready, sweeping left and right to clear the other offices. They entered the empty space to find two dead gunmen and one wounded. They each took a gunman and fired two additional rounds to make sure they were real dead.

They rushed back to Zapana who was wailing.

"Shut up, Joaquin," Wolf said. He gagged the prisoner to keep him from giving away their position to the remaining cartel soldiers. "You don't enjoy being on this end of an attack, do you? I bet you always had others fighting for you."

The hangar became a buzz saw of bullets. It sounded like the cartel was firing everything it had all at once.

Suppressing fire telegraphed a surge. He raised his head over the pockmarked office partition in time to see he was right.

Two gunmen ran through the open hangar man door, finding cover on the west wall. The curtain of bullets started again as two more gunmen ran forward.

Wolf turned to make sure Zapana was still in place with two of Gonzalez's soldiers nearby before engaging the attackers, but he was too slow.

Gonzalez and a sergeant dropped the gunmen with coordinated full-auto bursts. Then Carlos engaged the enemy on the west wall, directing the sergeant to put suppressive fire through the hangar opening.

One soldier with Wolf brushed by him to join the fight for the hangar. His M249 light machine gun was a welcome addition. Designed for sustained firing from its plastic box of two hundred rounds of linked ammunition.

Two more enemy gunmen sprinted through the opening, only to be cut down by the machine gunner.

"Grenade!" Carlos screamed.

With nowhere to hide, all they could do is drop. The muffled sound of the explosion made little sense to Wolf until he saw his friend looking down at his sergeant. Then Wolf saw the blood. The soldier had thrown himself onto the grenade to save Gonzalez's life.

A soldier yelled, "They're coming down both sides!"

Carlos put a hand on the dead commando's back, then stood with his M203 combination rifle/grenade launcher and two dual-purpose high-explosive grenades.

Wolf provided fire support as best he could from his position as Gonzalez worked his way to a spot in line with the enemy gunmen along the west wall.

He loaded the grenade launcher and fired, reloaded, and

then fired again. The dual-purpose warheads armed at forty-six feet, well before they struck the storage cabinets.

The small but effective charges turned the cabinets into shrapnel. Chunks of doors, parts, and shelves disintegrated into a hail of fragments. The wounded gunmen cried out in agony to God and their mothers as they died.

Gonzalez ran back to the offices, calling to Wolf. "Coming in!" "How are we doing?" Wolf said.

"Two KIA. Four tangos down in the hangar." "Check. I've got four tangos down here."

"Alpha Actual, Alpha Eight," the rooftop over watch radioed. "Tangos approaching fast, two more vehicles."

"Roger that," Gonzalez said, turning to Wolf. "Two more vehicles inbound. Go to the roof with the grenade launcher and see what you can do. We'll guard Zapana."

Wolf scrambled back up the interior ladder and crawled over to the sniper. "You take out the drivers. I'll try to catch the rest as they bail out of the trucks." Both men looked downrange and fixed their sights on looming targets.

The road into the hangar was a near perfect fatal funnel with nowhere to hide. The sniper dealt death to the first driver. Tires screeching, the truck veered hard left, crashing into a tree.

The second vehicle was so close to the first the sniper had to wait until the first swerved away to take a shot.

He missed the driver, but the round hit a gunman in the second row whose AK discharged into the roof of the vehicle, lighting up the interior with muzzle blast and no doubt scaring his companions.

Wolf lobbed a high-explosive round in front of the truck, causing the driver to swerve and slam on the brakes. This gave the sniper an easy shot at the driver and two other cartel soldiers in the cab with him.

As other gunmen bailed and scrambled to find cover, Wolf lobbed three more rounds at them, killing two and wounding several more. But several escaped death and pressed their attack.

The fighting intensified and the cartel soldiers were getting closer, with uncontrolled full-auto fire from the cartel AKs versus the short-burst, targeted firing of the defenders' M4s. Gonzalez radioed, "All Alphas and Bravos to the hangar now!"

A grenade exploded, then two more in quick succession. "Alpha Actual, we need support right now!"

"I'm headed back down. Do the best you can up here," Wolf said to the sniper.

"Yes, my friend—we will carry the day!" the sniper said. Wolf clapped him on the shoulder and scurried to the roof hatch and the ladder.

He had just run to Gonzalez's position when Wolf sensed the air waves caused by Black Hawks. He looked out the door to see one of the Lion helicopters arrive in combat assault mode, right on the edge of disaster.

"Cover!" Gonzalez yelled and pushed Wolf to the floor. The Black Hawk flared hard, the left-side door gunner unleashing high-speed death into the remaining cartel attackers from his mini-gun.

Between bursts, the pilot adjusted the Black Hawk to give the gunner the best line of sight into the hangar walls. The fight was over in seconds. Pieces of dead cartel gunmen and blood splattered everywhere.

After hovering for a moment so the door gunner could assess for any missed targets, he called all clear to the pilots. They headed for a concrete helipad a few hundred meters away.

Wolf saw Gonzalez was talking, but after the danger-close mini-gun he couldn't hear a thing. Gonzalez gave him a thumbs-up. Wolf nodded and did the same. The sergeant with an empty M249 squad automatic weapon was holding his calf and blood coursed from between his fingers. He was putting tentative weight on it, so it was a through- and-through gunshot wound.

"Let's grab Zapana and go," Gonzalez shouted to Wolf, who still wasn't hearing well.

Sergeant Major Dominguez and another soldier joined them.

"Sir, the hangar is clear and we set a security perimeter." Dominguez said. Then and he and a commando headed down the hallway at a trot, their weapons still ready just in case.

"We can't take Zapana with us and we can't give him to the police. I suggest we hand him over to the DEA. Can your brother arrange a pickup?" Gonzalez asked.

"I don't know," Wolf said. "We can ask."

Gonzalez looked around the office. "Where is he?"

"Over there," he said, pointing to a desk on its side he pulled away.

Zapana was lying on his back in a pool of blood, his unseeing eyes glassy and aimed at the ceiling. Wolf placed his fingers on the man's neck looking for a pulse. He ripped open Zapana's shirt and there were bloody lacerations in his chest. Two miserable pieces of shrapnel no larger than a fifty cent coin had killed their most promising lead.

He pounded the desk, and howled. The cartel had stopped their star witness from talking after all, though at substantial cost. So, who had won?

Two more gunshots rang out. Gonzalez keyed his radio. "Alpha Nine, are we clear?"

"Wes, sir, clear," Dominguez said. "Just cleaning up loose ends."

Carlos radioed for the Black Hawks to return and help care for the wounded and dead. There were plenty of each. Sirens rang out in the far distance.

Wolf scanned the video equipment. Most of it looked intact. Gonzalez walked in and sighed. "Wolf, we need to talk."

"What is it?"

Carlos gritted his teeth. It was clear it irritated him. "You have focused on getting what you wanted, and your choices have gotten my men killed. You lost the one remaining asset we had to bring the Cortes family to justice. Now we have nothing."

"I'm sorry for your men," Wolf said, "but the cartel killed them, not me." Gonzalez shook his head.

"You are not understanding what I'm saying. You only focus on what you want. Team is in your language, but not in your actions to-day. I consider you a friend, but not someone I can trust with the lives of my soldiers. I'm taking my team back to base. I must honor my dead and heal my wounded. I have families who have lost their fathers and husbands."

A spasm of sadness flowed through Wolf.

"Today there is no justice for my brother and his wife. There is no justice for your parents. Do me one favor?" Gonzalez asked.

"Anything, Carlos."

He handed a plastic shopping bag to Wolf. "Here is Joaquin's cell-phone and copies of the video. Give them to Cárdenas and tell him what happened here. Hopefully, he can make use of the material to further his investigation."

Outside, police sirens were close enough to be heard along with the helicopter turbines. Sergeant Major Dominguez was rounding up soldiers and getting them on the helicopters.

"We are leaving," Gonzalez said, "but I have one word for you, friend. Pensar-Think, Lance. Think." He tossed a keyring to Wolf and nodded his head to a dusty, doorless Jeep CJ4 tucked back in the corner of the hanger.

"It runs." Gonzalez nodded. "Have a good life." After Gonzalez left, he sat in a plastic chair and looked away from Joaquin's body.

What a friggin' mess. There were more dead bad guys than good guys, but none of this felt like winning.

A few kilometers down the airport access road, flashing emergency lights could be seen twinkling as they came over the rise. Time to go.

19

USSOCOM, Tampa, Florida

It had been ten days since the episodes in Mexico. After the funeral and a restless overnight on the reservation, Wolf went home to Tampa, Florida.

He lived alone in a three-bedroom townhouse on Tampa Bay. He had taken a few days off to decompress, but down time always felt like wasted time. With nothing new from the DEA, Cárdenas, or Gonzalez, he had to go back to his day job to preserve his sanity.

Every Wednesday at noon, he led a multi-service office group, civilian and military, on a run. Rain, sun, heat, humidity, it didn't matter. The eight-mile run was what everyone needed, especially Wolf.

Most were now stuck in desk jobs they never wanted. The run allowed them to blow off the stress and tension of entrapment in a cube farm.

It was sunny and humid, eighty-two degrees with ninety percent humidity. Classic Florida. It made the run especially challenging for two newbies who were being introduced to Wolf's lunchtime running agenda on a humid Florida day.

The group of nine men and three women were walking it off in the parking lot of the MacDill Air Force Base gym. Wolf was bent under the water stanchion soaking his head when U.S. Navy Master Chief Gunner's Mate Mack Hilton pointed at him. "Guys, did you hear we have a someone in our group who got shots off at the Sinaloa cartel?"

The group looked confused.

Hilton clapped him on the back of his soaked T-shirt, splashing sweat into the air. He looked around to confirm the group wasn't being overheard.

"Ladies and gentlemen, Lance Bear Wolf, Florida Army National Guard and our favorite intel nerd. He reached back to his SF training on his recent rtaining mission in Mexico. The report I read, suggests Wolf got after it with Sinaloa in a big way."

He took a swig of water. All eyes were on him.

"Guys," the master chief continued, "Our boy here captured a Sinaloa intelligence lead, interrogated him, and smoked some tangos for good measure."

Like most intel and special operators, he didn't like attention on him, much less on his activities, whether official or, in this case, unofficial.

"Let me set the record straight. Your ears only." Wolf asid as he used his shirt to wipe his face. "Yeah, I was in Mexico helping my parents drive back when Sinaloa gunmen killed my parents—" There were curses from several people. "—and a lot of other people. I worked with police and a new elite team called the Lions. Our interrogations turned up interesting information, but it's up to the Mexican authorities to deal with it." Wolf shook his head. "The people I worked with are first class, but their group is small and they're still under Mexican law. The system is so corrupt."

Kevin "Kit" Carson, an active-duty Special Forces Master Sergeant, blurted out, "Who on God's Green Earth gave you permission to operate down there?"

"No one. No one had to. There was a shooting in a restaurant, and I stopped the threat. Once they killed my parents, nothing was going to stop me from getting after their killers. I was fortunate to connect with the right people who saw the mission the same way I did." Wolf said. He still couldn't believe his mother and father were dead. But he felt pride they died as warriors.

"We did capture the cartel's intelligence chief. But he died in the cartel's attempt to rescue him." Wolf sighed. "Several top tier operators were lost too. I failed."

"Wolf, you did more than anyone has in a long time," Colonel Gates said. "We all wish we could have been there with you." The group nodded in agreement.

The acknowledgment from his colleagues buoyed his spirit. But now was not the time to celebrate. He needed to complete his plan for revenge

20

USSOCOM, Tampa, Florida

The U.S. Special Operations Command on MacDill Air Force Base juts out into Tampa Bay, surrounded on three sides by water. SOCOM's charter includes overseeing all special operations units. The command's daily business includes covert activity, direct action, reconnaissance, foreign internal defense, and unconventional warfare.

As a senior technical advisor to the head of intelligence, Wolf spent most of his time in conference rooms like the Secure Compartmented Information Facility he was in now.

The SCIF was designed for meetings at the highest levels of classification—those above Top Secret, as was the meeting he joined. Eight men and five women sat around a U-shaped table listening to a major from ops describe the planned interdiction of a high-value individual.

Just then, the SCIF door opened and the red warning light mounted above the door spun. A female in a well-tailored suit stepped into the room. In defiance of protocol, she did not close the door behind her but left it open a crack.

Through the opening he could see another person waiting. "Master Sergeant Lance Wolf?" she asked, though she knew who she was looking for.

"I'll be out in ten," he said, trying to keep the irritation from his voice. "Please close the door on your way out."

"No...now, please." Eyebrows raised around the meeting table. It wasn't a suggestion.

"Carry on," Wolf said. He rose and followed the woman into the hall.

"What's this about?"

"Lance Wolf, I'm Special Agent Elle Parker, Special Operations Command Counterintelligence." She held up her credentials.

"Okay.".

Parker pointed. "This is Special Agent Tim Brower. We need you to come with us."

Crap, this can't be good. What happened in Mexico wasn't ideal, but as a civilian on vacation, why did CI care?

"Okay, lead the way," he said in a chipper tone.

Parker led the way, with Brower following behind. They walked down two long hallways until they reached an unmarked room with an electronic lock. The office was sparse, just a table with four chairs.

"Sit down." Parker said.

He remained standing. "What's this about?"

Ignoring his question, Parker sat down and opened a file folder. She reached forward and touched a button on a console in the center of the table and the button glowed red.

"Master Sergeant Lance Wolf, you are advised we are recording these proceedings. We're here to question you regarding your recent activity while in Mexico. For the record, I am Special Agent Elle Parker, ID 1173 Alpha Delta. I am joined by Special Agent Tim Brower, ID 2031 Tango Sierra."

She looked up and motioned with her eyes for Wolf to sit. This time he did.

She flipped some pages. "Master sergeant, what were you doing in Mexico from January first to the fifteenth?" she asked.

"Time out, Parker. Am I suspected of having a vacation, or

committing a crime? What about reading me my Miranda rights? I'm sure you have heard of them."

She looked up from the file with a half-smile. "Why? Have you done something wrong? You are not under arrest. This is an informal administrative inquiry."

"So, I can go if I choose?"

Parker's face took on a thoughtful look. "Well, technically, I suppose so—but if you attempt to leave, you will be detained and face penalties derived from your violation of the national security provisions of your employment agreement."

Wolf clenched his jaw. "As you know, I was assisting my parents who were returning from Mexico. Until the Sinaloa cartel killed my stepfather and gravely injured my mother."

"Nothing else?" Parker asked.

"At the start. Then the cartel murdered my mother, too. I tried to assist the local police in bringing my parents' killers to justice."

"Master sergeant Wolf, wasn't your brother Bjorn wounded while trying to protect your mother?"

Where the heck is this headed? "Yes, he was. He saved her from a cartel attack."

"Did you kidnap a Mexican citizen and hold him against his will?" Parker asked.

"No. The local police and Army captured him."

"Tell us about your role in the interrogation of Joaquin Zapana and the subsequent gun battle at Los Mochis International Airport."

Wolf exhaled suppressing a smirk. Deny and probe. "Role?"

"You have history with Major Carlos Gonzalez, commander of the Mexican Army's Fuerza Especial Lion Squadron. They don't come more special operations in Mexico. You were both looking for answers to different questions, it appears, and may have joined forces in pursuit of each other's objectives." She said.

"I don't know what that mumbo-jumbo means. I was helping my parents return from Mexico until I brought home the bodies of my murdered stepfather and my murdered mother."

Parker snorted. "Do you expect us to believe you were not

involved in the abduction of Joaquin Zapana? You weren't at the airport for his interrogation? We know you worked the drug war in Colombia and have interrogator training."

Wolf smirked. "You may believe what you wish. I drive fast but it doesn't make me a NASCAR driver. As a cooperative American in a foreign country, I attempted to assist the police prior to the capture of Zapana. Then, after the murder of my mother, we spent most of our time coordinating with the funeral home on how to fly our parents back the reservation. I was alerted to the gunfight by a newscast at the airport as they escorted us aboard our flight to Phoenix."

Wolf hadn't told the whole truth, but he hadn't outright lied.

"So, unless you have something else today, I have a job to tend to."

Parker tipped her hand when she didn't respond. He stood and left, half expecting them to arrest him, half not caring.

He walked down to the basement and sat next to an unused mainframe computer, wondering when they would pull his security clearance.

No clearance, no job.

Revenge required access to classified information to move forward.

Someone stepped into the room and He turned. It was Colonel Gates.

"Wolf, I've been looking for you. Let's take a walk."

He followed the colonel up the stairs and out into the gluey Tampa air. His boss had a serious expression on his face.

"Wolf, what happened in Mexico?"

He considered him a mentor and someone he could trust. On active duty, Gates had saved Wolf's life when a solo mission exfil got nasty, and Russian Spetsnaz hunted him.

"I lost, sir. They beat me."

"No, they didn't. But I understand your loss was personal. I spoke with Major Gonzalez. You disappointed him with what he called a self-centeredness he'd never seen in you before. If it was a manifestation of a revenge mindset, you need to figure it out. The only way we stop the cartel is by acting as one team following our rules of engagement, our laws."

After Gates left, he stood for a moment, mulling over what he'd said.

Have I been self-centered? Maybe, but I'm not giving up. I need a team.

Wolf collected his thoughts, headed for his truck and smiled as his plan for revenge took shape.

21

K ojack's barbecue, Tampa, Florida

Wolf slept little that night. His every consideration on building his lineup. And what better place to start than a co-worker and his Florida Army National Guard team.

The next morning, his first stop was the cube where Staff Sergeant Kieran Kennedy worked. A nephew of a Massachusetts senator, he had his uncle's good looks and gigantic frame. His size synchronized with an IQ that was also large, and he had joined the Army to make his own money for college.

His expertise as the lead counter-drug intelligence analyst made him a strong first choice.

Kennedy accepted Wolf's invitation to meet for lunch at Kojack's, the best barbecue in Tampa.

Wolf was enjoying his sweet tea when Kennedy slid up next to him at the bar.

"Hey, soldier, come here often?"

Wolf smiled. "Only on Troop Tuesday, when I can spend more on my man."

Kennedy laughed. "Nice to see you in a pleasant mood. I was sorry to hear about your parents, Lance."

"Yeah, it sucks, but thanks. Let's order and go out back to the patio for some privacy."

Once outside waiting on their lunches, Wolf started the classic rock playlist on his cell phone and turned up the volume.

"Okay, brother," Kennedy said, looking around. They were alone and the music would keep them from being overheard by all but the most sophisticated eavesdropping devices. "What's this about?"

"Two things. I need to read you in on what happened in Mexico. Second, I want your input and advice. But before I start, you need to know I got a visit from a SOCOM CI agent, Elle Parker, and her sidekick, Brower. They had little real info, but they've been nosing around. Not sure why."

Kennedy's chin dipped, and he crossed his arms. "Okay, tell me what happened."

Their food arrived and after the server left, Wolf detailed the events. "I'll eat for a minute. Ask all the questions you want." Wolf dove into his BBQ ribs.

"Wolf, I appreciate your honesty. Everything you told me lines up with the Mexican police and Fuerza Especial de Reacción after-action reports I read. Of course, and whoever wrote them was trying very hard to minimize your involvement."

Kennedy took a bite of his brisket sandwich and chewed for a moment.

"The DEA went bat shit. You made them look bad, not to mention taking what they say was a valuable informant out of play. You got closer to the Cortes family than anybody ever has. But their big gripe was about you interrupting an undercover operation."

"That's BS," Wolf said.

"Maybe, maybe not. But you did an impressive job reacting to the cartel's moves."

Wolf frowned. "Not a win in my book. Too many outstanding people died."

"I hear you, but it happens in the fight with the drug cartels. The Sinaloa cartel is a drug production and distribution monster with trained intelligence, security, and enforcement units. Not your usual dirtbag drug gang."

"Yeah, it's what Colonel Gates said."

Kennedy nodded and took a sip of his sweet tea. "What else do you want to talk about?"

"Next steps."

"What next steps? What else can you do?"

"Well, I have some ideas." Wolf stared across the patio. "I can't let it go. I want to give what we got."

Kennedy was silent for a moment. "Think about what you're saying. If you hit them here, they will label you a criminal, even a domestic terrorist. If you hit them in Mexico, you'll be an international terrorist. A ton of hurt will come down on you. You'd be throwing away your career, and we would be lesser here not having your expertise because you're dead or in federal prison. I am with you, brother. I understand the pain. I hate losing, too. But direct action is too much."

Kennedy was right—this would not be the smartest thing to do. But every moment of every day filled Wolf with a growing feeling of loss, failure, and anger. It fueled his need for revenge. He had to make the Cortes family pay for what happened to his parents.

"What if we could do it under the radar?" Wolf said. "A small team, hidden within a larger team. A mission within a mission. Invisible, covert, deniable."

Kennedy furrowed his brow. "It might work with the right people and support."

"You know we've been ramping up our military support of the Mexican government," Wolf said. "Some in Congress finally see the drug cartels as a threat to our national security. I don't want to imagine what would happen if the cartel talent for moving dope applied to moving terrorists."

"Agreed. It would be disastrous if they worked with groups like al Qaeda."

Time for the truth. "I can hide covert missions inside the Guard's counter-drug operations. We already work with the DEA as we train for wartime missions."

"But how does it help you with your mission?" Kennedy asked.

"It's part of a concept which provides cover for action. But I need you on the team. You're the best intelligence analyst in the command. Not to mention, an expert on the Sinaloa cartel. I need you for targeting and operational awareness. I don't want to step into another agency's mission because it would raise our profile and jeopardize our objectives."

Kennedy saw the determination in his friend's eyes. There was no stopping him, and he need help. That's what friends and battle buddies are for.

"Can I count on you?" Wolf asked.

Kennedy sighed and folded the lunch check as he calculated joining Wolf in an unpredictable future. His mind wandered to questioning if federal prisons still used orange jumpsuits or some fashionable pastel.

He raised his head and stared at Wolf. "What's a little prison time between friends? Yes, okay. I want to make a real difference. Most of what I discover doesn't become actioned. We can't operate across the border, and we can't give the intel to the Mexicans. Catch-22, right? What we're doing now just isn't working."

He leaned in. "Yeah, count me in."

"Outstanding, brother," Wolf said with a wide grin. "Thank you. But first I need you to hear the obvious 'Mission Impossible' statement. If the Florida National Guard or, in your case, SOCOM, discovers what we are doing, they will deny we're official—because we are not—and they will lock us up. We could spend a very long time in Leavenworth making big rocks into small rocks."

Kennedy laughed. "You think? I know what's in store. You can count on me."

"Okay, outstanding. I'll start figuring out who else we can count on and inquire about logistics. I'll let you know ASAP."

"Copy. Oh, and if I'm buying a bunch of prospective prison time, you're buying lunch," Kennedy said with a smile. He sailed the paper airplane lunch check across the table. It landed in Wolf's barbeque sauce.

WOLF PLANNED WITH NEW ENTHUSIASM. He came up with a table of teammates with three selection factors: trust, invisibility, and agility. He needed to trust his people, but they also needed to trust him. Regarding invisibility, he could only choose people with little or no profile outside of the special ops community.

Candidates also needed the ability to adapt on the fly and complete the mission. This was a hallmark of special forces, but a genuine talent of a select few. Key criteria identified, Wolf created columns for weapons, demolitions, communications, and medical.

He sat back and looked at the list of his potential teammates. Army Captain Alonzo Franks and Chief Warrant Officer Jonathan Danner would his two picks for officers. The NCO included Sergeants First Class Henry Harris, Stewart Porter, and Tim Hughes, plus Staff Sergeants Mike Clinton and Oleus LeBlanc.

Wolf left off three teammates. Danny Connor was too ethical and would never break a law. Mikey Franklin was a great medic, but he was in college. And Pat Newton was a communications genius being forced out as he was in rehab, going to AA and NA meetings. Wolf added his brother, Kennedy, Carlos Gonzalez, Victor Cárdenas, and Dr. Mateo Munoz as support.

But this was just a recruiting roster. Whether the names on it would roger up to join a sketchy ad hoc task force of irregulars wasn't certain.

22

El Rancho Cortes, Sinaloa, Mexico

Alejandro Cortes had been in a funk since Joaquin's death. It was so bad cartel operations chief Martin Amaro called Eliana in Los Angeles to discuss what to do. Eliana didn't give him any advice, just a lot of cursing about Alejandro not dealing with his problems before they got out of control.

Amaro knew Alejandro and his intelligence chief had enjoyed a close relationship. He'd been part of several deep discussions, talking for hours about the science of guerrilla warfare.

Zapana received education on war and loved to integrate ideas from the likes of T. E. Lawrence, also known as Lawrence of Arabia, Robert Taber's seminal "War of the Flea," and Carl Von Clausewitz's "On War" into the construct of running the west coast portion of the Sinaloa drug empire.

Alejandro had trusted his friend Joaquin and knew the man would do anything for him. His death was a serious loss for his business but, in the way of guerrilla warfare, the number-two steps up and operations continue.

Throughout his life, Alejandro always felt like he was never worthy enough. He had earned little in life on his own, and the concept of personal accomplishment was foreign to him. He was the kid who always got what he wanted, even as his father would say, "You must earn your way on this Earth, my son."

It was hard for Alejandro to trust people—his was not a business that encouraged it. But something about Joaquin was different. Maybe he was wrong, but Alejandro had always felt Zapana respected him for who he was and what he'd achieved, despite it was on the back of others.

The press was blaming the cartel for his death. The story was the Army was trying to move a cooperating Zapana to safety when the cartel attacked and he died in the crossfire.

Alejandro closed the door to his office and motioned for Amaro to sit down.

"I am done grieving Joaquin's death and I've decided what to do next, Martin. No one kills one of our family and goes unpunished. I want the Americans dead. I want Gonzalez and his family dead. Use all the resources you need, but make sure it happens."

Amaro, ever the operational planner, smiled. "We have options that do not include another shootout, Alejandro. We can destroy their careers—"

Alejandro cut him short, raising both hands before his reddening face. "No, Martin. I want them dead for Joaquin's death. Do you understand me?"

"Yes, sir." He disagreed, but he dared not contradict Alejandro in this state.

"The gringo with Fuerza Especial must be military. A source told me he has siblings in Los Angeles and San Francisco." "I will find out everything I can," Amaro said.

Alejandro dialed his phone. A gruff man picked up the call. "Yes?"

"I have a job for you."

23

USSOCOM, Tampa, Florida

Special Agent Elle Parker was in the weight room. She was more impressive in sweaty workout gear, a Denver Broncos ball cap, a ponytail, and beads of sweat rolling down her neck than in her work clothes.

When Wolf sidled up to her, she was lowering a dead lift in a deliberate manner instead of dropping it like a poser.

"Agent Parker, what are you doing here?"

She rolled her eyes. "You remember I work on base, right?" She picked up a gym towel and blotted her face. "Most any question is inappropriate."

Wolf grinned. I haven't seen you in here before."

"Are you following me?"

"You wouldn't know if I was, but no." He smiled. "Sorry for blowing up at you guys the other day."

Parker took a sip from her water bottle. "No sweat, just the job. It was a sucky line of questioning, but you know. We had to make sure you're still on our team."

Wolf nodded. "Yeah, I get it." And he did, as much as he didn't want to admit it.

"Need any help?" he said, pointing to the bar stacked with plates.

"I'm good," she said. "I don't need any help to pull my weight."

Was that a sparkle in those green eyes?

SOCOM J2

Wolf had asked Kennedy to investigate a suspected trans-shipment facility in Santa Ana, Sonora, Mexico.

"I have updates," Kennedy said, pointing to an empty conference room. Once inside, he handed over a package. Wolf scanned the contents. Overhead pictures of a trucking company building and the surrounding area taken by an intelligence satellite. "If I'm right, this facility is a key hub in the drug transportation system into Arizona and the western states."

"How did you come by these overhead pictures?" Wolf asked.

"Lots of curiosity about this place. The Customs and Border Patrol, and the DEA's El Paso Intelligence Center, all have identified this facility as a place of interest. I called a guy." He smiled and didn't identify further. "Are you planning this location for your first mission?"

"It's in the top three. I'd like to identify two more and down select. Lots of opportunity between the Mexican states of Sonora and Sinaloa. I'll do a leader's recon first. We can use intel I gather to update this target package."

"Wolf, you're not going alone, right? Given what's just happened, it's not a great idea."

"I'll be okay, but I need to be sure. I've hunted mule deer in that area every year since I spent some pre-mission time at Fort Huachuca." Wolf smiled. He recalled when he hunted to fill the freezer versus kill bad guys.

"You remember the pre-trip and post-trip paperwork, right? It will produce one more trail leading someone to connect you to activity in Mexico."

"You're right, brother, but it's a risk I will to take. I'll study the package and let you know if I have any questions."

The plan was falling into place. Kennedy had come through with the pre-op intel, and now Wolf needed to sell the idea to the people he'd picked for his team. He called them and made plans to meet the candidates at locations in Tampa and St. Petersburg.

Wolf wasn't a salesman, so he would blend honesty, passion, and that together they could make a difference into his pitch. To his surprise, all seven men agreed to meet with him to discuss things further. A promising start.

Another surprise consumed Wolf's thoughts. Elle Parker. Her smile was stuck in his head.

24

USSOCOM, MacDill AFB, Tampa, Florida

Wolf sat off base across from his battle buddy Alonzo Franks. After four years on the same team, the captain was used to Wolf's sometimes unorthodox brainstorms. When Wolf proposed his plan, Franks had listened and asked questions.

"Wolf, I have to confirm that you know if the Florida National Guard or SOCOM discover what you're doing, you will spend the rest of your life in the stockade at Fort Leavenworth."

"Yes, sir, it's one potential outcome."

"Then the federal government. The Department of Justice will arrest you as an international terrorist. They could turn you over to the Mexican government. No telling what they'd do. You could end up a hero—or dead within weeks of being sent to prison. Most likely the latter given the desires of the Sinaloa Cartel. Have you thought about how it will affect the other men and their families if this goes sideways?"

Wolf had thought about it. He couldn't stop thinking about it. It didn't deter him.

Wolf sighed. "I know how this looks, like I'm asking you and the others to support a revenge campaign. But it's not about revenge anymore. I believe we can disrupt and damage the Sinaloa Cartel. My plan is to use a guerrilla warfare cell organization to limit exposure to discovery. The focus is to protect the team at all costs."

Franks stared at him. "Okay, count me in, but only for support. And then, only if I feel it's safe."

"Copy, good enough. Thanks. You have a family, and I understand. Thank you."

Wolf left the meeting with a dull ache baking his insides, knowing he had just lied to his friend for the first time.

Using the "higher purpose" of the team to exact his revenge, Wolf would have to hide in plain sight. The team would cease to exist if they thought it was all about Wolf's revenge.

Revenge for the deaths of his parents was an objective, but Wolf wanted more—he burned to destroy cartel drug production and shipments into the U.S.

But first, he wanted to see Alejandro and Eliana die.

The meetings with the rest of the team went well, each man accepting the risks and dangers. Wolf nodded with relief. He had his team of assaulters, and it was a damned good one.

But one important component was missing. A Mexico-based support cell to provide the team with local ground truth and logistics support. Priority one, acquire weapons and ammunition that cannot be traced back to the U.S. or the team.

After what had happened in Mexico, he wasn't sure Carlos Gonzalez would talk to him again, let alone help. It was clear Wolf needed more downrange support.

He wondered if former U.S. military expats might be the answer. Lots of military veterans had retired to low-cost regions. Military retirements go much farther in such places and attract a myriad of people with sometimes amazing histories.

Wolf dialed a number. "Hey, Sierra," he said when his sister answered her phone. "How are you and the family?"

"Good, thanks. And you? Staying out of trouble?"

Not one for small talk, Wolf got right to the point. "I'm good.

Listen, I was wondering if Mom or Dad ever mentioned meeting any expats other than their charter boat friend in Mexico?"

"You mean people who had moved down to Mexico full time?"

"Yes."

"Why do you ask, Lance? What are you planning now?"

"Nothing. I need to tie off loose ends with Lieutenant Cárdenas and meet anyone who had met Mom and Dad. It's a closure thing for me."

She huffed. "Besides the charter captain, the only people they mentioned are a couple who own a construction business. They build condos along the Mexican coast."

"Perfect. Where can I find their contact info?"

"In one of Mom's address books, I'm sure. They'd still be in storage."

It had been a month since the funeral. Wolf couldn't believe how much time had passed. Had he been spending all this time plotting revenge? A pang of sadness washed through him, but he couldn't lose focus. Not now. Not when act one was so close to kicking off.

25

Lance Bear Wolf's residence, Tampa, Florida

Wolf turned his second bedroom into an operations center. He blacked out the windows and put white-noise generators on the glass and in the vents to counter electronic eavesdropping.

Anyone wanting to find out what Wolf was working on would need National Security Agency level equipment, and no one would be looking into him yet.

Wolf thought ahead to the cross-border phase of operations. They could use his parents' winter house in Tucson as their forward base of operations. Anything closer to the border would be too risky.

Wolf's first half of the workday was supporting priority missions on three different continents. After lunch, he dropped by Kennedy's cube to grab an update on cartel activity.

"I just had an interesting visit. Come on, let's grab a conference room to talk." The seriousness in Kennedy's tone intrigued Wolf.

They went down a hallway and entered an empty room. "An officer contacted me from the Central America desk asking about Mexican Army Tier I organizations," Kennedy said.

"Okay, what's the big deal?"

"It was a specific ask about your buddy."

Wolf's eyes narrowed. "Gonzalez? Who's asking?"

This was unexpected. Someone else might be working their battle space.

"Helen Valo-Campbell. Major type. And she's a political specialist, which makes it all the stranger."

"What did you tell her?"

"That pulling the data would take a while with my other operational priorities."

"Did she ask about anything else?" Wolf asked.

"Yes, she asked about you. She tried to play it off as a casual ask, but it was more."

None of this made sense. "Why did she ask you about me when she could just look me up in the Command phone book?"

Kennedy just shrugged. "I do not know."

"Do you know anything about her?"

"No, but I'll have info on her by the end of the day." Kennedy shook his head. "I don't like this."

"Neither do I."

"It's an indication of activity in other channels we don't need. I'll put a package together on her and we'll see where it leads."

Wolf agreed. One more variable to worry about. Wolf changed the subject. "Any ground-level pictures of the Santa Ana facility?"

"No, just the overheads."

"Any SIGINT on the site or major players who base out of that location?"

"No. But since I gave you the package, I came into possession of a profile on the Cortes family's ground transportation lead. His name is Jose Torres. I'll make you a copy."

Wolf nodded. "I've asked this before, but it bears asking again. Do we have any assets inside the Cortes operation or any of their companies?"

"None that I've found. But it doesn't mean DEA doesn't."

Wolf handed Kennedy the team list. "Here are the team members. As you can see, we are short on auxiliary staff."

"Do you consider your team the guerrilla force, or an underground component?"

"I'd say we are the underground. We will do clandestine operations even though we aren't living in the area. We can work in some psychological operations that will lead to the Tijuana Cartel. Next week, I'm heading down to do the leader's recon."

"I still think you are crazy for doing that," Kennedy said.

"I hear you. I'll be careful. I'm flying to Tucson first to pick up contact info for a couple of expats who might be helpful."

"Good idea. Locals will be useful. Is your hunting cover story in play?"

"Yes." Wolf said. He'd bought a civilian hunting trip for Sonoran mule deer as a cover. With that, he could roam all over the area without attracting undue attention. He had found a ranch adjacent the trucking facility for a base camp and had his hunting permit.

"How are we going to communicate?"

Wolf handed Kennedy a business card with a handwritten number. Wolf had bought an MCI business-service package with voicemail and notification capability. Wolf programmed the voicemail system to send notifications to a pager.

"The passcode to access into the voicemail system is MuleDeer98. Capital M, capital D. The messages I leave will be descriptions of my hunting.

Wolf handed Kennedy a list of code words, a pager, and cellphone. "The cell belonged to my dad, so it's clean for now."

"You need to stay off the air as much as possible," Kennedy said. "You will be within spitting distance of Fort Huachuca."

"Not a problem for the recon. If we target the facility, I've got a communications plan to fool even the NSA."

26

S hipping Facility Santa Ana, Mexico

Wolf drove a rental Toyota pickup from Tucson to the hunting lodge just north of Santa Ana. At 0100 on his second morning in Mexico, he drove to within two miles of his target, then patrolled to the facility and hid in a juniper thicket.

Cartel guards walked past every six minutes without a clue. Between their patrols, he silently sang his death song and readied himself for war.

At 0300, the guards took a smoke break. When they did, Wolf cut into the chain link on the back of a post. He waited for another rotation of the guards, then dashed forty meters to the building, scaling a drainpipe to the roof.

He lay still as the guards came back around. Once they were out of range, he took a knee and scanned the roof, surprised by the exhaust vents in one corner.

Last time he had seen that type was in Russia at a covert biological weapons lab, the mission on which Colonel Gates had saved his life.

Pistol out, Wolf accessed a roof hatch and inside, he worked his way over to the corner where he'd seen the vents. Voices.

He climbed a storage rack and peered down at two armed men outside the door.

A building within the building. The roof, seven feet lower than the building shell, littered with electrical, plumbing, and vents. A tangled mess of opportunity.

Wolf crawled across the rack to the wall and used a roof truss to swing over the lab. He dropped onto a support beam. Five careful steps and he found an off-center vent revealing a table below. He set his rifle on the false ceiling and took pictures of three workers wrapping a brown material in plastic, most likely heroin. This would be the strike location.

Target identified, he turned to leave, but his boot snagged a wire and it threw him off balance. He struggled to land on the beam, dropping his camera and pack, the contents spilling and banging into the metal supports like a gotcha scene in a bad spy movie.

The guards jumped and opened the door to blank stares from the workers. Wolf brought his hunting rifle to his shoulder in case he had to fight his way out.

"Damned cheap construction," a guard said, and they laughed.

When no additional sounds ensued and the guards moved away, chattering about soccer stars, he gathered his spilled contents and jumped back to the truss.

More voices from the ground made the choice for him, so he worked his way along the wall, staying on top of the racks.

Twelve feet away from the ladder, Wolf lowered himself to the floor and froze. More rapid-fire Spanish. He was near the end of the rack, close enough to touch a guy who had a cellphone to his ear.

Wolf drew his Randall Model 18 fighting knife. The man ended his call and turned the corner. Wolf hesitated for a second, in recognition. It was Jose Torres, the Cortes lieutenant and cartel logistics boss.

If there had ever been a better, more perfect target of opportunity in Wolf's experience, he didn't remember it.

Wolf closed the distance between them, grabbed Torres' collar and drove the knife to the hilt into his throat, jabbing and slicing.

Torres gasped, grabbing for the knife, tearing his throat apart, but the wet struggle was brief and ineffective.

Wolf swept Torres' ankle in an awkward takedown, using his weight to leverage the knife, slicing Torres' carotid artery. The cartel soldier's legs kicked and flailed as the life drained out of him.

Wolf pushed Torres's lifeless body away and stood, soaked in blood and shaking. It was the first time he'd killed a man in hand-to-hand combat. That was too easy. He pushed down the urge to scream a war cry.

Wolf put Torres' pistol and cellphone in his own pack. His team would open the phone back home and plunder it for its secrets. He thought for a moment, then cut Torres' shirt open and carved the letters C-A-F in the dead man's chest—the Cartel Arellano Félix monogram for the Tijuana Cartel.

Wolf covered Torres with scrap plastic and slid him under a loaded rack. There was nothing to do about the blood pool whose streaks leading under the rack. It would make do. He was on the roof when the yelling started. Someone discovered Torres's body.

Men yelled empty threats of retribution, and the howl of angry automatic Kalashnikov gunfire tore at the peaceful pre-dawn sky. A new pump of adrenalin drove Wolf as he ran for his truck. Emboldened by his success and escape, Wolf wanted more.

27

Shipping Facility Santa Ana, Mexico

The reason for the early morning flight in the new Pilatus PC-12 kept Martin Amaro from appreciating the high-tech cockpit. What he did appreciate was how quickly he could get to Santa Ana. An hour ago, when he received the call, he'd been sleeping in his bed next to his wife.

He was told, about an attack at the Santa Ana facility, and someone had murdered Jose Torres. He was running operations and intelligence now, so this was the last thing Amaro needed on his plate. He turned back to his growing list of questions.

The pilot set the airplane down on a dirt road next to the facility and taxied to the end. The road included two wide cul-de-sacs at either end to permit aircraft to turn around.

The pilot spun the aircraft around to taxi to the waiting Range Rover. They drove three minutes to the facility and parked near the back door. The security shift leader held the door open for Amaro. They led him to an office in the production area.

"Walk me through the attack and your response."

"Yes, sir. Around four this morning, the guards outside the packing room heard a noise and did a quick search. Not seeing anything, they stopped to mention it to Mister Torres. He was on the phone and waved them away."

"Jose came to work at four this morning?"

"He often stayed very late or came in early. 'No interruptions,' he would say."

Amara thought it odd. "Okay, go on."

"Not more than ten minutes later, the guards heard another noise. This time, when they searched for the noise, they found the Mister Torres body with the letters C-A-F cut into his chest. As soon as they reported in, I called a full alert. We fired through the fences into the desert, hoping to catch the attackers. When we did not, I organized the men into search teams of three. I had them check the highways and back roads. I also had dispatch call all truck drivers to be on the lookout."

"You used the terms 'they' and 'attackers,'" Martin said. "Do you know if it was one person, or more than one?"

"No, I do not. But I talked to the men who heard the noise. One of them said the sound came from above. They thought it was shitty construction settling or something. We checked the area around the assembly facility and found foot and handprints on the storage racks. I think the attacker climbed up and over on top of the assembly facility." The onsite security boss handed up a folded piece of paper. "We found this hunting permit next to the ladder to the roof."

"Does it have a name?"

"No, sir. But I sent a team out to talk to the ranch owner. They should report back soon."

"So how did the attackers access the building? Did the alarm trip?"

"I am not sure. The alarm did not sound."

"Let's take a walk and find out."

Amaro started along the fence, spending most of his walk looking back toward the facility. He squatted down and surveyed the area. His eyes widened.

"Do you see the footprints?"

"No, sir."

"Come down here and look."

A set of prints were visible at an angle going to and from the fence to the building.

"Mark this post. Let's check the rest of the fence."

They continued surveying the property but came up empty. They returned to the marked post. Amaro couldn't find any indication the attackers went over the top. No hair, thread, or blood. He leaned on the fence, and it moved. Pushing it outwards, it opened from behind the post.

"Stay here."

"Yes, sir."

Amaro slipped through and found himself in a hide. The same boot pattern to the building was also inside. After identifying the route used in and out, Amaro reentered the property.

"Have two of your men follow the trail out of the hide and see if it leads to anyone." Amaro led the way back to the main building and stopped at the drainpipe. "Rooftop access?"

"Yes, sir, from the inside."

"Take me. I want to stand on the roof."

Amaro opened the roof hatch and stopped to look across the rooftop of the inner structure. The footprints went from the drainpipe to the hatch.

Back in a conference room, Amaro met with the site managers.

"This is what happened," Martin explained. "A lone man entered the facility through a cut in the fence and scaled the building using a drainpipe. Then he accessed the building through the roof hatch. At some point, he murdered Jose. The attacker escaped back through the fence. What we do not know is who, why, or if Jose interrupted their plan."

"But, sir, we know it was someone from the Tijuana Cartel, right?" the security shift leader said.

"Call it probable, but unconfirmed. Who did Jose call? Where is his phone?"

"No, sir. They took his phone and pistol."

"Okay. Any update from the ranch?"

The security shift leader didn't look up. "No, sir. We have not heard from them."

"Bring the security supervisor in here."

Seconds later the door opened, and the security manager stepped inside. With no hesitation, Amaro turned and shot him in the face. A dark hole opened on the centerline of the man's nose and the backside of his head splattered against the wall.

Ears ringing, Amaro turned back to the other site managers. "Prove your worth! Find me information. I need a phone."

They led Amaro to a private office where he called his operations center and spoke to the duty manager.

"I want Jose's cellphone call records for the last week. I want today's calls in an hour." He disconnected without waiting for affirmation.

Amaro stared out the window, trying to process all that he'd learned, when a knock on the door interrupted his thoughts. "Sir, the ranch owner identified the hunter as an American."

"Did he give you a name and description?"

"Yes, sir. John Ares. Five-ten, one hundred seventy pounds, black hair, green eyes. He is from Tucson."

Amaro called his duty manager. "Send someone immediately to check it out."

Could it be? The gringos at El Gran Pez were from Tucson.

Amaro had Joaquin's file on the Americans. Bjorn Anderson, a former DEA agent and pilot. He teaches at a university in Los Angeles. He has blond hair and blue eyes, six-two, and two hundred and twenty pounds. The sister, Sierra Morton, a doctor in San Francisco. Blond hair and blue eyes, five-eight, and one hundred fifteen pounds. Lance Wolf lives in Tampa. Black hair and green eyes, five-ten, one hundred sixty-five pounds.

He called Maria Camacho, his admin and de facto second in command, asking about Torres' calls and ordering her to dig into Wolf's profile.

"Jose made two calls. One to his girlfriend for five minutes, and a thirty-second call to a voicemail service," Camacho said.

"Call our contact at the phone company. I want to know who owns the voicemail service."

Amaro sighed.

Wolf won't stop until he kills Eliana, or we kill him. That I can handle. What scared him was Torres showing up at four in the morning making calls to an unknown voicemail service.

28

Lance Bear Wolf's residence, Tampa, Florida

The doorbell rang. Wolf glanced at his Casio Data Bank watch. It wasn't even five a.m. and he'd gotten home late last night. Go away.

The doorbell rang again, forcing him from bed, followed by urgent knocks. Wolf rose in his SOCOM T-shirt and running shorts and padded to the door with a Browning High Power in his hand. When he looked through the peephole, he sighed.

"Kennedy—what are you doing here?"

"Let me in."

"What's so important you're waking me up on an off day?" Wolf asked. As he swung the door open Kennedy hurried in past him.

"What the heck did you do? It's created a shit storm."

Wolf yawned and made his way to the kitchen. "I did a leader's recon," he said and turned on the TV, switching to CNN.

"That's not all you did. What about the dead Cortes family lieutenant?"

Wolf looked sheepish. "I did run into a little trouble."

"When did you plan on telling me this?"

"Tomorrow at work in the SCIF, not in my front room. Want coffee?"

"Yeah, sure. It's going to be a long day."

The ritual of making coffee gave Wolf time to wake up. He breathed in the rich aroma of Guatemalan Huehuetenango as he ground up the beans and let them brew. He handed Kennedy a steaming cup, and they went into the living room.

Wolf cranked up the TV volume and gave Kennedy a full debrief of his actions, from the time of crossing the border until he crossed back into the States. When he finished, they drank their coffee in silence.

Wolf replayed his killing of Torres, and Kennedy nodded. It was the right choice at the right time. He hadn't been out to kill anyone on his recon, but one less Cortes' lieutenant, the better.

It was a good five minutes before Kennedy asked his first question. "Do you still have Torres's cellphone?"

"Yes, but I want to give you his contacts and call log without connecting you to the actual phone. I'll give you the information tomorrow."

"Santa Ana is going to remain hot for some time to come," Kennedy said.

"Maybe, maybe not. The cartel has many other operations under way, and it may be a viable target sooner than you think. Plus, I think we can divert their attention."

"Sounds like you are getting ahead of yourself."

"I hear you, but they a have control problem. They can't be everywhere. The War of the Flea, brother—classic guerrilla warfare. What did you find out about our nosy Major Campbell?"

"Not a ton. She joined the Army when she was in her teens, two years later she went to OCS and worked her way up. She's married to Major Bruce Campbell. Nothing about her interest in you has floated to the surface yet, but I'll keep digging."

"Okay, there must be something. Those folks don't ask questions for nothing." Wolf took an exaggerated look at his watch. "And now, if you don't mind, I'd like to go back to sleep. I'll see you tomorrow."

Wolf locked the door and thought about how lucky he had been. The look on Torres's face as he bled out had come to him during the night. Now he understood what his stepfather Andy and his Vietnam buddies had told him. Killing up close stains your soul.

I should be happy at the outcome, so why do I feel this way? He turned off the TV and hit the sack.

The next morning, Wolf was in the communications division talking with the satellite operations duty NCO when Elle Parker appeared. She grabbed his elbow and whispered in his ear.

"We need to talk," Parker said, guiding him toward the door.

Damn, she looked good and smelled better. Wolf followed her out into the hallway.

"What'd I do this time?"

"Why don't you tell me? You take another trip to Mexico and more cartel dead bodies appear as if by magic."

"I went hunting in Mexico. The same as I have done every year since I spent time at Fort Huachuca."

"Right. I hope it's all you did. If not, you'll be in a world of trouble. One of the dead guys was the prime DEA source and they are not happy."

Wolf raised his eyebrows. They said the same thing about Zapana. Was it bull or was the DEA getting somewhere? There's going to be an investigation to figure out who killed the informant.

"Wait, are you saying I'm still under investigation?" Wolf asked.

She placed her hand on his arm. "Gotta go."

"Wait, why are you telling me this?"

"One, I hate the drug cartels like everyone else here. Two, I think it sucks you couldn't find justice for your family." Her small grin told volumes. "See you around, Wolf."

He watched her walk down the hall. She held his gaze as she stood in the elevator and waited for the doors to close. She was his type—physical, confident, and capable.

Let it go, Lance. Now is not the time.

And it was true. He didn't have time for a romantic involvement, especially with someone who seemed to be on the problematic side of the good guys.

Back in the intelligence division, Wolf found Kennedy in deep analysis mode. It appeared the outside world ceased to exist.

Even with all the noise and people moving about the cube farm, Kennedy's uncanny ability to focus amazed everyone. Wolf stood and watched as he sorted news clips, classified reports, and images among six twenty-one-inch monitors.

Scientific process combined here with a knack for seeing obscure and important connections. It identified him as a key player in the defense intelligence community. Kennedy's smile turned to a frown when he saw Wolf creep into his line of vision.

"Do you always have to sneak up on people?"

"Use it or lose it, Kennedy. What's making you smile today?"

"Not here. Conference room."

They walked across the hall to the big meeting room and closed the secure door.

"I've found some interesting information about Major Helen Campbell." Kennedy said.

"Okay,""

"A sister, Maya Valo, works for a non-profit in Mexico. She spends a lot of time with the Tarahumara natives down in Chihuahua. I think the cartel might be using Valo as leverage over Campbell."

Wolf processed the information. "Cartel leverage makes sense. After the death of Zapana, Alejandro wants me dead. Maybe he's using her to collect information on me and my Mexican connections? That would account for her interest in Mexican Tier 1 organizations. But what can we do with it?"

"We should give Campbell a managed package of what she asked for and see where it leads. But I'll add a lot of smoke and mirrors about you and Gonzalez. That way we can see how it comes back, and from what direction, with neither of you guys dying."

Wolf chuckled. "I like the not dying part." He held out two white three-by-five cards with phone numbers. "Here is the contact list and phone call record from Torres's cellphone. How long will it take to run them down?"

"A day or two in between mission priorities."

Wolf nodded. "Okay. Start with the contact list, I'm thinking there may be something interesting. One more thing. Parker told me I'm still under investigation."

"I thought she wasn't working you any longer?"

"She said one Torres was a DEA source.

"Great. Now we've irritated the DEA twice and who knows who else. You need to be careful with Parker. It could be a trap. The next thing you know, it's handcuffs and an orange jumpsuit."

29

On the road to San Juanito, Chihuahua, Mexico
Maya Valo hung her head out the window, her hair graceful and sinuous in the breeze. She was in the non-profit's old flatbed truck, driving out of Copper Canyon toward San Juanito.

Driving toward any city was a welcome relief from the poverty of the Tarahumara. The thought of a shower and a decent bed made her giddy.

Born in Mexico, Maya moved to the U.S. when she was ten. Her mother had awakened her in the middle of the night, shaking her awake. "Maya, get dressed—we must go." Her older sister, Helen, was fourteen at the time and looked frightened.

They crossed the border into the United States with some other people, ending up in El Paso. Her father worked at a chemical factory, and they lived in a one-bedroom apartment with many locks on its door.

Maya didn't understand at the time why they had fled Mexico, and it wasn't until she was an adult that her father explained they had run from the cartel. Her mother kept Maya and

Helen connected to their culture, so she spoke Spanish to them and cooked authentic Mexican food.

Maya and Helen went down unique life paths. Helen joined the U.S. Army and became a Central America specialist. Maya had always felt torn between two cultures and two countries. Her realization came in the fifth grade when her class had to do a family tree project. When she asked her mother for help, it felt like her world had expanded.

"We are Tarahumara, a proud people," her mother had said with tears in her eyes. "But we had no choice. We had to leave."

Maya tried to learn as much as she could to identify with the people of her culture. Now, fifteen years later, she spent most of her time in Mexico helping her people in any way she could. At first, the contradiction between her U.S. upbringing and the life of the Tarahumara rocked her.

In the U.S., anything was possible. She wanted to bring those same possibilities to the remote areas of Chihuahua. The Tarahumara lived in concert with the land. They taught her about life, love, and living. She had grown to love them and enjoy the freedom and beauty of running with them in the mountains.

Maya loved the people she worked with, but sometimes she missed basic creature comforts. That was why she and Billy, her coworker, were heading to San Juanito to pick up supplies and then take a day off. Bill Jensen—Billy to his friends—was a kind, well-to-do Midwesterner who'd volunteered for the non-profit and seemed to find joy from helping the less fortunate.

It took them a while to realize a truck was behind them. Billy made sure there was space to pass, but the truck wasn't budging. Maya ignored it and allowed the sun to bathe her face.

"I think the white truck is following us," Billy said.

"Don't worry, they will pass," Maya said, yawning. The sun was making her tired and relaxed.

"No, I'm serious. I think they're following us."

Maya sat up and looked back. Sure enough, the white truck she'd seen ten miles ago was still behind them. The unsmiling men in the truck looked serious. They didn't look like the rest of the farmers from this part of Mexico. A bad feeling crept over her.

"Go a little faster," she said, wanting to leave the serious-looking men behind.

Billy sped up, and the white truck did, too. Not thinking before doing, Billy tried to drop the tail by going faster, then faster still, until the speed got out of hand.

Not trained in high-speed driving, their old truck swerved from side to side. Maya screamed, and Billy slowed down. The mystery truck remained behind them, keeping a few cars-length distance for the next thirty minutes.

Maya knew something was wrong. They were on a road with very little traffic. There was no reason the white truck couldn't just speed up and pass them.

"I don't like this," Maya said. "What do we do?"

"Hold on to somethin'," Billy replied. He slammed on the brakes, and their truck skidded to the side of the road, expecting the trailing truck to pass. Instead, it came to an easy stop behind them. Billy jumped out, holding a tire iron pulled from under his seat.

Maya's heart was racing. A man got out of the truck. He had a smirk on his face. "You okay?" the man said, laughing. "Why you drivin' all crazy, man?"

Billy stood clenching the tire iron, veins in his head bulging.

"Are you following us?" he demanded, trying not to sound as nervous as he felt.

"No," the man said. He raised an old sawed-off Mossberg shotgun that was concealed behind his leg. "We are following her."

Billy turned to look at Maya as the shotgun blast hit him low in the back and legs, sweeping him off his feet and into the dirt. Other steel rounds from the double-aught buckshot shotgun shell rocketed past Billy and impacted the truck's tailgate and rear window, shattering it.

"Billy!" Maya howled as she jumped out of the truck and ran to her friend, oblivious to the swarthy man holding a shotgun.

Billy was bleeding badly, the femoral artery of his right leg pumping out his life into the dirt.

"No!"

She put her hand over the wound, trying to stop the massive flow of blood, but the pressure wasn't perfect, and the blood continued to leak. Too many holes.

"It's going to be okay," she whispered. "I promise."

The killer walked over and put the barrel of his gun to Billy's head. Maya looked up, and after a moment, pushed the shotgun away. The gunman stared at her for a moment, considering, and nodded.

"Remember," he said.

The killer returned to the white truck and made a U-turn in the roadway to drive off, leaving Maya and Billy on the side of the road.

Billy commented on the blue sky, not a cloud in it. A weak smile crossed his lips, and he died.

30

U SSOCOM, Tampa, Florida
        Wolf had never seen Kennedy like this before. His
        voice sounded rattled when he called and demanded they
meet for lunch.

When he arrived at Kojack's, Kennedy was sitting at the bar, tapping his foot.

"What's the matter?" he asked.

"Major Helen Valo-Campbell is what's the matter. She called me in and read me the riot act. She wonders why I don't know you."

"What did you tell her?"

"Nothing. She wants an updated profile on Gonzalez at 1600."

Wolf sighed. This was getting complicated. "Okay. We discussed giving her an altered-version of what she wants. Let's do that. I'll let Gonzalez know in case something bubbles up on his side."

"That's not all. I got copied on a cable from the embassy in Mexico City. The Regional Security Officer reported the murder of an American non-profit worker in Chihuahua. It's the same non-profit Campbell's sister works for, and the description of the dead man matches that of an aid worker Maya Valo reported killed a couple days ago."

Wolf froze. The report confirmed Campbell was being lever- aged by the cartel. But this event must be an underscore of intent. Campbell had been poking around well before this incident, so this new threat to the sister must mean the cartel thinks Campbell is wavering.

And if she's wavering, Wolf thought, we can turn her back to us. "Was her sister hurt?"

"No, but State thinks she's in danger. I want us to pull her out of Mexico to a safe place."

"Why?"

"What do you mean why? She's not cartel—she's collateral. We talked about not causing collateral damage. If we aren't careful, though, we might accelerate her death. If we extract her from the cartel's reach, we remove the leverage on Campbell, which chokes off the intel leak through her to Alejandro. It makes tactical and strategic sense. We have to do this."

Wolf looked at his friend, the silent tension growing between them. He was right. They couldn't let innocent people be killed. "I bet you have a plan?" Wolf said.

Kennedy's eyes brightened, and he leaned forward. "Yes, and we will have Uncle Sam to pay for it. We hold conferences via cover companies all the time to gather intel. Our conference will be called The Conference on Advancement of Central and South American Indigenous Peoples. I'll make sure Maya's non-profit sends her."

"All right! Let's do it, brother." Wolf said.

Distracted, Wolf drove home. He had never worked a mission where things went according to plan. There was always something— big or small—throwing a wrench in things. And his plan was getting more complicated by the minute.

When he arrived home, he grabbed a beer from the refrigerator, sat on the couch, and called Gonzalez. "We've identified a mole on this side," Wolf said. "She has a sister who works for a non-profit in Chihuahua. Her name is Maya Valo."

Gonzalez sighed. "We know of her. Someone killed her coworker, an American named Bill Jensen."

"We want her the States for her safety. Kennedy has a plan to lure her to speak at a conference in Tucson. She would have a purpose to come here."

"I hope this works," Gonzalez quipped. "I like my job."

"Same here. Once we have Maya safe, I plan to turn the mole and put her to use spreading disinformation. I'll keep you informed."

31

Gonzalez residence, Topolobampo, Sinaloa

Their house was a modest single-level ranch with a half-acre of land. Its most notable feature was the six-foot fence surrounding the property made from steel manufactured to be a very convincing simulation of wood.

Columns with lights dotted the fence every fifteen feet. Infrared beams buried in the columns provided intrusion warning. A wrought-iron gate topped with ornate spear tips sharper on purpose.

The home's interior was a traditional architecture of high-beamed ceilings, tile floors, and decorative wrought iron. In the kitchen, striking painted and glazed tiles. There was an old wood-burning oven and new gas range. When he came home after work, his wife was cooking, and tempting aromas would greet him at the front door.

Gonzalez hung his uniform jacket on a hook. His four-year-old son, Leon, ran toward him, and Gonzalez pulled him into a hug. He beamed as his son turned on his crystal radio, which he'd built in an old cigar box from parts and pieces he had gathered from his uncle and friends.

"I am proud of you, my son. Where is Mommy?"

His wife, Valeria, stood in the doorway. "What are you doing home so early?" She looked beautiful in a white blouse, red skirt, and red lipstick. Her dark hair framed classic good looks.

"I gave the team the rest of the day off. The new men are working out well."

Gonzalez kissed his wife and walked into the kitchen. His daughter, Sofia, stirred a pot on the counter.

"Are you helping, my love?" "Yes, Daddy."

"Can I have a taste?

"No, get out of my kitchen." His wife pushed him toward the door. "Go change. My mother is coming for dinner."

The meal started with a shrimp-and-avocado salad. The main course was a seafood paella, and the conversation was light and fun, and Nina, the children's abuela fussed over her grandkids. Leon and Sofia cleared the dinner plates and the smell of the caramel sauce let everyone know it was time for dessert. Valeria was famous for her flan. He was savoring a spoonful of it rolling around in his mouth when the perimeter alarm went off.

Gonzalez spun to face the security monitor mounted on the kitchen wall. At Wolf's suggestion, he had installed four wide-angle cameras that provided a three-hundred-and-sixty-degree view of the property. He saw a man dropping into the yard.

"We must go right now!"

Valeria grabbed the kids and Gonzalez led his mother-in-law into the den. They had drilled this action many times that child and adult alike knew precisely what to do, and in what order.

Gonzalez pulled back a bookcase that opened to a reinforced hidden room. He pushed them inside, motioning them to be quiet. He kissed his wife on the lips and pushed the bookcase back into place.

He strode across the room and reached under the desk for his pistol. He checked to make sure it was ready and placed it under his belt. Then he reached to the top of a bookcase for his Mossberg shotgun. As he was getting the shotgun down, the back door creaked open.

Gonzalez moved from bedroom to bedroom via adjoining doors

to stay out of the main hallway. He stopped in the bedroom near the back door and stayed low, cutting the pie in small segments until he saw the first gunman in the hallway. A second followed.

Slow is smooth, smooth is fast, He fired at the first gunman. The shotgun blast drove the gunman back into his partner, who sprayed the hallway ceiling as he fell backward. Gonzalez dove back into the bedroom and sprinted one more room away, pulling the door closed behind him. He waited for the inevitable clearing of the adjacent bedroom.

The sound of gunfire echoed down the hallway. Suppressing fire by frightened attackers unsure of their opposition, and then it stopped. That was his cue. He entered the room behind the gunman, who turned and gasped in surprise as Gonzalez fired. The point-blank double-aught cut the gunman in half.

Gonzalez eased out into the hallway and worked toward the front of the house. He heard a metallic banging in the kitchen. He slung the shotgun and drew his pistol. Another gunman had his back to the door, trying to quiet the hanging pots and pans he had bumped into. A fatal mistake. Gonzalez made a noise and shot the attacker in the shoulder as he spun. The gunman dropped his pistol and fell to the floor, yelling and pawing at his injured shoulder.

Gonzalez rushed over and kicked the pistol away. The cartel soldier was only eighteen or nineteen. His eyes were pleading, and he held up his hands in surrender, one dripping thick gobs of blood. The pool of blood under him was growing, so Gonzalez grabbed a towel and placed it to cover the wound, pressing hard to stop the flow.

"Press here," he ordered. "You will live today."

The kid groaned as he pressed on the towel, but his eyes were wide with shock and hope.

"You are not going to kill me?"

"Depends on what you tell me, who sent you?"

"No one. Sinaloa put a fifty thousand U.S. dollar price on your head."

"Sinaloa? You mean Alejandro Cortes."

"Yes, sir."

Gonzalez flex-cuffed the kid's ankles and called the police. Then he got his family out of the panic room. His wife and kids hugged him hard. Even his mother-in-law embraced him.

Valeria snatched the keyring for her silver Audi wagon as Carlos stopped her to hand over his pistol. She tucked it into her waistband, gangster style, and hustled the children toward the front door, away from the carnage.

"Come now, let's go grandma's house for some ice cream," his wife said as she shielded the children's eyes.

His mother-in-law had recovered from her brief flirtation with gratitude and pointed a damning finger at Gonzalez as she departed.

"You will get my daughter and grandchildren killed someday!"

Gonzalez had time to think about that statement as he waited for the police to arrive. This wasn't the first time someone had tried to kill him, hence the security system. But they had never attacked his family, and that spooked him.

The harder the government squeezed, the more violent the cartels became. It had become a contest of wills. The cartel against the government. A test of who could take more pain and suffering. The cartels were betting the politicians would be quiet when the body counts started affecting their reelection chances.

It was almost midnight before the police and crime scene investigators left. Valeria called to says she was keeping the kids away for the night. The crime scene would disappear before morning and when they returned, they would leave no trace except for a few bullet holes.

Despite the Lions' team taking positions in and around the house, a knot had settled in Gonzalez's stomach. Even with the extra security, he knew his family was no longer safe. They needed to leave Mexico.

32

The Blue Gorilla, Tampa, Florida

The cigar bar had become the Special Operations Command's unofficial off-base meeting place. Wolf was there waiting for Parker. It had been a busy three days. Yesterday, he'd bumped into Parker at the gym again and got the nerve to ask her out for a drink. She'd said yes.

Two nights ago, Gonzalez had called and said the Cortes' had put a price on his head and had sent thugs to kill him in his home. Carlos had been shaken up by the whole thing, but thankfully, no one in his family was hurt.

"I need to get my family out of Mexico, amigo," he said. "Can you help get them to the States?"

Wolf told him to get his family on a flight to North Carolina and he would make some calls. He called the Fort Bragg Special Missions Unit sergeant major. He and the commander agreed to sponsor Gonzalez's family at base housing reserved for international officers on training assignments. While he had focused on helping Carlos, Wolf realized he hadn't thought once about Eliana or the cartel.

When Parker walked in, Wolf's breath paused. The style of her clothes said Italian, smooth and clingy, all black. He smiled, looking her over before he realized she was watching him watch her. He jumped up and met her at the hostess' station.

She looked at him skeptical eye but allowed a slight grin. "Do I pass muster, Wolf?"

"Yes, you do. You look great."

"Thanks. How about buying a girl a drink?"

Most would say an eight-by-forty-foot wall of whiskey, bourbon, rye, scotch, brandy, and more was good for every drink combination possible in the free world.

If you didn't feel like spirits, they always kept craft beer on tap. As a proper cigar bar, they also stocked an extensive selection of imported tobacco products—but you could also get cigars custom blended and hand-rolled in the back.

"I'll take a Rip," Parker said to the bartender.

She knows her bourbon. Old Rip Van Winkle Handmade Bourbon was becoming rarer due to its popularity and was threatening to become collectible.

Wolf ordered a Yellowstone Bonded bourbon aged sixteen years. They sat at a table along the wall near the corner of the bar, facing the door. The exposed brick and dark-stained wood gave the place a comfortable feel.

Small talk came easy. They talked about themselves, where they were born, where she went to college, his finishing college, Army careers, her marriage and divorce.

And then it got crazy.

Three large men burst through the door and opened fire. There didn't seem to be any rhyme or reason—they just fired into the crowd.

As soon as Wolf saw the door fly open, he rolled out of his chair and pulled Parker down as bullets flew past his shoulder into the back wall. Wolf drew his pistol and Parker did the same, and together they engaged the gunman, firing their way. They each shot two rounds into his chest, ending his night.

From other sections of the bar, other armed individuals had also engaged the shooters in a withering crossfire that was effective. The other two gunmen lay dead just inside the door.

Threats down, there was an odd quiet, then men sounding off clear! Several people went from downed person to downed person, checking for injuries or homicides.

Wolf's right eye stung from gunpowder blast and it was watering. He turned to Parker.

"You, okay?" Wolf asked.

"Yes. You're crying?"

"No thanks to your muzzle blast," he said with a wry smile. "I'm fine."

"What the heck was that all about?"

Wolf looked away, pretending to dab at his watering eye with a table napkin, afraid his face would give away his lie.

"Not sure."

Unlike a shooting scene at a regular bar, no one here was screaming or running around. The calmness was almost clinical. Most of the men and women in the bar had seen combat.

A former Hillsborough County deputy sheriff turned government security contractor used his knife to slice open a dead man's long shirt sleeve, revealing a distinctive tattoo. The black and gold was clear for everyone to see.

"Latin Kings—evil dudes. What are they doing here? he asked.

Wolf stiffened and Parker noticed. She grabbed him by the arm and whispered, "Does this have anything to do with you?"

"As soon as they made entry, I knew they were looking for me."

A man Wolf knew as an SMU squadron commander pointed toward a dead gunman left of the door. "I saw him focus on you, Wolf. Why was that?"

An NCO acquainted with Wolf asked, "Is this connected to your Mexican activities?"

Wolf shrugged in a no comment kine of way.

"You slapped the hornet's nest, man. Time to take protective measures, right?" the NCO said.

"Agreed."

He turned to Parker. "Miss, I'd tell you to stay away from Wolf, but I see you can handle yourself."

At the sound of sirens, the SMU officer had one of his guys also call 9-1-1 to report the scene was secure and armed military and civilians were present to prevent cops from rolling in hot.

Wolf looked back to his and Parker's table. "Well, at least they didn't hit our drinks." Parker squeezed his arm. He took her demeanor as her way of saying, I'm here for you.

The arriving patrol officers, detectives, and gang unit were understanding and professional. Wolf didn't like the idea that his recent tangle with the cartel was becoming known across the SOCOM community, let alone the Tampa police force.

He wondered, could there be a SOCOM intel leak that needs attention beyond Major Campbell, an unknown one. He'd discuss that with Kennedy tomorrow.

After being questioned by police and released, Wolf had a conversation with the owner of the bar. He offered to pay for repairs, but the owner wouldn't have any of it.

"Hey, that's what insurance is for brother. Plus, we're 2A people here, and the rounds that count are in the bad guys. You all made me proud." He slapped Wolf on the back. Wolf thanked the man and gave him his card.

"I'm starving," Wolf said. "Want to get something to eat somewhere with no floor show?"

"Yes, I do."

Parker grabbed his hand and led him to her car. At the passenger side door, she spun him around, pushed him hard against the car and kissed him, deep and wet. Her lips tasted like sweet bourbon. She pulled back, they locked eyes, and she kissed him again, harder, their hips crushing forward to twist and grind. Wolf's senses exploded with her sudden passion.

Parker pulled away from him with a hungry look in her eyes.

"I don't want dinner—I want you. We're going to my place.

"Got a problem with that, Wolf?" Wolf's pulse quickened, and he smiled. "Nope.

33

Elle Parker residence, Citrus Park, Florida

Wolf awakened covered in sweat and gasping for air. Parker was hugging him.

"Lance, it's all right. We're at my place and you're with me."

Ever since he'd returned from Mexico, nightmares had haunted Wolf's sleep. Torres would appear at the foot of his bed, neck gushing with blood.

When he'd joined the military as an impressionable young man, taking another person's life at a distance with a rifle gave Wolf physical and emotional separation from the death act.

With Torres, he could still feel the man struggling as his life-force drained away. He had to make peace with the dead man's ghost.

"Torres was the first person I ever killed hand-to-hand. I guess I haven't processed through it yet," he said bluntly.

Parker kissed his cheek. "I get it. I'm here if you want to talk about it."

"Thanks," he said, but the last thing he wanted to do was talk about it. "But no, thanks. What I'd like now is a shower and a bucket of coffee. Not in that order."

They showered together, then Parker made Cuban coffee, dark and rich. Suddenly, her demeanor changed.

"I need to know, Lance." They were sitting across the kitchen island, and a serious look came over her face. "Tell me the truth. You didn't stop attacking the cartel after you came back from your parents' funeral." It wasn't a question. "Did you?"

His inner voice said to trust her, so he listened to it, regardless of the outcome.

"I did not," he said.

"So, you didn't go hunting deer in Mexico?"

Wolf rubbed his jaw. "How much do you want to know?"

"Everything. I'm on your side, but I need to know what I am dealing with."

There is something about how deep she sees into my soul. He considered how much to tell her.

"I was on a leader's recon at a facility in Santa Ana. I damned near got caught and had to kill a guy to escape. It was the cartel's transportation lieutenant, Jose Torres, so no loss, anyway. What I didn't know at the time was I had dropped my hunting permit somewhere inside the facility. The cartel guys found it and came looking. I had to drop them, too."

"You know better than to carry identification on a mission," Parker said.

"It was a hunting permit, part of my cover story, but yeah, I should have left it in the hide site."

"How did they find you at the Blue Gorilla?"

"Major Helen Valo-Campbell," he said.

She slammed her mug down on the coffee table. "What the heck? Major Helen Campbell, from the Command? She's working for the cartel?"

"We think so, but based on our assessment, we believe she's being coerced. She has a sister in jeopardy."

"That's what they all say at first."

"No she is. Her sister is an aide worker for a non-profit in Chihuahua, Mexico. She works with a native tribe there. The cartel killed the sister's coworker as a warning. She's caught in a dangerous situation. We're working to get her sister out of the country to safety and then flip Campbell."

Wolf didn't know how deep he wanted to get into it all. Kennedy was still getting Maya Valo to come to the States on the pretext of attending the conference.

"I don't think you should go back to Mexico, okay? You have a lot of eyes on you now, and the incident last night will bring more." Tears filled her eyes, and Wolf didn't know why.

"Have I said something wrong?" he said.

Parker shook her head. "I know what it's like to need revenge, to lose someone you care about."

Wolf took Parker's hand. "Have you ever wished you could get back at the bad guys who killed your teammate in Bosnia? Yes, I know about her murder."

"Yes."

"Ever want to take the fight to the enemy?"

"Yes," she whispered.

"I think I've found a way, and I have other men who have signed on to the idea."

"Why?"

"What we have been doing to stem illegal drug flow is not working, so it's time for a different approach if there's to be any hope for change. Guerrilla warfare by genuine pros, small actions with outsized impact. Hit them where it hurts, in production and transportation. Turns out the facility I was at does both."

She leaned over and kissed him, pulled back, and looked into his eyes. "All right," she said. "I'm in."

Wolf spent the rest of the morning filling Parker in on every detail. Then they spent the rest of the weekend together not thinking about anything but each other.

34

El Rancho Cortes, Sinaloa, Mexico

Alejandro sat in his office. While playing with his pistol, he might appear distracted to the unknowing. He could see Martin Amaro and Maria Camacho walking across the courtyard. In a moment of frustration, he cursed and stood at the open window, firing his pistol over their heads. The noise was deafening.

His bodyguards rushed in, and he waved them away. Amaro and Camacho, unclear on whether or not they had been targets, lay prone in the gravel until their boss turned away.

Alejandro's upbringing had been one of discipline and severe punishment for failure. Discipline equals freedom. Punishment teaches success. The life lessons of his father were never far away from Alejandro's thoughts, and he spent his days trying to achieve his dead father's expectations.

Amaro and Camacho appeared side by side in the doorway.

"Another miserable failure. What punishment makes sense? You clowns have embarrassed me again." The two underlings stood still, hoping it rendered them invisible.

"If you weren't so goddamned important to the organization,

Martin, I would shoot you right here!" Alejandro shouted. "I expect more from you both."

He scowled a moment more, staring at his pistol. Then, "Martin, what will it take to kill this damned Wolf?"

"Alejandro, forgive me, but the Latin Kings are at fault. They moved without our permission or coordination."

He waved his gun side-to-side, and they flinched. He expressed his anger by stalking around the office, deep in thought. He had wanted to keep Wolf an in-house problem, but now the man was becoming an international irritant.

Alejandro's mind raced through different options. If he contacted El Chapo about the Latin Kings, he would see it as a failure on his part. He needed to save face. He turned back to Amaro.

"I want the Latin King who survived, the driver asshole who lacked the courage to enter the bar, I want him dead. We will not tolerate their failure."

He turned to Camacho. "Wolf is more dangerous than we thought. Will he continue to attack us?"

"Yes, Alejandro, I believe he will. Revenge is a powerful poison. It takes time to leave the mind."

"Where will he strike us next?"

"It will be here in Mexico. I believe Wolf was collecting intelligence on Jose's facility, so it is also a likely target. But he will also attack our transportation and production sites. The U.S. Army trained him in guerrilla warfare."

"Why not attack us in America, closer to home?"

"Two reasons, boss. First, he does not want U.S. law enforcement agencies investigating his activities." She took a tentative step forward. "Second, our U.S. operations are decentralized, and they change frequently. I think he will attack us here in Mexico where our production and shipping hubs are fixed and relatively easier to compromise."

Alejandro clicked his tongue as he thought about what to do next. His eyes raked over Camacho, and for the first time he saw her in a different light—as someone he could trust. She had come out of the shadows like a jaguar on its prey.

"You both can go. Make sure they die tonight."

"Yes, Alejandro." Amaro said.

After they left, Alejandro sat for a minute. He was not an introspective man, but considering the travail of recent weeks, he was beginning to feel older than his years. He wondered if it had become time to escape the cartel never be seen or heard from again.

He walked into the courtyard and stared into the fountain. He took a gold coin left at the fountain for the kids to make wishes with and rolled it between his fingers as his thoughts coalesced.

Maria's comment about Wolf not wanting U.S. agencies investigating his activities was a weakness he could exploit, but Alejandro's plans for the gringo went way beyond getting him in trouble with his bosses.

He smiled before a dark determination came over him. I will hurt him in ways he cannot imagine.

Alejandro walked back into his office and called the number left with the answering service. The Tomador de Almas—the Taker of Souls had never failed to deliver.

35

NGO conference, Tucson, Arizona

Wolf had driven back onto MacDill AFB to speak with Kennedy, who he found was focused on solving the Campbell issue.

"I leave tomorrow for the conference. It kicks off Wednesday. We should have Maya secured by Thursday and then we can move on Helen."

"All set for your exfil?" Wolf asked.

"Yes, we spend the night at your parents' place, and I have the tickets to Asheville."

"I had a friend from Fort Bragg make sure the cabin is all stocked and ready."

"I wonder if she likes to fish?" Kennedy wondered aloud. Wolf shook his head, smiling. "Stay on task, brother."

"Roger that. Now get out. I have work to finish," Kennedy said.

THE CONFERENCE REGISTRATION desk was busy. There was a positive vibe in the air as the conference attendees readied for the keynote speakers. Maya Valo fidgeted with her wireless mic setup.

Kennedy imagined most people would still be in shock after seeing a coworker killed right in front of them. Maya seemed a little nervous, but her presentation on her NGO was full of beautiful imagery, funny stories, and positive results. Her passion for the mission and her people was easy to see.

The audience gave her an appreciative round of applause, and several attendees waited after her presentation to talk and trade business cards. Valo came over to where Kennedy sat and parked next to him.

"Thank you for this opportunity," she whispered. "I appreciate it."

He nodded and smiled as the next speaker began.

The rest of the day included more speakers and workshops. Kennedy was never too far away from her, but not so close that it was creepy. At the day's end reception, Kennedy smiled as she approached him.

"I wanted to say thank you again." She reached forward and touched his shoulder.

"I appreciate that, Maya, but no need. You did an impressive job, and your passion for the work is clear for all to see."

"I also needed a break."

"I'm glad this worked out." Kennedy said, "I know several wonderful trails nearby if you'd like to go for a run."

"How do you know I run?"

"You work with the Tarahumara, you have no choice," Kennedy said before chuckling.

Maya laughed. "I am Tarahumara. Being back with my people taught me you can run until all your troubles and worries fall away. It cleanses my soul and clears my head."

Kennedy took her to Fantasy Island, a little-known mountain biker trail system, which gave them a cross-country run with multiple loops and easy elevation changes.

He was proud that he had gotten his running to a low seven-minute-mile pace, but Valo still crushed him. She ran like the wind, skimming the ground, black hair flowing in the breeze behind her. They ran for five miles, and she barely looked warmed up.

"More?" he asked.

"Yes, this is wonderful."

"Okay, the next loop is six miles this way."

Maya bolted off, and he laughed. Then she slowed and Kennedy watched it start. Small at first, as Maya wiped tears from her face. Kennedy hugged her, and she hugged him back, sobbing.

They stood together for several more minutes before she whispered a quiet thank you into his shoulder. Then she pushed him backward with a grin and bolted off again down the trail.

36

B arrista del Barrio coffee shop, Tucson, Arizona
Kennedy sat in the coffee shop with his thoughts and a steaming dark roast. Maya would hate him when he told her the truth.

He was never one to let his feelings get mixed with a mission, but the moment he had seen Maya, an excited, tingling rush of blood had flowed over him. He glanced to the coffee shop entrance and saw her. He waved her over.

"Morning, George," she said and smiled. "How are you after our run?" She slid into the booth opposite Kennedy. His cover had included the fake first name; one more lie to apologize for later.

"I'm great, and you?"

"I feel better than I have in a while thanks to you."

"So, tell me a little about yourself," Kennedy said, sipping his coffee. "Any siblings?"

"It's just my sister and me. Our parents have passed away. They worked hard to get us to the United States to give us a good life. I miss them." she reflected on her parents' passing. They had worked to provide for her and her sister. "What about you?"

"Parents, one brother, and two sisters, all in the Boston area. I see them once or twice a year. What does your sister do?"

"Army intelligence, both she and her husband. They can't talk about it, but I fear something is going on. I hear the stress in her voice."

Kennedy's ears perked up. "Sorry to hear that, Maya. What do you think?"

"I wonder if it has to do with what happened to my friend Billy."

Kennedy tried to choose his words. "It's possible. The cartels are very adept at leveraging weaknesses in people for their own gains. They are experts at intimidation, like with the killing of Billy."

Maya cocked her head. "Why do you think it was intimidation?"

"Well, you said your sister is in Army intelligence. You were out in nowhere Chihuahua and your friend Billy was killed. Do you think they wanted your sister to get the message that you could be next?"

The color drained from Maya's face. "Who are you? How do you know such things?" She jumped up and turned for the door.

Kennedy ran out after her. She was leaning back against a car, hands over her mouth, crying. He walked over and stood next to her.

"Maya—"

"Please," she said through tears, "please leave me be."

"Maya," he said in a softer voice. "Listen to me. I need to tell you some things first."

She looked up at him, her eyes glossy from big tears that rolled down her cheeks.

"My real name is Kieran Kennedy. I work for U.S. Army intelligence. You and your sister are both in danger. We believe the cartel killed Billy to send her a message that you would indeed be next if she didn't cooperate with them."

She stared at him, perplexed. Her expression transformed from shock to confusion to anger.

"Maya, my job is to get you to safety, and to bring your sister back over to our side to help us against the cartel."

"My sister is not a terrible person!" Maya exclaimed.

"We know. But we need to keep you safe so that we can help her. We aren't going to turn her in. In fact, we want her right where she is. But for her to be effective, she needs to know you are safe." Kennedy sensed Maya's shock leaving her, replaced by resolve.

"When the sicario killed Billy, he looked at me and smiled," Maya said. "I knew I wasn't their target, and it must have had something to do with my sister. As soon as you said intimidation, I knew it had to be true." She wiped the tears from her eyes with her sleeve. "What can I do to help?"

"We need to hide you here in the States until we finish our work, and then maybe you can go back to your regular life. Back to helping those in need."

She paused for a moment, taking it all in. "When do we start? It's Kennedy, right?"

He smiled. "Yes, it's Kennedy. Let's get back together at lunch and I'll tell you the plan."

37

E l Rancho Cortes, Sinaloa, Mexico
Alejandro had called one of his most-trusted assets, the Tomador, to fix his problem. Wolf's attacks had emboldened the Mexican federal police and defense minister. Their military counter-drug teams were impeding cartel business.

Alejandro would not let an emboldened Mexican Army interrupt the business any longer. A few more wins and the U.S. would push until the Mexican government caved. Next would be large-scale counter-drug operations with American partner agencies. Drug suppression operations on a warlike footing that multiple U.S. presidents had wanted for a long time.

Holding the phone away from his ear, Alejandro flinched as El Chapo screamed vile obscenities at him. El Chapo was losing faith in him. If Alejandro's soldiers couldn't kill Wolf, then El Chapo would grab the brother and sister and use them for leverage.

After being cut off mid-sentence, Alejandro needed some good news, so he called Eliana. She answered on the first ring.

"How are you, sister?"

"Excellent, brother. It is good to hear your voice. I trust you approve of my work here."

"I approve and El Chapo is happy," he said. No need to burden her with El Chapo updates at this point. "He says this is your calling."

"Good to hear. We have taken several new prime locations and two new distribution networks. I sent the details to Martin."

Alejandro hid his frustration with El Chapo and laughed. "Yes, the Félix brothers are not happy. Have you seen Cousin Jimmy yet?"

"Yes, we are using his company to buy new warehouses."

"Good. I need you to ask him to do something for me. It's our Wolf problem."

"Ahh, yes. I heard about the Latin Kings screwup. Why don't you let me take care of it for you?"

"Eliana, you are doing so well in L.A. that I hesitate to interrupt that focus. What I do need you to do is pass on a message that Jimmy can pass to his friend, the governor of Florida. I need Jimmy to motivate the governor to investigate Wolf. Once the investigation starts, he'll not be able to attack us. We will help them put Wolf in prison."

Alejandro detailed Maria's skillfully crafted allegations. "I will call Jimmy tonight," Eliana said.

"Perfect. Keep up the excellent work."

Eliana disconnected the call and thought about her initial desire to get back to the center of power alongside her brother. But L.A. was suiting her. Here she was free to grow the business without the looming shadow of Alejandro.

The fight against the Tijuana Cartel was her mission, and she was good at it. What she had not counted on was the unfamiliar feelings growing in her with pregnancy.

Her hormones were changing as she adapted to the unfamiliar form her body was taking. A maternal side she had not known was making itself apparent, and it was becoming a nuisance.

She dialed Jimmy's cell, he answered on the first ring.

"Eliana, my dear. How nice of you to call. How are you?"

"Good, cousin, thank you. Getting big as a damned house. Listen, primo, we need you to make a call to your friend in Florida."

"Anything for la familia."

"One of my men will courier the message to you. We need this call as soon as possible. A man is hurting the family and our business, and other methods have been, um, ineffective."

"I understand. I will make the call today."

"We will not forget this, Jimmy. Tell your wife I will call her to schedule lunch. And tell the children Aunt Eliana sends her love."

38

Bjorn Anderson residence, Los Angeles, California

Bjorn finished his coffee and rinsed out the cup before placing it in the sink. Would today be the day his wife, Lisa, would sleep through his morning routine?

When he bent over to check his briefcase for lecture materials, he felt a pinch. He adjusted the pistol in his waistband holster. His new Glock 19 shot well, but its length took getting used to when wearing it concealed.

He raised his head and saw the most beautiful creature staring at him. Golden-blond hair in a ponytail, blue eyes, and a trim, athletic build. She stood in the doorway sporting her favorite sleepwear, a Rangers Lead The Way T-shirt.

"Sorry, babe. I thought I was Ninja this morning."

"Oh, you were. My brain kicked off so there's no sleeping in."

"No rest for a mad scientist, right?" He kissed her on the lips and lingered.

They walked out the front door together, pausing as they always did, so Bjorn could perform his customary security scan. It had started as part of his father's awareness training for the family and had been further ingrained during his time on active duty.

Regardless of the point of departure—patrol base, base camp, restaurant, or house—the process was the same.

As he turned to say goodbye, his brain registered a threat, the movement of an unexpected, unfamiliar vehicle slowing in his peripheral vision. He instinctively pushed his wife back into the house and pulled the door closed, drawing his Glock and took cover behind a planter box. Time slowed as the two shooters pushed rifles out the car windows and let loose.

Bjorn executed a near-ambush, immediate-action drill, firing to stop the threat. The front-seat passenger's head exploded as he sent two bullets through his right eye. A chunk of his head blew splattered of red and gray over the face of the driver, blinding him for a beat. That was more than enough pause for Bjorn to keep firing at the second shooter before the car sped away. He performed a combat reload with a full magazine in case they came back.

Immediate danger gone, Bjorn ran back inside the house to his wife, who was curled up behind the leather living room sectional.

"We're clear, honey. Are you all right?" He knelt and ran his hands over her body checking for injuries.

"Idiots! Now I need to wear my vest too. I hate that thing." She rose to her knees and embraced her husband. "When is this crap going to end?"

They had met when he was a DEA pilot, and she was a new scientist. Unlike her professor husband, she was still a sworn federal agent. She had thought her street combat days were behind her, so Bjorn felt guilty about this new threat following him back home.

She hated the cartels. She had seen autopsied brains firsthand and the irreversible damage drugs cause. But he knew she was by his side no matter what. He could ask for no more committed partner.

Police summoned by frightened neighbors could already be heard in the distance. Bjorn gritted his teeth and unloaded his weapon, just for drill, placing it in plain view on the coffee table.

The local police knew him and Lisa so neither would be pushed about the shooting. Bjorn's and neighborhood residential video surveillance cameras would support their accounts of the attack.

Bjorn had detected that he and his wife were being watched, but always from a distance, and by different personnel each time. He'd concluded wrong that it was related to her DEA job.

This morning's attack, on the other hand, suggested it had to do with his parents' deaths and his brother—that meant Sinaloa.

He frowned. "I don't think that was for us specifically. I mean, sure—they'd have killed us if they could. But I think it was meant to send Lance a message."

Bjorn asked Lisa to call 911 and let them know the shooters had left the scene trailing DNA and that civilians with unloaded weapons were on scene.

The gangs in Orange County and Los Angeles proper were known to out-gun the police. The all-clear was a public service.

The neighbors peeked out of their houses. A drive-by shooting had never happened on this street, much less this community. Sirens were close now. Bjorn walked into the street, pulling on surgical gloves from his medical kit.

He picked up a folding-stock AK that had fallen from the shooter's window when the man's head exploded, and he unloaded the weapon. He put the rifle back on the street among the spent brass. He was returning to the house just as police cruisers skidded to a halt at both ends of the street. Bjorn automatically stopped walking, raised both arms away from his sides, and slowly turned around.

He called over his shoulder to Lisa.

"Would you call work and tell 'em I'll be late, hon, please?" He smiled. "They'll understand."

Within seconds, more squad cars were blocking the street from both directions and establishing a perimeter.

Bjorn took a deep breath and turned back to the half-dozen police officers tiptoeing forward with weapons raised.

"Coffee, officers? It's going to be a long day."

ONCE A PERFUNCTORY SEARCH of Bjorn for weapons was completed, the police presence stood down and he invited officers into the kitchen. Lisa, now in black jeans and T-shirt over her soft armor vest, offered them coffee.

Her DEA badge holder was clipped to her belt in a casual manner, but she knew it would make a difference to the police.

She and Bjorn presented the cops a step-by-step replay of their morning until they finished with their point of view of the incident. Their video surveillance captured the entire event, start to finish, at just nine seconds.

Bjorn downloaded the corroborating video and gave it to the patrol sergeant on a USB drive.

Initial interviews concluded and with best wishes from the police for a better day, it was done. When Lisa and Bjorn stepped outside with the cops there was a crowd of neighbors gawked at the damage.

The crime scene had been processed. CSI counted fifty-two AK rounds that had in short order torn up the front of the house and the Anderson's Land Cruiser. Lisa was already on the phone with a USAA insurance representative, scheduling an assessment.

Minutes later a news truck arrived from KCBS-TV Channel 2. The neighbors remained and gawked, eager to hear any juicy gossip they could pass around before it was on the noon news.

Then came round two, with detectives and the insurance adjuster all needing answers to the same questions. Pots of coffee and delivery pizza added to the blur of the day.

After rounds of talking through the shooting Bjorn called Sierra and learned her house had also been damaged in a drive-by event— at the same time as Bjorn's.

"For Christ's own sake, is everyone okay?" he asked.

"Yes, we're all fine here. Shook up, of course. We can thank Lance for installing the cameras and the alarm system. It caught the driver's and shooters' faces along with the car's license plate. They fired into the master bedroom and sprayed the front door. Thank God the kids' rooms are in the back of the house."

"How are the kids taking it?" Bjorn asked.

Sierra sighed. "They are asking questions and we told them what happened. Bad people shot at our house. We told them it was a case of mistaken identity, and we aren't in danger now." She paused for a moment. "When is this going to end? I mean, mom and dad gone, and now we have to worry about our own lives."

"It's okay," Bjorn said. "I know this is scary but trust us. Lance and I are doing everything we can to make sure we all remain safe."

"But how do I know this won't happen again? What if I'm at the hospital, or at the store, or what if the kids are at school?" she asked. It was a legitimate question.

It was one thing for Wolf to live on alert and always be looking over his shoulder. Lisa and I are used to such precautions, too. But now it involves Sierra's family.

"You know," Sierra said, "I'm all about saving lives, delivering babies and stuff, right? But I have to admit my dark side wants those cartel assholes to pay hard for what they're doing to us."

"I know, I know," Bjorn said as a wave of guilt washed over him. "What are you going to do next?"

"I'll wait to see what the police come back with on a threat assessment. If it comes back high, I'll take my family on an extended vacation."

Bjorn understood. "My pissed-off wife is taking leave to visit her grandmother in Alaska. I'm staying here, though. If they keep sending them, I'll stack them like firewood—and I'm expecting more, so I put the plates in my vest."

"Just please be safe. We've already lost our parents." The line was silent for a moment. "I don't want to lose my brothers, too."

39

LAX International Airport, Los Angeles, California

Two days later, Wolf spider-sensed a tail as he walked out to the airport passenger pickup area. At least this guy didn't look like a cartel dirtbag. More than likely DEA or FBI—which meant they intended him to spot the surveillance.

Regardless of the agency or the reason, a tail would complicate his plans. He rounded a corner and caught a quick reflection in a window of the man following him—tall, dressed way down, well built, Ray-Bans.

He might as well have been wearing a raid jacket with a big yellow FBI on the back. If it was a check-in tail, no worries. That would be easily enough to shake. But if it was a full surveillance package, he would have to work countermeasures into a plan that didn't allow time for them.

On the sidewalk Wolf raised his face to the California sun and stopped for a moment to take in the dry heat. He liked Los Angeles because he'd never spent enough time there to dislike it.

A vehicle horn honked, and he saw his brother parked a few cars away, waving out of the sunroof of a brand-new Mahogany Pearl

Toyota Land Cruiser. USAA had totaled the last one without argument.

Wolf opened the rear passenger-side door, dropped his weapons case and kit bag into the back seat and hopped in. "You notice, we're being followed?"

"Yeah," Bjorn said. "It's almost like they don't care if we know."

"True that," Wolf said, laughing. "Ours or theirs?"

"Ours is my guess. I'd say DEA."

"I was thinking FBI, but either way. Why do you think DEA?"

"Central casting. Long hair and cheap clothes. FBI dresses better."

"Ah, says the connoisseur of fine attire," Wolf teased. His brother always dressed nicely. Off-duty, Wolf lived in frayed jeans, old sneakers, and faded T-shirts.

"Are you thinking they have a full surveillance package in play?"

"Possible, I guess," Bjorn said, glancing in the rear-view mirror as he signaled and pulled into traffic outside the Arrivals terminal. "Not sure yet. I can't imagine we rise to that level of attention. But let's give it twenty-four to see how it settles in."

"Did you sweep the vehicle?" Wolf asked, wondering whether his brother had checked for electronic tracking devices.

"No, but I picked this one off a dealer's lot this morning myself and stood by as they prepped it. Then I drove straight here."

"Okay, close enough for government work, right?" They laughed, releasing tension. "While we're headed back to your place, I'll fill you in on my ideas."

Wolf went through his plan to get the Tijuana Cartel to target Eliana directly. Bjorn asked a few probing questions to focus their intentions. Wolf could always count on his brother's smarts to make even good plans better.

As they neared the Bjorn's house, Wolf's eyes went wide at the broken glass and other perforations in the house. "Bro—that's a crap ton of incoming. Will insurance take care of it?"

"Yeah, we're all good. I talked to Sierra, and they suffered the same, but are okay."

"Glad to hear that!" Wolf said and sighed.

Bjorn switched off the vehicle in the driveway. "Lisa made some dinner before she left. I can microwave us up some chow like nobody's business."

Wolf was grateful for the food and the comforts of home, if a battered one. He didn't got little of that on a bachelor's lifestyle. After they'd eaten and were seated comfortably in Bjorn's spacious living room with Bourbons, they discussed their next moves.

Through the blinds and the masking tape temporarily holding the front bay window glass in place, they saw a dark blue government- issue Chevrolet pull to the curb a few houses down from Bjorn's driveway. He logged into his laptop and called up exterior video, panning the camera to the interesting blue Chevy.

He shook his head. "Hmm. Minders, looks like. Good thing I have the dirt bikes in the shed out back."

"How does that help? Won't they be too loud?"

"No, I set them up street legal. Not loud at all. That's a gas company easement behind the house and we can scoot down it for blocks before we decide to get out on the street. When and where is the meet?"

"Zero-two-thirty tonight at the Elsinore drop zone."

"Okay, I'm getting some shuteye. I'll be awake at zero-one. You'll smell the coffee."

"Roger that. If this works and Eliana reacts with her normal fit of rage, tomorrow will be an outstanding day."

Bjorn disappeared down the hall. With a sheet and pillow, Wolf set up his resting place on the couch. It was quiet, and even though he was amped up about what would go down tomorrow, his eyes were heavy. He let the darkness of the room lull him to sleep.

The smell of coffee brewing woke him up. He walked into the kitchen. Bjorn was leaning against the counter and slid a cup his way. "Here you go."

"Thanks. Is the car still here?"

"No. And no replacement that I can see. But we should still take the bikes, just in case. Long as they see the truck in front they'll think we're still here."

"Agreed. How long will it take to get to the drop zone?"

"Thirty-five minutes, plus or minus. We can hit the road and get in our observation post early."

"The skydivers will still be partying, so we walk in the last half mile. We can use the office park and hangars for cover."

After they finished their coffee, they grabbed their backpacks and pushed the motorcycles down the grassy easement for a couple of blocks before starting them.

It took less time than expected to reach their destination. From their offset observation position along Cereal Street, Bjorn and Wolf had a direct view into the drop zone parking area. The party was still going, but the meet site was empty. A bright blue-and-chrome 1964 Chevrolet Impala SS arrived and flashed its lights twice.

"There's my signal. I'll stay in the open," Wolf said as he checked the Glock Bjorn had given him.

The plan was for Wolf to keep his back to Bjorn, so the chem light in his left rear pocket remained visible. If shit hit the fan, Wolf would toss the chemical light toward the bad guys to help Bjorn identify targets.

The deal went down without a hitch. Wolf traded ninety thousand dollars for two kilos of cocaine. He watched the seller drive off and he memorized his license plate number, though it was probably stolen. Wolf turned and walked a roundabout route back to the motorcycles.

Back at the house, Bjorn stared at the cocaine stacked on his kitchen table. "What have I gotten myself into?"

Wolf laughed.

"What's so funny?" Bjorn asked.

"I bought two keys of cocaine using ninety thousand dollars of Cortes money, and when I sell it, I'll make another forty thousand," Wolf said.

"No kidding, the money was the cartels?"

"Yes. Cárdenas gave it back to me right before they deported us. Now, let's taint this crap and get it on the streets."

40

L ance Bear Wolf's cabin, rural North Carolina
      Kennedy looked forward to the safety of Wolf's remote
North Carolina cabin. He saw no reason to deviate from the
initial plan. Stay out of sight for two weeks before heading down to
Tampa and a reunion with Maya's sister.

At the Asheville airport, Kennedy and Maya headed for baggage
claim. The two-stop, five-hour flight from Arizona to North Carolina
went off without an issue. Once they had their bags, they headed for
the rental cars.

Outside, Kennedy stopped and asked a leather-vested bearded
guy standing next to a Harley for directions. The guy used his finger
to trace out the route west to Brevard on the paper rental car
company map.

Kennedy thanked him and they placed their bags in the back of a
refrigerator-white Ford Explorer. Headed out on the two-and-a-half-
hour drive, he and Maya didn't speak much, mostly just comments on
the lush green mountains as they drove west.

Kennedy stopped in Brevard for fuel. Several bikers—including
the one he had asked for directions—pulled into the plaza at the
same time and parked at the Burger King next door. As the bikers

went inside the fast-food joint to get lunch, the directions guy gave Kennedy the hand signal for all clear. Kennedy gave the man a thumbs-up, then turned and smiled at Maya.

"Want a drive-through lunch? It's another forty-five minutes to the cabin."

"Sure, I could eat."

Kennedy topped off the gas tank, and they drove next door to order from the drive-thru lane. The rest of the trip was uneventful, finishing the drive west on S-64. They turned off on RT-281S.

It was three more miles before the markers on the telephone pole signaled the left into a brush-covered driveway with a locked gate. Kennedy opened the lock and swung the gate in, then drove up the driveway to park on the far side of a weathered concrete pad. Before going inside, he trotted back down the driveway and locked the gate behind them.

It was another a half mile of switchbacks up the mountain to the cabin. The large trees, mountain laurel, and rhododendron provided a cool, dark backdrop to the steep hillside. Kennedy took his time inching around an enormous boulder, taking most of the road on his left.

It looked as though it could start rolling with no notice. When they emerged out on top, Maya broke into a wide grin.

"Wow—it's beautiful!"

Kennedy pulled to the left along the driveway. Before them was a genuine Appalachian cabin built up over many years around what had been a logging bunkhouse and kitchen.

Fruit trees surrounded it, giving the air a sweet fragrance. Kennedy took their bags to the back door near the kitchen and turned on the liquid natural gas tanks. The screen door creaked as he let them in.

The cabin was an encapsulation of another time, though with enough modern additions for year-round comfort. Kennedy went to a utility room and turned on the lights, hot water heater, and a wall furnace. He started water heating on the stove and offered Maya a seat at the kitchen table.

"Kieran, this is a wonderful place," she said. "I can't wait to explore the woods and the waterfalls we drove by."

"Have you seen the movie, The Last of the Mohicans?"

"Yes, I loved it."

"Well, they filmed parts of it around here. We can run the same waterfall Hawkeye did."

"How fun!" Then her face darkened. "Are we safe here?"

"Completely." His sheepish smile telegraphed a secret. "Those biker guys who followed us are my friends Army buddies. Specialists, kinda. They've been escorting us since the airport and would have known if someone had been following us. And I'm certain they would have done something about it."

"It's not the Army uniform my sister wears."

Kennedy laughed. "No, and they don't do what your sister does.

"I can't tell you who they are, but they are experts."

"You have a lot of secrets in your business."

"We really do," said Kennedy. He changed the subject. "Listen, I need to take a quick power nap. The house alarm system is on, so don't open any doors, please—an the alarm here doesn't mobilize the police." He didn't elaborate on the mysterious comment. "The water is hot if you want tea or coffee."

Kennedy took the smaller bedroom and set the alarm on his watch for seventy-five minutes. He had just found the right position when he felt Maya slide in behind to him. She snuggled, putting her arm over his. Her warm breath on his neck took away the stress. He exhaled and relaxed, and fell into a deep sleep.

41

Eliana Cortes warehouse, Los Angeles

Eliana was drinking her post-workout smoothie. A high-tempo cardio workout on the elliptical had her drenched in sweat.

She wondered if she would have to change her workout schedule. Would her taste in food change with the pregnancy? Would she look like a beached whale afterward, like all the other sloppy cartel wives?

She'd never hung around the wives. This was all new to her.

She sat outside on the deck and took in the morning sun. She enjoyed the view of the Hollywood hills before the smog rolled in.

At first, she had been angry at Alejandro for banishing her to the States. It had taken a few weeks for her to say goodbye to her old life in Mexico. Los Angeles held immense promise.

The phone rang, startling her. "Please meet me at warehouse three," her U.S. operations lead, Enrique Velasquez said. "We have an issue, Señora."

No time to shower, Eliana toweled off and changed into dry black sweats. Aron Lopez, her deputy, had the black Range Rover waiting for her.

Lopez gave her a brief description of the issue while Eliana's anxiety percolated. She hated surprises and surprise trouble most of all.

Warehouse three was a cavernous but well-lighted space, a working area that held more than twenty workers, with discrete rooms for efficient packaging of heroin, cocaine, marijuana, crack, and other portfolio drugs for distribution.

Another area held workers processing a large table covered by a breathtaking quantity of money and a half-dozen currency counters.

The workers knew better than to show they recognized Eliana, and she ignored them. She took the stairs two at a time to an old second-floor office with painted-over windows.

Seated on the right side of the table, a long-time Cortes distributor looked at the floor and wrung his hands, mumbling to himself. She powered into the office so hard that the door was flung open and struck the wall hard, shattering the door glass.

"What have you done to our product, idiot?" she shouted. "Users are getting sick, and they think it will kill them. Our product is dangerous and now you've destroyed our reputation."

Word was spreading to stop using Cortes cocaine because it might kill.

"I, I didn't do nothing, Señora," he said. "I swear on my children I never touched it."

"Then why are customers in our prime market getting sick?" she screamed. "Why are they getting sick!?"

"I do not know."

"Has the product ever been bad before?"

"No."

"Then you must have done something to it. Admit it to me now and you will live." He wouldn't, of course, but the threat was necessary.

She had to figure out the cause of the contamination in her product and shift any blame for it onto someone else.

"No, please—your man said we had bought it from the Tijuana Cartel."

Eliana waved her hand. "Our man said what? It was product we had what?"

"Yes. Your man gave us a great deal for two kilos. Better than normal. I saved many dollars for you."

"Was he your regular contact?"

"No, he was new. But he knew the passwords."

She slapped the top of his head because he hadn't dared look up to her face.

"Get out, idiot. Your people will take anyone needing medical attention to clinics. Tell your customers we will replace their dangerous product with good."

When the man was too frightened to budge, Eliana swung a powerful right into the side of his face, knocking him to the floor. "Now go!"

Soldiers grabbed the man by his arms and assisted him out of Eliana's sight.

She threw a chair. It was her job to keep the customers happy. If Alejandro found out about this there would be hell to pay, and she couldn't think of any scenario where he wouldn't find out.

She glared at Lopez, her face reddening. "That idiot took contaminated product from the Tijuana Cartel, those motherless bastards. I want them hit and I want them hit hard—now."

Lopez tried to inject some space for a cool-down into the discussion. "I suggest waiting until tonight, boss."

Eliana's face was brilliant red as she grabbed Lopez's chrome handgun from his shoulder holster and jammed it hard under his chin. His eyes went wide with fear as she shrieked.

"I suggest you shut up!" she screamed in his face, angry spittle flying into his eyes. "I said we hit them now, right now! I want them dead. Do you hear me?"

She pulled back the hammer on the Colt Python revolver Lopez favored, and the cylinder clicked as the .357 Magnum round rotated into place.

"Hit them now!"

"I will make the calls!"

Eliana stuffed the pistol in his chest and strode down the stairs into the warm California air. She was breathing heavy and sweat poured from her as if she'd done another power workout. I need to stop this damage before it gets out of control and kills me.

ELIANA WAS BEING DRIVEN downtown for a meeting when a car, later identified as full of Tijuana Cartel gunslingers, thought they would make a name for themselves.

They pulled up behind Eliana's Range Rover and blasted away, not noticing their gunfire was ineffective against the Rover's armor plating and bulletproof windows.

The Rover skidded to a controlled one-eighty-degree stop in the road, facing her attackers.

Her security team dismounted out both side of the Rover into a wedge formation and unloaded their Colt M16 carbines the car full of teenagers.

They shredded the Tijuana soldiers with well-trained military precision. When the return gunfire died, Eliana jumped out and emptied her Sig P226 semi-automatic pistol into the attacker's car.

Her shots ending three of the five men whose ghastly gunshot wounds hadn't yet killed them.

Then a security man walked up with two fragmentation grenades with longer fuse times. He pulled the pins and dropped them into the car full of dead cartel soldiers and trotted back to the Range Rover.

She glanced in the side mirror and watched the car exploded into a bright orange ball of flame.

On the advice of Sonny Garcia, her head of security, Eliana switched from managing the Tijuana Cartel strikes from her office. Lopez was frightened enough to follow her orders to the letter or die trying.

Instead, she was driven back to her residence to work a burner phone like a congressional call center seeking votes. She assured her distributors they could count on her product.

After fixing a terrible mistake in processing, they were now churning out fresh product. Eliana would make it worth their while to remain loyal to the Sinaloa Cartel.

Several callers voiced their concerns about the negative effect of all the shooting. She agreed it was unfortunate, but necessary to balance the scales. She had just ended the call when her front door crashed open with men screaming in English and Spanish.

"LAPD! Police—show me your hands!"

Her security team alerted but didn't have enough time to draw weapons in response, a good thing. They knelt and placed their hands on their heads with fingers interlaced.

Eliana cursed under her breath. She reached to the side and dropped the throwaway cellphone into one of the many fish tanks in the house, then placed her hands palms up in her lap. Three LAPD SWAT officers in full combat gear focused on her, their red laser sights trained on her chest.

Two police lieutenants then entered, flashed badges and identified themselves—one from Homicide, the other Narcotics.

"Eliana Cortes, you are under arrest for murder." They displayed the warrant. Five counts of murder. They said they had video proof of her shooting at a car and there were dead bodies to back it up.

That was fast. "I want my lawyer."

"Don't speak." They hauled her up from the couch and two female officers entered and pinned her arms behind her, placing handcuffs around her thin wrists. Extra snug.

The SWAT officers searched, cuffed, and loaded the security team into a van for transport. A female officer searched Eliana and found her ankle holster. She held up her pistol like she'd just won the Super Bowl. Then they escorted her to a waiting squad car. It took less than twenty minutes before word leaked out.

Eliana Cortes, sister of a top leader in the Sinaloa Cartel, was in custody for killing Tijuana Cartel soldiers.

42

Sybil Brand Institute for Women

The district attorney could have kept Eliana in the county jail, but he liked the thought of her being pushed down to live with the everyday trash in Sybil Brand, some of whom were her dope customers.

The bailiff placed the chain and cuffs around her belly below the small baby bump, so it hurt to sit. She nursed a powerful thirst, but the faucet was right over the holding cell toilet, and she couldn't bring herself to use it. It wasn't until after she had gotten through the intake process that they gave her a small bottle of water.

Even the meanest women criminals in California hated the Sybil Brand Institute for Women. The Northridge earthquake had damaged the facility, and its minimal repairs completed to keep it operational. Just long enough for the planned move to the new Twin Towers facility. Until they were ready, there was no other place in L.A. County to put its two thousand female inmates.

Broken, infested, and rank. For a first timer, it was jarring, demeaning, and dangerous. And even more so for a nominal cartel princess. Status in the outside world didn't matter. Inside the Institute, Eliana was at the bottom.

The morning after, the bright sunlight hurt her eyes as they led her out into the yard. Everyone there stopped what they were doing and stared at her in silence. For the first time in Eliana's life, she felt scared, and she put on what she hoped was a fierce, don't-mess-with-me face.

A group of five husky women walked over and Eliana steeled herself for a fight, turning into the threat and balling up her right fist. She was a weak puncher with her left.

The women stepped right into her personal space and encircled her. Eliana never felt more vulnerable in her life, but her fear didn't show on her face, just in a neck vein that pulsed fast. She took a deep breath and snarled.

"What?"

After a moment, the biggest woman smiled.

"Relax, baby girl. I'm Renae. Your brother sent us. We're here to protect you."

Relieved, nodding and exhaling, Eliana walked with them to a table, where the leader chased the occupants off.

Eliana ignored their bitchy looks. The group leader, Renae Relleno, had painted-on eyebrows and crooked teeth. She was tall and big-boned, not some- one Eliana wanted to mess with. She was happy Relleno was on her side.

"The Tijuana Cartel has put a price on your head in here, love. We will eat, sleep, and shower with you to make sure you're safe," Relleno whispered. "It ain't cheap, but hey, your brother's payin'."

She looked around at the hard women, believing now that she might make it out of the Institute in one piece. She was only waiting for arraignment, which had to happen within forty-eight hours, not counting holidays and weekends. I could stand on my head for forty-eight hours, she assured herself.

The rest of the exercise period was uneventful. Eliana made sure she memorized the faces of the women holding long stares and posturing with their teams. No doubt there were Tijuana Cartel women in the general population.

The bounty on her head could turn a few lesser criminals into potential first-time killers. Not the best situation, but manageable.

On the way back to her cellblock, two amateurs made a move. The first, a decoy, charged from the left, drawing the crew away from the actual attacker, who thought she would go unnoticed and slide in from the right.

But Eliana had years more experience. The attacker grabbed for Eliana, catching her jumpsuit. Eliana grabbed the woman's wrist, but instead of twisting it away, she held it in place.

Then she used the fulcrum point to spin into and break her attacker's elbow. The sickening crack and scream spun two of her crew around. Eliana blocked the left-handed shiv coming in on a wide arc, then she back-kicked her attacker's knee, dislocating it and dropping her to the ground.

The attacker lay on the floor, wailing. As Eliana backed away, her crew pounced on the attacker, beating her to a bloody pulp before they hurried off.

Back in her dank cell, the crew took the other three bunks. The remaining two inmates made themselves welcome next door.

Eliana thanked them, assuring she would not forget their help.

Exhausted, she lay down on her thin mattress and closed her eyes, trying to imagine herself out of this place.

Her hands cradled her stomach. She showed little, like many women in the first trimester, but she felt her body changing more each day. Tears trickled down her cheeks, and she rubbed them away.

Joaquin, I miss you.

She daydreamed of their last time together. Zapana had shown her the transformative power of love and devotion. His honest attention to her needs was in stark contrast to the youthful men on her crew she had used for her own pleasure. He had shown her another side. She would never admit it, least of all to him, but she had loved him.

The thought faded when she scratched at her arm. She pulled back her sleeve, revealing the PENSAR brand her brother had caused. It ignited an angry fire that she did not attempt to quench.

One day, brother.

A dozen angry women walked toward her cell. A soft whistle and her protective crew jammed into the cell's doorway. The group leader, a large, threatening woman with a man's haircut, stared through the cell bars and laughed.

"You think they keep you safe, princess?" she sneered. "You will beg for death before we open your throat."

Eliana stood up and stared the woman down. Guards converged on the cell then and cleared the passageway with threats of discipline. The group laughed before the guards moved them along.

That night, Eliana didn't sleep.

43

E l Rancho Cortes, Sinaloa, Mexico

Alejandro lay on his oval bed, embracing his wife while staring at the ceiling. Anyone seeing a picture of the scene would say it intimate and loving, but Alejandro wasn't present.

The opulence of the master bedroom was in stark contrast to the dirt floor, rope bed, and single naked lightbulb he'd lived with as a child. He kissed his wife and climbed out of bed, heading downstairs for breakfast, thinking about his sister's latest jam-up.

Eliana, it never stops.

When he was told they had arrested his sister for attempted murder—and multiple counts at that—his first reaction was to laugh. He couldn't help himself. The news was too fantastic.

But it pleased him that she had responded to the problem. Someone acting the part of a Cortes supplier had sold bad cocaine to one of their most important distributors in Los Angeles.

It was communicated throughout their network and hundreds of people were getting sick. It had almost destroyed their reputation.

Eliana had swooped in and fixed the cocaine problem, but she created another. The first rule of cartel reputation management is not to be caught.

That's what underlings were for. Now she needed to be bailed out or broken out, and the latter was not the best method. Alejandro rubbed his temples. Why must he always come to his sister's aid? He wondered if she would do the same for him.

He called his cousin, California State Senator Jimmy Cortez.

"Alejandro, how are you?" Jimmy said with enthusiasm. He was wary because his cousin didn't call very often, but he always called for a purpose.

"I'm angry, Jimmy. I'm sure you have heard about Eliana. I need you to get her out of jail now, before she gets hurt."

"Yes, I did hear I don't know what you think I can do, but I can't—"

"Jimmy! You are not listening. I'm telling you I want my sister out today. Tonight, at the latest. I have arranged protection for her, but nothing is certain in that place."

"Alejandro, I can't do this. The system needs its own time to work—"

"Do I have to remind you what will happen with one call to the L.A. Times?" Alejandro barked.

Jimmy fell silent. It was a painful memory from Alejandro's weekend-long party for Jimmy's fortieth birthday. On the last day, as Jimmy sobered up and laughed about how much fun he was having, Alejandro had shown his cousin the high-quality videos made of him with three women, though it wasn't quite accurate to call fifteen-year-olds women.

Alejandro sent Jimmy home with the videos as a warning and a memento.

"Okay, okay," Jimmy said, relenting. "I will see what I can do."

Alejandro slammed down the phone without saying goodbye.

He missed Joaquin and his counsel at these crucial moments. He would know what to do.

Forty-four minutes later Alejandro sat alone with his coffee, reading through the stack of reports he received every morning, when his phone rang.

"It's done. they will release Eliana tomorrow morning," Jimmy said.

JAILERS WOKE Eliana at three-thirty the next morning. She was getting out, no questions asked. Eliana passed a slip of paper to Renae Relleno and told her to call the number when she and the crew got out. They all had bonuses and jobs waiting.

Eliana changed back into her street clothes and, in less than an hour, they escorted her through secured portals and a sign-out office to the double front gates. Outside, a black Range Rover idled for her.

As they drove into the garage at her home, she saw the patched-up front door where SWAT had made its no-knock power entry and shook her head.

That door was a hand-carved custom piece, and she'd loved it. She surveyed the mess the police had made as they searched the house, then went to the bathroom to start a long shower.

She luxuriated in the hot water as she washed her hair twice to make sure there was no part of jail residue left on her. She was on her bed applying moisturizer when the phone rang. Caller ID said UNKNOWN, but who else could it be?

She sighed and took a beat before pressing the Accept button.

"Eliana, are you okay?" Alejandro asked. He seemed sincere, which meant he was faking. "No lingering effects from jail?"

"No, brother. I'm well, thank you." She rubbed another dollop of moisturizer on her punitive tattoo and grimaced. "Thank you for getting me out."

"I have news you will find interesting." She rolled her eyes. "What is it?"

"Your men got a description of the seller from the distributor." He paused. "It was Wolf who sold your man the bad product."

Eliana clenched her fists. A volley of swear words in English and Spanish flew out of her mouth in jumbled, uncontrolled rage. "He's attacking us in the States now?"

"Yes. We need to end this now. El Chapo and I agree you should lead the effort to kill Wolf. You are the only one we trust."

No, I won't do it. I just want to have my baby in peace. In the moment, Eliana's internal response came from a maternal place. She was tired of fighting and killing.

"What do you propose?" she said in a noncommittal way. "I'm already under scrutiny. I may not be the best choice to handle this matter."

"We're putting a one-hundred-thousand-dollar bounty on Wolf, making it look like it came from you. El Chapo will appreciate that you are taking care of the problem. You can choose your connections or mine, but we need this done pronto."

Her body tensed. It was one thing to say no to Alejandro, but another thing to say no to El Chapo. He never took no for an answer.

"I need the Tomador," Eliana said, her voice low. She wasn't afraid of much, but she had seen the man's eyes once and they were black pools of emptiness. The Tomador was the best of the best, according to Alejandro's security lead. Fifty-four unsolved murder cases.

No witnesses, no DNA, disciplined perfection. Some said he was ex-Army, and others said they raised from an orphan to kill without emotion or remorse. He worked on his terms and his time. All you needed to know was that once he accepted a job, it was done.

"Good, I contacted him about Wolf, but will turn him over to you and have him fly to Los Angeles as soon as possible. I will have him make contact at the warehouse, okay?" Alejandro asked.

"No, Alejandro," she blurted with irritation. "What's wrong, Eliana?"

"Nothing," she said. "I'm just tired. Have the Tomador go to Tampa and wait for my instructions. Wolf will head home."

"Smart," her brother said. "This is why I need you."

"Text me a number for the Tomador's burner," she said, disconnecting the call and falling back on the bed.

This was only the beginning, and she wasn't ready for it.

44

B jorn Anderson residence, Los Angeles, California
"Lance, get in here," Bjorn yelled. Wolf finished pouring his coffee and headed into the living room. The major head-line scrolling across the bottom of the TV screen screamed cartel murder suspect released from jail. Video evidence found corrupted.

Wolf mumbled. "Well, at least we caught their attention. Can you imagine how pissed off Alejandro must be?"

"No, but I like the thought of it. He has to deal with the bad-product backlash. And there are more reports coming in of users near death. It will haunt them for a while."

Wolf took a sip of coffee. "Maybe some users will also start questioning their life choices. You know, I thought I had to get in the gutter to fight them, but that's not the way. I like them killing each other. They care only for themselves. It's their own downfall."

Bjorn nodded. "You act like you're taking the high ground, but this war has just started. Keep an eye out for the gutter."

Meantime, magic was being prepared in the garage.

Lizzy Armstrong's resemblance to Eliana was closer than Wolf had thought possible. A Hollywood makeup artist had done an exceptional job transforming her into the woman in a photograph.

Armstrong was a stunt double and personal-protection specialist by trade, but today she would play Eliana Cortes.

Wolf handed her a lightweight under-clothes bulletproof vest as she surveyed the array of weapons on the table. She decided on a 9mm Glock for the evening's work. Her job is for show, the Glock for defense. If needed, she would help them break contact.

Bjorn rolled into the double-wide garage in a rented black Range Rover. He got out and said, "Do you think they'll mind if they get it back with holes in it?"

Not that it mattered. Bjorn had rented it with fake credentials. "I bought damage insurance," he said.

Wolf and Lizzy shook their heads. They finished loading their magazines and double-checked their weapons.

"All right, the mission is simple. Kennedy and I have identified four gang locations. Lizzy drives us to the target, Bjorn and I shoot the place up and throw the Molotov cocktails, then we head for the next site. Three minutes at each site. In and out, run and gun, home in time for a nightcap."

"I'll stop the Rover where they will catch us on security video," Lizzy said. "After tonight, we'll all be eligible for Academy Awards."

She blew on her painted fingertips and pretended to buff them on her top. "I'll be Best Actress, of course."

"Perfect. The objectives tonight are to get 'Eliana' seen and to start a war."

"Roger that," Bjorn said.

"Yep, got it," Lizzy said, raising an approving thumb.

"Okay, we leave in thirty minutes," Wolf said.

Run and gun. From Wolf's perspective, action at the first two sites went down as planned, ending with Lizzy's single-finger salutes to the video cameras as the Range Rover pulled away at high speed.

The third site was a hangar at the Compton Woodley Airport. Kennedy had identified the site as the Tijuana Cartel location for small batch loads of premium cocaine for the Hollywood crowd. The studio big shots expected the very best, and they got it.

Wolf realized the gap in their intelligence when the site security team fought back with unexpected ferocity.

Wolf yelled to Bjorn, "These guys didn't get the 'easy in, easy out' memo."

"Yeah, looks like 151 Original Block Pirus from the tattoos."

These were no-joke gangbangers, some with actual military combat experience. Their firepower was impressive—M16s, AKs, and compact Heckler & Koch MP5 sub- machine guns.

But while they were better than most gangs, they were still a pyramid organization with one leader at the top. They knew little about decentralized leadership or organization, so their com- bat effectiveness slowed a ton when Wolf dropped their boss.

The bullets tore through the man's throat, exiting out his brain stem and decapitating him. Stunned gangsters watch his body crumple to the concrete, but only for seconds, and the gunfire picked back up with a ferocious surge.

They stood in the open, firing everything they had, spraying and praying. Bjorn and Wolf started dropping bodies, but the sheer wall of gunfire coming at them pinned them in place and prevented maneuver.

Wolf turned to see Lizzy leap from the Rover and skip several rounds under a car, taking out a shooter's legs. Then she strode around to the front of the Rover and ripped off a few more shots before standing tall and flipping them the bird.

She slid back behind the wheel and roared in so Wolf and Bjorn could dive in the back. As they drove off, Wolf broke the silence with a chuckle.

"That was crazy, huh? Thanks, Lizzy. Nice work."

"Did you see her standing out there in front of the Rover? Price- less!" Bjorn said.

"No, brother, I didn't see it. I was dropping tangos," Wolf said with a smirk.

"You two stop! I was just doing the job with my customary charm and panache."

The next morning, the headlines screamed all over the news.

Gang Wars Escalate, Death Count Rising.

Wolf sat in front of the TV with his coffee, switching channels to get different reports of violence. The sheet of paper on the coffee table had a crude grid with two rows, one each for Sinaloa Cartel and Tijuana Cartel. The vertical columns included known gang territories and a "W" for winner.

Bjorn walked in with the coffee pot and topped off his brother's cup. "How long you been up?"

"Thanks for the refill. Since about zero-five. Thirteen reports of gang violence so far and it keeps growing."

Bjorn clapped his hands together.

"Outstanding! Eliana will be their priority target now."

45

Lance Bear Wolf's cabin, rural North Carolina

Maya's love of the North Carolina mountains grew with each hike. Streams, waterfalls, and the Horse Pasture River were all in stark green contrast to the alpine desert of Copper Canyon, Mexico.

Kennedy introduced her to fishing with corn and dough balls, simple bait to catch rainbow trout. Beautiful to look at and even better to eat. Their thoughts and stress of the recent past melted away.

It was the exact reason Wolf had purchased the old homestead for getaway and decompression. They sat on the back porch overlooking the forest, drinking coffee. Kennedy held his cellphone, waiting for it to ring. And it did, at 0830 on the dot.

"Excuse me, I have to take this," he said, and stepped inside. "All good?" Wolf asked.

"Yes, thanks." Kennedy paced around the front room. "How's L.A.? From the news, I see you did your thing out there, too."

Wolf chuckled. "Yeah, mission accomplished. I need you to come back, though. It's time for phase two."

He knew Wolf would want him to come back, but he'd been dreading it. Part of him didn't want to leave Maya alone. Or at all.

"Okay, understood," Kennedy said.

"Will Maya be okay alone for a while?"

Kennedy paused. Would she be okay? She had been through so much, but this was how it had to be for now.

"She'll be fine. I'll leave in an hour," he said.

Kennedy turned to see Maya standing in the doorway. Her expression had changed from blank eyes to a clenched jaw and an aggressive stance.

"I am going with you!" she snapped.

"Maya, you can't. I don't have a place for you."

"We will figure it out. I am not staying here by myself."

"But Maya—"

"End of story. I'm packing, then I'll help clean up before we go."

Kennedy smiled. What would be the harm in her coming with me? He could keep a better eye on her if she were close. The change of plans might piss off Wolf. But as Maya stared at him with those big brown eyes, he relented.

"Okay, we'll figure it out. Go pack. I'll shut everything off."

Maya kissed him on the cheek and turned to go when a shot rang out, splintering the right side of the doorframe. Kennedy dragged a stunned Maya to the floor.

"Follow me, now!" he ordered.

They crawled into the bedroom. Kennedy reached up to a decorative wooden emblem carved into the nightstand and pressed it twice, paused, then two more times, then once.

Then he stuffed his Glock into his waistband, extra magazines from the nightstand in his pockets, and pointed to a panel in the bathroom dropped ceiling. They crawled that way and Maya pushed the ceiling panel aside. Above it was an attic access panel she pushed up and out of the way.

She was standing on the toilet when he whispered in her ear, "Mind the bats."

Maya was wide-eyed. "What?"

"There are bats in the attic. They won't hurt you. Go!"

Maya squirmed her way inside and Kennedy followed. He replaced the ceiling tile then closed the access panel. He held Maya's hand as they walked on a large hand-cut wooden beam over to the fireplace chimney.

The chimney had been hand-built with stones polished smooth from eons of river water. When they reached the chimney, Kennedy guided Maya over to the far side. It was dark, musty, and there wasn't much airflow.

"Why here?" she whispered. "We could have gone down the other side of the mountain."

"We don't know how many gunmen there are," he whispered.

They held their breath as the front screen door creaked opened. For the next few minutes, they listened as someone took their time and cleared the house from front to back. Their attacker stopped on the back porch for a moment before walking around to the front door.

"I will find you," a man's voice said. "Why don't you come out and make it easy for all of us, man?" The voice laughed. "As a favor to me."

Kennedy could see Maya's face screwed up, her hand pinching her nose to stifle a sneeze. She put her face in the crook of her arm, and he leaned into her, his forehead touching hers. She sneezed.

The attacker chuckled. "Don't y'all go nowhere, hear? I'm getin' me some coffee."

Kennedy heard noises that sounded like the fridge opening. Then the man dragged a kitchen chair along the floor before flopping into it with a humph. Maya jumped when the man slammed a cup into the sink.

"I know you're up there. I'll find the access soon enough." He kept up his version of psychological warfare as he stomped around the cabin. Kennedy could see the effect it was having on Maya. The fear and anxiety etched in her face. So, he smiled and made the rotating crazy sign next to his temple with his finger, hoping to get Maya to smile.

"Not sure who he thinks he is intimidating. We'll sit tight," Kennedy whispered. "Help is on the way."

They heard him rummaging around in the bedroom.

"Mister, I'm only here for the woman. But since you're protectin' her, you got to go, too."

He trashed the bedroom, smashed the mirror, and kept making excessive noise, hoping to terrorize his victims. It was only a matter of time before he came into the bathroom.

"Well, well. Where could everyone be?" Ceiling tiles fell to the floor until he laughed again. The hatch flew open.

"Okay then, guess y'alls ain't as smart as I's led to believe, huh? Who said the good guys always win, dipshit?"

The bats stirred and squeaked. Kennedy saw the rifle come through the opening first. Their attacker stopped for a moment, waiting for his eyes to adapt in the gloom. The attacker brought himself halfway through the opening.

Kennedy took a deep breath and raised his Glock. He could see the night sights glowing in the dark, so he aimed where he thought center mass would be and pulled the trigger twice. The man screamed and cursed as he fell forward.

"I hate a blowhard," Kennedy murmured.

The gunshots had awakened the bats now. They swarmed like angry bees around the gunman as they lunged for the lighted opening filled by his bulk. With the wounded man engaged in swinging at the bats, Kennedy took a supported position and emptied four more rounds into the gunman. Kennedy ducked back behind the chimney to reload before peering around the corner. He waited for the bats to leave before moving.

Their invader was motionless.

"Stay here," Kennedy said to a frightened Maya.

He inched his way over to the hatch. The rifle sling held the man's body in place, the AR-15 bowing from the weight. Kennedy used his Swiss Army knife to cut the sling, dropping the dead man to the bathroom floor where his lifeless head slammed to the floor and left an exploded red bloodstain on peel and place vinyl tiles

Kennedy jumped as two large-caliber rifle shots echoed outside the cabin. He backed away from the hatch at the sound of footsteps on the porch.

"Kennedy, hey, ya mama called," a voice yelled into the house.

"Is it raining in Omaha?" Kennedy said, relieved.

"Cats and dogs, brother," the voice replied with a laugh.

The code phrase protocol satisfied, Kennedy said, "We're coming down."

Maya startled for a second at the sight of the green faced young man helping her descend from the ceiling. It looked like he was wearing the forest on his back.

When she stepped off the toilet, she saw the bloody dead man and gave back her breakfast into the bathroom basin. Kennedy held her hair back and placed his body between her and the dead man.

She finished vomiting and Kennedy gave her a warm washcloth for her face.

"Why don't you go sit in the front room? I'll bring you some water," Kennedy said. She nodded and tiptoed out of the bathroom.

"Two tangos KIA on the north side," Oleus LeBlanc said.

Kennedy nodded, clapping the man on the shoulder of his camouflage ghillie suit. "Great to see you, brother."

"No worries. It's one of the best drill weekends I've had in a long time." LeBlanc gestured to the assassin on the floor. "Outstanding job taking out the big guy."

"I wouldn't say that," Kennedy said. "I got lucky."

"All looks the same on the scoreboard. It's how you handle yourself under stress that shows mettle. Don't sell yourself short, brother. You did warrior work today."

Kennedy stood a little straighter. "Thank you," he said.

"You all right to drive?" LeBlanc asked.

"Yeah."

"All right, let's get you on the road." LeBlanc pulled off the ghillie suit and draped it over a kitchen chair. "I'll stay behind to make sure you're not being followed and do the clean-up."

Kennedy and Maya gathered their things and headed for the car.

They were soon on the open road, heading toward Florida. The cabin faded in the distance but the experience there had not.

"Who was that guy who helped us?" Maya asked. Kennedy's eyes remained on the road ahead. "One of us."

"What about the bodies?"

"He will take care of them. You are going to learn we're a big family and we take care of our own."

They drove on, each lost in their own thoughts. Maya had been silent for the last hour, and Kennedy wasn't sure what she was feeling. He cared for her, and it all became known to him in the cabin.

All he could think about was keeping Maya safe and how he would never forgive himself if something happened to her.

"Pull over," she said, jarring him from his thoughts.

"What? Why? There's a rest stop just fifteen miles—"

"I said pull over here, please."

Kennedy did as he was told and came to an easy stop off the roadway in the grass.

It was quiet and remote with no other traffic. She had a look on her face, and he worried she was in shock. Then she leaned over and kissed him long and hard on the lips.

Maya pulled back and took a deep breath. "Kieran Kennedy, just so you know, I love you."

"Wh-what?" he said.

"You heard me."

He stared into her brown eyes, and in that moment everything in his life became clear. He loved this woman and would protect her.

"Maya, I love you too, but you need to know this life will not be easy. The cartel is after us and my friends. They will not stop until we or they are too dead to continue."

"I don't care. I'm ready for what comes."

"Well, one thing's for darn sure—it's coming."

46

Tampa, Florida & Imperial Beach, California

Back in Tampa and flush from his results in Los Angeles, Wolf pushed forward with the cross-border portion of his plan.

It was time to carry the fight to the cartel's home turf. An advantage of working at Special Operations Command was his ability to cultivate relationships with people who could make things happen.

His friendship with the Special Forces National Guard Advisor, Colonel Neil Gates, and the Command operations counter-drug task force, paid dividends.

First thing Monday morning, Wolf checked in with the planning cell. They had a working list of six operations they needed to source. The one that caught Wolf's attention was a DEA request for support along the Arizona/Mexico border.

"What's the mission, sir?" Wolf asked.

Lieutenant Colonel Eli Stoner stood over a large map table with a pointer. He traced a line northwest of Nogales to the break in the Arizona border where it turned straight west.

"The DEA is looking for a team to do training in this area and report back lines of communication."

Wolf nodded his understanding. It wasn't perfect, but it would work. And it couldn't hurt to mend a DEA fence.

"Any other teams or units in the area?"

"Yes. There will be two reserve Marine Corps armored recon companies to your west." He circled an area of desert scrub. "There will be Customs and Border Patrol operations in your area. But, as you know, they are reactive. Just ensure they aren't reacting to you."

Stoner looked up from the map table.

"If you want the mission, your team needs to launch in ten days or less."

"Roger that, sir. We can make that happen."

Wolf called his Alpha Company, 3rd Battalion commander, Major Ted Stanley, and briefed him on options. The officer listened, asked about the other missions on the list, and got to the point.

"Master Sergeant Wolf, are you ready for this?"

"Yes, sir. We need the team training. It aligns with our strategic vision for the group and our company. We will continue to support 7th Group and our South America mission, but I see a pivot coming. We will be back in the Middle East, and we need to be ready."

"I will get the battalion commander to green-light the mission. I'll also have Support Company ready the isolation facility. See you in three days."

"Yes, sir. I'll alert the team and work with the head shed to get our mobilization orders cut with a funding cite from the DEA."

Wolf went back to work, smiling. The DEA was going to pay for his revenge program.

~

FULL APPRECIATION for and understanding of her situation did not come to Eliana right away. There was no epiphany, no bright light of comprehension to provide razor-sharp insight.

She was not engaged in a fight for turf or the respect of customers. After the disastrous contaminated cocaine event and now the brutal attack on the Tijuana Cartel blamed on her, it all came down to a simple to understand fight for her life.

She needed help from professionals and agreed to a plan brought by an Israeli contractor. Like Pablo Escobar and Osama bin Laden, she was to be in continuous movement.

Never in one place more than twenty-four hours. Very limited and short-duration burner cellphone use. Use of couriers for most communications. If she stuck to the protocol, she would survive.

Since the Tijuana Cartel had bought into the war started by Wolf, the number of people looking for Eliana numbered in the hundreds. Not to mention California and federal law enforcement.

Terrified for the first time in her life, she suspected everyone, even those in her own crew. She hadn't slept more than three consecutive hours in two days. When she did, it was with her new Sig P226 pistol in her hand.

The privileged life she had lived in Mexico, even in Los Angeles, had not prepared her for the anxiety of being prey. Cigarettes and excessive coffee had their effects on her—in fact, the coffee might have been the worst of all. Dark circles under her eyes, no makeup.

She needed a good meal, a hot shower, less stress and lots more sleep.

She would get none of those things today.

The Tijuana Cartel had other plans for her.

The Cortes safe house in sleepy Imperial Beach south of San Diego provided clear fields of fire all around with the Pacific Ocean as the ultimate escape route.

They had chosen this location from other options for its security and proximity to Mexico only a short distance south. Eliana and her team were exhausted and looked forward to twenty-four hours in one place to regroup and reconstitute.

Only a few more miles and they could rest.

The Tijuana Cartel identified Eliana's convoy before it turned off Highway 805 onto Highway 905 west. Once spotters confirmed Eliana and her team were staying at a house on Seacoast Drive, they waited until the early hours of the next morning to attack.

Eliana was sleeping in the master bedroom in her clothes when it started. The handset radio on the table next to her Sig came alive with shouted alarms as gunfire erupted from the street side.

When Elaina stood, the concussion of multiple explosions knocked her down. The radio barked RPG! RPG!

As she got back to her feet, Enrique Velasquez, her ops chief, stumbled past and fell dead, blood spurting from a massive chest wound.

Eliana grabbed her handgun and tried to hide in the master bedroom, not thinking that the wall facing the ocean was all glass. She listened to her radio as her security lead directed a counterattack.

Then different-sounding gunshots rang out before a machine gun began spraying the house. Eliana heard another burst of gunfire and an explosion from the south and saw two men sprint into the Pacific. Defectors. Cowards.

As the tempo of fire increased, Eliana saw something had changed. The gunfire was coming from too many directions at once. How many attackers were there?

Over the din of the gunfire, she heard her security lead, call for the helicopter. The Imperial Beach Airport was less than three miles away by car, but even with the pilots on ready standby, it would take minutes to spool it up, and hop over to the beach outside of the safe house. They might as well have called for a taxi.

Another garbled radio call, pincer, pincer! Eliana didn't know what it meant. The transmission laced with panic. She was overwhelmed. All she could think about was her baby and its safety. Saving the baby came first.

Garcia radioed to fall back to the Alamo—an armored last- stand structure dug into the beach and disguised as a large cabana. They would defend from there until the helicopter arrived. The remains of her security team encircled Eliana and quick-timed out of the house, firing at muzzle flashes arrayed behind the safe house and at points along the beach.

Wisps of sand sprang from the ground with bullet strikes, but without light or night vision, the Tijuana attackers weren't hitting any defenders. The Cortes team, shooting from the protection of the Alamo, fared better.

At the sound of the helicopter overhead, the team waited at the door. The pilot radioed Garcia to standby for a command to exit. Inside the Alamo, the team formed a protective diamond formation around Eliana, and Garcia ordered her grab his belt and not let go. He counted down from three.

Their attackers responded to the incoming helicopter by moving around the house and rushing the Alamo in two groups. They came from both sides in a pincer movement. Their lack of training had them shooting wild in a moonless crossfire, which took out some of their own, but that isn't what killed most of them.

The unlighted helo hovered about fifteen feet off the deck. This obscured the aircraft with a man-made dust storm while the gunners fired their machine guns into the helpless Tijuana Cartel, dismembering some and vaporizing some others.

The pilot had night vision, and his gunners mowed down the attackers wherever he turned the helicopter.

It was over in seconds.

Garcia led the security team out of the Alamo, and they raced across the sand to the helicopter, which had settled on the beach. The gunners jumped out and joined the security team as they loaded Eliana into the helicopter and Garcia followed.

As the helicopter rotors gained speed, her soldiers formed a perimeter in case any attackers were playing possum. As the chopper rose, the security team sprinted back to the house for mop-up. Police sirens were growing louder in the distance.

The helicopter rose, spun to face the sea, and had surged forward only a few dozen feet above the surf when two men rose from the breakers with rifles and filled the nose of the chopper with bullets.

Eliana screamed as rounds penetrated the pilot's chest and emerged from the back of his seat to puncture the rear bulkhead, just missing her abdomen. The turbine engine began making ugly sounds and smoke filled the cabin.

The pilot slumped forward dead, pointing the helo toward the Pacific.

Garcia, who had flown helicopters in the Mexican Army, scrambled into the open copilot's seat and seized the controls, but he was long out of practice. His control inputs were exaggerated. Eliana screamed again when he lost control and the helicopter nosed hard into the Pacific.

It flipped when it struck the water, landing on its side, the rotors destroying themselves slapping the ocean. The weight of the engine filled the helicopter over and it filled with water as Eliana struggled with her belts in the dark cold of the ocean.

Her thoughts were only for her unborn child, and then she passed out and had no thoughts at all.

The noise of slapping water woke Eliana. When she tried to sit up, she groaned at pain in her lower back. No, please, no, she thought. It's not time.

She reached around to feel her back and winced but relaxed at the realization that she had sustained only a grazing bullet wound. Eliana pulled the blanket back over her head, not caring who had her or where they were going. She closed her eyes and dropped into a deep sleep.

47

El Rancho Cortes, Sinaloa, Mexico

Alejandro was a nervous wreck waiting for word of his sister's safe return. Since receiving a report of the attack, he had gotten only one cryptic message—Inbound.

As the hours dragged on, his cursing and banging on the walls kept everyone away. No one dared interrupt him.

The safe bet was to run the business and stay out of the way. And there was plenty of work to do. One of their biggest markets was in shambles.

First the bad cocaine, then the turf war, and now the fallout of the gunfight at Imperial Beach. What was next?

The phone rang. It was Martin Amaro's Caller ID. "Is she okay?" Alejandro shouted.

"Yes, she is safe and well. Canto has her," Amaro said. "They will bring her to Topolobampo."

He explained the assault on the safe house, the frenzied defense and retreat, then the escape and helicopter crash. The backup exfil team reached the helicopter in time to pluck her and Garcia from the water, then bolt south to safety.

"I also have something you must see," Amaro continued. "It's important. I'll be there in five."

Alejandro didn't even bother with a goodbye. He just hung up and paced.

Amaro arrived. "Boss, look at this."

He pushed a videotape into the player. The resolution captured at night under sodium vapor streetlamps was grainy and terrible. On the screen there was what appeared to be Eliana and two masked male shooters.

There was something about Eliana's movements. The woman looked like his sister, but it wasn't the way she moved. Almost like a man—or a soldier. Not the fluid, cat-like movements of the Eliana he knew.

"What is this?" Alejandro said.

On the screen, the men stood on either side of the woman, firing weapons at unseen targets. The muzzle flashes lit the scene like photo strobes and the grainy image would pop in bright, high-resolution contrast.

The three stopped firing and got back into the Range Rover. As the vehicle sped away, the female driver extended her left arm out of the open sunroof and raised a middle finger.

"I don't think this was Eliana," Martin said.

"What does this mean?"

"The Tijuana Cartel hits point to Eliana, but it wasn't her."

Alejandro grabbed the wall to steady himself. His eyes blazed as he spun.

"Wolf."

Alejandro and Amaro left on a forty-five-minute drive to the waterfront. They discussed the video and its implications. As they reached their destination, Alejandro leaned forward to see two enormous men walk up the dock with Eliana between them, hunched over and hobbling, head lowered, a blanket wrapped around her like a protective shield. More men waited in the RHIB.

Alejandro ran to her, his face showing alarm for his sister. "Eliana, are you okay?"

She looked up at him with red, dark-rimmed eyes and answered. Her voice dull, her energy reserves gone.

"No. Those pigs tried to kill me. I will kill them all. You will see."

"Martin, pay these men," Alejandro said. Pointing to a man standing at the helm of the RHIB, he said, "Canto—I am in your debt, my friend."

Canto nodded, placing his right hand to his heart. "Your servant, sir."

Amaro walked to the boat and threw four medium canvas gym bags onboard. Fifty thousand dollars for each man was too much, but it was neither his business nor his money.

Alejandro walked Eliana to the Rover. "Let's get you home and rested." Her head lolled onto his shoulder. Her glassy eyes fixed on nothing. "Then we will make plans for the Tijuana Cartel."

The ride home was silent. Eliana embraced by sleep, her breathing shallow and smooth. Alejandro's breathing matched his sister's and as his heart rate fell to a healthy level for the first time since he'd heard of the attack.

His thoughts drifted to the mystery of the surveillance videotape. It didn't matter whether or not it was Eliana on the tape. The Tijuana Cartel believed it was her, so that was the new reality.

The Tijuana cartel had crossed an unspoken line when it came to the two families. It was time to protect his, and he started by assigning four of his best former military operators to protect Eliana.

He would take the extraordinary step of stopping the Tomador mid-job, for now. Alejandro's faith in him was high, as was the lump sum added to the assassin's standard fee.

Whether it was his American enemies on the tape or not, they would have to wait. Wolf wasn't going anywhere, and if he did, Alejandro's sources would let him know.

He needed to strike back for the attack on Eliana. Then he would avenge Joaquin's death and stop Wolf's plan for revenge, whatever it was.

He would show everyone who was boss.

48

E lle Parker's residence, Tampa, Florida
        Wolf couldn't shake the feeling that something had
        changed at Elle's house. He attributed the change to his
excitement at the upcoming mission.

Steaks and potatoes on the grill, Caesar salad, and ice-cold beers.
A simple meal to fuel their talk of the mission, the team, communications, and contingency plans. Parker was showering and Wolf was
flipping the steaks when Kennedy called.

"I don't know what all you did in Los Angeles, but someone other
than me may connect the dots. If they do that, it'll be bad," he said.

"Yeah, I guess it's possible." Wolf said, glancing around to see if
Elle was nearby. "The good news is the cartels are fighting each other,
as planned. We also got the DEA border support mission booked. Not
a perfect location for our planning, but you know. Close enough for
government work."

They exchanged a few more minor details and then Wolf begged
off the call. He checked the steaks and took them inside to rest.

Standing in the kitchen doorway was Parker dressed in black
running shorts and a Broncos T-shirt with John Elway emblazoned
across the back.

"I'm not sure what's prettier, Ms. Elle Parker—you, or these steaks," he said with a grin.

"Well, Mr. Lance Bear Wolf, if you can't figure it out, you might be sleeping in the wrong house."

"Okay, let's see. Both are hot and tasty, but you are definitely spicier. Not super filling, and yet very satisfying—"

"Stop, you cornball," Elle said, shaking her head. "I'm starving. Let's eat."

They talked over dinner and a smoky Argentinian Malbec. The conversation was easy and unhurried and without deeper meaning as they sought to learn more about each other.

Wolf held back his planned cross-border movement and the offensive on the central Cortes business. If questioned, she could tell the truth and profess ignorance of his activities, and it was better if she had no information about any plans or actual movement of the team into Mexico.

She asked if Wolf knew anything about the news report of a cartel gun battle at Imperial Beach. Wolf was truthful and told her what he had learned.

The police, with support from DEA, confirmed the dead were Sinaloa and Tijuana cartel members. They suspected that Eliana Cortes had been there and had escaped.

He told her about the report he'd read of two Navy SEAL chief petty officers living in a house down the beach. They had heard the gunfight, called it in to 911, armed themselves and went to investigate.

They were fired on by the Tijuana Cartel and had returned fire before relocating to the safety of the pre-dawn Pacific.

They watched the attacking force's pincer movement and took fired again right before the helicopter lifted off. So when it turned in their direction, they opened up on it with precise shooting into the cockpit. The helicopter crashed after a few seconds of errant flying. Someone, at the last second, had deployed inflatable floats that slowed the helicopter decent into the Pacific.

They recounted a large RHIB that moved to the crash site and deployed divers who rescued two people, a man and a woman, and then headed south.

Eliana must have nine lives.

After dinner they fell asleep on the couch watching Mystery Science Theater 3000, only to get up before dawn to crawl into bed.

Come morning, Wolf stayed for coffee, kissed Elle goodbye, and headed back to his house to work. He called the team. The company commander had pushed him to add two newbies to the mission, fresh out of training group.

Wolf hesitated at first, but they were smart, fit, and eager to please. He agreed to find a purpose for them.

The Arizona and Mexico border was a region the team had never seen, but they could make the DEA mission whatever they wanted, and it was what Wolf planned to do.

His basic concept of operations was to split the team. This would cover more area and permit him to keep his strike team separate prior to heading south to the actual target.

He covered the walls in maps, terrain analysis, plans, radio frequencies, and lines of communication.

Wolf's proactive interaction with the command operations division gave them a head start. He knew the basic mission location and targets of interest, so the team focused on their mission analysis and intelligence preparation of the battlefield.

He'd already convinced Captain Franks that a split-team operation would cover the key targets in the shortest period. A quick read on activities in their sector would let them adapt for maximum effect.

Wolf and his senior communicator, Sergeant First Class Henry Harris, met in private to focus on covert communications while south of the border.

"Line of sight is out of the question," Wolf noted. "Look at the terrain. Rugged isn't a good enough word to describe it."

The topographic maps laid out before them told a grim story. The Sonoran Desert was anything but a flat, sandy expanse. The red-brown lines highlighted contours of elevation. When depicted close to each other, it illustrated steep terrain.

"High-frequency radio will work, but it's slow," Harris said.

"The risk is too high to take satellite radio with us south of the border," Wolf added.

Harris grinned. "I have an idea. We can leave the new guys behind to communicate our situation reports. I can teach them to use the radio and Digital Message Device Group." Harris paused before continuing. "I'm thinking we can give them pre- planned messages to cover the time we are on target. Isn't one of the new guys the commander pushed us to take a communicator?"

Wolf nodded. "Yeah, and the other is a demolitions sergeant who can pull security. They'll excited to have a high-profile part of the mission. And I've got a line on a satellite phone prototype we can test."

"Nice! A friend at 10th Group got to test one for a month."

"So, we our standard radio as our primary means of comms, the survival radio is our alternate via Guardrail aircraft, and the SATCOM phone prototype is our contingency and emergency. Plus, we'll have our panels and glint tape for visual comms," Wolf said. "Sounds good."

Wolf didn't mention Kennedy's part of the plan. His training flights in the test bed Beechcraft King Air-based Guardrail RC-12H would replace the need for a ground-based signals intelligence team. Kennedy's excuse to be part of the training mission was his need to train on the Guardrail's newer Common Sensor System platform.

Known in the Army as an airborne SIGINT collection and precision-targeting location system, the RC-12H aircraft with Kennedy at a prototype onboard analyst station would provide early warning of cartel activities.

It would take a bit of influence for the battalion to support the deployment of an RC-12, but integration with airborne intelligence, surveillance, and reconnaissance platforms fit the training profile. And DEA would pay the bill. The remaining critical path task was to create a safe weapons cache south of the border.

Wolf grabbed a beer and walked out back, dialing Carlos Gonzalez from Andy's old phone.

"Major Gonzalez." "Carlos, it's Lance."

"Hello, my friend! How are you?"

"Good, amigo, very good, thanks. I need a favor."

"Okay. What do you need?"

"I need seven AKs, ammo, Semtex, high-explosive and smoke grenades in a cache south of Sasabe."

"You have a target?"

"Yes, in Sonora."

"Good. Rifles and grenades are not a problem. But I do not have access to Semtex, location?"

Wolf gave him the coordinates. "Can you have it in place in a week?"

"Yes, it will be there for you. And thank you again for keeping my wife and kids safe."

"For you, anytime brother!"

49

Valo-Campbell residence, Brandon, Florida

The house on a suburban street east of Tampa blended in with the others. Simple designs in light tan with white trim. Bright flowers and occasional palm trees punctuated the layout.

The temperature and rainfall lent itself to year-round gardening. Sidewalks were water-stained orange to dark brown from the sprinkler systems. Chalk marks lined the street and sidewalk where children had been playing moments before the call to dinner.

The front door opened, and a woman pointed at Maya. She was crying in the arms of a man. Kennedy recognized them both from their Department of the Army photos. It was Major Helen Valo-Campbell and her husband, Bruce.

Maya wiped moist eyes as she exited the car, running to embrace her sister in a long hug.

"It's all right. I'm here now," she whispered. Kennedy stuck out his hand. "Kieran Kennedy, sir."

"Good to meet you, Kieran. Call me Bruce. Please come in."

The sisters sat on the couch hugging, their tear-stained faces soon producing smiles and then laughter as they caught up on the three years the women had gone without seeing each other.

Bruce led Kennedy into the kitchen. "Beer?"

"Perfect, thanks."

"So, how did you meet Maya?"

"It's a complicated story. Maya should tell you when she's ready."

Over the next hour, Maya briefed her sister- and brother-in-law on what had happened since Billy's death. Helen didn't say a word as she sipped her iced tea, engrossed in the story.

Kennedy could tell Bruce wanted to ask questions, but Helen's look kept him at bay. Maya left out Kennedy's role as conference organizer.

When the tale was told, Helen stood, moving around the coffee table to hug and thank Kennedy. Bruce stood, shook his hand, and slapped him on the back. "Nice work."

Kenney smiled. If she is working for the cartel, versus being coerced, she's playing this like a pro.

Helen beamed. "How about dinner? Anyone for roast pork, yellow rice, and black beans?"

It was a warm Florida night with a hint of a breeze. The outdoor dining was next to the screened-in pool, and it was casual and fun. They talked as new friends do about growing up, family, the Army, and how lucky it was they all worked at a great command.

As the sun set, the screened porch kept the larger insects out. The bug zapper snapped and popped as it did its job on the smaller ones that did make it in.

It was close to eleven when Maya and Kennedy retired to the bedroom on the other side of the house. They held each other, kissed, and fell into a deep sleep.

Kennedy woke to the smell of coffee. If there was anything he liked more than wine, it was excellent coffee. He wandered toward the kitchen where Helen greeted him and embraced him in a long hug. She poured a steaming mug of black coffee, and he accepted it with a smile.

"Thank you again," she said, "For saving my sister."

"No problem."

Kennedy had seen Helen's attempts to read him over dinner and again later as they got to know each other. He was sure she understood he knew more about her than he let on in front of Maya and Bruce. Helen looked down for a moment, considering, then stared out the kitchen window.

"Come with me, bring your coffee." She led him out to the pool. It was quiet, and the sun wasn't yet too hot. She looked forlorn. "I need to tell you a story."

For the next twenty minutes, she confessed her situation and the jam the Cortes people 'd put her in. Kennedy had known or suspected most of the story.

The cartel had been a part of her life since her family had taken their illegal crossing into the U.S. when she was a child, she said. The cartel started by El Padrino had, over the years, forced her family to support drug activities, two or three times a year. Never violent, always in the background, moving people and product.

When Helen turned eighteen, she joined the U.S. Army, but the cartel had stayed in touch. They encouraged her to switch branches from logistics to intelligence.

They even sent her birthday and wedding gifts. Over the last two years, they began to ask for more specific information. It seemed harmless. Profiles on Mexican government officials, regional economic forecasts. But as of late, their requests had changed.

Now they asked for everything she could get for them on an American soldier named Lance Wolf and a Mexican Major Carlos Gonzalez, the leader of the special forces group Escuadron de León.

As a political-intelligence analyst, she did not have direct access to some of the information and told them so. They didn't care. They reminded her of the exemplary work her sister Maya was doing and what a shame it would be if something happened to her.

"You were being groomed for a long time, Helen," Kennedy said. "Maya was the leverage."

"I didn't know what to do," Helen said with tears in her eyes. "Their intel requests seemed innocent enough, but I should have known better. I thought going to my chain of command would get Maya killed."

"That was a potential outcome. But neither the cartel nor command knows Maya is here."

Helen exhaled, and her weak smile was all Kennedy needed to see to realize now was the time. "How would you like to get back at them for all the years of abuse, and the attack on Maya and Billy?" he asked.

Her eyes squinted. "How is it possible?"

"We are working some opportunities to disrupt the Sinaloa Cartel's business. We can use your help with deception operations."

She furrowed her brow. "But wouldn't it just make us a target here? They can find people. It doesn't matter where you go."

"To be honest, it might. But we can protect each other better here —with you on our team."

Maya walked into the room. "I'm tired of being a target, Helen. I've already joined their team."

Bruce popped in. His shirt drenched with sweat. "Oh, hey, I didn't think anyone was up. I would have invited you all to join me on my morning run."

"Go jump in the shower and we'll make breakfast," Helen said.

She waited for Bruce to leave, then she turned to Kennedy.

"I'm in."

"Me, too," Maya added.

Kennedy smiled. Everything was falling into place.

After spending the weekend with Maya's family, Kennedy flew out for a six-day training period to Fort Huachuca. Raytheon was on contract to provide training before installing and testing their system integrated with the Guardrail CSS-3.

A week later, Kennedy acted surprised when the aircraft commander told him of their upcoming mission. Their testing would support a special forces training mission with the DEA.

"It will cover the Buenos Aires National Wildlife Refuge here in Arizona and the border area over to the Tohono reservation," the pilot said.

"Excellent," Kennedy replied. "Looks like I'm your analyst for the tests." He told the pilot he would see them soon. Before heading back to Tampa, he dropped in to see an old friend who had taken over as operations sergeant for the Signals Intelligence school.

"Look at you, Master Sergeant Danny Hester—archduke of all you survey!"

Surprised at Kennedy's ambush, Hester stood with a huge smile and the two men embraced. "Kiernan Kennedy, my brother from another mother! What secret squirrel crap brings you out here?"

"I'm training on the CSS-3 and Raytheon's Guard."

"Good, it's about time you updated. When was the last time you worked an airborne mission?"

"Two years ago, and it was the Southern Command-configured Crazy Horse system."

"Are you good to go on the new system?"

"Yes. I just spent a week with the new system and learning the Guard. I'll be back in two weeks to fly a SF support mission as a test. When I get back, I need to push temporary no-go frequencies out to the school."

"What's the problem if it's training?"

"It is a classified multi-agency mission that includes training and live operations. We don't want trainees interfering."

"Sounds like it's big. I'll make sure it gets pushed."

"Thank you. It's important. Lives depend on it."

50

L ance Bear Wolf residence, Tampa, Florida
Wolf took a two-hour lunch break to run back to his house and prep, replacing the mission maps, pictures, and load-out lists with target information.

On a folding table, he arranged six packages by operator: Jon Danner, Mike Clinton, Oleus LeBlanc, Hank Harris, Stew Portes, and Tim Hughes.

Each package had the same basic site data and intel but differed by responsibility and action on target. The team arrived around dinner time, so he ordered pizzas and had Clinton run for beer. This would be an all-night session. Pizza, beer, and small talk out of the way, the team took their places at the table. Wolf pointed to the map.

"Our area of operation is near Sasabe, Arizona. It's bounded by the Tohono O'odham Nation Reservation on the west and the Pima County border on the east. The strike target is three hours to the southeast by road. We know they package and ship drugs from this location. It's a bonus site. We'll destroy the capabilities, equipment, and drugs found there, disrupting distribution into the U.S."

They started with the helo load plan, offset from the cache, recovery, and movement from the cache to the objective rally point.

Next, they considered setting security, breaching of the building, destroying the target, and exfil out a different route. Their plan also included improvised explosives using likely materials at hand. The communications plan was a critical element, as was time on target, and contingencies for each element of the plan. Total mission time from infiltration to exfil was three hours and twenty minutes.

"Looks solid, guys. Did you consider ways to shorten the mission time or time on target?"

"We had a couple of ideas. Portes thought we should go the Son Tay route. I had to remind him they crashed the assault helo in the compound. Easy in, not so easy out." Danner said.

"All right, we can meet back tomorrow to get this memorized. I will shred all of this before we isolate. See you guys tomorrow."

The team left and Wolf had a moment of doubt. Not about their ability to complete the mission, but whether he should involve them in his crusade.

They didn't know his personal motivations, just the cartel objectives. They did volunteer, he reasoned. They hated the cartels and their carnage as much as he did.

The next night they walked through the mission again. Each man committed his part of the plan to memory, which included taking over for a hurt teammate if it came to that. They were ready and hungry for the fight.

Two days later, Alonzo Franks issued the warning order. Across Florida, the teammates packed their last few items and said their goodbyes. Except for the two new guys, all the women had seen their men go off to war before. This was just training.

More money for a kid's college fund, or a bathroom remodel. For the young single guys, it was pocket money or maybe a down payment on a Harley or a Ford F-150 diesel with tires too big for the street.

But to a man, there was the craving to be part of something consequential.

Wolf spent his last night before deployment at Parker's house.

Elle found the isolation phase and special forces adaptation of military planning and decision-making process interesting.

She had operated in an intelligence battalion as part of Big Army during the first Gulf War. She had also deployed to Bosnia and lost her best friend there. She knew war.

Her training and wartime experiences were a world apart from Wolf's, but they shared a bond. Wolf treasured it and her ability to understand his motivations. Wolf could be himself, and Parker liked him.

He hoped Parker would be by his side when it was all done.

Camp Blanding Joint Training Center, Starke, Florida
Pre-mission isolation was going as planned. A Judge Advocate General lawyer walked in unescorted. He appeared to be a desk jockey until you noticed the Ranger scroll combat patch and Combat Infantryman Badge.

"Franks!" a voice boomed. The captain and the JAG slapped each other's back as men do who have shared war.

"Steve—what the heck are you doing here?"

"I got a slug assignment to brief a weekend warrior SF team prepping for a DEA funded training mission in Arizona," Gates said.

"I thought you got out," Franks said.

"They dangled law school for four more years and I thought, why not?.."

The captain grinned and turned to the group.

"Everyone, this is Major Gates. We jumped into Grenada together just after getting to our first Ranger platoons."

There was something familiar about him, but Wolf couldn't put his finger. The way Gates spoke, the way he smiled.

The JAG nodded. "Take a seat, men. Most of you have heard this before, but I have to present it by the numbers."

He described the rules of engagement. In short, you couldn't shoot until shot at first. You couldn't detain anyone or represent yourself as law enforcement. The team had a few questions related to different scenarios.

But it always came back to the bad guys had to engage first. Unless you thought one of your teammates was in mortal danger. But you'd better be able to prove it.

Briefing over and departure pleasantries exchanged, the lawyer headed into the hallway outside the briefing room, followed by Wolf.

"Sir, do you know Colonel Gates at SOCOM?"

"I do. He's, my father."

"He's a great man. I consider him a friend and mentor."

"Yeah, he's a great, my bias aside. I know something about your background and recent experience, too. Did you know my father and your stepfather were on the Son Tay prison raid together?"

Wolf paused. "No. Andy never mentioned it."

"You won't find it anywhere because they worked for the Agency. It's how they got their Silver Stars. My father is keeping watch on you because he promised your father he would do so."

"My stepfather asked yours to watch out for me?"

"Yes, and he takes it serious. Now, you may intend to go to war with the cartel or you may just want your pound of flesh. It's up to you. Just make sure these men know the full spectrum of your actual intent. That way, it doesn't catch them out when the shit hits the fan."

They shook hands. "Bonne chance," Gates said, and exited.

Wolf stood big eyed, mouth open catching flies. He wondered whether the cautionary speech had come from his colonel mentor or an insightful major.

Regardless, he couldn't believe his father had been on the famous operation to rescue POWs in North Vietnam. When this is over, I need to find out more about my stepfather was.

At 0500 the next morning, the team met for a quick workout and breakfast before diving into the day. At 0845, the company and battalion commanders and the B staff entered the room. At 0900, Franks kicked off the mission brief.

At the end of the briefing, battalion commander Lieutenant Colonel George Kamis stood up and addressed the group.

"Captain Franks, Master Sergeant Wolf, I commend you and the men on an excellent and well-constructed plan. He turned to Company Commander Major Ted Stanley. "Ted?"

"Sir, I say it's a go." He raised an approving thumb.

Kamis nodded with a grim smile.

"I agree. You are a go."

Wolf smiled. His plan was working.

52

El Rancho Cortes, Sinaloa, Mexico

The Tijuana Cartel had almost killed Eliana, but worse, they had humiliated the Cortes organization through her. They had forced her to flee to survive and it was not a look that generated a long life in El Chapo's organization. One that prized death before dishonor.

Nobody embarrassed her and lived to cherish her discomfort.

Not for long. Nobody.

She was packing a bag when Alejandro came by her bedroom to check on her.

"Where do you think you are going?" he demanded.

"Back to L.A. to get our turf back from the Tijuana scum and those filthy Félix brothers."

"I will send someone else."

"No, you won't. I am going."

"I forbid it. You can't go when you are like this."

"Like what? I will not let them beat us, ever."

"You will put the baby at risk."

"Put the baby at risk...because you suddenly care, is that it? What about, 'It's too risky for you, Eliana'?" she scoffed. God, I wish Joaquin were here.

"You know what I mean."

"Yes, I do indeed, brother. It's very clear to me."

She held out her arm and pointed to her scar. It ignited a fire within her every time she saw it.

"Pensar. Think, remember? You should try it. I have a plan to reclaim our turf, rebuild our network, and kill the Félix brothers. I will destroy the Tijuana Cartel forever."

She was going to hire every scumbag from Mexico to Monterey and kill everyone associated with the Tijuana Cartel.

She had already contacted gangs who hated the Félix brothers and bought their loyalty.

I will use the Tomador to keep Wolf busy worrying about his close friends, so I can operate without interference.

"I don't like this, but there is no better plan, sister," Alejandro admitted. He embraced her, and she even accepted he was sincere.

It felt exceptional to be working again. It energized her and revenge fueled her. She had brought on three gangs to serve as shock troops.

At the top of her list were the best of the three — the Sinaloan Cowboys. They were a fierce Mexican group and distributors of El Chapo's cocaine to the greater area street crews. Stone cold-blooded, they were renowned for being armed to the teeth and they had no fear of authority.

Next, the Mexican Mafia, a prison-based gang operating in the Los Angeles area. What Elaina appreciated most about them was their disciplined members and capability for strategic thinking. They controlled a significant portion of the Hispanic street level thugs, which numbered more than a thousand.

And, for shock and awe, there was the Mongols. A violent outlaw motorcycle gang that distributed Sinaloa cocaine, heroin, and PCP throughout Southern California.

She was taking a strategic approach. Her demands for an existing operations overview and an intelligence briefing said to all that she had turned from reactive to proactive. She was becoming a leader with vision.

This would be bad for many people sooner than later.

53

Davis-Monthan Air Force Base, Tucson, Arizona

Wolf slept little on the flight out west. He woke when the Air Force C-5A Galaxy touched down. His wheels were already turning. Franks and Wolf would soon get a bird's-eye view of their area of operations via airborne reconnaissance. They would integrate their findings into final mission planning and rehearsals.

Then, during the night of day three, they would insert and move to their positions. Pre-planned resupply drops into the area of operations would occur throughout the following twelve days with exfil on the thirteenth.

Davis-Monthan Air Force Base, also known as the Boneyard. A sprawling location housing row after row of decommissioned aircraft, many of which Wolf and the others had flown on in the early years of their careers.

The 55th Rescue Squadron provided an unused hangar for the mission helicopters and offices for the Forward Operating Base. The Company B team took the office on the second deck. Wolf's ODA moved into a ground-level office and began blacking out the windows. Franks briefed the two intel analysts who were added to the team at the last minute.

Harris had the newbie comms and demo sergeants set up his SATCOM antenna and run the wire through a window. All connections and settings confirmed, he entered the net, testing voice and data communications.

Then they repeated the process with the newbie's kit. They marked their operational status on a chalkboard they had borrowed from another hangar.

"LeBlanc," Wolf called out to his weapons NCO. "Where are we on weapons testing?"

"The Tucson Police Department range is six miles from here. We coordinated with them for indoor night fire and to test our night vision goggles. The L-T over there said he's holding the range free all week, so we can go whenever we like."

"Outstanding! Put it on the board." he said, switching his attention "Hughes, do you have the med kits ready to go?"

"Finishing up, adding tourniquets, and we're solid ." The team's lead medic was a combat decorated and a Tampa firefighter/paramedic when not in uniform. Wolf hoped they wouldn't need his considerable skills.

"Everyone carries their own bag, right?"

"Yes. Five hundred milliliters of saline for everyone."

"Demo, you've got the prototype night vision and laser rangefinders ready to go? Plenty of batteries?"

"Far as I can tell, nothing has changed since we left isolation. Batteries are all topped off."

Murphy's Law. Anything that can go wrong will go wrong. He continued to observe the team as they prepared. The casual joking would transition to war faces when they camoed up.

Hand signals would replace talking. Real-life or training mission, it was the same to Wolf and his men. He remembered some ancient wisdom that he'd learned when he was a Ranger newbie. Train like you fight, fight like you train and bleed in training so you don't in battle.

"Listen up!" he shouted. Everyone in the staging hangar stopped what they were doing and turned toward him. "I want everyone ready to launch before we head to the range. We will be ready to insert starting at 1800 today."

He walked outside. This was as good a time as any to test the SATCOM phone. He dialed Kennedy's office. "Kennedy, it's Wolf on SATCOM." The half-second delay had him thinking Kennedy had not answered.

"Copy, Wolf. Some latency but reading you four by."

"Roger. Any updates for me?"

"Yes, the deception plan is ready, I will execute when you signal."

"Okay, consider the next call from this number your signal."

"Roger that, out here."

He had given Kennedy complete freedom to create the deceptions. Kennedy's actions would drive Alejandro's stimulus responses. To include sending a kill crew six hundred miles west of the strike location and having his focus drawn to the border.

He headed upstairs to the B staff. On the second deck, an operations sergeant pulled him aside.

"Master sarnt," he said, "Ops has moved your infil time forward twenty-four hours. Got a hot request from the DEA to have you in place by zero-five tomorrow. They expect a High-Value Individual to attempt a border crossing in the next twenty-four to forty-eight hours."

"Who's the HVI??"

"They wouldn't divulge her name."

"Her?" he asked, his interest piqued.

"Yeah. Notify your team. You leave at zero-deuce."

He couldn't believe his ears. Eliana? It didn't seem possible, but what other female they would consider high value?

Wolf confirmed the launch update with Franks and Danner. The captain provided the update to the rest of the guys.

"All right, listen up," Franks announced, quieting the murmured conversations. "We are going tonight at 0200. DEA thinks an HVI will pass our way and they want us to track her so they can police her up. Ensure you accomplish any remaining critical tasks between now and 2100. We'll eat and test fire as planned. If you need help, ask."

THEY BOARDED an Air Force bus for the quick ride to the one-hundred-yard indoor police range. They fired their sidearms and zeroed M4s on semi and full auto. With the lights off, they donned their NVGs and turned on the AN/PAQ-4C infrared aiming lights. They rechecked their zero and practiced immediate-action drills.

Zero defects.

Satisfied the team was ready to defend itself, Wolf ordered everyone back to the base. They cleaned their weapons, then checked and cross-checked each other until 2100, when he called the men together.

"Long day, guys. Good job getting ready. Anyone not doing something else, curl up somewhere and get some sleep."

His voice echoed in the cavernous hangar space. "Be in your sticks at 0100."

54

D avis-Monthan Air Force Base & Mexican Border, Arizona
They sat on cracked tarmac still radiating the day's
fierce heat. Franks led alpha and Danner Bravo.

They inspected their men and waited for the load order.

Wolf talked with the pilots and reviewed the flight plan again.
These pilots were professionals, full-time Army 160th Special Operations Aviation Regiment pilots. They reviewed primary and
secondary landing zones one more time. And the crew chiefs,
inspected the MH-60M Black Hawk helicopters.

He scanned the sticks, calculating the hurt they were about to put
on the cartel. The whine of Black Hawk turbines interrupted his
thoughts of revenge. When he saw the crew chief's load signal, he
gave a hand to each man, helping them stand. They were a fearsome
sight.

Wolf nodded at each member of the strike team within the team.
They faced a point of no return. A pivot to a new level of engagement
with the drug cartels. They were ready to bring the pain.

It would damage an unconventional enemy, causing untold death
and damage to countless lives and families tonight in unconventional

ways. He would not admit it, but he felt exhilaration at the prospect of putting a hurt on the Cortes organization.

THE THREE-MAN ALPHA insertion was on terrain as steep as the topo map had promised it would be. The pilot nosed in, then slipped sideways. The team exited the helo and hugged ground. The helo took off, showering them in dirt and small rocks.

After nine minutes of additional flight time, he and Bravo in the second helicopter touched down between two ridges. They were out before the wheels touched down, holding a defensive perimeter.

After their taxi left, they moved a hundred yards west, where they stopped for a security check. Five minutes later, he used hand signals to move to the rally point.

They were in the cartel's backyard.

At the rally point, Danner set security and Wolf passed the word to take ten for water. The initial stage of their mission was to surveil lines of communication—travel routes, in military terms.

Often drug mules interspersed themselves among migrants walking or driving. They were often easier to identify because their packs were heavier and often square from the kilos of cocaine or vacuum-packed blocks of marijuana.

They were not the principal target.

As the golden rays of sunrise warmed and brightened their surveillance sectors, the vista before them came alive. An expert in celestial navigation, it still amazed Wolf when the two-dimensional map unfolded before him into three-D reality.

The team was in place and outer positions were reporting at their pre-assigned intervals. Everyone took a turn on the binoculars and spotting scopes. Between sunrise and 0900, two of the three positions called in SITREPS describing foot traffic.

Harris sent the updates via SATCOM. The rest of the day was uneventful. Movement increased when the sun set but were easy to follow via the white flashlight beams sweeping the countryside.

The forward observers worked together to back-azimuth the contacts and Wolf and Danner took turns plotting eight-digit grid coordinates. They added them to the SITREPs they forwarded on to B team.

At about 2200, the migrant groups turned off their flashlights and packs of illegals bedded down for the night. One group started a fire for cooking, but it was extinguished for being too bright in the night.

The rest of the night was quiet except for the occasional coyote yipping in the distance. Without the light pollution of urban areas, the stars were so bright they crowded out the major constellations.

Wolf thought how small he was when compared to the view before him. Small, but tonight...not inconsequential.

55

University of Arizona Cancer Center, Tucson, Arizona

Kennedy and Helen Campbell sat in the living room with the blinds closed. There was a phone with a recording device sitting on the coffee table. Her eyes flirted between the phone and Kennedy. He fidgeted with a pen, spinning it between his fingers like a rock band drummer.

"Whenever you're ready," he said.

She dialed the number, and a woman picked up after the third ring.

"I've been trying to reach you."

"Maria, I'm sorry, I—"

"What did I say about using my name?"

"I'm sorry," she said. "I have more information on Wolf."

For the next fifteen minutes, she relayed what they had prepared. Wolf and his team were on their way to Los Padres National Forest north of LA to support a DEA. Maria seemed excited to get such actionable intel.

"Los Padres? Are you sure?" she asked.

"Yes, positive. Please don't hurt my sister." The call disconnected.

Kennedy smiled. "I think she's taken the bait."

The following morning, Kennedy took a flight to Tucson. It was a two-legged affair; Tampa to Houston, almost an hour-and-a-half layover, and then Houston to Tucson.

He slept on the first flight. On the second leg, he worked through the rest of his plan to divert the cartel's attention while the team attacked the target.

He had studied the sensor system specifications and done the math. He'd also checked with a friend—a Nuclear, Biological, and Chemical NCO in the 82nd Airborne. He'd agreed that liquid radiological waste material was safe for testing sensor systems, with the appropriate clean up.

When Kennedy collected his rental car, he made sure he had the additional insurance permitting him to venture into Mexico. Then he headed north to the University of Arizona Cancer Center. He gave his name at the front desk. The receptionist directed him to an orderly who told him to park at the loading dock around back.

When he arrived, the man was waiting with a cart carrying two insulated five-gallon buckets. They were both sealed with custom-made lids that were further secured with a silvery tape a lot like metal.

The sides of the buckets bore the black on yellow symbols that looked like a three-bladed window fan. CAUTION RADIOACTIVE MATERIALS.

"Officer Zankowitz? My director told me to give this to you. You need these for training?"

"Yes, thanks." He displayed his Customs and Border Patrol ID. "We have some new radiation-detection equipment to test."

"Okay. You know how to dispose of the waste when you're finished?"

"Yes, we do. Thanks."

Kennedy popped the rental car trunk. He placed the buckets of radiological waste in the back, covering them with a blanket and his duffel bag. Then he headed for the Best Western in Nogales.

He would wait there for word of Wolf's launch across the border. The Best Western was newer, and his room had a large, wall-mounted flat-screen television and plenty of hot water for the shower. He paid in advance for three nights just in case there was a delay.

After a stop at a hardware store, Kennedy stowed the protective gloves, a face shield, and a plastic rain suit in the top of his pack. He'd also bought construction-grade plastic bags and a paint roller with a handle that extended to twelve feet. It was an important part of the plan. Painting the waste down both the sides and, if possible on the tops of the semi-trailers. He settled in for the night at his hotel room, going to bed early.

Kennedy went for a run the next morning before dawn, then showered and headed to the free breakfast. Back in his room, he read the local newspaper and the Phoenix- based Arizona Republic.

As a former wrestler, he often used pushups to burn off extra energy. He stopped his count at one hundred and six when his cell-phone rang.

"We're a go. Execute at 0300."

The call disconnected. Nightfall could not come soon enough.

56

U ndisclosed desert location, Mexican border, Arizona
Wolf briefed Bravo at 2100. He would take everyone except the new guys and execute an area recon. The plan was to leave the newbies to man the radio.

Wolf and the strike team dropped off the backside of the mountain at 2300, taking their time in the rugged terrain. Even with night vision, the route was rocky and shadowy, and no one wanted to be the guy who twisted an ankle and slowed everything down.

They got to their landing zone thirty minutes early and set up a security perimeter. At 0055, the men turned on their infrared strobes. They placed them in an L-shape, with the long end pointing toward the approach and departure azimuth.

At 0100, a civilian Sikorsky S-76 swooped in and landed in a sandstorm. Bjorn had borrowed the bird from a wealthy Texas cattle baron he knew from his DEA time.

The rotor disk created static electricity, firing off spectacular blue sparks. LeBlanc retrieved the strobe lights, and everyone boarded the helo. Wolf jumped in with his back to the pilot's seat.

The other teammates were strapped in and dressed head to toe in black, including helmets and dark goggles. As the helicopter climbed skyward, Danner handed Wolf a headset. He clicked the trans button twice to let the team know he was in the net.

"Welcome aboard, brother," Bjorn said on the intercom from the pilot-in-command seat. He smiled at the sound of Bjorn's voice. "Do you remember how to drive this thing? This ain't no Schwinn."

"You're asking now?" he laughed. "A bike is a bike, bro."

"That's what I said!" a female chimed in. It was Sierra.

"What are you doing here?" he yelled into his mic, recognizing her.

"Are you nuts? This is not cool! Land this thing right now."

"Don't be stupid," Sierra snapped. "I want payback too, and you can use a real doc. I mean, Hughes is good, but I'm better." She turned to him. "Sorry, Henry. No offense intended."

"None taken, doc," Hughes responded. "I'm stoked you're here."

He keyed his intercom and barked, "I am not."

It took twenty-four minutes via an indirect route to get to the pre-positioned weapons cache. They tossed the parachute bags full of Russian firearms on the helicopter and lifted away.

Wolf expected used junk but found brand new Kalashnikov AK-103s. The chest rigs were Spetsnaz design, with full mags and four grenades for each man. And there were two suppressed Makarov pistols, all in like-new condition.

The flight route took them east of Saric, La Compania, and La Cebolla. They hopped over the last ridge and dropped into the valley north of Santa Martha. Bjorn landed the helo in a wash eight hundred meters north of Santa Ana and five hundred meters west of Highway 15.

As soon as they exited, the team started movement to their forward positions on the northeast side of the logistics center. Bjorn lifted off to the designated holding area on the west side of the mountain.

Wolf led the team to the fence ninety degrees clockwise from his last location. Nothing about the large facility had changed since his last visit. No electric or vibe wire, no cameras. He wondered if the cartel had fixed the cut from his earlier mission.

There were more men patrolling, but it was still a four-minute gap between patrols. Clinton cut the wire on the back of a pole. From their current location, it was a sixty-meter run to the back door. At the door, Wolf and LeBlanc stood security with their suppressed pistols while Danner picked the lock.

Once inside, they started clearing their way to the production and packaging part of the building. All was going as planned until they turned a corner and found a guard standing there smoking a cigarette.

Wolf was fast, and he pulled the Makarov's trigger twice. The pistol suppressor did little to quiet the report as one round ricocheted after passing through the guard's skull. Then Danner killed a responding guard with his AK.

"Well crap, so much for being stealthy," Wolf grumbled.

He and LeBlanc holstered their pistols and switched to their AKs. LeBlanc squeezed Wolf's right shoulder. They were first to enter the drug packing area.

The door they entered was at one end of a long room filled with tables parallel to each other. Twelve women were working the assembly line in their underwear, black lights illuminating every lurid white morsel of coke being measured on scales.

Blocks of brown product sat at the far end. The guards leering at the scantily clad women were slow to react to intruders in the near darkness.

Two died in an instant as Wolf and LeBlanc assaulted. A third grabbed a woman as a shield and started backing away to the rear exit door.

Wolf held the gunman's attention by pleading for his life Spanish while LeBlanc set up his tricky shot. A beat later, the gunman's brain stem was separated by LeBlanc's kill shot, covering the hostage in blood and brain matter.

The other women screamed and hid under the tables. He told them in Spanish to leave and they grabbed their clothes and following his medic out.

Wolf turned to Clinton, the team engineer. "Figure out how to blow this place." "Roger that. Give me your grenades."

He handed his grenades over and strode to the loading area. The ladies Hughes had attempted to escort from the building wouldn't leave. They were banging whatever they could find on the heavy industrial lock, sealing the doors of a CONEX. Several women pointed and cried.

What the heck? Wolf trotted over and got the women backed off. He pressed his head against the door and what he heard made his blood run cold. Voices were yelling. They sounded young.

"Boys and girls inside?" he asked, pointing to the container.

A frantic older woman said, "Yes, yes!"

Hughes looked at Wolf with a blank stare. "What's happening? This is drug cartel location, right?"

"Find a fire ax, sledgehammer, anything we can use to pry this open."

Danner came racing around the corner and skidded to a stop. "It's getting hot out there, boss. More bad guys just arrived. We gotta go."

"We can't yet," he said. "There are kids inside."

Danner cursed a blue storm. "All right, work it. We can hold 'em for a bit," he said, and ran toward the sound of gunfire.

Clinton ran up. "Place's ready to blow."

He looked at the container scene with fresh eyes. "Hey, what's goin' on here?"

"Okay, copy ready to blow. But first we need to open this trailer."

"What's in there? Product?"

"Yeah, but not the kind you'd expect—kids, we think." Wolf said.

Clinton slipped out of his tactical backpack and reached inside to grab a handle. When he stood up, he was wearing a big grin and holding an industrial bolt cutter.

"Gimme some room," he said. Wolf stepped aside and Clinton stepped in with the tool. He gripped the padlock hoop in the powerful cutters and grunted as he squeezed. The lock was cut a few seconds later.

Wolf clapped him on the back. "This is why you are our favorite engineer, brother."

"I'm your only engineer. But thanks," he said.

The women had pulled opened the tall metal doors, allowing dim lights to illuminate the interior. The CONEX container had fourteen tweens and younger inside, with six gallons of water and a white plastic bucket for waste. There were bags of snacks strewn around, but no proper food.

To Wolf's surprise, they were not Mexican. They looked Asian but spoke what Portes identified as a coastal Peruvian dialect.

While Clinton and Portes were looking after the kids, Wolf ran over to Harris and called Bjorn on the radio.

"Nighthawk, Outlaw Actual—need immediate exfil main building rooftop."

"Outlaw Actual, Nighthawk. Roger on the way. ETA four minutes. Out."

Wolf ran back to the loading dock. "Get them to the roof. Bjorn is inbound."

"On it," Portes said. He spoke Spanish in a calm voice. "Time to go, ladies. I need your help to get the young ones to the roof."

"I'll pull rear security," Clinton said.

Wolf nodded. "I'll get Danner and the guys."

Clinton dropped the magazine from his AK-103 and eyeballed it for load, opting to replace it with a full mag. He slammed it home and waited to ascend the ladder until all the women and kids had followed Hughes up it. He faced out until it was his turn.

Wolf and the rest of the guys lit up the growing crowd of gunmen, then he raced up the ladder. He heard the distinctive oil-can sound of bullets hitting the chopper as it approached, but there was no smoke or scary engine sounds. Danner, Harris, and LeBlanc provided covering fire. The children panicked, but Portes and Clinton kept them together.

Wolf ran over to Bjorn's door. "Change of plans. We're going Titanic here—women and children first. Portes and Clinton will stay with them for security."

Born flipped up his night vision goggles. "It's getting pretty hot. You sure you'll be okay?"

"Yeah, no sweat. We'll see you at the exfil LZ." The brothers clasped hands at the thumbs and Wolf ran back to edge of the roof and fired.

Sierra helped women and children board. Everyone had a child in their lap.

Bjorn cranked up the power, flew backwards into the darkness before turning left ninety degrees to disappear into the night.

57

Cortes Facility Santa Ana, Mexico

Wolf jumped the stairs two at a time and found the guys in a first-floor office. The firefight had subsided, and the silence was deafening.

"Why aren't they attacking?"

"Looks like they're waiting for reinforcements or reloading. Or both. Did I hear our ride leave?" Danner asked.

"Yes, Bjorn is taking the kids to safety."

Harris kept scanning his sector while cursing. His intensity infused the rest of the team. "Scumbags don't ruin enough lives with their drugs. Now they're trafficking children?"

"Well, they lose all around on this gig. We'll exfil after we draw these scumbags them into Clinton's surprise." he said.

"We got this, brother," LeBlanc said. "It ain't nothing but a thing."

Wolf admired the simplicity of the saying. Just another thing to do. And a commitment that each would give their all for their teammates.

An explosion from the back of the facility implied one of the booby-traps had worked. He ran to check and found two dead bodies at the back door.

He dropped a gunman running for cover, then moved a forklift to block the wrecked doorway. He ran back into the production area and grabbed a sealed package of cocaine for each cargo pocket. Then set his radio transceiver for Clinton's big surprise.

By the time he got back to the team, Wolf's emergency radio vibrated. "Outlaw Actual, Nighthawk, over."

"Go for Actual," he said.

Without digital satcom relay, the terrestrial signal was scratchy and laced with static. Bjorn would still be flying at tree-top level, so the signal was weak. But the message was understandable.

"Nine vehicles headed your way via the main road, maybe one or two klicks out. Time to saddle up, over."

"Roger that." Wolf looked at the men.

"Put on your party hats. We got company comin'."

Everyone ran to the wall and peered out the windows to see nine trucks pulling up outside the perimeter chain-link fence. The driver of the vehicle at the head of the convoy revved his engine and launched toward the locked gate. He smashed it open in a shower of sparks and flying chain links.

The team opened up as one, killing the driver and a lone gunman stupid enough to stand in the bed. The dead driver's right foot pressed the gas pedal to the truck's floor. The unguided truck slammed hard into an eighteen-wheeler in the loading dock, grinding to a stop.

Another group was pushing a truck forward as the cartel soldiers hid behind it for cover.

Danner turned to Wolf. "There's too many of them. It's time to go."

"Agreed. Let's give them the back if they want it so bad. We'll bug out through the front." They withdrew and stacked at the entry door. On the count of three, they flowed out and across the darkened parking lot.

They fired on the move, slipping through the broken gate and into the desert darkness. Harris and LeBlanc killed the last two gunmen on the near side of the building and opposing fires stopped.

The team ran a seven-minute pace. After the second mile, they stopped for a breather and Wolf extracted a cellphone from Harris' pack. He pressed a shortcut key that dialed a stored number. When it rang four times, Wolf pressed the hashtag key and disconnected the call.

Wolf switched to his radio and the channel for Clintons' surprise. He keyed the mic. At the cartel compound, there was a mammoth explosion. To a man, they smiled at the gigantic orange and white fireball as it lit up the night. Secondary explosions took out extended sections of the building when the fire reached more unstable chemicals.

They had to hustle. About three-quarters of a mile behind them, a noisy truck stopped, and they could hear men talking in Spanish. From out of the darkness came bursts of automatic gunfire.

The cartel soldiers couldn't see the team in the pitch dark but sprayed random shots in their direction.

As they dropped to the dirt, Danner spun around. Wearing night vision goggles, Harris and LeBlanc responded with a near-ambush immediate-action drill that silenced the attackers. This gave Wolf the cover he needed to help his teammate to his feet. But he wasn't getting up.

"I'm hit, boss ..." Then he coughed and a wad of blood sprayed into the air.

"Chief, talk to me! Can you move?"

"Yeah, but no PT this week, okay?"

"You got it, stay with me, brother." he pulled Danner up into a one-arm carry and started quick-timing toward the LZ.

"Oh man, it hurts to breathe ..."

He grunted with every step as his friend and team sergeant lugged him through the desert. Behind them, Harris, Hughes, and LeBlanc kept firing and throwing grenades to discourage any contact.

Wolf tripped, and they both flopped onto the sand. Danner coughed up blood, his chest wound bleeding red and frothy. Punctured lung at minimum, possibly a full collapsed one. And where the bullet had migrated was anyone's guess.

"It hurts to breathe."

"No worries, we got you."

Wolf tore open Danner's vest and shirt and checked for an exit, not finding one. He swiped at the entry with his drive-on rag and covered it with a pre-cut piece of plastic. He taped it on three sides so air could exit but not enter the chest cavity.

Then he readied an eighteen-gauge IV needle in case Danner exhibited signs of a tension pneumothorax.

"Hughes!" When he skidded in on his knees, he assessed Wolf's work while Wolf radioed Bjorn.

"Nighthawk, Outlaw Actual. Exfil LZ busted. Moving to LZ Golf. Be advised, medevac nine-line follows," using the Army casualty message format relaying Danner's condition and where he wanted Bjorn to land.

He took over monitoring Danner's wound and handed the radio mic to Hughes to transmit the necessary information.

LeBlanc ran over. "I think your buddies have stopped chasing us." He looked down at Danner. "How bad is he?"

"Ready to fight, junior," Danner answered.

"Right on, Chief," Wolf said. "Ten-twelve more minutes to the LZ. The chopper is waiting with beer, pizza, and pretty girls."

Hughes finished the radio call and knelt next to Danner. "Lemme get in there for another minute." He examined field dressing and saw he was already breathing better. "I think you'll be fine, Chief. But damn, some folks'll do anything to get out of PT."

Danner grunted. "I can still do more pushups than you. Let's go." Hughes and LeBlanc helped him to his feet and took off, holding him by the belt. Harris and Wolf pulled rear security.

Over his PRC-90 Wolf heard Bjorn radio, "Actual, Nighthawk, tangos one-five-zero." the voice said. "Heads down, coming in hot."

He double-clicked the transmit button.

Bad guys were one hundred fifty meters aft and closing. Too close. The trucks stopped, headlights in a row. Mechanical dogs pushing their prey to exhaustion, expecting an easy kill.

The air filled with bullets snapping by way too close for comfort.

Hughes and LeBlanc bent low but keep chugging forward. Wolf and Harris dropped to prone positions to engage the shooters. They selected their shots and fired back at the green tracers, hitting most with just one or two tries. The opposition was being depleted, but it was slow and eating up a lot of precious ammo.

He heard the helicopter flying in fast and low and expected the sounds of an AK, but this was different. They didn't know it but Sierra was on the M-60 machine gun. She used tracers to walk the bullets into the first vehicle and down the line.

Bjorn wheeled around for a second pass and Sierra dominated the remaining vehicles and personnel. Bjorn completed the last run. Sierra had killed many and forced the rest of the cartel soldiers to retreat.

Wolf watched the last two drivable trucks turn off their lights and back out. They left the fight at high speed with some of less trained cartel soldiers running to catch up.

As they got up to move, Harris caught one in the outer thigh, a through and through, not life threatening.

"Oww, you bastards!" He grabbed the leg with his hand, but it wasn't bleeding much. "Some butthead always has to shoot last, right?"

"You okay?" he asked.

"Yeah, just winged me but it's annoying all get out. I'll be all right. Gimme a minute to wrap this thing."

Harris drew combat dressings from his kit and wrapped them tight around his thigh, covering the bullet entry and exit wounds. Then he cinched his drive-on rag around the dressings and powered off on point while Wolf and LeBlanc carried Danner. It was only about two hundred meters to salvation.

They pushed through the dust storm created by the helicopter and got to the door as the wheels touched down. Sierra pushed aside the M-60 pedestal and helped pull Danner aboard, checking his wound as Bjorn lifted off.

"How's Chief doing?" he yelled over the noise.

"He'll be all right," Sierra said. "I'll insert a chest tube, and he'll survive until you get him to treatment."

"Where are the kids?"

"At a holding site. We will get them out after we deliver you guys back over the border."

They sank into the canvas seats and Wolf exhaled as Santa Ana disappeared.

Time to count the wins. Drugs and facility destroyed. A couple dozen cartel killers dead and dying against only two wounded on our side. Not bad for first contact.

58

Undisclosed desert location, Mexico
      Bjorn landed in a wash near the original pickup, dropping off his passengers.

LeBlanc ran off to retrieve the team gear. Wolf got Portes, Clinton, and Harris in a fighting position overlooking the border crossing route they'd identified in their planning.

Several sets of tire tracks ran through the area. Then he went to help LeBlanc.

A short time later, Wolf met the helicopter with the Russian kit. Clinton and Hughes changed into their American issue while Wolf talked with Bjorn.

"The precious package is safe?"

"Yeah, consider it taken care of."

"I appreciate that. One more thing. Can you put the this stuff back in the cache for me?" Wolf asked.

"Yeah. I expect you'll want it for another vacation," Bjorn said.

"Possible," Wolf said with a grin.

Wolf hustled back to the men. "Time for us to re-enter the training mission," Wolf said before switching to his PRC-90.

"Big Top, this is Nighthawk, requesting immediate medevac my position. Nine-line follows." After completing the transmission to the B staff, Wolf switched frequencies and radioed the newbies.

"Caravan, this is Nighthawk. Shut it down. Rendezvous at OP Four ASAP."

"Roger that. We heard gunfire, you all okay?"

"Negative. Medevac inbound. Out."

He turned his attention to the guys. "Okay, listen up. Command and the DEA are going to investigate, so let's get our story right. We came upon a drug exchange. No idea who they were. Two lifted Chevy trucks with big sand tires. We were observing and getting ready to call it in when a helicopter running a nose light spotted me and started shooting. Fired upon, we returned fire. They bugged out. I requested evac. Harris caught one in the leg and Hughes worked to stabilize chief. Check?"

One by one they acknowledged the story. Wolf showed them the tight packages of cocaine he'd liberated from the Cortes cartel warehouse. "Here is proof of the exchange, that was dropped as the subjects fled. Make sure Chief understands."

A few feet away, Danner snorted. "I'm shot, you idiots, not deaf."

Minutes later the newbies came stumbling in, exhausted from their rushed movement over the foothills. Wolf nodded.

"Just in time for exfil. It's a long walk home."

Two helicopters arrived. The first was the MH-60 combat medevac to take the wounded to the Fort Huachuca hospital. The second would transport the rest of the team back to the forward operation base.

We loaded everyone and everything on the right chopper and the birds lifted off toward different compass points. They had only been airborne a few minutes when the copilot of Wolf's bird yelled, "Break left!"

The pilot executed the maneuver without question, flaring the helo and breaking hard left before nosing over to pick up speed. The copilot flipped the countermeasures switch, firing off flares and engaged electronic systems designed to fool possible incoming missiles.

Rucksacks became weightless, then slammed back to the deck. If the doors had been open, they would have flown out of the helicopter.

He glimpsed Bell 206 Jet Ranger helicopter streaking north at less than fifty feet off their nose. Too close.

The pilot came over the intercom. "Wolf, channel three."

"Go."

He cursed in a heavy Southern drawl. "Dang drug runners, for sure. You need to be ready when we land. It's chaos back at your Command."

59

Davis-Monthan Air Force Base Tucson, Arizona

On arrival, the B staff collected their weapons, maps, and the cocaine. Then they brought back Hughes and Harris from the Fort Huachuca hospital and began a full start-to-finish after-action inquiry.

The team stayed on the story with plausible minor differences to account for their differing individual viewpoints of what had occurred. At the end of the interviews, the company commander advised Group Headquarters was sending its investigative unit. They would start again in the morning.

No longer in isolation, Wolf and company watched television news in the hangar's Day Room to catch up on recent events. The big news was CBP had detected radioactive material on five eighteen-wheelers and two smaller trucks at the Nogales border crossing.

The DEA confirmed all the trucks carried enormous quantities of dope believed to have Sinaloa Cartel origin. He slapped Harris on the back and whispered, "That, my friend, was the second part of Kennedy's deception plan. Worked like a charm."

A wide-eyed Harris smiled as he shook his head. "Priceless."

Wolf walked to a vacant corner of the hangar and called his brother. "All good there, brother?"

"Mission accomplished," he said. "I delivered the packages and Dr. Mommy has headed back home."

Each of the strike team members plus Bjorn and Sierra had given up their emergency blood-chit money to the kids. Twenty-seven thousand dollars would help the church help the children. Send them home or provide new lives new life in the U.S..

Plus, there was a little something for the brave women who didn't run away from danger but fought for the kids.

Wolf felt a wave of satisfaction flow through him. He gave a thumbs-up to the team, and the strike team nodded in return. The newbies, confused as ever, each gave him two thumbs up.

The trafficking of children disturbed him to his core. With Joaquin Zapana dead, it left one man with the money and the means to deal in human flesh. Cortes ops boss Martin Amaro was of Peruvian decent, which made it even more bewildering.

Why take such a substantial risk? His brain swirling, it was sheer exhaustion that dragged Wolf into sleep.

It was mid-morning when the Group Headquarters investigative team arrived with all its straphangers. They had to move the investigation out into the hangar to accommodate all the staff officers and administrative personnel.

They divided the hangar into two pods of investigators and looked at every angle of the operation. From the pre-planning stages through the minute-by-minute of the mission and exfil.

A captain wearing Quartermaster branch brass arrogantly questioned LeBlanc on why his sniper rifle was dirty. LeBlanc had to explain to the clueless young officer he didn't clean his weapon after he sighted it in. It would change the point of aim.

Just then, Kennedy and a private first class entered the hangar. He nodded at Wolf as he strode by. The 9mm pistol on his hip and a locked pouch in his grip indicated he was transporting classified material. The other soldier, a youthful intelligence private, looked nervous. His nametag said WAYNE.

Sergeants from the individual investigation teams escorted them into separate investigation pods. Wolf watched as Kennedy pulled out a map and what looked to be a printout on green-bar paper. He couldn't see the private, but he had an uneasy feeling about him being here.

~

KENNEDY SAT across from two officers and two senior NCOs. He hadn't talked to Wolf, so he hoped their pre-planned stories still matched. His pre-flight adjustments to the new Guard tech and sensor logs would back up the team's story. He tried explaining how to follow the sensor logs, but no one understood what he was describing.

"Okay, okay, I think we got it. That will be all. Thank you, Staff Sergeant Kennedy," the senior officer said.

He packed up his classified pouch and stood by waiting on Wayne. He could make out what they were saying in the second pod. One of the interrogating officers had taken an aggressive approach with the young soldier. He even threatened him with court-martial and spending the rest of his life at Fort Leavenworth. He invoked the image of Wayne breaking big rocks into little rocks for the rest of his stinking, no-account maggot life.

"Your sensor logs don't lie, private. Why do you?"

The kid was the superior subject-matter expert in the conversation and was unmoved by his interrogator's attempt to hard-case him.

In his disarming, down-home Kentucky way, he broke it down to the panel like he was explaining it to a child. He pushed the back-woods accent a bit more than he did when dealing a potential date met off base in a bar.

"Sirs, it's like this, see—those logs ain't lying, it's true. But it's the setup on them old schoolhouse sensors. They be Vietnam era, maybe even Korea. They old, sir. Older'n me and you and can't no longer hold they calibrations. We use 'em when we have to 'cause they're what we got, see? But they ain't reliable, if y'know what I mean. The signal you think came out of Mexico could have come from anywhere in a hunnert-mile circle, including a big chunk of Arizona."

A couple of other panelists asked perfunctory questions to justify being present, amounting to nothing. Frustrated, the interrogator ordered Wayne to leave before they changed their minds and sent him to Leavenworth.

He walked past the staff sergeant on his way out. "How did it go?" Kennedy whispered.

"It went mighty fine," he whispered back. "Mighty fine."

On the way out, Kennedy let Wolf know Danner was improving.

"All good?" Wolf asked.

"Mighty fine," he said, smiling. "Mighty fine."

That afternoon, they staged the space as if it were a court-martial. Wolf huffed, this supposed to be intimidating. Who do they think they're playing with?

The team sat to the right side of two six-foot tables pushed together where the investigation panelists sat. The absence of military police in the room was a good sign.

Wolf sat next to Captain Franks. "We good here?" Franks whispered.

"Yes, sir."

Board president Lieutenant Colonel George Kamis ordered each of the investigation leaders to summarize their findings. One by one they stood up and gave their reports, some affirmative and some pointless in their negativity.

Bottom line was the ODA had acted within the boundaries of their orders and the Uniform Code of Military Justice. The men had displayed respect for the rules of engagement, only returning fire after the wounding of two teammates.

"I am in full agreement with your assessments. This ODA upheld Special Forces values and honor while operating under constrained rules of engagement." Kamis said and nodded in their direction. "Well done, men." He raised a gavel and struck a wooden puck. "You are returned to duty, and this proceeding is closed."

Board members milled around picking up their folders and briefcases.

The team stood waiting on dismissal. The LTC came over to Wolf and extended his hand. He took it and they shook.

"Well done, Lance," Kamis whispered. "I know you've had a rocky few months. And while I don't know if this was an extension of that, I appreciate you are too smart to get caught embarrassing your Army or your nation."

"Thank you, sir."

The colonel leaned in. "Keep looking for ways hurt Sinaloa and I'll green light the missions."

"Ah, yes, sir, will do."

60

E l Rancho Cortes, Sinaloa, Mexico & Garden Grove, California

Maria Camacho briefed Alejandro on her investigation. She had uncovered the source of the radiation that resulted in the confiscation of their drugs.

Her team's search of a wide area included every disturbed pile of dirt and all the derelict cars. They emptied every trash can and dumpster within twenty-five miles. It took time, but they found the empty buckets of radioactive waste used to paint the trucks.

In Alejandro's mind there was only one person who could implement a plan so bold in concept and execution. Wolf.

There was growing anger north of the border. The National Security Council labeled the Sinaloa Cartel a terrorist group and a Weapons of Mass Destruction threat. Throughout the southwest, vehicle border crossings closed.

The U.S. government added all Cortes-linked businesses to the terrorist watch list. Then the president ordered the Financial Crimes Enforcement Network to freeze and seize all the cartel assets they could uncover.

Alejandro and Maria met to discuss her plan to leverage the Mexican Army to hit back. Their contact would turn over the radioactive buckets to a U.S. Army counterpart with a request for processing. If the process worked like her source said, the American Army would turn over the evidence to the FBI's world-class forensics team. They would process everything for fingerprints and even DNA.

FBI would analyze trace droplets of fluid to uncover radioactive fingerprints leading back to the manufacturer. One domino after another would fall and they would snare Wolf in the trap. The U.S. government would do their work for them.

Alejandro's radio cracked to life. "El Chapo is here."

They stood. "Get Martin," he ordered his assistant. The security team entered first, followed by El Chapo and his central states distribution lieutenant.

He was five-six, but the two hulking bodyguards flanking him made him look smaller. Built like a combination fireplug and bulldog, it was a bad idea to his will to overcome every obstacle.

"Sit down!" El Chapo ordered.

Alejandro and Camacho sat. He pointed at her. "Not you."

She looked at her boss and stood. Neither would lock eyes with the big boss.

A drop of sweat rolled down the back of Alejandro's neck, but he didn't dare wipe it away. His cousin was quick to violence.

"You have turned into a major problem, Alejandro. The last month has been one incident after another. You have lost product and money and now our southwest distribution routes are closed."

"Cousin, we—"

El Chapo held up his hand, and he stopped talking. He looked at Amaro when he walked in. "Stand next to Maria." Amaro obeyed.

Alejandro panicked. "We can solve these issues and repay your losses," he blurted.

"No, you cannot fix the problems!" El Chapo shouted. He sat trembling in his chair. Few who were addressed in that tone by this man ever celebrated another birthday.

"Your incompetence is very clear. There will be new management and I will handle this myself. And when I'm done, I might let you have the business back. But first you must repay the Colombians."

Alejandro's heart sank. Everything was going wrong, and he couldn't do anything about it.

"Yes, sir!"

"We can't ship overland in the southwest. New ideas are required, so I brought Manny to keep product flowing using central U.S. routes to make up the losses. Martin, you will now report to Manny." He waved dismissively at Alejandro. "Not this scarecrow."

El Chapo pointed at Camacho. "Why is this amateur even here? Get rid of her, right now and find an intelligence professional."

Camacho only hoped she was going to be fired, and not disappeared.

"Where is Eliana?"

"She left for Los Angeles."

El Chapo pulled out his gold-plated 9mm Beretta 92X and walked over to Alejandro.

"Please, God. Please don't let him kill me."

El Chapo tapped Alejandro's shoulder with the tip of his gun.

"You have hurt my business. And that is hurting my relationship with the Colombians. If you were not the son of Romulo Cortes, I would kill you where you sit."

El Chapo spun and raised his pistol, shooting Camacho twice in the chest. She was dead before she hit the floor. Walking over to her lifeless body, he smiled and shot her again. He looked directly at Alejandro and said, "See? The new management is already providing value."

THE WAREHOUSE IN GARDEN GROVE, California, sat in a nondescript blue-collar section of the city. A block over from the intersection of Blades Avenue and Monarch Street. It was perfect now that a new thirty-foot Airstream trailer was in place.

Eliana had gotten word of El Chapo's visit and its results. Now it was her time to prove her value to him. She had recovered all but a few former customers, with promises to replace the dangerous product, and more for their trouble.

Soldiers were returning to her fold and recruiting from outsiders had picked up. This meant working for Eliana Cortes was again a desirable thing.

She was on the road meeting and paying some of the most violent gangs in L.A. to do her dirty work. For some it was money, others product, and some a cut of the take from a particular corner. She worked with everyone, building offensive and retail coalitions for the future.

El Chapo would see these results and the millions of dollars she would generate. He would promote her into a place of honor in the cartel. She hoped it would include superiority over her brother.

Then it would be a party.

When Eliana got back to the warehouse, she walked into the trailer, closing the door behind her. Her team understood a closed outer door meant privacy inviolable.

She prepared a hot shower and afterward sat quietly on the queen-size bed, rubbing her belly with coconut oil. Her serenity fled as thoughts of Joaquin crossed her mind. She missed him so.

There was much work yet to do, and Wolf's death could not come soon enough. She lay back in her terrycloth robe and relaxed on the bed. Everything in its time, she thought. I will not forget.

She ate a snack of carrots, celery, and hummus. Then jotted some notes in her planner before drifting off into a late-afternoon nap. Deep in her dream state, she pushed a stroller through a city street devoid of people or vehicles. Then a single shot rang out from afar and her happy-family dream transformed into a horrifying nightmare.

A dark, hooded figure ripped her baby from the stroller. Then it smashed her baby against a wall. When the creature spun around and pulled a flowing hood from its head, the man was Wolf.

Eliana's panicked screams woke her and drew her security team pounding into the trailer, firearms in hand. She waved them off.

I can't let anyone find out about my baby.

61

USSOCOM, Tampa, Florida

"What are you doing back so soon?" Kennedy asked when Wolf stepped into his cube.

"Battalion commander sent us home. I told him we wouldn't do that in war. It didn't help."

"How is Danner?"

"Good, eighty percent. He'll be home by the weekend. He's a tough one."

Kennedy tilted his head toward the SCIF. Wolf badged in, and he followed behind, then locked the door.

"That was one scary op."

"You did an outstanding job. I think you're a natural. I appreciated your over watch while airborne. Hard to believe your sensors can range so far into Mexico," he said.

"That wasn't me airborne. It was that kid, Private Wayne. I couldn't be two places at once, so I enlisted his help with the Guardrail while I slimed the radioactive waste on the Cortes trucks."

"I thought the story was he intercepted our transmissions from the schoolhouse."

Kennedy chuckled. "Right, 'the story.' I have a question about your movement. Wayne mentioned you flying back and forth across the border several times. What was that about?"

"Child trafficking. Someone was moving kids in twenty-foot containers. We found some at the cartel compound and Bjorn and Sierra got them to safety."

"What? The drug cartels don't human traffic."

Wolf frowned. "True enough. It's been front and center in my thinking since we popped the lock on the CONEX that held them. We believe the kids were Peruvian. There is only one name making any sense for that."

"Martin Amaro," Kennedy said.

"The same. He manages and operates the extended cartel network. Peruvian descent. He has the means and the money to finance the scheme. Maybe he was freelancing, getting a little enterprising for himself?"

"If Alejandro or El Chapo found out he was risking the goose that laid the golden egg, they would roast him alive."

"Yeah. We'll keep that info in top of mind in case we can use it somewhere. Tell me more about this Wayne. What's his story?"

"Turns out Wayne is a supernatural signals intelligence analyst. A friend of mine at the schoolhouse let me know about him, so I read him in on a classified mission. That was him on the other end of the radio. He is one in a million. When the time is right, I want to recruit him full time." Kennedy changed the subject. "I need a break. Let's go out to eat with the ladies tonight?"

"Good idea. I can use one, too. I'll see if Parker is available. Meet at Crabby Bill's 1830?"

WHEN THE FOURSOME arrived fifteen minutes early, the line at Crabby Bill's snaked around the building. The hostess best guessed an hour or more to get a table.

Wolf grabbed Parker's hand. "Follow me."

He led them around back to the kitchen door where he was a

tattooed mountain of a man greeted them. He introduced him to his companions.

"Guys, meet Anthony Delvecchio, best Ranger chef in recorded military history. You haven't eaten until you get a bucket of his steamed spiced shrimp."

"I do hold my own, y'all." He laughed and shook Wolf by his shoulder. "Where you been, man? Don't see you no more."

"Oh, you know, brother. Out checking on people's democracy and stuff."

Delvecchio laughed a booming guffaw. "I know that's right."

"Is the special spot free tonight? The front is jacked up with tourists," he asked.

"For you, brother, I'd evict anyone was there, but yeah. C'mon in and get you that table."

Tony led them through the kitchen to the chef's counter and ordered his staff to set it for four. Wolf and Elle had discussed the menu on the way over.

So, he ordered beer and two dozen oysters with extra horseradish. Calamari, grouper, red snapper, and crab cakes with coleslaw rounded out his order. Kieran and Maya placed their orders, and the impressed waiter scooted to fulfill them.

The four were in good spirits. It felt good to depressurize and enjoy a meal among trusted friends, something he was desperate for.

While they were waiting on their dinners, Wolf excused himself to use the bathroom. On the way to the head, he saw Colonel Gates and his wife at a table with another couple.

"Sirs, ladies. Good to see you again, colonel. I hope I'm not intruding. I just wanted to say hello."

The colonel stood and man hugged, then introduced him to the table. "Always good to see you in one piece. Before you go, how is Chief Danner?"

"He's doing well, sir. He'll be home this weekend."

"Excellent. Let's talk at lunch tomorrow."

Wolf returned to the chef's counter.

"What took you so long? You get stage fright in a public restroom?" Kennedy asked.

"No. I saw Gates out front. He wants to 'talk' tomorrow at lunch." He flashed a tight-lipped smile.

The rest of the meal was memorable, as usual, and the conversation was fun, but something nagged at Wolf. Parker looked striking, as always, and her smile sparkled. But he felt distance between them, and he didn't like it.

62

Tampa, Florida

There was only one other person besides El Chapo who made Alejandro nervous. The Tomador de Almas "Taker of Souls" stood about five-nine, with jet black hair and eyes. His eyes could make you confess your soul before he took it.

He had been in the service of the Cortes family for twenty-four years. The tools he favored ranged from knives to crossbows to rifles that could kill from a mile.

After the arrest of Miguel Angel Félix Gallardo in 1989, Romulo Cortes chose to align himself with the new boss, Joaquín Archivaldo Guzmán Loera, also known as El Chapo. Having El Chapo as extended family helped him make the choice, as there was still some honor and loyalty attached to it.

The Tomador's work made known the cartel's power, reach, and relentless focus on protecting its business. With the cartel's resources rivaling a nation state, the Tomador was the supreme court and executioner all in one. He was a force of nature.

Alejandro handed him a gym bag that contained an envelope with several new target photos and a hundred thousand dollars.

"Boss, this is too much money. I still have the fifty thousand from the earlier contract, the contract I have not yet fulfilled."

"You earned it protecting my sister during her recovery. Now I want you on a plane to Tampa as soon as possible."

"Yes, boss."

The Latin Kings provided the Tomador a safe house on the north side of Tampa. Its location provided security and privacy with multiple routes of ingress and egress. The gangsters gave him the keys to a nondescript Ford Explorer, a long-term lease in the name of a shell company.

When he got to the house, the Tomador found a packet on the kitchen counter. Inside were photos and details of his target and directions to a farm north of Brooksville, where he would find custom-made ammunition, a rifle built to his precise specifications, and the space to zero the rifle at distances up to a thousand yards. He would head to the farm in two days. But first, he needed to acquire the target.

He began familiarizing himself with the area around Wolf's house and his likely routes to and from work.

63

Kojack's Tampa, Florida

The next day was a typical hot and humid Tampa day. Wolf found Gates sitting in the shade at the corner of the veranda in a chair facing the street. They ordered and didn't have to wait long for their soft-shell crab sandwiches to arrive.

"Seems like trouble has a habit of following you," the colonel said. "Tell me what happened during your training mission."

"Well, sir, that may be." he started to reply with a laugh as he bent down to pick up his napkin that had blown off the table.

Zip – thwack - boom.

The front of Gates' chest exploded across the table. Screams, shouts, diners scrambling, chaos. He stared wide-eyed but un-seeing, then his lifeless body slumped over the table. A second shot rang out and carved a groove into the table where he'd been sitting.

Wolf dropped and drew his pistol while he scanned his surroundings. He surveyed the area and found what appeared to be a repairman on a telephone pole, but the man wasn't holding a weapon.

The sniper fired three more rounds in Wolf's direction. He moved left and, before pulling Gates to the tiled patio floor, fired three shots back at the rooftop he suspected concealed the sniper.

He dragged Gates back toward the bar through the jumble of chairs and tables left by the fleeing lunch crowd. He knew it was useless, but he checked the colonel for a pulse. There wasn't one.

The bartender, a retired Marine, ran over holding a Glock in one hand and a towel and tablecloth in the other. "Are you hit?"

"I'm okay." Wolf said and wiped blood and bone from the back of his neck and head. Then he covered Gates with the tablecloth and lowered his head for a brief, silent request to his spirit guide. The request ended with I'm killing every one of them.

Police sirens were coming. He stood. The cartel was trying to kill him, and in the process, killed his friend. There was no turning back now.

You want me, you got me.

The lunch crowd had fled, but the street was filling back up with spectators since the shooting had stopped. He called Kennedy and briefed him on what had occurred.

"Call 9-1-1 and tell them armed civilians are on this scene," he said. "Then, I suppose brief Ops and get the casualty assistance office engaged."

"Will do," Kennedy said. "But you also need to know, your friend Victor Cárdenas is dead."

"What?" Wolf growled.

"Major Gonzalez called. Said they got him coming home from work with an IED. Gonzalez mobilized a team from his Lion Squadron, and they got Cárdenas's family to safety."

"No, no, no ..." Wolf rubbed his weary eyes. "He was a such good man." His heart pounded. There were so many deaths, and for what? Because he wanted revenge? Gates had told him revenge was a dead-end street. And now the cartel had killed people he loved and admired.

"Something or someone has gotten to Alejandro," Kennedy said. "He's acting out of character, so my guess is El Chapo has motivated him."

"The cops are here," he said and ended the call.

Wolf put his unloaded handgun on the floor, stepped back, and raised his hands. Officers approached and entered the restaurant with weapons drawn. They ordered him to kick his weapon and magazine across the floor to police, then told to knee. Then they handcuffed him and brought him to his feet, and searched.

Once he'd identified himself and provided a thumbnail sketch of what had happened, they removed Wolf's cuffs. A detective who was a reservist on base recognized him, and they talked at length about Gates murder.

The site commander brought in a group of officer trainees to deploy a barrier system providing privacy for the CSI team. The evidence techs split up. One started at the table, the other drove over to the condo building. A crime scene specialist asked for Wolf's shirt, citing the need to test it for DNA and particles from the bullet that had taken Gates' life. He was ready to give it up.

The bartender offered Wolf a T-shirt with the bar logo emblazoned on the back, and he was happy to pull it on.

His mind was already in Mexico. Guilt crowded his thoughts out and it weighed on him. Cárdenas had always been in the cartel's crosshairs for being a cop, but his death directly resulted from knowing Wolf. I can't let this go unanswered.

It was early afternoon when police let him leave the crime scene, and he went home to shower off and make a drink. The cartel needed to be stopped, and soon, before they threatened other innocent lives in his orbit.

The question hanging in the air was how best to do that and not get more of his family or friends killed.

Parker called. "I heard what happened. Are you okay?"

"I wasn't shot."

"That's not what I asked."

"Yeah, I'm good, thanks."

"I'm coming over."

When she arrived, she hugged him hard. "Lance, are you all

right?" They stood at the kitchen counter, not speaking. Wolf stared into a coke that he'd fortified with Jim Beam. There was intensity in the silence.

"What are you going to do?" she asked.

Wolf's eyes narrowed. "Take some vacation," he said, low and angry.

She could see that he was already in different geography, working through future tasks. She feared she knew what that meant, but all she could do was offer support.

"Do you want me to leave?"

"No." he said. He put the coffee cup on the counter and pulled her close. They spent the rest of the afternoon on the couch. Parker read, and Wolf stared off into space. She ordered delivery Chinese food. The bar shooting was the top news story on the six o'clock, so she changed the channel to the British ITN Channel.

Heartache and death were the headline stories in Europe too, so she turned it off.

Wolf read Marcus Aurelius. He was not interested in the stoic indifference of the moment but how to deal with it. He picked up a book by Japanese philosopher and martial artist Morihei Ueshiba, the founder of Aikido. He visualized getting inside the cartel's qi, redirecting their energy and resources, forcing the end of their reign.

Unlike the peaceful founder of Aikido, Wolf's vision was not to subdue. His was to destroy. He sighed and changed from daydreaming to planning his vacation.

Kennedy and Maya dropped by to share their condolences. He was polite as Kennedy told them about the pop-up wake the office staff had arranged at the Blue Gorilla.

A viewing and funeral would take place the following Wednesday. Gates' wife Dana wanted Wolf to speak. HE hoped Carlos would do the same for Cárdenas.

He would call Gonzalez in the morning. He was going to need his help once again, but this mission would be solo. No team, no safety net. No margin for error.

A saying from the famous Japanese swordsman and ronin Miyamoto Musashi's "Book of the Five Rings" placed Wolf on his terminal path.

"To win any battle, you must fight as if you are already dead."

64

Pinecastle Range Complex, Lake County, Florida
Unknown to but a few special access program-cleared personnel, the Navy and a landowner in Florida operated a training and staging area.

Its primary use, covert missions headed into the Southern Command area of operations. He made the two-hour drive north from Tampa to Pinecastle and checked in.

Wade Micanopy, the president of Micanopy Enterprises and a direct descendant of the Chief Micanopy who had led the Seminoles in the second Seminole war, ran the facility on behalf of the Navy.

As a natural extension of his patriotism, the Agency and special operations community also had free use of his adjacent land for training and pre-mission workups.

"Istonko, Hello Wolf," Jimmy said in his native Seminole.

"Kehee, Hello Jimmy," he said in Crow.

Jimmy nodded. "I got your message. Got you all set up, brother."

He spent the afternoon on the pistol range with a Makarov PB he had picked up at a local gun show. He used the shoot house to practice strong-hand and weak-hand shooting, combat reloads, and immediate-action drills.

He practiced one-handed reloading and clearing of malfunctions. He cleared rooms, lighted and not, making use of his high levels of rhodopsin to power the rods in his eyes and see in darkness like a cat.

Done for the day, Wolf cleaned the pistol and walked over to the facility chow hall for dinner. Wade's cooks always did a good job, but it was the surprise of finding old teammates present on other acres for their own pre-mission training that made the meal special.

They shared their condolences for Wolf's losses and their hate for the cartels. They talked about everything but current operations, as warriors do.

Wives, kids, and the latest RUMINT—rumor intelligence—on their friends, and a growing focus on the Middle East. Wade brought out a bottle of Jim Beam and everyone drank to each other's successes, lies, and war stories before calling it a night.

The next morning, after a breakfast of biscuits, sausage gravy, and eggs over-easy, he began his day with a folding-stock Kalashnikov AKMS he had bought at the same gun show where he'd snagged the Makarov.

He opened the spam can of Romanian ammunition and loaded six thirty-round magazines with twenty-eight rounds each.

Out on a deserted range, he followed the same training pattern as with the pistol, finishing up just after noon. He grabbed a burger and a couple of waters from the dining facility before stopping in the operations building to sign in for the demo area.

"First customer of the day. Only customer of the day. What do you need from me, kid?" asked the armorer, a grizzled retired U.S. Marine Corps master gunner.

Wolf handed the master gunner a sheet on which he'd checked various boxes. His signature was at the bottom.

"Two grenades, one pound of Semtex, four caps, fuse, igniters, two number-ten time pencils. Three twenty-ounce Diet Cokes."

The armorer handed him a clipboard. "Sign here for the range. Back in a minute."

When he returned, he placed a heavy brown cardboard box on the counter and countersigned Wolf's request chit.

"Outta Diet Coke."

He smiled. "No worries this will keep me busy."

He spent three hours recreating what he planned to build once in Mexico. He didn't need the time pencils or grenades, but they were fun to improvise with and examine the effects.

On the way out, Wolf gave Micanopy the Makarov and AKMS in thanks for the use of the facility.

"If you can't be safe, be violent, brother," Micanopy said with a wave.

"Safety is not part of the plan, bother," he said, head out the window before turning to focus on the road.

As WOLF DROVE from Phoenix across the border into Mexico, he completely missed the magnificent vista and stark beauty of the Organ Pipe Cactus National Forest. Under the seat next to him was a bag filled with Sinaloa Cartel high-value-target profiles and operational intelligence.

His first task was to retrieve the Russian weapons cache near Sasabe. Once he collected the weapons, the plan would become kinetic and terminal. The urgency driving him demanded action.

Guerrilla warfare as taught in Special Forces was all about maximum damage with minimum force. Strategic thinking applied to a tactical battle space.

Wolf was about to put his knowledge of the Cortes organization and its capabilities to a stress test.

He took his time driving to the coast, splitting the ten-hour drive into two peaceful days. He ate at the Soggy Peso and slept on Los Algodones Beach. For a moment, his trip had the trappings of a real vacation instead of prelude to war.

But war suited him. The closer to Los Mochis he got, the better his mood. He took a left on High- way 114 to sleepy Batebe, Sinaloa.

Carlos was waiting in the pre-arranged cantina meet location. Wolf thought he looked older.

"I should arrest and deport you," the Carlos said as they shook hands. "You should not be here. You can still go home and let the Cortes struggle with what you have already done."

He ignored the plea. "Good to see you too, Carlos. Did you bring what I asked?"

"Yes, and I have some Semtex this time. Is this another team mission?"

"Yes—army of one."

Gonzalez pondered that for a moment. "May God be with you, my brother."

"Thanks, God's not riding with me today."

THE CORTES RANCH stretched north from Charay to Macoyahui. Five miles wide at its base and ten miles long at its tip, the triangular property was his target. It would be suicide to try to hit the well-protected main house.

Wolf's plan was to start at the north end of the ranch and ride south, leaving havoc in his wake. He sang his death song and remembered his parents and dead friends. It felt strange to attack the Cortes family with a pellet gun, but it was the perfect delivery device.

In four hours, Wolf went through forty frozen pellets of toxin in the ranch's stalls and pens. Alejandro's prize bulls, cows, and Eliana's beloved horses would all be dead before the day was over.

Along the way, he poured gallons of gasoline and antifreeze into water tanks and wells. A little gas was all it took for three barns and the nearby fields to burn.

He wanted to stop and watch, maybe get a shot off at Alejandro, but he stayed true to his plan.

Mission number one accomplished, he headed toward Puerto Vallarta. The quarter moon and the cool night breeze were welcome partners on the drive south.

Soon, he would sing his death song again.

65

By The Sea RV Park, Puerto Vallarta, Jalisco

A lump formed in his throat as Wolf pulled into the seaside RV resort where his parents had last stayed. *The one time I accept my mother's offer to join them and it ends in death.*

He walked down the pier to Master Chief, a forty-five-foot deep-sea fishing charter boat that looked as solid as its captain.

John Irwin, U.S. Navy Master Chief Boatswain's Mate retired, gripped Wolf's hand. He stared at Wolf for a second or two, his deep ocean-blue eyes searching. Remembering.

"You remind me of your mother."

"Thank you. I appreciate that."

"I have no words for the loss of your parents. They were remarkable, loving people and I will miss them always." Irwin frowned. "The cartels are some nasty dudes."

Wolf's dry smile held no mirth. "So am I."

"I've heard. Your father bragged on you." He swung his arm over his shoulder like a father would. "How can I help you?"

"I've got some work to do, and I'd like to charter your boat. At some point soon, I think my being on the road will be too risky."

Wolf handed over a claymore bag. The bag didn't contain mines.

Irwin opened the flap and whistled.

"Twenty-five thousand for your help, another five thousand for fuel."

"I don't need your money, Lance, but it will pay for food and gas. Get your stuff on board and I'll put the vehicle in a friend's garage. No worries about security. He's working a contract in Costa Rica."

Wolf boarded the boat and Irwin introduced him to its secrets. Weapons and demo stowed, Irwin fixed some sandwiches and handed Wolf a soda.

"I think yours is Diet Coke, yes?"

Wolf chuckled as he accepted the ice-cold can, popped the pull tab and took a long drink. He handed the chief a Makarov PB. "Do you have a machinist that could hush-puppy this for me?"

"Hush puppy? Why don't you just take mine?" Irwin said, reaching under the table to retrieve a copy of the suppressed Smith and Wesson Model 39.

"Deniability. That's why I have all this Russian gear."

"Oh, got it. That's smart. Yeah, let me have that. I'll get him to work on it."

Wolf laid a map on the galley table. It amounted to a battle plan. Capitalized P's, and A's stretched from Puerto Vallarta to Los Mochis.

Chief ran his hand over the map, spending time to inspect each marking. He looked up at Wolf and laughed. "Targets. I love it. 'P' for production and 'A' for aviation?"

"Yes, I'm thinking the entire organization will come alive once I kick this hornet's nest, so I'm not sure about timing."

Irwin pointed to the map. "If you work this right, you can do two of these in a single night. But you'll have to pre-stage."

"What makes you think that?"

"I did a little running and gunning in Nam. It's where I met your stepdad."

"Phoenix program?"

"Yes. Andy said you knew Neil Gates. Sorry to hear about his murder."

"Thanks. I'd like to hear some more about those days and Andy when we have time. But for now, any suggestions?"

"Keep it random. Doing the same thing more than once will get you killed."

"Roger that. Do you have location where I can make some improvised?"

Irwin winked. "I do. You were a weapons guy, how'd you wrangle the demo schools at Indian Head and Harvey Point?"

"I volunteered when our demo guy's wife had their first kid. Great training and now, for the first time, useful information."

Wolf spent the afternoon at a rusty workshop next to the charter boat office, creating his improvised explosive devices. Semtex and grenades for the bang.

Old nuts, bolts, and chain links for the bloodbath. He took his time drilling into skydiving altimeters he brought, adjusting the trigger settings for different altitudes.

Mated with Semtex, he loaded them into surplus claymore bags. To secure his work until needed, He created a temporary hiding place for the IEDs in the ceiling over the charter office.

Back at the boat, Irwin had two large steaks covered in Montreal seasoning ready for the grill. He handed Wolf a beer and asked if he liked grilled vegetables.

He could tell Irwin wanted to know what had happened with his parents but wouldn't ask, so he recited history by starting with his parents' actions at El Gran Pez.

Then he recounted his brother and sister's help at the hospital and the fight at the airport. He kept Gonzalez's name out of the retelling. But at the end, he mentioned the killing of Gates and Cárdenas.

The next morning in the workshop, Wolf selected the best of the rifles and stripped it down, laying out the parts and inspecting them for wear and function.

He reassembled the rifle and ran through its immediate-action drills. He wanted the same level of muscle memory he had with his M4.

He donned the Russian chest rig and thigh holster, working through different scenarios and drills. Slow at first, then faster and faster until he flowed from AK to pistol and back without looking or thinking.

He ran the same routine with rifle to knife and pistol to knife.

Irwin entered the workshop greasy, sweaty, and smelling like gasoline from tuning the engines. "You're right-handed but left-eye dominant?" he asked.

"Yeah, one of the weird ones." Wolf shrugged.

"No, it's cool," he said. "Let's grab a bite at a dive I know. After lunch, you can practice with your weak hand."

Weak-hand practice took most of the afternoon. After getting to an acceptable level of fluidity, he turned to adjusting his combat rig.

His equipment ready, he headed back to the pier where Irwin had returned from a fishing charter. When he got on the boat, he dropped his kit bag and laid the map on the galley table, marking each target with a number.

Wolf assessed all his objectives with a critical eye. It was an enormous task. Were there too many targets? Were there too few?

"Master Chief, can I see you for a minute?" he said.

"Sure, 'master sergeant.' You can call me John, you know."

He laughed. "Force of habit. Yeah, I guess we don't have to stand on ceremony, right?"

Irwin gazed at the map. "What do the numbers mean?"

"Just numbers at this point. Thinking about what you said about not creating a pattern."

"There has to be a strategic first choice. Think bigger. Besides disrupting their operations, what is your ultimate endgame?"

Wolf's face hardened. "I want Alejandro and Eliana Cortes dead at my feet."

"I get it but let me tell you where I would start: Aviation. After your radiation event at the border, ground transportation must be affected. So, they must be relying more on air. Attack the planes and you are mission complete in two or three nights."

"Makes sense." He said and marked the map with red circles. "I'll focus on aircraft, but add in some production sites so as not to create a pattern."

Then he grabbed a notepad and made a mini map with coded reference marks and reminders only he could decipher. He hid grid coordinates in his Casio Data Bank watch and switched the language to Russian.

He took a minute and walked up on deck. The sunset presented its usual spectacular colors. Wolf took a moment to appreciate the view.

It was clear now why his parents had loved this place. For the beauty, and because his stepfather had a friend with whom he had shared the unbreakable bond of combat.

His parents died because they chose not to run away from the danger confronting them. It was in their blood to help others.

The apple doesn't fall far from the tree, he thought and spun to go back inside to grab his kit bag.

"See you in three days, master ch—uh, John. If I'm not back in four, do what you want with the weapons and gear."

Irwin shook his head. "Be smart, kid. Keep your ass and head down."

He nodded. Can't get my revenge if I'm hiding. It's time for in their face violence.

66

North of Mazatlan, Mexico

The moonless night was as dark as a West Virginia coal mine. Wolf drove the last two miles to his hide site with the headlights off, using night vision to navigate. He pulled the vehicle into a large stand of brush and dragged camo netting over it.

He armed a control panel and deployed battery-powered motion detectors then inserted an earpiece before trying for some shuteye.

What's the command to shut off my brain?

When he awoke a few hours later, the birds were chirping, and the heat of the morning sun warmed his skin. He stretched, feeling refreshed, and took a long drink from a water jug while surveying his position.

He scanned for signs of larger animals. Dogs, cattle, anything that might give him away if it alerted. He checked for human traffic, finding none.

Satisfied that he was secure for the moment, he calculated the distance and time to his first target, to the second target, and to the third. The rest of the day was long. He was used to hurry-up-and-wait, and this personal mission was no different.

Go now, his internal voice said. Wolf chuckled to himself and told the voice to wait.

"We'll attack soon enough," he whispered back. "We go when I say we go."

The ability to practice patience when surveilling people, convoys, and facilities for days and weeks on end had been a strength brought through from childhood.

He focused on staying hydrated and snacked on protein at regular intervals to keep his blood sugar level consistent. In the day's heat, he reset the alarm system and took a nap. Forty-five minutes later, he woke up soaked in sweat.

As he stood outside the Jeep, the breeze chilled him.

When the sun started to set, his adrenalin kicked in. He donned battle gear and painted his face an angry zig-zag pattern in green and black. He checked his weapons and kit once more before he stopped and sang his death song.

As he drove to the first target, the pattern of the targets jumped into his consciousness clear as a blue-sky morning. A subtle pattern, but distinct among the production sites and the airfields, created in the name of efficiency over security.

The azimuths for the airfields intersected nothing. No fields of marijuana, no mountainsides of coca, nothing.

There had to be an intermediary point for processing and packaging. Somewhere deep within his subconscious, he felt a connection. He set the thought aside to focus.

He stopped a mile from the first objective, concealed in the undergrowth on the far side of a ridgeline. He crossed through a nearby saddle and circled the runway and hangar until he could approach from downwind.

From his position just inside the tree line, he could make out the silhouettes of two airplanes, a Cessna 208 Caravan and a three-engine Britten-Norman BN2A Trislander.

No dogs, but three guards. Two at a time they patrolled the hangar and airplanes. The airstrip, just once.

Wolf watched them for an hour. Not once did they walk the tree line and there was no indication they ever had. Wolf removed his combat rig, taking only his pistol belt and two claymore bags. He worked his way through the tall grass to the Trislander.

He had to stand to reach the landing strut pod to place the IED. The wheel struts had a maintenance panel high up near the wing with just enough room.

There was little chance of the pilot uncovering it during a pre-flight walk-around. Pilots always checked the landing gear, tires, and brakes, but few ever checked the empty area best left to the mechanics.

Wolf retraced his steps back to the tree line, adjusting the grass as he passed to minimize his imprint. Moving around the hangar, he stopped at the road leading into the airfield and listened for movement. Hearing none, he sprinted across the road into the woods on the far side.

His line to the Cessna was on the wrong side of the aircraft to access the cargo pod. His only option, given the guards and access panels, was an approach from behind the aircraft.

Hidden from the patrolling guards but visible to anyone exiting the hangar, it was his only option.

Wolf slid up next to the building. He could hear a soccer game on a TV. Wolf low-crawled around the light from the corner to the rear of the Cessna.

He sat up and opened the pod hatch, placing the IED as far back as he could reach. He closed the hatch and rolled to the centerline face down in the shadow.

An overweight sentry with a slung rifle walked by, calling in for the soccer score. A voice yelled out, "One, zero!" The guard grumbled turned and plodded down the runway.

He made his way back to his combat rig and out to the Jeep. One down, two more to go. Target two was identical in layout and security, but with two Trislander aircraft.

When he got to target three, he saw the cartel's air ops had been enhanced. The aircraft looked new, and here there was a full squad of guards.

One walked too close to a small hut next to the hangar and two huge German Shepherds sprang out, snapping and barking at the guard.

Wolf suppressed a laugh as the guard jumped away in fear and a dark stain spread in the crotch of his khaki pants.

He took a deep breath, exhaling to settle himself. His need for vengeance denied him the option to pass on the target, however well defended it seemed to be.

The new plane could haul more and go farther than the other aircraft he'd seen. Wolf bet they transported leadership.

A Beechcraft King Air and a high-performance Pilatus PC-12 gleamed in the half light. They were well cared for, top-of-the-line civilian planes used by CEOs or as an ambulance in remote areas of the world.

The right landing gear wheel well was the best choice for IED placement on the King Air. On the Pilatus, the upper rear area of the nose wheel.

The area around the hangar and his targets was as bright as a car dealership. There wasn't a single viable option while the lights were on that allowed him to escape with his hide intact.

He eyeballed the black insulated cable leading from the hangar out to the wooden power pole. About twenty feet up was a gray transformer the size of the ones you would see near a house.

Right above it was a fuse. He knew that using the suppressed Makarov was his best option now that the machinist had built the slide lock.

Without the sounds of a cycling slide and with subsonic ammunition, the pistol was noiseless.

He crawled to thirty feet from the fuse and took careful aim. The shot destroyed the fuse with a loud pop of brilliant sparks. The lights in the hangar and most of the com- pound went dark.

Wolf ran to the planes.

The dogs barked and yelped as they found the end of their chains. The guards yelled, running in a pack back to the area of the transformer. He could hear them talking in rapid-fire Spanish about not seeing ghosts where there were none.

The final consensus by the clueless guards was that the darn thing had just blown out on its own.

As he sprinted back to his Jeep, he gave thanks that the sentries didn't think to unleash the dogs. For a moment, he thought about the pilots and their families. Regrettable, but they'd made their choice.

Anyone who works for a cartel is my enemy.

67

S   outh of Culiacan, Mexico
        Two more hours before daylight was just enough time to
        do a recon of the area that Wolf suspected held the pre-trans-
portation facility.

There had to be an intermediate location for processing the raw
material. Any building or complex of buildings used in drug manufacturing required considerable amounts of electric power.

Fixed or portable, power was the indicator he looked and listened
for. He tracked high-voltage lines to a substation with poles that fed
thick insulated wire into conduits buried in the ground.

He flipped down his night vision goggles and scanned the tree
line, looking for cameras. Out here it was safer to use the passive
NVGs instead of an infrared flashlight.

There was a high chance that some of the surveillance video
would cover the infrared spectrum. It would be like shining a flashlight right into a sentry's eyes.

There were six units focused into the clearing. At the nine o'clock
position from his point of view, he could see a dirt road and a dark
shadow. An underground facility? He searched the perimeter,

confirming the entrance and finding vents. At one vent there was an ether smell, and further on several air intakes.

In the back of the Jeep, Wolf found his solution. He had one chance to get it right. With no time or place to practice, he stood within five feet of the substation fence and spun a chain over his head like an Argentinian cowboy throwing a bolo.

He released the chain and thought he had wasted the opportunity. But one end caught an insulator connector and grabbed hold, then the other end wrapped over the charged line from another pole.

Sparks started flying as Wolf ran, and the transformer blew up with a violent thump. That was going to hurt. He pushed hard and arrived at the Jeep nervous about the coming dawn.

The sunrise cast golden rays as he redeployed the camo net and added branches and foliage to increase his concealment. He drank a long pull from a water jug and ate an MRE. Belly full, and satisfied with the night's achievements, he set the alarm panel for the motion sensors and dropped into a comfortable position.

The next morning, Wolf had to know if his plan had worked.

As dangerous as moving in daylight could be, he used an hour and forty minutes to get line of sight to a cell tower. He checked in with Gonzalez, who said the TV news was reporting the destruction of five aircraft. Five of seven—a seventy percent success rate.

Later in the afternoon, he fumbled the simple task of field stripping the Makarov. His sluggishness was a byproduct of feeding on hate and adrenalin instead of food and decent sleep. Not confident he could stay hyper-vigilant for much longer, he forced himself to drink and eat before surrendering to a power nap.

He drove further north, to the first target of the night. It appeared to be another packaging facility. He could see the ghostly images of the workers and guards through the plastic-sheet-type walls.

He crawled close to the north end and its debris field of empty fifty-five-gallon plastic drums. To his front, five drums stood on a wooden pedestal with hoses running back inside the facility. Using his Swiss Army knife, he pricked a hole in a drum. The smell of acetone didn't surprise him. They were making meth.

Wolf enlarged the hole and used a stick to create a channel for the flammable fluid back into the woods where the liquid pooled in a depression. With a grin, he pulled Andy's Vietnam Zippo lighter and ignited the acetone fumes.

He didn't wait to watch and sprinted away down a game trail. He didn't get forty feet when he felt the heat and shockwave of the first explosion and bits of flying debris crashing through the surrounding vegetation.

A secondary massive explosion almost knocked him on his butt before sucking the air out of the area.

His initial plan was to poison water and destroy the school buses used to transport the workers. He gave the school bus idea and its psychological impact a second thought. Would the poor folks so desperate for money stop getting on buses if he destroyed two or three? No, their poverty made the choice for them.

There was a moment of guilt, but it passed. I'm not ready to stop.

68

North of Culiacan, Mexico
Lessons learned from his target interdiction and exploitation courses came back to him as if he had just aced the tests. Wolf scanned the marijuana farm through the NVGs, looking for targets of opportunity.

A lazy quarter moon floating in wispy clouds provided ample illumination. He identified a primary well pump and three smaller distribution pumps. There were two diesel generators, but not much else.

Unlike the aviation targets, the guards at this facility stayed in their bunks, probably stoned from taking some of their compensation in trade. Wolf stood at the foot of each bunk. Left to right, one head shot each. No one stirred.

That's what you get for choosing the wrong profession.

He disconnected power and placed a Semtex charge on the backside of the relay panel, connecting his electric blasting cap on either side of the motor relay.

To the cartel, it would appear the starting of a generator caused an electrical fault that caused the pump to detonate. He rolled a barrel of diesel fuel over to the well, unscrewed the metal cap, and laid it over on its side gushing fuel.

Location prosecuted, he headed to his last, encountering a large black steer . He suppressed a smile, his mind creating a visual of the notification. "Former Green Beret Master Sergeant Lance Wolf gored to death in a road rage incident. Location, date, and time for BBQ to be announced."

This target was the most difficult. Wolf hid the Jeep and patrolled his way to it, staying off the switchback track. The terrain was rugged and hard to navigate in the forest's darkness.

They appeared to be alert and trained. Wolf took his time to inspect the objective. There were two bunkhouses full of workers and a third full of men with rifles in racks next to their bunks. Why all the soldiers out here?

Wolf thought back to the grainy aerial photo of the area Kennedy had provided. It hadn't revealed its true value. As he scanned the area, it stunned Wolf to see an immense field of opium poppies, twenty acres or more.

His mind raced. Guards, workers, cooking vats, poppy fields. He pulled back into the jungle to assess his options. No team. No Air Force to drop napalm on the entire crop at once.

What can I find to cause some mayhem?

He moved silently between the guards and found diesel, gasoline, and propane under an open-air storage canopy. Combined with his remaining kinetic assets, one grenade and two Semtex charges on five-minute timed fuses, it would have to do. He entered a small shed and set the grenade to booby-trap a stack of opium paste.

He poured gasoline over everything and dribbled it out to the stainless-steel opium cooking vats. He placed the two remaining Semtex charges on the propane tanks and pulled the Russian version of the M-60 fuse igniters.

Five minutes, time to go.

As he headed back to the wood line, the crack of bullets zipping by confirmed the sentries had spotted him. Crap, he thought, time to get loud to keep them occupied until the big party starts.

Wolf spun around and pulled the trigger of his AK twice, hitting the closest guard in the center chest. As the man dropped, another took his place, then three more.

They were popping out of the ground like mushrooms after a spring rain.

Then the lights came on in the bunkhouses. Wolf unloaded the rest of his magazine into the guards' bunkhouses, hoping to hit as many as possible.

Changing magazines on the move, he ran straight down the mountain, trying his best to not fall. The road was just below, but his momentum was too fast and when the hillside sloped away, he was airborne.

Wolf slammed his ankles together, hoping to land feet first. His instinct was to execute a rolling parachute landing fall.

He hit the dirt and rolled upright in one smooth move. Bullets tore at the dirt as he sprinted away then stopped behind a thick tree to catch his breath. Nothing hurt or seemed broken.

Random gunshots tore through the woods, but they were unfocused as his pursuers didn't know where he was. He fired controlled bursts on full auto, dropping two more attackers and slowing the rest for a second.

When they ducked for cover, he ran again. Sunrise filtered through the trees and that didn't work in his favor. He saw the next drop-off early enough to slow and slide down the embankment to the road. He turned right and sprinted, jumping off a boulder back into the woods.

The group chasing him emerged out onto the road, yelling loud frustrations at each other. He fired a full auto burst into the gaggle, reducing their number to only four.

He was about to engage the rest when he heard a truck rounding the switchback. Wolf ran through the trees, skidding to a stop at a forty-foot drop.

He spun and fired back as bullets cracked by. The guards were attacking him from three sides. Someone, likely former Mexican Army, called out maneuver commands.

He took a moment to read the situation and decided it was time to Superman.

He backed up several steps and hurled himself off the drop toward a copse of pine. His trajectory took him into the trees, but they didn't slow him down.

A branch caught his ankle, and he flipped over, face-planting on the rocky ground. A world speckled with impact stars spinning in his head, a stabbing poked at his side, and he didn't dare even touch his face yet for the intense pain and likely broken facial bones. As Wolf was trying to focus on what to do next the darkness took that decision away from him.

He didn't know how long he'd been out. As he gained awareness, Wolf moved muscles and limbs to see if his parts were still usable. Every movement tested his threshold, but he was breathing, lucid, and not captured. That was a good start.

He felt a trickle of blood on the side of his swollen face. He raised his head for a look-around and his neck dared him to do that again. At least there were no pursuers nearby, though he could hear their shouts and crashing through the woods searching for him.

He took a few painful breaths and slid up to rest against a pine tree and collect his wits. He did a self-assessment, finding a large gash on his forehead and cheek. He had broken or dislocated his left foot, but his boot contained the swelling.

He checked his AK, it was still functional. The front sight was bloody and his NVGs were gone. He could tell he had his Makarov by the pain in his thigh. He took it out of the holster anyway to check that it still cycled.

Wolf's first order of priority was mobility, so he rotated onto his side and placed his right boot over his left. He gritted his teeth, jerked back, and felt his ankle pop back into place.

He stood and was slow to place weight on his injured ankle. The pain did care, it seared up his leg. Wolf took a long drink from his water bladder. He looked back at the trees hiding him from his pursuers. They weren't far away, so he hobbled off toward the Jeep.

The trek back to his ad hoc base camp was slow and painful, but

Wolf gritted it out. He didn't waste time repacking the camo net. He had driven only about two kilometers when he rounded a corner and found cartel soldiers waiting for him.

He backed up as rounds hit the vehicle in several places. Hurt and angry, he continued to back up another hundred meters and stopped. He shuffled around to the back of the Jeep, tossing aside a blanket and retrieving his see you later message.

He peeked out from around the back and fired an RPG-7 at the cartel truck rounding the corner. The warhead detonated between the cab and the bed, a lucky direct hit on the fuel tank.

The two gunmen in the cab and three in the bed died in an instant. It blew another two of their comrades back as the truck lifted and rolled onto its side.

Wolf dropped the launcher, took a couple of steps and fired on full auto to make sure they were dead. At the Jeep, he reloaded the tube and gulped some water. It was time to bug out.

The sun was high, its warmth soaking his aching body, the humid air growing hotter as he left the mountains for the coast. After an hour of driving, he pulled to the side of the road, undressed, and poured water over his body.

He wiped away as much blood and dirt as he could, then used the rearview mirror to apply steri-strips to close the gashes on his face and forehead.

Wolf changed into clean clothes and taped his black-and-blue ankle before jamming it back into his boot and lacing it up tight. He checked and topped off the Jeep's radiator, then drained the jerry can of fuel into the gas tank.

Wolf stayed on back roads until almost dark. He knew he should wait for night but he didn't care.

I'll kill as many as I can before they get me.

69

Puerto Vallarta, Mexico

Back at the Master Chief, John guided Wolf's head into the light and examined his wounds. "Looks like you kicked over that hornet's nest, bud."

"Something like that." Wolf's left eye had swollen shut.

A dark bruise colored the left side of his face.

He used alcohol to clean the wounds. "Don't be a baby," he said as Wolf flinched.

"No. Just dislocated. I fixed it myself."

John chuckled. "Those gashes look bad. Do you want me to pull them together with butterflies?"

"Yeah, thanks."

He prepped the gashes and sprayed them with medical adhesive, then sealed them tight with butterfly closures.

"You'll live, brother. Couple of weeks and these will be barely visible enough to tell lies in the club about how you got your dueling scars."

Wolf chuckled. "You should have seen the other guys."

He took four Motrin 800s and slept the last of the night in the galley with ice on his face and ankle. He woke to Irwin replacing the bags of melted ice with fresh ones. He raised himself into a sitting position and groaned.

His body felt like both Major League Baseball All-Star teams had beaten him with a bat. He moved slow and deliberate, stretching through the pain.

He peered at Chief through his good eye. "How long did I sleep?"

"Thirteen hours."

Wolf put the new ice pack on his face. He took a second to breathe into the cold. "Anything in the press?"

Irwin made a face. "Yeah ... but not what you would expect, kid."

"What?"

"Here's the short version. The Mexican government has labeled you a terrorist. There is a million-dollar bounty for your capture. It's on every TV station and in all the newspapers."

He tried to rise and fell back onto the bench. He knew his actions risked putting himself in the crosshairs of the cartel. But he was impressed, the development was inspired. Cerebral, not muscular, uncommon for dope kings.

He had to hand it to the cartel. They got him on this one. Labeling him as a terrorist? It was smart. Too smart for Alejandro. It couldn't have been Martin Amaro—that snake had a lot to lose if his child trafficking came to light. Then he realized who was behind it.

El Chapo.

"Here, look." Irwin handed him a paper.

AMERUCAN TERRORIST LANCE WOLF, the headline screamed. An old picture of him accompanied the story. The blurry color photo from another guy's Facebook album of photos on Grenada.

The Mexican government offered a million-dollar reward for information leading to the capture of Mexico's most wanted.

Irwin laughed. "The picture must be close to twenty years old."

"Yeah," Wolf said, a wry half-grin creasing his face. He stared at the photo and thought about his brother, about Kennedy and Parker.

A sinking feeling swept over him when he wondered whether he'd ever see them again.

That bounty was a lot of money. Would someone he knew turn him in?

"I have to go," Wolf said.

"How you going to drive?"

"Get me to the Jeep. I'm putting you in danger just being here."

"Will you stop? The hit must've rung your bell good, kid. I like it."

"Like what?"

"The danger. Let them come. This old man still has danger in his blood."

"Okay, but this is a good time to, how'd you guys say it in Nam?—di di mau?"

Irwin let out a booming belly laugh. "Yes, little brother, we'll di di. Let me go ashore for supplies and we'll cast off."

While the chief was out, Wolf hobbled to the back of the galley and opened the hidden compartment. He grabbed two AKs and started his breakdown and function ritual.

Checks complete, he loaded four magazines for the AKs and three for the Makarov. He stashed the weapons in the compartment and was struggling to climb the steps up to the main deck when Irwin returned.

"Just like your Andy, stubborn to the bone. Sit here while I stow this stuff and then we're outta here."

Chief started the powerful engines, taking them back to a fast idle before casting off the lines. He scaled the ladder to the flying bridge.

He took the boat out of the harbor through the Bay of Banderas to the Pacific, turned north and added power to the engines until the boat leveled out on its trim tabs. He set the autopilot for north-northwest.

"It's twelve hours to Cabo. We'll stop there for gas. Maybe you should go below and get some more rest, kid." He smiled. "I got a feeling you're going to need it."

He stayed topside for a time, basking in the sun for an hour before heading below deck. He slept for four hours, ate some soup, and fell back asleep.

The pitch change in the motor sound woke him. He felt the boat coming off plane, the front settling. He tried looking nonchalant as he climbed into the galley, but he caught the fuel attendant noticing him.

Thirty minutes later, the fueling was complete, and they headed out of Cabo toward San Diego. Fifteen minutes out of the harbor, Irwin spotted a cigarette on a clear intercept course. He shouted to Wolf to stay below.

"Mexican Coast Guard if we're lucky, but most likely cartel. They're going to board us. I'll come to a stop." Irwin handed him a mask and flashlight.

"You'll find what you need behind a brass hatch in the keel." Irwin throttled back, and they settled into the calm water. "Get ready."

Wolf slipped on the dive mask, grunting at the pain as he tightened the strap for a good seal. As the cartel came alongside, he slipped into the water.

He dove to twenty feet where he could see the two hulls now alongside each other. Oriented, he swam back to the underside of Master Chief, turned on the flashlight, and found a brass hatch flush with the hull.

Inside was a Draeger rebreather used by special forces around the world. It didn't leave a bubble signature like regular scuba gear.

Wolf donned the Draeger and shined the flashlight deeper into the compartment. What he found looked like a homemade limpet mine wrapped with a length of time-delay fuse.

Right on, John!

The cartel cigarette boat's fiberglass hull negated any magnetic means of attachment, so he kicked toward its stern. Four massive Mercury outboards gave the boat its incredible speed. Mounted to a steel plate designed to handle the output of the motors, it was what he needed.

He broke the surface and listened. The crew was aboard tearing it apart in their effort to find him. The mine attached itself to the cartel boat with a soft click and he initiated the fuse.

He swam to the far side of the Master Chief. The cartel boat pushed away then roared off at full throttle. He waited until Irwin signaled the all-clear with two taps on the hull.

Back aboard, he found Irwin's face bloodied, his nose broken along with two fingers. He pointed them at Wolf, and they splayed in different directions.

"Grab them," he ordered. Wolf grabbed the man's fingers and Irwin yanked his hand back, which made a sickening grating sound along with his painful, jaw-clenched grunt. "Did you place the mine?" Irwin asked. "Yeah, on their stern plate."

"Then those bastards have ten minutes max before they report for duty with Davy Jones."

"It would have been smarter to let them go, I guess, but they're cartel, so screw them," he said.

Irwin grimaced. "Teach them to mess up my boat."

Irwin was stuffing Kleenex up his nose to stop the bleeding when the mine detonated. The bright flash of the gasoline-fed explosion was spectacular. Wolf dropped the binoculars, turned, and smiled.

"Lesson delivered."

Irwin started the engines, increasing the power until she was on the trim tabs again and headed for San Diego. "I'll take the first watch, kid. Get some rest, I'll wake you later."

He understood this pain-free period was temporary. The adrenalin would wear off soon and the aches would return. But his swim in the cold Pacific had helped, and he felt reinvigorated. He washed down four more Motrin 800s with water and lay back, his last thought before falling asleep Elle Parker.

Four hours later, Irwin woke him up to take his turn on watch. The boat was on autopilot, no steering or course corrections needed, and Wolf's only job to keep a lookout for commercial shipping.

The Milky Way and his favorite constellation, Orion, shone bright among billions of dusty stars in the night sky. Alone on the bridge, the boat humming along on a calm ocean, Wolf appreciated why men and women went to sea.

He tallied his wins. Would they all be for nothing? Would the U.S. government take the terrorist designation seriously? If Mexico as a sovereign neighbor nation made official requests for Wolf to be surrendered, it could go either way. And he still had work to do.

Alejandro and Eliana Cortes still walked the earth, and in his darkness, he was willing to give his own to make it happen.

70

USSOCOM Intelligence Division, Tampa, Florida
Kennedy sat at his desk, smiling at the news. The official memo noted his selection for Intelligence Warrant Officer training. He had an official billet number and instructions to report to the Fort Huachuca school three days before class to in-process.

His happy moment crashed to a stop when Marine Corps Colonel Eric Davidson appeared at his cube.

"Kennedy let's go. We have an appointment with the boss." When a full-bird colonel and the commander of the intelligence operations section refers to the boss, it only means one person.

Kennedy's mind raced as they walked to the front office with the rest of the counter-drug team members. The group entered the large lobby and were led by the executive assistant into the command conference room.

At one end of the long table sat the one-star Chief of Staff Brigadier General Horner, Judge Advocate General Brigadier General Stokes, and the respected chief of J2 intelligence, three-star Lieutenant General Mitch Courtland.

A stern-looking woman in civilian clothes entered the room and sat next to the J2. Everyone stood as SOCOM Commander General Anthony Davis entered and went to the head of the table.

"At ease, at ease," Davis said. "Take your seats."

It took several seconds for everyone to sit and settle. The seniors sat at the conference table and subordinates sat in chairs along the walls on two sides.

There was a moment of stillness and then Davis spoke.

"This morning I received a direct phone call from the Secretary of Defense relaying concerns the president and Secretary of State have with our Master Sergeant Lance Bear Wolf," he said, and paused. "The Mexican government has labeled him a fugitive terrorist and have instituted a nationwide hunt for him. They are asking for our help."

Kennedy struggled to keep his composure. He looked at Davidson and shook his head. Davidson's hand gesture said to stay quiet. The counter-drug team looked at each other, not sure what to think, or whether somehow, they were in trouble too.

"Staff Sergeant Kennedy, Colonel Davidson tells me you know Master Sergeant Wolf and can provide insight on recent events."

Kennedy rose from his place along the wall.

"Yes, sir, I know him. I'm not aware of the events of which you speak, but I can tell you what I know."

He recounted the murder of Wolf's parents at the hands of the Sinaloa Cartel and the Cortes family. He also reported on the attacks on Wolf's brother and sister, the Blue Gorilla attack, the one that had killed Colonel Gates, and the killing of and Mexican police Lieutenant Victor Cárdenas.

"As far as I'm aware, sir, Master Sergeant Wolf is on leave in Tucson attending to family matters and not in Mexico as claimed," Kennedy added. "If I may also say, sir, I believe this smear is a lie and the work of the Sinaloa Cartel using their sources and influence inside the Mexican government."

General Davis looked at the room. "You all know Alexandra Jones, our J2 deputy." He gestured to the woman on Courtland's left. "Alex, do you have a location?"

"Yes, we do." She glared at Kennedy, and he thought he might pee in his uniform pants right here in front of God and everybody.

"Master Sergeant Wolf is at his brother's house in metro Los Angeles recovering from a fall from the roof of his parents' house in Tucson."

Davis said, dryly, "Are you saying he has not, in fact, been in Mexico blowing up expensive airplanes and killing innocent farmers?"

"Sir, I'm saying we know where he is. We cannot say what he has been doing since he left Tampa."

The general looked to his JAG.

"Sir, Wolf is a Guardsman, not active Army, but of course he still falls under the Uniformed Code of Military Justice. To my knowledge, this is a first. A foreign government labeling an American as a terrorist."

"Options, anyone?" Davis asked.

Colonel Davidson stood. "Sir, I suggest we get the National Guard Bureau to put Master Sergeant Wolf on orders. Get him back here, then we can sort this out."

Kennedy surveyed the room. It did not appear to be a witch hunt. No one had advocated they turn him over to the Mexican government.

"Sir, if I may ask, what is the sentiment in Washington?" Kennedy asked.

Davis sighed. "No one is jumping to turn Wolf over to the Mexican government. But they want answers. Colonel, I'm placing you in charge of getting Wolf back here as soon as possible. Let General Horner know if you get any resistance from the National Guard."

"Yes, sir."

"Okay, that's all." Everyone stood when Davis stood, and they remained at attention until the general left. Kennedy surveyed his teammates. Their shaking heads and whispered conversations added to the shocking tone of the meeting.

"Come to my office, Kennedy," Colonel Davidson said.

"Yes, sir,"

Kennedy strode to his cube and started dialing. He left a fast voicemail for Parker. Then he called Bjorn and held on until voicemail picked up.

"It's Kennedy. Call me ASAP."

He made his way to Davidson's office, took a deep breath, and knocked before entering.

"Sir."

"Close the door and take a seat."

Davidson stood, looking out the window. He turned and sat on the front of his desk. "It doesn't take a genius to see that every time Wolf takes leave cartel members die in Mexico."

"Sir, since the breakup of Félix Gallardo's super cartel it's been war down there. Even here. We received intel that the Tijuana Cartel attempted to kill Eliana Cortes in Los Angeles."

"Don't patronize me, son."

"No, sir. I was just—"

"Stop. I know you and Wolf are buddies. I just hope it doesn't connect you with all this. I would hate to lose you." Kennedy chose not to respond, discretion being the better part of valor.

"I'll be in touch as needed. You do the same. Now, get back to work."

Kennedy spent the rest of the day collecting reports of violence in Sinaloa. It painted a different picture than the constructed story coming out of Mexico. Emergency services were denied access to aircraft "crash" sites.

Doctors reported deaths of cartel gunmen versus farmers. There were hints and inferences at destroyed product and production capability.

He understood the information would be of little help if the government turned Wolf over to the Mexicans. But it might mean something if the government prosecuted him in America. That the American government supported acts of terrorism on foreign soil was old news. It might be the leverage needed to keep Wolf out of jail.

He packed up for the day and headed toward his car. The parking lot was near empty. He grunted when he looked at his watch. He needed to pay more attention to the time.

He was starting his car when Parker jumped in the front passenger seat, startling him.

"What the—?"

"Drive off base," she ordered.

He drove, inventorying Parker's body language, tone of voice, and hyper vigilance. He headed north on Dale Mabry. They ended up in Rowlett Park. She got out without a word and walked toward the river.

She scanned the near empty park and selected a bench. They sat and Parker exhaled.

"I need answers. Has Wolf lost his mind? Are the stories true?"

"Can I call you Elle?".

"Sure."

He understood her anxiety. Getting involved with Wolf could do that to a person.

"One thing I know is Lance has not lost his mind." he said, hoping he sounded convincing. "He is not insane, nor is he a robot without feeling. When the Cortes group killed Colonel Gates and Lieutenant Cárdenas, he was furious and sad at the same time."

"I'm not sure I know him anymore," Parker said. "When I think about his dark side, my stomach churns. I don't I want to be with a person like that."

Kennedy nodded. "You've been to war. You understand. This is a war, not a declared, but a real shooting one. And the U.S. and Mexican governments haven't demonstrated the will to win it."

"But we have laws and a moral duty to follow them. It isn't right that Lance has declared war, even if it's against the Sinaloa Cartel we all despise." Parker said.

"I understand. Many honorable men have dark sides. We don't deny it. We are not weaker for it but stronger, because we embrace it and know when to use it. We use it for our country, our loved ones, our teammates. Maya and I would be dead if I had no dark side."

"That's my point. Has Lance lost his self-control, his humanity?"

The sky darkened, matching the mood. A heavy rain fell from the heavens that caused them to run back to his car and leave the park. Kennedy gave in to the storm and pulled over beneath an overpass for lack of visibility, which was an appropriate metaphor.

"I don't think so. Talk to him when he returns," he said knowing he couldn't see a path forward with Wolf, either.

71

Navajo Nation, northwestern New Mexico
Wolf helped Irwin dock and secure Master Chief, before heading to Bjorn's place in Orange County.

His plan was to stay with his brother to get his strength back. Then head back to Florida with a stop by his parents' house in Tucson to re-insert himself into his cover story.

Kennedy called Wolf on his second day in L.A., telling him of the federal shitstorm about to be unleashed. Wolf needed to be scarce a while longer.

It was Bjorn's idea to buy a student's car for cash. Wolf would drive from Los Angeles across I-10 to Tucson. After a day of rest and reflection at the house, he'd drive across the southern U.S. to get home at an unhurried pace.

But Wolf had a stop to make first. Once he'd stopped, he didn't care if the authorities captured him. But he would make the stop.

The Navajo Reservation in New Mexico, like many others throughout the U.S., had a broad-spectrum tired appearance that contrasted with gleaming new casinos. Wolf had not seen Sam and Ethel Nez in ten plus years. But they welcomed him with open arms despite his rolling in before dawn.

Ethel tended to his wounds. They sat on the back patio, drinking coffee and talking about his parents as the sun peaked over the horizon. They were old family friends: Wolf's stepfather and Sam had served together in Vietnam.

Ethel was slow to rise, announcing it was time for breakfast. She looked the same, just older and grayer. Her beautiful silver hair was long and braided in the traditional fashion.

"I'll fix your father's favorite," she said, shuffling off to the kitchen. "You will eat."

Sam watched his wife depart with a smile, then his face got serious and he turned to Wolf.

"So, what have you been up to? Is what the papers say true?"

Wolf shook his head. "Yes, and no. I did attack the Sinaloa Cartel. I destroyed some of their airplanes and damaged a couple of farms. They were growing marijuana and opium, but I did not kill innocent farmers. I killed enemy soldiers."

"Sounds like a hard mission," Sam said, nodding. "I know what that is like."

"Yes, sir. I know you do."

"Sam, can you help me?" Wolf asked. "I need your guidance and strength to finish my journey."

Sam nodded.

He made a call to tribal elders, and they prepared a sweat lodge. Wolf spent the rest of the day in prayer with his ancestors and parents. Wolf used cedar, sweetgrass, and bear root throughout the sweat. He pushed himself in meditation, forsaking his body as the last round of pours hit the stones. The spirituality of the sweat released the demons who scoured his soul, and he felt whole again.

At sunset, Wolf was renewed in body and spirit. He slept all night without waking and awoke ready to take on the world.

Sam and his Ethel rose with Wolf at dawn. Once Wolf packed his beat-up car, she hugged him, called him her son, and made him promise to be safe.

Sam put his arm around him and whispered. "People will hate you for being different and for not living by greater society's standards. But deep down, they often wish they had the courage to live the way you live, Lance Bear."

Then he spoke in his Wolf's native Crow. "Show them the path, Xaxxe Akduxxiile—fearless warrior."

Wolf pounded down the road with stops for fuel and bathroom breaks. He overnighted in Shreveport for six hours and was back on the road for Tampa before sun up. Wolf phoned Parker once but got voicemail. He longed to hold her, tell her everything was okay and that they would be okay.

He pulled into his driveway after the marathon cross-country drive. He was fatigued, but in a good way, like he'd just maxed an annual PT test. His heart rate and mind settled as he approached the front door.

When he opened it, he could see someone had been inside looking for something. Though there wasn't any unless the searchers had brought it with them.

"Crap," he said to the empty room. How they did it without serving him a search warrant was interesting, but irrelevant. He'd not been available.

He checked his things. Weapons, ammunition, and critical documents were untouched in his hidden safe room. But his office was empty.

The paper trail of his life—taxes, credit-card statements, expense reports, receipts, computers, even the printer—were all gone.

First things first. Organize your thoughts and story. Wolf grabbed a pen and paper, then thought better of it. No need to leave potential evidence of the lies he would tell.

I'm going to fail my next polygraph, he admitted to himself.

Pounding on his door jarred him from his thoughts. He looked through the peephole and exhaled.

"Brother, I'm glad you're here," Kennedy said as Wolf opened the door. "I've been waiting for you to get home."

He glanced over his shoulder as he entered, laughing at the rusty old Chrysler sedan in the driveway. "That's the best car you could get?"

"You said anonymous."

Wolf grabbed beers and handed one to Kennedy, turned on the TV and upped the volume. He recounted his time in Mexico, starting with meeting John Irwin. He worked through the airfields and the underground facility and continued with the farms, leaving out his killing of the guards.

Kennedy nodded at the mention of opium poppies. Wolf made light of his lacerated face getting into a fight with his AK as he's played superman into the trees.

Kennedy poked. "I think it's an improvement, though."

Wolf finished with an admission that he'd succumbed to the voice in his head that demanded revenge on the cartels.

Kennedy stood up. He stretched and shook his head like he was trying to dislodge what he'd just been told.

"If I hadn't put the mine on the fast boat that boarded Master Chief, those guys would have had nothing to report. And the cartel would still wonder if I was in Mexico."

Kennedy looked serious. "Yeah, well. Command wants to talk to you. Good news is they have nothing, and the front office is being cagey. But it seems predisposed to back the home team—that's you. The FBI and DEA are taking the Mexican government's lead and investigating you as a terrorist. Not a good label to have right now. You need to play the victim card all the way."

"Okay."

Wolf let Kennedy out and reactivated the house alarm system. He was planning to go to work in the morning, just like any other workday, even if it meant his detention. It was important to act as if was just another day, and seem above suspicion, if possible.

But what Kennedy told him had changed the calculus. Until this point, he'd gotten away relative unscathed way. He wondered how different tomorrow would be.

72

USSOCOM, Tampa, Florida

Wolf parked his truck in his usual assigned spot so anyone following could see him head into work. To be seen in plain sight was part of the plan.

The command was just coming off its overnight watch status into full operation at 0530. Wolf was in well ahead of his boss, so briefing him would wait.

He headed to the operations center to get a handle on upcoming ops requiring technical surveillance support. The duty officer looked at Wolf's beat up face for a long, uncertain moment, then began his situation report.

The update was longer than normal. The ops tempo had surged fourfold since he left. It would be a busy week.

He needed to have his intelligence support packages approved and in place early to minimize the time he would spend being questioned. His team was a good one, experienced and innovative.

They would make sure operations went off without a hitch.

Wolf had finished prepping the second package when he sensed movement over his shoulder. He looked up to find Parker standing in his doorway, her blank expression belying the seriousness of the day. "Come on in."

Wolf stood and hugged her, and she returned it. Parker touched the scar on his face. "Lance...look at you. Are you okay?"

He closed the door and spun. "I'm fine. The fall from the roof banged me up."

"Don't bullshit me. I thought you were dead or in jail. To be honest, who you have become scares me."

"Elle, I'm the same person I always was. You're still getting to know me. Yes, it was touch and go for a bit, but I hurt them, and they couldn't stop me. Now they're using political influence here to put pressure on me."

Parker crossed her arms. "When they find out the truth, they will bury you."

"They won't find the truth, at least not enough to convict me of anything. I'm the victim here. My parents are dead. They targeted my brother and sister with drive-by shootings. They sent gangsters to kill us at the Blue Gorilla."

Parker sighed. "The FBI has our files."

Wolf swallowed the lump in his throat. "It's okay, it's their process, right?. There's nothing actionable in them."

"The FBI will cross the border and talk to the police and Major Gonzalez."

Wolf put his hand on her arm. "I know. That works for us. It will be another dead end for them."

He stepped back and sat on the edge of his desk. "Look, you and I know they're going to question me for the next couple of weeks. At some point, they will question you, too. I suggest we go on living our normal lives. I'll suspend team activities until this blows over. Sound like a plan?"

Parker nodded but said nothing. The one thing he didn't count on was his relationship with her failing. If it happened, he wasn't prepared for it.

The FBI doesn't wait around to question suspects. To Wolf's surprise, they waited until office hours before showing up in his cube and holding out their credentials. So stereotypical, he had to suppress a laugh.

"Mr. Wolf, I am Special Agent Mark Townsend of the Federal Bureau of Investigation. This is Special Agent Timothy Clark." They pocketed their cred holders. "We need to talk."

"Sure," Wolf said affably. "Conference room, okay?" The agents nodded, and he led them to the room where Wolf sat at the head of the long table. They arrayed themselves on either side of him.

Clark pushed record on a small digital recorder and place it in from of Wolf, its bright red LED eye staring him in the face.

"Master Sergeant Wolf, you have the right to remain silent," Clark began. "Anything you say can and will be used against you in a court of law. You have the right to an attorney and to have one present before questioning. If you cannot afford an attorney, one will be provided for you. Do you understand these rights I've just read to you?"

"I do," Wolf said.

"With these rights in mind, are you willing to speak to me now?" Clark asked.

Wolf smiled. "Yes, let's talk."

Wolf spent the next two hours providing his day-by-day account of his actions and the events surrounding his parents' deaths. He left out his active role in Joaquin's capture and interrogation.

When asked, he acknowledged his knowing Major Carlos Gonzalez and police Lieutenant Victor Cárdenas. Townsend focused on the Blue Gorilla assassination attempt. Clark asked about his Sonoran mule deer hunting trip and recent visit to Los Angeles.

Then Townsend acknowledged it was his team who entered Wolf's house to gather evidence of possible improper use of government funds. The terrorism label had negated the need to serve a search warrant.

Wolf liked these agents. He appreciated their measured and low-pressure questions. But taking a liking to them, or anyone else associated with his investigation, could be dangerous. So, he let it go and replied to questioning with simple yes or no answers as much as he could.

As they left, Clark waited for Townsend to get out of earshot and then whispered to Wolf. "There's something shady about the Mexican government 'evidence,' so keep your chin up." Then, in a louder voice. "Here's my card. Please call if you remember anything else you think will be helpful."

"Thank you, Agent Clark."

Wolf held the card, then flipped it over.

California Senator was handwritten.

73

USSOCOM briefing room, Tampa, Florida

Wolf could tell from the looks he got the entire Command had heard about the FBI interview. Military admin staff who had never been downrange had labeled him a pariah.

The operators, men and women who had seen combat, nodded and whispered their support. Back in his office, he finished another package before calling Kennedy.

"Let's go for a run."

They met at the gym and ran out past the golf course toward the beach at an easy pace. As they passed the three-mile mark, Kennedy picked up the pace. "Did the FBI want what I think they wanted?"

"Well, they used terrorism as the excuse to no warrant search my house. On top of that, they're investigating me for misuse of government funds and murder."

Kennedy stopped. "What? I get the terrorism and funds misuse, but murder? Where did that come from?"

Wolf rolled his eyes. "The FBI said I'd have to request it through the courts. But one agent gave me a lead. It's a senator from California."

"Jesus. Politicians. I'll see what I can find out." Wolf took off sprinting.

"You know that doesn't work!" Kennedy shouted. It took longer than he expected to catch Wolf. As he passed him, Kennedy said, "Maya is faster than you, loser."

"Maya is faster than both of us!" Wolf said.

It was the DEA's turn in the late afternoon. Wolf went through his story again, changing it up from the FBI version, but not in a material way. The lead agent danced around, admitting Jose Torres had been an informant.

His death must have ended an important flow of information. Wolf didn't care. Their propensity to turn someone and leave them in place made no sense. To let the cartel continue to flow drugs into the U.S. pissed him off, but he hid it.

The interview ended close to dinnertime. He walked the agents out, shook hands, and assured them he was available as needed.

Wolf jumped in his truck with Parker on his mind. It didn't take long to see he was being followed by four shadowy men in a black Suburban with dark window tint.

Wolf reached for his pistol. His sixth sense screamed at him, prepare to fight. Then a government-issued sedan elbowed its way between the tail and his truck. Bad guys and FBI, he thought. Offsetting penalties.

The bad guys broke off leaving just the FBI. The G-car with two men in it backed off to a respectful distance, and Wolf relaxed. He was happy for the timely support the FBI had provided.

At home, Wolf went straight to the intrusion detection LED he had hidden in a bookcase corner. There it was, flashing its warning. Intuition and recent events said it wasn't a false alarm. He moved into a close combat handgun stance, Browning High Power at the ready.

He scanned the hallway, looking for the smallest sign of disturbance. His mother would have said, "It's your warrior spirit protecting you—listen to it, let it speak to you."

He cleared the front bedroom, then the bathroom. His first sign was in the kitchen. A butcher knife was not in its place.

Then he cleared the middle bedroom and garage. He found the second and third clues in the master bedroom. Fingerprints on family pictures.

In the laundry room, Wolf pulled a hinged storage rack away from the wall and stepped into his gun locker. He rewound the video recorder to the time of the first hit and stared into the screen at the intruder's masked face.

Average size and build, nothing remarkable. No visible tattoos or scars. Precise foot placement. It had to be the assassin.

Wolf imagined he was adept at blending in, hiding in plain sight, moving without being noticed in public. He would be almost impossible to track and kill.

To gain entry, he had defeated the alarm sensor on the side door of the garage, disabling the siren and flashing light. His moves had been precise.

No gloves, not worried about leaving fingerprints or DNA. Wolf finished watching the video and replaced the recorded tape with a new blank one. He would fix the disabled siren and light later.

In the shower, he wondered who had sent the intruder. Eliana made the most sense, but he wouldn't rule out Alejandro or even El Chapo. Once again, anyone and everyone around him was in danger.

As he drove over to Parker's house, he executed a surveillance detection route, pulling to the curb after a left. He spotted a government car as it drove past. There was no telling how many other cars were following him.

Come on, let's finish the fight!

74

FBI field office, Tampa, Florida

Wolf's world started coming apart at 0500. He and Parker had stayed up all night, working through what he had done in Mexico.

He was honest about his descent into darkness and his fight to not become ruthless like the cartel but failing at that. But he kept his bouts of pure evil to himself. If they scare me, he thought, they'll make her run.

Parker made Cuban coffee. Wolf watched as the thick condensed milk poured out of the can. He was taking a long pull of the hot and sweet drink when the doorbell rang, and he caught movement out back.

They both grabbed for their pistols. Walking to the front door, he peered through the side window to see five men in suits. The man in front was holding up a leather folder with FBI creds and a gold badge.

"It's the FBI." Wolf handed her his weapon. "Hide the guns."

He opened the door all the way and kept his hands in view so the agents could verify he did not present a threat.

"Good morning, gents. How can I help you?"

"Sir, my name is Special Agent Bill Steadman. We're from the FBI. Would you step outside for me, please?"

"Agent Clark go on leave?"

Steadman drew breath to answer, but Parker appeared then, her own badge swinging from a beaded chain around her neck. She pushed Wolf aside and stepped in front of him.

"What are you doing on my property, Special Agent Steadman?"

"Ma'am, we're here to bring Lance Bear Wolf into custody."

"May I see a warrant for this arrest?"

"No, ma'am, not at this time, but it's on the way."

"Well then, my profound advice is you get the heck—"

Wolf laid his hand on Parker's shoulder and took a step forward.

"Elle, stop. It's okay. I'll go with them."

"What? Why? You know you don't have to go with them, right?" Her head tilted and eyes widened.

"Yeah, I know, but I have done nothing wrong, and arguing only forestalls the inevitable." He turned to Agent Steadman. "Right?"

Steadman nodded behind his Ray-Bans. "Yes, sir, pretty much it does."

Cuffed and held by an agent on either side, they took him to a car.

"Aren't you going to read him his rights?" Parker demanded.

"Ma'am, I see you're a badge carrier, so I suppose you well know he doesn't need his Miranda warning unless we're asking him questions. I promise you I'm not the interrogator, just the delivery man."

He pulled a business card from his shirt pocket. "This is me, if you have questions."

"No worries," Wolf said to Parker. "I'll call you to come get me."

They took him to Hillsborough County and processed him like any other criminal, fingerprints, pictures, and a different agent read him his rights.

They put him in an interview room and hand- cuffed him to the table. The FBI followed their rote script, leaving him alone to stew.

Thirty minutes later, a new suit walked in. He was followed by what had to be a newbie fresh from the FBI Academy based on the anxiety shown on her face. They took seats opposite Wolf.

New Suit was a good six-two, square shoulders, a decent college football player, no doubt, but not good enough for the NFL. Dark tan. Pearly white teeth.

New Suit laid out what appeared to be a copy of Wolf's military service record and two folders. One labeled MEXICO and the second labeled LOS ANGELES.

He reached for his credentials, holding it out at eye level. "I'm Special Agent in Charge Andrew Stockwell. With me is Monica Helms." She nodded.

"Kicking off with the SAIC. Nice touch. I'm not that important, to be honest. So, how can I help you?"

"Mr. Wolf, before I start, you are aware of your Constitutional rights, correct?"

"Yes, sir. But it's Master Sergeant Lance Bear Wolf, for the record. I believe you are recording, so let's get the details out early."

Stockwell nodded. "All right, understood. Do you wish to have an attorney present before we go any further?"

"I reserve my right to an attorney, of course, but it isn't necessary at this time."

"Mr. Wolf, the FBI, in its role as lead agency, is investigating you for terrorist acts and homicide. You are also under investigation for misappropriation of government funds and property in the commission of your crimes." Stockwell sat back with a wry smile, as if his work was already done.

"For the record, I want to state that I am the victim here, and the allegations against me are false."

"Thank you, Mr. Wolf. Let's start with your service record and training. Most is redacted, so let's focus on your training. It gives you a unique perspective and the skills to commit your crimes, does it not?" Stockwell asked.

"I've committed no crimes and you have yet to allege any. What it gives me are the tools to protect and serve my country."

"Please explain this acronym SOTIC."

"Special Operations Target Interdiction Course." "And this one: SAFARTAETC."

"Special Forces Advanced Reconnaissance, Target Analysis, and Exploitation Techniques Course."

"So, tell me how and where you have used these courses in the support of our nation?"

Wolf laughed. Stockwell did not take it well, and his irritation showed. Helms fidgeted, unsure of how she was expected to act.

"I'm happy to tell you about basic training and my time as a Ranger, and my Special Forces selection. You are not cleared for the rest. So, why don't we just move on to your Mexico folder?"

A red-faced Stockwell pushed Wolf's service record to the side. He made a big show of laying out the evidence of his alleged terrorist activities in Mexico. Back and forth they volleyed. Accusations and denials.

Stockwell never admitting the photograph showing a dark, blurry figure wasn't usable in a court of law.

"This is you firing the weapon, isn't it?" Stockwell demanded.

Wolf leaned forward to view the pictures and laughed.

"This is your evidence?" He placed an index finger on the silhouette of a man shooting. "A first-year law student wouldn't have to work very hard to convince a jury that this is Bigfoot."

Wolf punched holes in every line of questioning. They stopped for lunch and Wolf got jail food: a dry bologna sandwich, potato chips, and a Diet Pepsi. He asked for more coffee. He knew it was going to be a long day.

Stockwell left the room to take a call. He nodded at Helms, and she resumed questioning. To Wolf's surprise, she was good. He guessed she had a master's in criminal psychology.

He understood why she worked alongside Stockwell. She turned up the emotional volume, playing on his grief, anger, and hate for the cartel.

"He left you holding the bag, Agent Helms."

"You can call me Lance."

Okay, so this is a new direction.

"We have a witness from the Blue Gorilla who heard you say, 'I want to kill them all.'" Helms said. "And now we know you meant all Mexicans."

That surprised Wolf. "Okay, yes. I said it. I was angry at the cartel, but that was heat of the moment, just anger, not action. I have no beef with the average Mexican or anyone else."

"Of course, you turned to violence, didn't you? You needed revenge. You couldn't protect your mother and that failure enraged you against others you saw as the reason for her death."

They must have gotten access to his psychologist's notes. So much for doctor-patient confidentiality. He hadn't told a soul of his visits to the woman he referred to as his headshrinker.

The paper trail of his payments for the sessions was the likely tipoff.

Helms walked behind him. "Your mother died because of you, didn't she? You are a weakling. A scared little man who couldn't save the woman who gave you life. The woman who protected you your whole pathetic life."

That was workman-like, but over the top. Wolf knew this game, so he pushed back.

"Let me guess—your daddy wanted a boy, didn't he? He wanted a son to keep the bloodline going, and what he got was you. Your birth must have crushed him."

Wolf had a solid feeling that she wouldn't appreciate blatant misogyny. The red face and lowered eyes told him he'd hit pay dirt.

"You're not a real sworn agent, are you? You're a criminologist. A support puke, a civilian. At least if you had made it through the academy, your father could have bragged about it at the golf club.

"Sorry, honey, but you're a disappointment to your family and your profession, and always will be."

Time to bring her in.

"Helms, look—I know you because I am you. I was my family's disappointment, too," Wolf said. It was a lie, but this was theater.

"So, let's stop the bull. I need you and the FBI to team with the Mexican government to bring the cartel to justice."

Stockwell burst back in the room. He cursed under his breath, telling Helms to take a break. She left in a hurry without looking back at Wolf.

"Listen, dirtbag, we have your call records." He waved a printout in front of Wolf's face that had a line item highlighted in bright yellow. "Whose number is this?"

Wolf looked at the number and smiled. "You already know."

"Yes, we do. Major Carlos Gonzalez, your Mexican partner in these crimes."

"You know, Stockwell, in my line of work I expect a certain level of professionalism. Until now I didn't think you were plain stupid, but now I'm not sure. Let me save you and your team some time."

Wolf told how he had met Gonzalez and his team, and the connection to Hector and El Gran Pez. He explained how Gonzalez had helped Cárdenas in his police investigation. The rest he left unsaid. Stockwell nodded. Something about him changed. Wolf sensed a new confidence.

"Tell me, Mr. Wolf, who does this number belong to? Never mind. Let me tell you. It belongs to the DEA. It is a protected number known only to one deep-cover cartel informant."

The number from Jose Torres's cellphone? Brain racing, Wolf inhaled, visualizing his programming. He pictured himself falling backward into a warm pool of emptiness. It was a protective measure taught by the Agency.

Stockwell noticed the change and slammed a fist into the table. "Answer me!"

Wolf had a blank stare. His response was in a monotone and unflinching. "Lieutenant Cárdenas didn't tell me. He just asked me to call the number."

"You know we're going to check your story and find your lies."

"Be my guest. I can't tell you anything, no one answered."

By early evening, Stockwell decided he had finished his work for the day.

"How about my call?" Wolf asked.

"Yeah, sure."

Stockwell released him from the interview table and the two agents led him to an adjacent office with a desk phone. The agents stood by as he dialed Parker.

"Elle, they're keeping me. I'll be in front of a judge tomorrow."

"Call Gates for me. I love you. Be careful."

75

Orient Road Jail (ORJ), Tampa, Florida

At the Hillsborough County jail, known as ORJ, they locked him in a cell by himself. Wolf scanned his surroundings and exhaled. On the positive side, he thought, I won't have to fight tonight.

The jailers woke everyone at 0330. At his in-processing, he had learned the times to eat—0400 for breakfast, 1000 for lunch, and 1600 for dinner. Wolf stayed by himself during breakfast, perusing the inmates to figure out who might help him if he needed it.

He was one of the best-trained men in the place, though, and thought he'd fare all right solo.

After morning lockdown from 0500 to 0800, cell doors opened, and officers walked his pod out to the yard for a break. He walked over to two guys he identified with eagle, globe and anchor tattoos.

"How much longer you here?" he asked the former Marines.

"You takin' a friccken' survey?" the man asked.

"I'm Wolf. You guys served together in the 1st MARDIV Recon?"

"So what?"

"I worked with some of your buddies in Colombia, recon training for a special counter-drug unit."

"We were there, too. Been here three, got three to go. I'm Amato, this is Russo."

Wolf swapped handshakes with both men. Russo held his grip, looking at Wolf.

"Hey, you're the guy from TV they're calling a terrorist, right?"

"Yeah. It's a lie, but it's me."

"The Kings tried to kill you at the Blue Gorilla?" Amato said.

"Yeah. Sinaloa sent them."

Amato scowled. "The Kings are expanding beyond drugs and moving in on our business."

"I might need your help in here if they send someone. I can pay for protection."

"Not a problem. We got your six, brother," Russo said.

The inmates went from the yard to lunch. Wolf sat by himself, his new friends facing him a table away. Wolf was about to eat a forkful of Salisbury steak when Amato shouted a warning.

Wolf spun to clear the bench, crouched, fork at the ready. A man stood there looking like he was going to attack, but still talking himself into it, a definite meth head. Eyes wide as saucers and eyes blood red from lack of sleep. The meth head was clutching a four-inch shiv.

Wolf grabbed his tray as those eating around him cleared out. His attacker dove, screaming his slashes wild.

Wolf blocked the shiv with the tray and buried the sharp end of his fork in the man's arm. As the attacker pulled back, he dropped the shiv and grabbed at the fork. Wolf side-kicked the meth head's knee, breaking it with a sickening crack.

The man's scream changed to one of pain as he dropped. Wolf knocked him out with a left to the jaw. Then he walked over to the wall and assumed the position as correctional officers rushed over.

He looked over his shoulder at Russo and Amato, who had blocked the aisle among the milling crowd of onlookers. He nodded, and they relaxed to let the officer's pass.

Without a word, two bulls shackled Wolf's hands and feet, dragging him to a holding cell. Wolf was trying to get comfortable when a lieutenant and two massive officers opened the cell door.

"Get up, Wolf. I saw the video. You can go back to your cell." "Thank you, sir."

As he was being escorted out, the lieutenant stopped and whispered to Wolf. "I hope what they say about you is true. I lost a young nephew to drugs. Someone needs to take the fight to them."

They kept Wolf in his cell for protective lockdown until the marshals transported him to the FBI field office for more questioning. Stockwell started again, this time with the LOS ANGELES folder laid out across the table.

He tried to link Wolf to the Eliana hits and destruction of U.S. government property at the Compton airport. Photos taken from security video cameras at the various sites showed two men throwing firebombs and shooting at various warehouses.

Stockwell pushed across the table a grainy photo of Lizzy Armstrong as "Eliana," with Wolf and Bjorn from an off-angle video camera. As hot as it had been, Wolf's insistence on full coverage from head to toe, had blunted any chance of identification.

"Think about it, Stockwell. All the history between El Chapo and the Félix brothers. Add into the mix the Cortes running the West Coast business for the Sinaloa Cartel, and it's an all-out war with these people.

"Talk to the guys at the DEA. Did you know it was the Tijuana Cartel that tried to kill Eliana south of San Diego?"

Stockwell paused, considering what Wolf had said.

Am I finally getting through to this guy? Wolf wondered.

The door opened without a knock and Stockwell spun to see who had interrupted his interview. Wolf sat stunned, staring at Army JAG Major Steve Gates standing in the doorway, all dress green uniform, spit-shined jump boots, and tan beret.

"Special Agent Stockwell, meet Army Major Steve Gates, Judge Advocate General." Wolf said with a sly grin.

Gates looked at Stockwell and spoke in his well-modulated command voice.

"Agent Stockwell, be advised that under the provisions of 32 USC 110, Part 564, Subchapter E, this man has been mobilized to active-duty status in the Florida Army National Guard. As he is no longer a civilian, I am now his legal representation. You may leave now so I may consult with my client."

He pointed an index finger at Stockwell. "I'll instruct you to hit pause on the recorders."

The SAIC frowned, collected his documents, and slammed the door as he left. Gates waited a good two minutes to allow time for the room recorders to be switched off.

Wolf dragged the table with him as he stood to shake hands with Gates.

"Real good to see you, sir. Was that mumbo-jumbo for real?"

Gates laughed and shrugged. "I don't know. More or less. I get the titles and subchapters mixed up from time to time, but it sounded good. The fact is they brought on you on active duty and I am your lawyer for whatever happens next."

Gates frowned. "That could be good news or bad news for you, of course. SOCOM assigned me and I've already petitioned the court for a hearing tomorrow morning. The fibs have plenty of hearsay, but no actual evidence to prosecute you with."

"Roger that." Wolf said, shoulders dropping.

"For now, keep to your story." He shook Wolf's hand and grasped a shoulder. "One more night in ORJ and we'll get you home."

Gates opened the door. "Special Agent in Charge Stockwell, thank you for the courtesy. Please join us. I have instructed Master Sergeant Wolf to continue answering your questions."

Wolf suppressed a smile. Stockwell looked confused. The smug look on Gates's face seemed to have worried him.

"Mr. Wolf, let us get back to your attack on the warehouse at the Compton airport."

"That's Master Sergeant Wolf, Agent Stockwell. And I caution you not to assume facts not in evidence." Gates said.

Stockwell cleared his throat. "Yeah, we covered that before you got here, but whatever. Master Sergeant Wolf, we have photos. Our photo analysts estimated the heights of the two males, and they match those of you and your brother."

"How many pairs of brothers in the United States do you suppose have those same dimensions?" Wolf said inside a chuckle. Stockwell bristled.

"He's right," Gates said. "There must be hundreds of thousands or more given the two hundred and seventy-five million people in the U.S."

Stockwell's face again took on the appearance of a bright red Beefsteak tomato.

"I'm done here," he said, rising and storming from the room.

"It's for the best," Gates said with a grin.

Two U.S. Marshals entered and shackled Wolf. Gates told him to be ready this next morning for transport to a hearing with Chief Judge Douglas Stevens.

The marshals escorted him to the sidewalk and handed him over to ORJ corrections officers. At the jail, the officers and Wolf approached the outbound phone bank on the way back to his cell. "May I use the phone, please?" Wolf asked.

"Sure. Keep it short," the officer said.

He called Parker collect. She answered on the first ring. "Elle, it's me. How are you are you, sweetheart?"

"Good...Lance, are you okay? Major Gates called and briefed me. I'll be there for you tomorrow."

"I'm good. I made friends with a couple of former recon Marines, just in case."

"Well, update du jour, the command is investigating me too now, and they're hammering Kennedy."

"I'm sorry I got the two of you involved in all of this."

"We made our choices. I would do it all over again. I love you."

The officer interrupted. "Wolf, it's time."

"Gotta go. See you tomorrow."

Wolf's cell door shut with the familiar clang of steel on steel. The electronic deadbolt thudded into place.

It was library night at ORJ, and a friendly inmate pushed a book cart around the pod. Moby Dick caught Wolf's eye. He spent the next six hours reading. The visual painted by Herman Melville's master-piece was familiar. The final chase taking place over three long days, culminating in three attempts to kill the whale. Each one ended in disaster, but Captain Ahab kept going. In the last attempt, he got caught in the harpoon line. He drowned as the behemoth white whale dove to the depths of the sea.

Melville's famous line stuck with Wolf as he fell asleep.

"To the last, I grapple with thee. From Hell's heart, I stab at thee. For hate's sake, I spit my last breath at thee."

Wolf was fighting an unseen enemy in his dreams. He was drowning in a quicksand of white powder when the jail loudspeaker woke them up a 0330. He sat next to Russo and Amato, and they ate in silence.

The eggs and famous Jail House Fire Hot Sauce wasn't any more appealing than it had been any other day. Back in his cell, waiting for the marshals, an officer appeared with a suit bag.

"Wolf, your wife brought this for you."

Wife. I like that.

He shaved, using the icy water to lubricate his face. The five-cent, single-blade, plastic razor scraped more than cut away his stubble. He shined his boots with the can of black polish and piece of cotton T-shirt Parker included in the bag.

The ritual of shining his jump boots was calming. A smile broke across his face at the reflection in the toe. Countless instructors and senior NCOs over the years had told him discipline in the little things added up to discipline in life.

Discipline equals winning—first over yourself, then over your enemies.

76

United States District Court for the Middle District of Florida, Tampa, Florida

Elle adjusted his tie. They were at the federal courthouse and the marshals had given her fifteen minutes with Wolf.

He felt closer to her than ever, and he couldn't wait until this was all over and he could wrap his arms around her for long periods of time.

"You ready for this?" she asked.

"Yes. Gates will do the talking."

"I pray this works out. I want you at home."

Wolf hugged Elle as best as his shackles allowed.

"Me, too. This is just the first step, though. Stockwell wants to put me away for a long time."

"Lots of external influence at play, and who knows who's applying the pressure." Elle said.

"I gave Kennedy a lead, but I'm not sure he can work it if he is getting hammered."

"Who?" Elle asked. "Maybe I can get somewhere." Wolf whispered, "One of the California senators."

She looked stunned then recovered. "Okay, I'll run it down. I'm not sure what committees they serve on, but it's a good place to start."

"Ma'am, excuse me," the marshal interrupted.

"It's time to go, master sergeant."

Gates waited for him in the courtroom. They unshackled him and he sat next to his lawyer, with a bailiff and two U.S. Marshals behind him. Two bailiffs posted on either side of the judge's stand.

At the prosecution table sat Carolyn Moore, the U.S. Attorney for the Middle District of Florida. Next to her was a second chair from the DEA legal office, and Stockwell.

Following the initial identification of the parties for the record, Judge Stevens got right to the point.

"Ms. Moore, on what grounds are you detaining the defendant?"

Moore stood up and laid out the case and evidence gathered from the agencies involved. The judge asked pointed questions for which the prosecution did not have ready answers.

"Thank you. Be seated."

The judge stared at the prosecution table. "Special Agent Stockwell, I'm shocked and appalled at the poor quality of this action. You have no facts to argue, just inferences, innuendo, and poor investigative work." The judge turned to the defense table. "Major Gates."

Wolf's lawyer rose to his full height of six-two, resplendent in the same Army uniform as his client. It was impressive.

"Your Honor, the defense agrees in full. The agencies involved, and the FBI as lead, have nothing concrete to substantiate their spurious claims against my client. Assertions we believe created and pushed by the very drug cartels Master Sergeant Wolf has worked to bring to justice. He and his family are the victims here. The Sinaloa Cartel has tried to kill my client twice right here in Tampa. Once at the Blue Gorilla and the other ending in the tragic death of Colonel Neil Gates—my father."

He paused for a moment to let that last part sink in. "What are these federal agencies doing about those acts of terrorism on U.S. soil?"

"Major Gates and Master Sergeant Wolf. First, let me say, you both have my deepest condolences and sympathies at the dreadful loss of your family members. They were exceptional men, heroes, and patriots, who protected this nation without consideration for themselves or their safety."

Moore stood. "Your Honor, if I may—"

"You may not, Ms. Moore," Judge Stevens said with crushed ice in his voice. "You will sit down and be quiet unless acknowledged by the bench. Any additional outburst from your table and I'll hold you in contempt." He turned to his chief bailiff. "Randy, if any member of the prosecution speaks without being spoken to, I want them cuffed and placed in a basement cell."

Stockwell drew a loud breath to protest, but Moore elbowed him in the ribs. "Shut it," she hissed through clenched teeth. "I'm not going to jail because you don't know how to do basic police work."

The bailiff stared hard at the prosecution table, longing for someone to dare to speak.

"Master Sergeant Wolf, please rise." Wolf and Gates both came to their feet.

"Master Sergeant Wolf, I cannot in good conscience dismiss this case outright, as thin as it appears to be at this point. The court can't allow you go free until the FBI completes its investigation. What I can do is order you into house arrest and direct Major Gates to be responsible for you. You will surrender your passport and you are enjoined from possessing firearms. You will wear an ankle bracelet and take regular visits from an officer of the court. Do you understand my instructions?"

"We do, Your Honor." Gates nodded his assent.

"All right. The officer will escort you downstairs to get fitted. Then you can go home in the custody of Major Gates and Captain Parker while the FBI gets this sorted out." He banged his gavel once. "This proceeding is adjourned for now."

Wolf glanced at Stockwell, whose normal surfer's tan was a purplish red glow of hate framed by a scowl.

He ought to get his blood pressure checked.

The bailiff escorted Gates and Wolf downstairs where a court tech configured, tested, and then locked Wolf's ankle bracelet in place. He shook it a couple times to confirm the fit.

"You're free to go, sir. Out that door and two rights. You'll be on Polk Street." Wolf thanked the man. He and Gates donned their berets and stepped outside into a sunny day.

"I will come by your place in an hour," Gates said. "In the meantime, do not mess with your tail. Drive straight home and stay there until otherwise directed by me." His face got serious. "That is an order, master sergeant."

"Roger that, sir." They shook hands. "And thank you." Wolf saluted Gates, and they went different directions.

Wolf walked into the parking garage where Parker waited. They embraced, then got into her car and drove off. As she turned left out of the courthouse parking structure, he noticed a dark blue sedan following behind them, not trying to hide.

At his house, the sedan pulled right out front. Before disappearing through the front door, Wolf nodded to the agents and gave them a thumb's-up, and they returned it.

Elle pulled him close and kissed him hard. Wolf exhaled long and loud, then inhaled to quiet his mind and focus his thoughts.

"I need to change out of my monkey suit."

He changed into jeans and a T-shirt. They sat in the living room, and it felt good to sit on a comfortable couch instead of the hard jail seats.

"Time to think this out. What do we know? One, the cartel is using its influence and fake evidence to manipulate the Mexican government. Two, the Mexican government, more likely a few cartel stooges, are providing fake evidence to the FBI or DEA, or both. And three, Agent Stockwell is taking their input at face value. So, how do we discredit the Mexican side of the investigation?"

"We only have one friend in Mexico now, since they murdered Vic Cárdenas," Elle said.

"True, and Carlos also may be under investigation."

They sat in silence, mulling over the pieces of the puzzle. When the doorbell rang, it surprised Wolf to see Kennedy and Gates.

"C'mon in. Beer, water? What can I get you?"

"Water, thanks," Kennedy said.

"Sir, anything for you?"

"Lance, it's just Steve here, if you don't mind. I'll have a water too, please. I know it makes me sound like an officer weenie, but I'll take sparkling if you have it."

"Not a problem," Wolf said. "I keep San Pellegrino for my friends."

He distributed the drinks, and everyone found places to sit.

"We were discussing cartel influence into the Mexican government," Elle said. "They have provided fake or 'enriched' evidence. And the FBI seems to be swallowing it whole without verifying its authenticity."

Steve nodded. "Yeah, not the usual FBI rep for detail, is it? SOCOM JAG has had a word with the director of the FBI's Inspection Division, they were at West Point together.

"SAIC aside, Washington will supervise Stockwell from here on out and do his duty under the Constitution or get replaced. My view is, the evidence is insufficient for prosecution. But it's enough at face value to keep you in their investigative gaze for a long time."

"There is nothing for you to do, brother," Kennedy said. "Maybe you haven't listened to your voicemail yet, but Command suspended your clearance until they complete the investigation. And Treasury has frozen all of your accounts, credit, and banking."

"Steve," Wolf said, "before you got here, Elle and I were talking about our one potential asset in Mexico, Major Carlos Gonzalez. He's the Escadron de Leónes commander."

Elle stood and stretched. "He could be under investigation, too."

"You have to call him, because I can't. I haven't told you the rest of what's happening." Kennedy said.

"Out with it, brother. Let's get all the bad news on the table so we can deal with it."

"The NSA is looking at your training mission and my RC-12 re-certification. They have the aircraft system logs. They'll figure it out."

Steve looked confused. "I don't want to ask this, but I need to know. Figure what out?"

Kennedy, Elle, and Wolf looked at him as one. "How much do you want to know?" Wolf asked.

77

L ance Bear Wolf's residence, Tampa, Florida

Wolf's company had him on paid family leave from SOCOM pending a positive outcome, but it wouldn't last.

The cost of revenge continued to increase. It consumed everyone near him and those he loved. The death and destruction had him feeling cornered.

He was banging his head against the wall. Pensar, darn it—think! His mother whispered inside his head. "Wolf, start over."

He smiled at the memory. One of his mother's most valuable lessons was simple on the surface and yet so impactful in practice.

"Don't accept your day, start over. Don't accept how you feel, acknowledge it, and start over. Choose an attitude of gratitude. You always have a choice. Take charge and live with intention."

Thanks, Mom! This fight isn't over until I say so.

KENNEDY'S ORDERS for Warrant Officer school were cancelled and replaced with orders to Korea. It was the day of his sendoff party, so Wolf cleaned the house while Parker shopped for chicken and steaks.

They compartmentalized, putting the investigations and butchering of their careers on hold.

Fajita seasoning on the chicken and steak combined with grilling veggies smelled wonderful. Their laughter filled the space, and it felt like fun, food, family. It lifted everyone's spirits.

Kennedy stopped Wolf in the kitchen. "I'm no longer officer material according to the assignment chief."

"I'm sorry to hear that. Lots of stupid going around."

Kennedy shrugged. "It's okay. I've got the Agency begging me to come to work for them, and I might. I can retire after this enlistment."

"Good idea. You'll do well in a place where they reward smarts and innovation. I could even see them wanting you for a field agent—Bond. Kieran Bond." Wolf laughed.

"Bond is English, I'm Irish. That'll never work." Kennedy said with a smile.

"Wolf," Parker called out. "I need your help on the grill."

"Let's get back to the important things in our lives," Wolf said to Kennedy as they headed outside.

They were all sitting at the picnic table around loaded plates of food when Kennedy grabbed Maya's hand. "We have something to share with you," he said, smiling at his friends.

Wolf and Parker stopped eating and smiled back. "Well, go on.

"Tell us"?" Parker asked.

"We're getting married."

A chorus of approval filled the air, and everyone stood to hug. The guys laughed, and the ladies cried. Wolf raised his beer to toast. "Here's to—"

The bullet struck Parker's back mid-point on her right scapula, exploding just above her right breast and lodging itself in Maya's chest. The sound followed a split second later.

Wolf looked up as he pushed the ladies to the ground. His eyes found a glint of light that could be coming from a rifle scope. He drew his pistol from under his shirt and unloaded a full magazine at the spot. "Shoot me, you cowards! Shoot me!" he screamed.

Nothing.

Kennedy pulled linen napkins off the table and pressed them hard against Maya's sucking chest wound. The seal was imperfect, and she had trouble breathing, but the bleeding slowed.

Wolf heard the FBI powering into the house. He did a fast wipe of his pistol and tossed it into the shrubs. Then he knelt next to Parker and assessed her entry and exit wounds.

The front door exploded open as FBI agents charged in, weapons drawn rushing the back yard.

"Put your hands where we can see them!" the agents screamed. "Lie flat on the ground! Do it now!"

Wolf never stopped working on Parker, and his inflamed anger driving him to act.

"Screw you! I'm saving her life."

He tore open her shirt and unfastened the front-closing bra. Wolf's med bag was already on the table from addressing a grill burn, so he pulled it to the ground and threw Kennedy a combat bandage.

"You might wanna find some cover there, Sparky," Wolf growled, looking at the agent closest to him. "Sniper, three o'clock, one hundred and fifty yards. Fourth floor."

The agent took a quick look before crouching. He repeated Wolf's sniper call to the other agents, and they tried to get small. Another agent requested SWAT and EMS.

"We need to seal these wounds to prevent tension pneumothorax. I'll walk you through it," Wolf said.

He sealed Parker's back while directing Kennedy to check Maya for an exit wound. Parker stared up at Wolf, tears welling up and rolling fat down her terrified face as she grunted through the pain. He'd seen the look before on people who thought they were dying.

"Elle, listen to me. You're going to be all right. I will not lose you."

She gripped his arm as he cleaned the exit would and applied the chest seal. She was breathing better. Wolf had seen plenty of combat wounds, and while these were bad, he thought they were survivable.

Kennedy shouted. "No exit wound here."

Wolf tossed his medical shears to Kennedy, telling him how to make a three-sided chest seal. "Once you get the seal in place you need to watch her. Let me know if her lips turn blue or if she gets short of breath."

The FBI agents had formed a protective perimeter around the house and had evacuated neighbors from nearby houses in four directions. Sirens meant more help was close by.

Tampa SWAT surrounded the house as EMS arrived. Wolf briefed the SWAT team lieutenant, and he sent out a search team to find the sniper.

The paramedics worked through their assessments and nodded. "Outstanding work, guys. We got it from here."

Kennedy and Wolf followed the gurneys out to the ambulances. Kennedy jumped on board with Maya. Wolf was about do the same with Elle when FBI agents grabbed him from behind.

"We can't let you go. You're under house arrest."

Wolf exploded, pushing backward into the agents. When one let go to catch his balance, Wolf spun, tripping the other agent backward onto the lawn. He was about to charge when Kennedy bear hugged him.

"Not now, brother, not now! Elle is going to need you, and not from a jail cell. Don't make it worse. I got this. I'll call Gates."

Wolf shook him off and stomped back into the house with death glares at the FBI agents. He was on autopilot and unnoticed as he picked up the brass in the backyard.

He accounted for all the brass. On his knees, cleaning the spilled food and blood mess, he realized how futile all this was. The cartel was going to get him, or his own government would. What was the use in delaying the inevitable?

It was only getting innocent people hurt and killed, but wait, he was also getting bonus points for destroying Kennedy's career.

I'm getting my ass kicked and my friends killed.

They transported Elle and Maya to Tampa General. Gates arrived about forty minutes later and found Wolf sitting at the backyard picnic table, staring into space, surrounded by bloodstains.

Wolf looked up, eyes red. "What?"

"Let's go. We got dispensation to see Parker. You get thirty minutes plus travel time."

Wolf dashed to the sink and ran cold water over his head. "I was worried she wouldn't make it, that she wasn't—"

"I know."

When they got to the hospital, Wolf ran to the nurses' station. "Elle Parker? Where can I find Elle Parker?"

Gates caught up with him. "This way, soldier. She's in ICU." The elevator made its way to the fourth floor.

Wolf stopped outside Elle's door, took a deep breath, and put on a warm smile. When he stepped into the room, it horrified him to see her connected in the same science-fiction visual as his mother.

The charge nurse was in the room reviewing Elle's chart.

"We came close to losing her to a bullet fragment that nicked her vena cava. She came close to bleeding out." The nurse looked at her sleeping patient. "She's under mild sedation now, but she's a tough one. She'll make it." The nurse patted Wolf on the shoulder and departed.

Gates pulled a chair over to the bed and steered Wolf to her side. He squeezed her hand and meditated on her face, relaxed and tranquil. By her face alone he thought she looked uninjured and was maybe just asleep. The beeping and clicking machines around her brought him back to crushing reality.

His thirty minutes over, Gates said it was time to go. Wolf leaned over Elle and whispered, "I love you." He straightened, sighed, and walked out. Kennedy was waiting in the passageway.

"Brother, are you okay? How is Elle?"

"I don't know, on either count. How is Maya doing?"

"They say she'll make it."

A chill ran down Wolf spine only to be replaced by a fiery fury of rage as the realization washed over Wolf.

"Alejandro hasn't been trying to kill me—he's been targeting everyone around me. Think about it. The assassin has attacked and or killed everyone important to me. My family, Carlos, Cárdenas, you and Maya. Colonel Gates. Death by a thousand cuts."

Kennedy looked to Gates.

"Major, request you agree to serve as my legal counsel."

Gates nodded, looking unsure.

"Attorney-client privilege applies henceforth, correct?" Kennedy asked.

Gates looked puzzled. "Um, yeah ... sure. Why do you need legal representation?"

Kennedy just shrugged. "Call it a hunch."

78

Lance Bear Wolf's residence, Tampa, Florida

Wolf spent the day reading Marcus Aurelius, Seneca, Sun Tzu, and Taber's influential guerrilla-war manual "The War of the Flea." A visual of Parker bleeding on the backyard grass kept interrupting his thoughts.

Where did I go wrong? What have I missed?

The phone rang, and he jumped. It was Gonzalez with a condolence call Wolf would not remember later. Gates dropped by to tell him FINCEN had finished its investigation of financial misappropriation allegations and found no evidence of impropriety.

They had restored his financial accounts and unfrozen his assets. Good news, but not what he prayed to hear. Parker's condition had not improved. She was still in critical condition, and she dominated his thoughts.

The doorbell jolted him out of his focus on Parker. It was Sergeant First Class Pat Newton, who Wolf hadn't seen since the planning phase of the expeditionary Mexico mission. Newton was a frequent relapsing alcoholic. He was a wizard with communications gear, but his personal life was a fiasco.

Wolf wondered why he was here as he let him in.

"Hey Wolf, hadn't seen you in a bit and thought I'd check in. You okay, brother?" Newton asked, extending his hand. Wolf paused a moment before accepting the handshake.

"Yeah, good. Good, thanks. I appreciate you coming by, but I've got to prepare for my next round with the FBI."

"Sure, sure. Understood, man, yeah. You got my digits, right? Ping me anytime if you need anything, okay?" He raised a hand and waved. "Just wanted to check in, ya'know? See you when I see you, man."

Wolf didn't have the time or inclination to deal with Newton's baggage. He closed the door behind him and turned off the lights.

Wolf was asleep on the couch when Kennedy banged on the door. Wolf let him in.

"What's so important?" He rubbed his eyes. "You need to see this. Wake up, man, this is important." Wolf stretched, yawning. "So ..."

"Elle and I found the connection. California State Senator Jimmy Cortez is Alejandro's cousin. The family changed their last name when they immigrated. Turns out the senator is also a wealthy commercial real estate developer. Guess who he buys property for?"

"Yeah, I get it. Alejandro. Turn the information over to the FBI."

"Why? We can use the information against them."

"You can. I'm done. I've caused enough damage. My results are at the hospital."

"No, we're winning. El Chapo must be ready to burn them and move on."

Wolf's blank stare made Kennedy back up. "Have you tallied the score? I have. I thought we were winning, too. But it's a lie I've been telling myself and all of you. Don't make me list it out. I can't."

THE COURT GRANTED Wolf permanent authorization to visit Elle in the hospital for one hour a day. Six days had passed since the shooting, and she was showing little sign of improvement. He would sit in the chair at her bedside and hold her hand and wouldn't take his eyes off her.

He was just leaning back in the chair when she started convulsing and machines beeped louder and faster.

Wolf rose to the door to call for help, but he'd only drawn breath when the room filled with doctors and nurses. A nurse hustled him into the hallway with Gates, who had been waiting in a chair outside the room. Twelve long minutes later, the doctor asked Wolf to come back in.

"Mr. Wolf, what you witnessed was a grand mal seizure. It shouldn't be a persistent issue unless Ms. Parker has undiagnosed epilepsy. We treated her with meds to reduce brain swelling and we'll continue to monitor her for additional indications."

"Yes, sir. Thank you."

Wolf spent the last minutes of his visitation time reading to Parker. Gates opened the door and nodded.

"Time to go."

When he got home, hunger pangs reminded him he had not eaten. He grabbed a Ramen and bags of frozen shrimp and peas. The water was near boiling when he touched the pot by mistake. In the scream of nerve endings punished by heat, he inspected the burn mark like a book collector examining a signed first edition.

He stuck the burned finger in the icy stream of the kitchen faucet, a second wave of pain bringing on a grim smile. That's me. Burned, blistered, and in pain.

Wolf's eating robotic. The doorbell rang. He looked through the peephole, pulled back, and looked again. Must be the military's turn.

Time for the general court-martial. On his porch stood Colonel Davidson, Major Gates, and Staff Sergeant Kennedy in dress green uniforms. He opened the door.

There were two black Chevy Suburban's idling at the curb.

"Good morning, sirs. Kennedy. Come in, please."

They entered but made no moves to be seated. This was not going to be a long visit.

"What can I do for you, colonel?" Wolf asked.

"Master sergeant, you are a mess. Get cleaned up. Dress greens. We're taking you to the Command."

Wolf's eyes widened. "Yes, sir."

Kennedy opened the refrigerator, bypassing the beers for waters all around. They were engaged in small talk, when nine minutes later Wolf reappeared. He was clean-shaven and in dress greens so perfect he looked like he'd just walked out of a recruiting poster.

"I'm ready, sir," Wolf said. "May I ask what the Command wants?"

Colonel Davidson stood. "Very well. General Davis requested we bring you in."

79

USSOCOM Commanders conference room, Tampa, Florida
They drove to the Command in silence. Wolf figured
Big Army, and the FANG had reached the limit of their
tolerance for him.

They would court-martial him into dust to demonstrate the military could and would police its own. At the headquarters building, they used General Davis' private entrance to access a secure elevator.

They walked to Davis' command suite and the general's executive assistant pointed to the commander's conference room.

On each side of the door were awe-inspiring photos of Medal of Honor awardees from the special-operations community. Above the door was a handmade scroll that read Always in the Fight.

Wolf kept his emotions in check as he entered the room. He knew the deputy commander and the commander of JSMC, who had also entered the room. He stopped short when he recognized the man sitting at the right of the commander's chair—Matt Scanlon, Agency Deputy Director for Operations.

Wolf didn't know whether to be angry or just resigned to his secretive fate. It was out of his control either way.

Someone called Attention! and everyone stood when General Davis entered the room.

"At ease, take your seats," Davis said.

Electronic door locks slid into place and several displays indicated the Top Secret/SCI sensitivity of the meeting. A red panel lit up over the outside door reading room in use–do not enter.

"Gentlemen, please sign the NDAs in front of you and consider yourselves read into the Shadow Tier Special Access Program. I've just come from a call with the president and the joint chiefs. They have agreed to move our concept forward with concurrence from the Agency Deputy Director for Operations." He nodded to Scanlon. "To quote the president, 'It's time to take the fight to our enemies.'"

The general continued. "Master Sergeant Wolf, you and Staff Sergeant Kennedy are no doubt wondering what I'm talking about. Colonel Davidson will provide the background."

"Sir." Davidson said as he moved to the front of the room. An Air Force sergeant darkened the room and put a PowerPoint slide on a screen lowered in front of the room.

"Gentlemen, by this time you have heard of Master Sergeant Wolf's family tragedy in Mexico, the multiple attacks on him here in Tampa, and ongoing FBI-led investigations."

He used a laser pointer to indicate different circled areas on a map of North America. Heads nodded all around. "What we are seeing is a complex web of lies and disinformation concocted by the Sinaloa drug cartel, using their influence in the Mexican and U.S. governments. Since the death of the master sergeant's parents, we have tracked the movements of Wolf and Kennedy."

Wolf watched Kennedy close his eyes, frown, and shake his head.

Davidson continued. "I cross-referenced their movements with incidents of violence, deaths, and disruptions to cartel operations on both sides of the U.S.-Mexico border. My findings are these. Our innovative and daring soldiers have done more to affect the Sinaloa Cartel and interdict illegal drugs in the last six months than the U.S. war on drugs has since its inception."

Wolf closed his eyes. This must be the compliment before the summary prison sentence.

"What they have confirmed to leadership," Davidson continued, "is the depth of untapped experience hidden in the National Guard units and Army Reserve. Master Sergeant Wolf and his team of part-time warriors bring the unique skill sets and real-world experience we need for a serious war on drugs. Many Guardsmen and Reservists have valuable civilian skills complimenting their military training that negate the need for specialist additions to a team. The counter-terrorism operating tempo is increasing faster than we can produce Tier I operators. If we intend to fight our drug war in earnest, the time to do so is now. The time is right to create Shadow Tier."

Wolf and Kennedy were stunned by what they'd just heard. For the first time since Elle's shooting, Wolf could see a future. A powerful one.

General Davis turned to Scanlon. "Matt?"

He stood. "We're in total agreement and we have the approval of the President of the United States to proceed." He looked at Wolf and Kennedy. "Gentlemen, you will work in coordination with our Special Missions Division and the Commander JSMC."

Davis smiled. "Colonel Davidson now the unit Commander. Major Gates, we have promoted you to rank of lieutenant colonel and you are the unit JAG. Master Sergeant Wolf, we promoted you to sergeant major and retired you at that permanent rank from the Florida Guard. You are the Shadow Tier Deputy Director of Operations."

Wolf blinked. What just happened?

"Staff Sergeant Kennedy, we promoted you to Chief Warrant Officer Three and retired at that permanent grade. You now work for the Agency as the Shadow Tier Deputy Director of Intelligence."

"Wolf," Colonel Davidson said. "All of your charges, military and civilian, are dropped, with the personal apology of the director of the FBI. And you need to thank just promoted Lieutenant Colonel Carlos Gonzalez of Escuadron de Leones. He uncovered the cartel moles and lies behind your accusations."

Some of it wasn't just accusation, Wolf mused, but he kept that thought to himself.

General Davis and DDO Scanlon met Wolf and Kennedy at the head of the table and shook hands. Colonel Davidson interrupted the revelry.

"Mr. Wolf, there is an acknowledgment we need from you before embarking on the mission of this new organization."

"Yes, sir, what is that?" It felt strange to be addressed by his commander as a mister.

"From now on, we expect you to put team and mission first, always."

Wolf stood a little taller. "Sir, opportunities like this are once in a lifetime. Team and mission first, always."

"I knew we could count on you. Our first tasking is to complete the capture or elimination of Alejandro and Eliana Cortes, and if it presents itself, El Chapo."

80

Tampa General, Tampa, Florida

Free of his ankle bracelet, Wolf spent more hospital time bedside with Parker. She was more awake and coherent now, and the doctor expected a full recovery. Wolf was ecstatic over the news.

Parker didn't remember the party or the shooting, but she looked at him with the same intensity as before and that was enough.

She grinned when they talked about Kennedy the nerd trying to take care of a woman as strong-willed as Maya. They had scheduled Parker for surgery in two days. The thought of reconstructive breast surgery embarrassed her, but Wolf tried calming her fears with his usual dark humor.

"Sweetheart, it's all good. We'll get the doctor to bump you up a size or two and head home happy."

Parker smiled. "You're a pig, Lance Wolf! You can't handle what I have now, snake eater."

"You're right!" Wolf laughed. "I'm also the one who will love you forever plus two weeks."

"See, there you go again. It's all about you."

"No—it's about us," he said.

The doctors released Maya to finish her recovery at home. Kennedy attempted to hover, but Maya wouldn't have it. She told him to go back to work and finish the mission.

Wolf's and Kennedy's new offices off West Cypress in Tampa needed everything. The many technical installations and improved building security that would occur under the team's new facilities manager, a retired Seabee master chief.

Until then, the Shadow Tier would spend most of its time on MacDill Air Force Base in a SOCOM Secure Compartmented Information Facility.

The first order of business was an upgrade of secure comms devices. The NSA delivered the latest in encrypted cell and SATCOM phones along with pagers. The Agency provided additional means of covert communications and electronic drop boxes.

Kitted out, they engaged in detailed planning for their first mission. Operation Thor's Hammer began.

Kennedy hired Lizzy Armstrong and got her on an Air Force executive transport plane from the West Coast. The Agency supplied a field operative who had been investigating reports of the Sinaloa Cartel's collaboration with Al Qaeda.

Wolf hired his former strike team as contractors and processed them for their TS/SCI security clearances.

The SCIF was subdued when the entire hybrid civilian-military team, old and new, met for the first time. Wolf's former military teammates, known quantities, were uneasy with new, unproven personnel.

"Mr. Kennedy?" Wolf said. "Care to begin?"

Kennedy shook his head, still not comfortable with the title.

"Ladies and gentlemen, let me introduce two new members of the team. Lizzy Armstrong has operational experience working with Wolf and his brother during the cartel turf war in L.A.. She has experience working undercover and is an expert in disguise and sub rosa operations. She saved them both at one site when the bad dudes decided not to cave and run."

Kennedy continued. "Our second new member, codename Francisca, is on loan from a three-letter agency. She has been working the

Tijuana and Sinaloa cartels, focused on uncovering ties to terrorism. Francisca left deep cover to join us. You understand the implications. You will get to know them both a lot better as we execute Operation Thor's Hammer. Wolf?"

Wolf stood. "Thor's Hammer—the primary mission is to capture or kill Eliana and Alejandro Cortes. The secondary target, should it present itself, is to kill or capture El Chapo. To do this will require multiple objectives to align for mission success. We are ramping up the cartel war. We are going to capture Eliana Cortes and use her as bait to draw her brother Alejandro across the border. Mr. Kennedy has your assignments. I want multiple courses of action. Be ready to brief when we meet back here tomorrow at 1300."

The group dispersed and Wolf suppressed a grin. But something kept nagging at him. He took Kennedy aside.

"Now that my mind is clearer, I've been thinking about a visit I got from an old teammate, Pat Newton. Like the rest of the team, he came by the house to 'offer his support,' but this time was different.

Wolf took a big breath. "This is hard for me to say—but I think he gave my address to the assassin."

Kennedy's tone was immediate and ice cold. "Give me his info."

81

USSOCOM SCIF, Tampa, Florida

After lunch, the team assembled to present their updates. Clinton briefed logistics. The core elements of travel, safe houses, security, food, weapons, and vehicles were in process, waiting for final approval. The quick consensus was everything was solid. He approved.

Harris presented comms. He described potential gaps based on location activity, with downtown L.A. the most complex. Wolf asked questions about alternative means of comms, relay stations, and pagers. Harris had it covered, including radio frequency harmonic interference. Its net effect blocked transmissions. His proposal to shut off the offending paging service during key portions of the operation brought nods of approval around the table. He approved.

Intelligence was next, and a hot topic. Kennedy's plan required immediate movement to the primary safe house. Their number-one priority was activating informant networks and placing technical surveillance packages, all focused on finding and setting Eliana Cortes's location. Kennedy described the concept for his surveillance teams, and an Agency version of the Army RC-12 Guardrail was on standby at John Wayne Airport. Wolf and

Kennedy agreed to a combined advance and intel departure in twenty-four hours.

Oleus LeBlanc briefed support. It was simple, but a key test of the Shadow Tier concept. It included bringing in National Guard Special Forces and Navy Reserve operators from SEAL Team Seventeen at Coronado to bolster staffing. They would support the operation by operating the safe houses, providing security, acting as the armorer, and installing and maintaining the comms nets under Harris's guidance. In certain cases, they would assigned them to an assault unit.

"How do you think it's going, 'Mister' Kennedy?" he said with a hint of sarcasm.

"Funny, 'Mister' Wolf. Good for their first time together. Francisca and Lizzy are working with the team."

"Are there any integration issues?"

"No. They're pros. They can handle themselves and anyone who tries gets in their way."

He smiled. He had experienced his own dose of Francisca wonderment. Her stunning good looks seemed incongruent with her training and deadly capabilities. Lizzy, attractive in a tomboy kind of way, had proven herself. She was more than capable of completing her part of a mission, and both could work undercover without raising the slightest suspicion.

She stood. "Our first objective," she said, "is to capture and/or kill Eliana Cortes. The following COAs are the best options to accomplish Phase 1 of the mission. One, we capture a high-ranking Tijuana leader and offer him to her. Two: Find, fix, and assault Eliana's location. Three, we make her think the Cali Cartel wants to make a deal. Let's start with option one. Thoughts? Feedback?"

Wolf thanked Francisca, then continued. "One keeps to the concept of having the cartels fight each other. Better to have them kill each other without us in the line of fire. Who would you target and how?"

Lizzy stood.

"The who is Javier Arellano Félix. He spends enormous sums on parties and prostitutes. The how includes setting up a front business to serve the L.A. elite via a fake escort service. We will use Francisca's connections for an introduction. She will setup a meeting to deliver sample services to 'win the business.' With the right drugs and a simple deception, we will capture him. Then we call Eliana's security lead to offer Javier for a price, and she jumps at the opportunity to kill one of the Félix brothers."

"Thank you, Lizzy. Option two?" Wolf asked.

Danner walked to the head of the table. He was just about recovered from his expeditionary injuries and looked good to go.

"Direct action. Assault her location, but with a twist to lower risk. We know she is location hopping for additional protection. She prefers houses near airports where a getaway jet is nearby and uses Airstream trailers for living space inside warehouses. By destroying or denying several of her current options, we can reduce her choices to one or two sites. We can deploy a nonlethal gas, rendering her guards ineffective, and bring her in with minimal risk."

Kennedy asked, "How would you disperse the gas?"

"Via the air conditioning and heating system."

"Russian Spetsnaz have been testing different compounds against the Chechen separatists," Kennedy said. "The results have been inconsistent. Our scientists do not recommend use except in extreme situations, and then in smaller contained spaces."

Wolf said, "I like the idea. It's still an option. Innovative thinking, team. Three?"

Francisca took Danner's place at the head of the table.

"Three plays to Eliana's ego. I will pose as Cristina Santa Cruz London, the daughter of the Cali Cartel leader and her old friend. I will connect with Eliana, asking for a face-to-face meeting. The hook will be my father wanting to work with her to bring Cali cocaine into Southern California. I will ask for an exclusive deal bypassing Alejandro. I have a source telling me she hates her brother and wants his place at El Chapo's table." She looked around the table. "Shocker, I know, right?"

Wolf smiled. "Playing on Eliana's ego. Excellent work, team.

Three viable options, each one a prospective player." He glanced at his watch. "Okay, let's take thirty."

The group dispersed, and he headed to his office. Kennedy followed. Wolf looked distracted.

"I have seen that look before on you before. What are you thinking?" Kennedy asked.

He crossed his arms. "Tell me if this makes sense to your big brain. Execute option one to get the Tijuana Cartel after Eliana. It will occupy her frame of reference. Then execute three. If the Tijuanans keep her distracted, it helps shorten the buy-in time for the Cali opportunity. And one is the backup plan in case she doesn't bite on three."

"Your logic is a surprise. Executing one as a backup is smart and lets us bring it into play if needed."

"Good. How is Maya recovering?"

"Very well. She kicked me out of the house. Told me to go kick some butt and finish the mission."

"Her time with the Tarahumara people strengthened her. She was born with warrior spirit. "

"All you Genuine Americans say stuff like that," he said.

Wolf laughed, slapping his friend on the back. "I'm going to teach you some respect for your elders, white man."

The teammates filtered back into the conference room past Kennedy and Wolf and the meeting resumed.

"While you were out, K-man, and I gave your options a scrub. What we came up with is a hybrid approach. Execute option one to get the Cortes and Tijuana cartels fighting again and hold Javier while executing option three. The fighting keeps Eliana distracted from a deep inspection of the Cali request to meet. If she gets nervous and backs out, we play the Javier-for-a-price card."

Kennedy said, "We see complexity and additional risk, but we like the backup idea. Danner?"

"I'm in. As long as we stay in sequence, we can respond to Mr. Murphy's weigh-in." Murphy's Law, whatever can happen will happen at the worst possible time—brought laughs and nods around the table.

"Lizzy and Francisca?" Wolf said.

Francisca spoke first. "We will be busy, but it looks doable." Lizzy agreed, as did the rest of the team.

"Okay, good. Now on to objective two, getting Alejandro to cross into the U.S. This time I want you to break into two teams. One team will work on the setup, and the other on the capture-or- kill component."

They spent the rest of the afternoon on refining the setups with a focus on the psychological aspect of denying Alejandro's options. In effect, presenting him no other alternative but to rescue Eliana. His narcissistic ego was a lever they could pull at any time. The capture-or-kill portion of objective two was more complicated, considering Alejandro would not cross the border alone. His security team would be well armed, trained, and unafraid of dying. A key element of the plan would be the need to limit his team's ability to maneuver and resist.

Kennedy pulled Wolf aside. "We forgot to include Steve Gates." "You're right. I've got to adjust my thinking."

"Yeah, don't we all. We just missed extended jail time. Let's not put it back on the table." Kennedy smirked.

Wolf walked to the front of the room. "Most of you know me, but anyone needing a primer can find it in the secure C-Drive under Profiles. Up front, here's something you need to know about me. I dislike asking ...for permission."

The group broke into some laughs, no kidding smiles, and nods of quiet approval.

"Some folks claim I'm not too keen on asking for forgiveness, either." More laughter, louder this time.

"This isn't about me, though. I am one hundred and forty-three percent focused on us bringing Alejandro and Eliana Cortes to justice ... or killing them. I don't have a real preference either way. Keeping you all from having the month I just had is our top priority.

We will follow our Rules of Engagement and do what's right. Agreed?"

The team replied in unison, "Roger that."

Five minutes later, Gates joined the briefing, his face sporting a devious grin. "I was wondering when you would call me."

"Thank you for joining us, sir. Danner, please recap our plan for the major."

The recap took twenty minutes. Gates asked a few questions and then said, "I understand. Thank you. So, let me start with this. The Shadow Tier finding, or as some of you may know it, the Memorandum of Notification—our official establishing charter—is on the president's desk. Meantime, you may train, purchase authorized equipment using Uncle Sam's money, deploy, and begin operations. It is a formal notification to the intelligence committees and in no way affects your mission unless the president changes it, which is unlikely given his desire to take the fight to the cartels. Questions, comments, concerns?"

Wolf said, "All right. If there are no questions, we're done. We'll see you in L.A."

As the room emptied, Kennedy grabbed Wolf's arm. "Hey, how is Elle recovering?"

"Doing very well, thanks. Her latest surgery went well.

"She's a tough one. She'll push her limits as her recovery progresses."

"That's great news. How about you? Are you still singing your death song?"

"Not since Mexico. You can bet I will before we go to war in L.A." He took Kennedy by the shoulders and gave him a little shake. "War is easy when you're already dead."

82

Shadow Tier safe house, Los Angeles, California
Big-city safe houses are a different breed than the storied hundred-acre estates of Virginia and Maryland.

A joint FBI- Agency team had designed this unremarkable safe house to run complex operations. The selection criteria included access and escape routes, security, and an ability to harden the site. Toward that end, the government owned this entire block.

On the north corner was an operating brake-and-transmission repair shop that had no idea of its actual landlord, which provided an excellent cover for vehicle and personnel movement. Next door, there was a Motorola distributor selling the full line of radios, pagers, and cellphones. Its roof jammed with antennae.

The safe house included everything the team would need. Office space for ops, intel, and comms teams, sleeping quarters for up to twenty, a full kitchen, and a trauma room equipped to perform emergency surgery. The basement had the gym and armory.

There was access to Highways I-5, I-10, and the infamous California 101. A concrete wall put in place by CalTrans protected from surveillance. The adjacent houses could accommodate eighteen to twenty personnel. Any additional bodies could make use of rental properties in the area and shuttle in through the automotive shop.

Wolf met Francisca at the Beverly Wilshire where the Félix grab would take place. The fake escort service they crafted up operated out of the Doheny suite, a luxury space for sophisticated tastes that they crammed with the latest in surveillance gear.

"When can we start?" he asked.

"We're already in play. My asset is setting up the introduction."

"What additional help do you need from us?" he asked.

"I need two men to help with transport once we secure Javier. I imagine he will be very excitable. I'd like a secure room at the safe house to hold him."

Javier Arellano Félix loved to mix with the highest levels of the Hollywood elite, especially the women. He wasn't shy speaking about his special bizarre sexual preferences nor about his willingness to seek those who would satisfy them. This was the hook being used to lure him to his capture.

Francisca told Wolf that he felt so comfortable with her that his security detail was just one man.

Wolf got a solid five hours of sleep in a row, which was one hour more than he got on the night before a mission. The Beverly Wilshire was more than comfortable enough. Up early, showered and dressed, it still caught him by surprise that when he went to the closet, there were no Army uniforms hanging there. He slurped down some poor hotel room coffee and joined the team.

He leaned against the wall behind the surveillance techs and stared with them at the video feeds flowing in from the room next door. On time, LeBlanc escorted Javier Félix and a bodyguard to the private elevator that carried them to the fifteenth floor.

Lizzy opened the door to the main salon. Francisca stood at the panoramic curved window with her back to them. Lizzy said, "Ms. Barbosa, your appointment is here."

She kept him waiting with a hint of indifference as she played with her drink. Turning, she smiled and held out her hand. He crossed the room and bent to kiss it, drawn in by her magnetism. She motioned to a loveseat, and they sat close.

"Javier, would you like one?"

A nod was all he could muster. Francisca waved and a white-coated waiter, a Navy Reserve SEAL arrived at her elbow.

"Please bring my guest a tequila." She placed her hand on Félix's arm. "1800, of course."

The waiter went to retrieve the libation.

"Javier, darling, shall we have our bodyguards wait outside? The only danger you face here is delirious exhaustion. They will scare the ladies and ruin the mood, no?"

"This is true. But first, allow them to clear the suite." Félix gestured to his man, waving him in with two fingers. "Arturo."

Pointing at Lizzy, Francisca said, "Help him."

Quicker than efficient, Arturo cleared the suite, then headed outside with Lizzy and LeBlanc in tow. He accepted the tequila from the undercover waiter and the withdrew. Wolf was relaxed as he watched them exit on the surveillance video feeds. He could tell she had complete control of this guy.

"Now we can focus on you, Javier. Tell me about all your desires. Leave out nothing."

He laughed. "May I call you Francisca?" She nodded assent. "Good. I am a simple man with simple tastes." His tastes took another twenty minutes to describe, most of them a retelling of lurid past exploits with other women intended to impress her.

"I see. So, tall, blonde, blue eyes, athletic, and if she reminds you of a submissive Uma Thurman or Robin Wright Penn, all the better."

"Yes ... or you, my sweet..." Félix whispered, leaning in.

She smiled and denied the attempt with a subtle turn of her head away. "Not today, mi amour. We must get to know each other first. But today is my gift to you."

She stood and paused just long enough for Félix's eyes to roam her curvy topography.

"May I get you another drink before I bring the ladies in?" "Yes, please."

They had coated his glass and several others with an in- visible compound of Ketamine and Propofol. Félix should already be feeling its effects. She refilled her wine glass and handed the second tequila to Félix. He pushed back.

"Please, you must join me to seal our friendship."

"Thank you, but I prefer my wine." She smiled. "Tequila makes my clothes fall off."

"No, I insist. I want us to share a drink to our relationship."

Wolf couldn't read him. Was this a test or a genuine gesture?

He keyed his hand mic. "All teams standby."

Outside the front door, Armstrong and LeBlanc shared some small talk, using their angles to hide the drawing of their weapons from Arturo.

Francisca smiled, took the glass and sipped from the drink, passing the glass back to him. He finished it in one macho swallow and stood with a smile. Wolf watched him. Was he wobbling a bit?

"Well done, love. Now, before we begin, where is the bathroom?" he asked. Francisca pointed to her left.

He got three steps before collapsing to the tile floor. His head slammed with a loud thump and she screamed for effect, collapsing back on the ornate sofa. The sedative mixture in the sip she had imbibed was causing dizziness, but she had taken in a frac- tion of what Félix had downed, so she remained conscious. Arturo heard the commotion and rushed through the door with his Glock ready.

He pulled a small plastic box from his suit jacket and put a pill under Félix's tongue.

"He has cardiac issues sometimes," Arturo said. "You have gotten him drunk and too excited."

Wolf keyed his mic, but stopped as Armstrong and LeBlanc closed the distance on the distracted bodyguard. When he looked up from his prostrate boss, expecting help, he got a single suppressed shot through the left eye. Armstrong handed her Welrod MK III pistol to LeBlanc and went to help Francisca.

Wolf keyed his mic. "All stations report."

The team reported back in sequence from all the hotel locations. "All clear."

Wolf left the surveillance room to walk next door. The blood pool was small and already coagulating. "I'm glad they didn't carpet. How is Francisca?"

She spoke up. "I'm right here, you know. I'm a little pixilated right now, but I'll be good to go in twenty or thirty minutes."

Clinton helped Armstrong and LeBlanc separate the bodyguard from Félix and into a body bag. They folded him in half at the waist and deposited his body into a hotel laundry cart, then covered it up with wet towels. They smeared the top couple of towels with a brown substance that was a convincing simulation of human feces. No one was digging into that cart for some time.

Hughes inspected the unconscious Félix. "Hey, I'm no doctor, but our target is dead."

He looked in the pill container that had fallen from Arturo's hand and shook his head. "Heart attack. This is digitalis. He had a weak heart."

Wolf stood with his hands on his hips, head down and thinking.

"Okay. Not a problem. Guess Arturo didn't get there in time after all."

He keyed his encrypted radio. "Outlaw One. Roll our paramedics and let's get our baggage loaded. Everyone else back to position one. We'll hold a fast hot wash and move on to the next phase."

The next phase of the mission was about to test all their preparation and more. He remembered what Seneca said.

Luck is what happens when preparation meets opportunity.

83

Shadow Tier safe house, Los Angeles, California

They sat around the conference table, waiting. There was a phone connected to a device that would scramble the number and transform Armstrong's voice into Eliana's.

"Ready?" Wolf asked. Armstrong nodded. He dialed Benjamin Félix, Javier's youngest brother, on Benjamin's secret cell number.

"Benjamin, it's Eliana Cortes. I have Javier. Pull your people out of L.A. or I send his pieces back to your mother in a garbage bag."

He exploded into the phone. He wasn't notable for subtlety. "Do you know who I am? Do you know?"

Lizzy/Eliana laughed. "Your mother didn't tell you, idiot? I am not in charge of your family tree. It's full of monkeys."

A long silence ensued. "You are dead—you know you are dead, don't you? Nothing about L.A. gets decided until I see proof of life," he said.

"No need. You will have it tomorrow. L.A. is now mine. It's long pastime for you to leave." Wolf disconnected the call.

"Will he take the bait?" Kennedy asked.

"He didn't blink or ask how I got the number," Armstrong said.

"Got right to business. When you have seven brothers fighting the Sinaloa Cartel, I guess you get used to dealing with threats."

The team spent the rest of the day collecting intel, working through phone logs and cellphone registration records. The SIGINT crew was on the move, scanning every known Eliana location and sighting. He looked at Eliana's organization chart, wishing they had more of the blanks filled.

He suspected the known associates were at least two levels below what they needed. Kennedy's only option was manpower- intensive surveillance. Several of the recent additions had Cold War experience in collection activities against Warsaw Pact nations. One Green Beret Warrant Four had run covert ops in Berlin. Wolf had confidence the suspects board would fill in. Like most targets, focused effort brought results.

He walked around the corner to the intel center. "Kiernan, has SIGINT found anything?"

Kennedy shook his head.

"Nothing yet. I'm investigating the report that she has an RV or trailer inside her warehouses. That way she can move sites every twenty-four hours like Escobar did, but stay close to her business activities. I'm starting with Airstream, looking for dealers that have completed cash transactions in the last six months."

"Do they have RFID tags like the Department of Energy Safe Secure Transport escort vehicles?"

"Good question. We'll check that."

Wolf headed to the gym. Francisca and Lizzy were there, taking turns with the heavy bag.

"How are you feeling, Francisca?" he asked.

"Good, thanks. But I'm going to need a waiver for my next urinalysis," she said, smiling.

They laughed. "Because you took one for the team with your convincing swallow of doped tequila, we're closing in on Eliana Cortes," he said.

Kennedy ran into the gym, his broad smile infectious.

"Airstream doesn't tag at the factory, but the SOCAL distributor does. We have a list of sales for the last two years with buyers' names, addresses, and models."

"Now we're cooking. Get everyone not in the field to the conference room. Team brief in fifteen," Wolf said.

"All right, settle down. K-man has assignments for you. We have a large data set to work before we can begin targeting."

He was explaining the assignments when a tech stuck his head in the door. "Police reports of new gang-on-gang violence are filtering in."

"This is what we hoped for—a precursor to all-out cartel war. Tell the field teams to be on the lookout for convoys of blacked-out Range Rovers. It's likely that Eliana will stay true to form and come out shooting at some point," Wolf said.

Kennedy closed the door. "We need to talk about the RC-12. The attenuation effect caused by the metal roofs of our likely targets means we have to fly lower than normal. I am worried we might spook Eliana."

"That's a problem. Can we deploy ground units? Use the RC-12 to radiate and use ground crews to pick up the signal?"

"Good idea, but we would require a defined target area for it to work. I have another idea. It may be crazy, but I think it will work."

"You know me," he said with a smile. "I like crazy."

"Since we can't improve the sensitivity of the equipment, we must improve the sensitivity of the operator. We should bring in that kid who helped us at the inquest, that Private Wayne dude. He displayed exceptional capability during your training mission."

"Where is he in the training pipeline?" he asked.

Kennedy laughed. "Graduated. After our interaction, he went all Rambo. Signed up for jump and Ranger school. He just completed jump school and is awaiting orders for the Ranger Indoctrination Program."

"Good. Let's pull him before he gets orders. We can use our influence to get him reinserted when the time comes. What's his clearance level?"

"Should be interim TS, at least. I'll get an upgrade expedited.

"We can have him on-site in two or three days," Kennedy said.

"Anything come of the Newton matter?"

"Yes. DEA observed him with a known member of the Latin Kings. We pulled his cellphone logs, and his call pattern connects the dots."

Wolf clenched his fists. He didn't want to believe he was an informant. "It'll wait till we get back to address this," he said.

"Roger that. On the good news side, we have identified twenty-one large Airstreams acquired with cash."

He nodded. "We fly as soon as the kid gets here."

He stocked the refrigerators with beer, wine, and waters, and bought pizza for a casual Happy Hour to let the team know his appreciation for their hard work. The teams were putting in long days before longer and more dangerous days ahead. The Shadow Tier concept was working.

Late in the evening, Wolf and Kennedy sat in the intel center, their glasses glowing from the Glenallachie single malt Scotch whiskey twenty-seven years in a sherry cask, perfect for sipping and deep thought.

He stared into his glass. "Most people never see the grind that happens before the action. They hear stories about how good or bad an operation goes, but not the months of intel collection, processing, and decision-making."

"Listen to you, professor," he chuckled. "It's true. Most of intel is not glamorous and makes no one famous unless it's in the negative. All the hard work and the positive outcomes thrown into the secure vault of history. All you can hope for is to play your own role in keeping the free world safe."

"You sound like a true believer, brother," Wolf said. Kennedy raised his glass. "I am that."

They finished their musings and drinks. Tomorrow we tighten the noose, Wolf thought as he headed for his room. He was taking off his shirt, thinking about getting some much-needed sleep, when his cellphone rang.

"Sir—we need you in the intel center right now. LAPD is in

pursuit of vehicles matching our target," the out-of-breath analyst said.

He threw his shirt back on and sprinted upstairs. "Situation?"

"Listen," Kennedy said. The receiver set to monitor all police frequencies cracked to life.

"Two-Adam-Fifteen. Shots fired, in pursuit south on Chavez of a black-in-color Range Rover, license plate Sam, Paul, Zero, Six, Nine, Zero, Six."

"Patch that into comm three," he said as he grabbed a handset radio and K-man grabbed binoculars.

They ran out the back to a ladder used for maintenance where they climbed to the roof. A new report quickened their pace.

Wolf walked to the peak and pointed north. "They're on I-10 now. They'll come right by us." he said and indicating the highway.

Kennedy raised the high-power binoculars to his eyes and said, "Bet you a quarter they don't make it. CHP will cut them off at I-10 and 101 interchange."

They could hear the intermittent gunfire, hear sirens, and see police emergency lights. CHP was blocking I-10 south at the Los Angeles River.

He smiled. "You are going to owe me."

Just then, two sets of headlights blazed their way. They listened as the rate of gunfire surged, then watched as the Range Rover blocked the highway. Someone bailed out of the front passenger seat and blasted away with a heavy machine gun, its throaty roar echoing off nearby structures. Police car headlights swerved left and right, and the squeal of brakes pierced the night.

"Those are some brave cops down there," Wolf said.

Out of nowhere came a Jet Ranger helicopter that landed fast on an unpaved heavy-equipment yard on the far side of the highway.

Kennedy pointed while still looking through binoculars. "Check that out—can you make out the chem light? And there she goes," Kennedy said as the helo lifted off. He fished in his pocket for a quarter.

"Keep your money. We have work to do. If that was Eliana and she goes into hiding, she might crawl into a rabbit hole. We may never find her."

84

Eliana Cortes safe house, Los Angeles, California

Her icy calm hid her thoughts as she marshaled her resources for a counterattack. She had talked with Alejandro about her latest near miss and convinced him to let her go all out against the

Tijuana Cartel.

This has to be the last push, she thought. If I fix this, El Chapo will take care of Alejandro.

She decided that her shock troops for the looming battles would be the Sinaloa Cowboys. Their reputation came from utter disregard for human life, and they had only fierce, selfless loyalty to the cartel. They preferred death over getting caught.

She stood in the middle of her warehouse in Redlands looking at the group of hard men before her. She attributed their nervousness to the fact that the masked Tomador stood next to her. She told her crew the Tomador de Almas had a mission to complete that would pave the way to victory.

She said to the warehouse foreman, "Give the Cowboys the heavy pack. Semtex, grenades, AKs, and RPKs."

"Boss, that package is going to Venezuela—Fuerzas Bolivarian- as de Liberación.".

Eliana drew her Sig and pointed it at the man. "Not anymore... this is war! I will own L.A."

Her lieutenants and their crews had rushed to hire every gang with a grudge to mobilize against the Tijuana Cartel. From teens to jobless older men, they scooped up anyone they could get their hands on. They would overwhelm the Tijuana Cartel with their numbers and firepower. Eliana's focus was a blitzkrieg of violence that would leave her enemies nothing.

She took the Tomador aside, handing him a green canvas messenger bag.

"Here is fifty thousand dollars. I want you to kill Benjamin and Javier Félix." She didn't know Javier was already dead. "You have five days."

The Tomador nodded. "It will be done," and walked out.

She spent the evening pushing her teams forward. She relished the body count. It provided immediate feedback on progress. She understood the body count was retail and lower-level crew, but it underscored to others that doing business with the Tijuana Cartel was unhealthy, denied them money, and hurt their reputation.

Eliana permitted herself to smile as the reports came in. There had been a successful ambush of the South Side Street Villains 13 gang, a Tijuana Cartel-aligned crew on the south side of Olympic Park. The snipers had taken elevated positions on Los Angeles Memorial Coliseum that provided them clear vision into the Lot 4 parking area. Their suppressed large bore sniper rifles disabled the vehicles with a few easy engine and tire shots, and then they supported the assault team with over watch protection.

The gangsters never knew what hit them. The assaulters killed all but one member of the Villains, letting him live to spread the story.

Eliana looked out of her trailer and saw men unloading wounded from the back of a pickup. Stupid men! she thought. What are they thinking? She stormed over to the leader and got in his face. "Are you stupid? We can't help them here! Take a van and get them to clinics in East L.A."

As they drove off, she motioned to her security detail lead. She leaned forward and whispered, "Wait until they are in East L.A., then get rid of them all. I will not tolerate stupidity anymore."

Walking back to her trailer, she rubbed her belly, talking to the baby bump. "Be good, my love. I have work to do. Then we can rest."

85

S hadow Tier safe house, Los Angeles, California
The conference room buzzed with the news of the shootout less than a mile from the safe house and Eliana's perilous escape by helicopter once again.

"Last night's event presents us two questions," Wolf said. "One: Why do we not have Stingers to use against her helicopter?"

The room erupted in laughter.

"I'm only half kidding," Wolf said. "Was Eliana attacked during movement, or did she come out shooting? It's important that we understand her mindset. Two: Does she stick to her plan now using her current hides, or drop out and disappear? Her profile suggests she will stick to her plan, and we will too. It's how I want to move forward for now, at least."

As the team filed out, Kennedy lingered.

"We have landline information for each of the remaining sites, just in case we can't find her cellphone."

"I doubt we will find phones on the other end of the lines, but I could be wrong. Have them tested, we'll might get lucky."

It was nearing lunch when SIGINT radioed.

"Outlaw Six, Big Eyes. Be advised we have located a promising suspect warehouse. Detecting a dozen cellphone signatures and encrypted radio transmissions," the leader said.

"Copy, Big Eyes. Get a surveillance over there now. Is any- one nearby?" he asked.

"Four is three miles away." There was a pause. "A yellow box truck and a black sedan are leaving the site, headed west on Redlands Boulevard."

"Break-break. Outlaw Four, Six, can you intercept?" he asked.

The team leader responded. "Roger that."

A shift change replaced the SIGINT watch for the rest of the afternoon. Four continued updates as they followed the truck and cars to a warehouse next to Long Beach International Airport. They peeled off after seeing the convoy enter an industrial building.

Team Six closed the distance on foot, finding a position seventy-five yards away with a view of an enormous open roller door. The angle of the sun made it impossible to see its interior. They took pictures of Cowboys and tattooed gang members leaving with heavy duffel bags.

One skinny kid dropped a kit bag and an RPG rocket fell out. He scooped it up and headed out. Within ninety minutes, the cars had left the site, and the truck headed back to Redlands.

The surveillance team reported in and Wolf had Danner radio all teams the safeguard code Romeo-Tango-Foxtrot. Ready To Fight.

Each team stopped to kit up. Body armor on, Glocks and M4s checked, stun and frag grenades ready.

Wolf had just declared weapons hot to all squads. Across greater L.A., Shadow Tier personnel prepared for the war to come. In a matter of hours, Los Angeles would once again explode in violence between the Cortes and Tijuana cartels.

Wolf smiled. Cartel versus cartel. Gang versus gang. They would hurt each other for weeks on end, all without a clue that the U.S. government had initiated it. But his smile gave way to the sad reality that innocents might die.

He had created region wide violence he couldn't control.

86

P ublic street, Los Angeles, California
The violence grew fast and flared in intensity. The blood-shed continued to flourish throughout the night. Well before midnight, TV news outlets used on-screen graphics with blood-red terms such as War Zone, Battleground LA, and Hornet's Nest.

The press called the mayor out for lack of leadership, and the governor mentioned calling out the National Guard.

Wolf recalled his teams as the fight progressed. Between the cartels and police, now was not the time to get caught up in a cross-fire. They took turns spotting activity from the roof and monitoring radio transmissions. The rest of the team worked the intel collected by the SIGINT and surveillance teams.

A tech and two members took a black Suburban and drove to the Redlands site to change batteries in the leave-behind technical package. The uninterrupted intel increased their confidence that Eliana had moved to and operated from that location.

The lead informed Wolf they were on the way back when they encountered the war first-hand. They had turned down a street the Tijuana Cartel had decided was perfect for an ambush.

"Contact left!" the tech called out.

He punched the accelerator to bust out of the kill zone, but a dump truck rolled forward from an alley and blocked the way. As they backed up, a garbage truck blocked the opposite end of the street. In a move that would save them from the initial onslaught, he backed onto the sidewalk parallel to the cars and the team dismounted to return fire.

The Shadow Tier operators reacted with automatic violence of action in their rehearsed immediate-action drill. They met the spray-and-pray shooting of the cartel soldiers with deadly efficient aimed fire of their own. When the tech turned and fired on the dump truck, the driver panicked and drove off, opening an escape route. The crew piled back into the Suburban and raced out of the kill zone.

Back at the safe house, the hot wash was quick and to the point. Danner congratulated the tech for his quick thinking. Wolf wrote himself a note to promote the guy and gave the guys the rest of the night off. They left the ops center, exchanging back slaps and high-fives.

More than a few members requested to roll with the next battery swap. Wolf found Kennedy asleep in a chair in the intel cell. He was talking with SIGINT when K-man roused from his nap.

"What? What do you need?" he asked.

"Two things. How many sites do we have left? And do we need to fly them tomorrow?"

"Four sites, and yes. We now have more altitude to work with, so it's a low probability of detection option."

"I've never heard LPD used that way, but it makes sense."

"I just made it up, and it does. I said so."

"Someone needs more sleep," Wolf said with a smile. "As do I. I'll be in my hooch if anyone needs me."

John Danner said, "Aye-aye, skipper," and waved. "Nighty-night."

∽

"WOLF, wake up, man. You need to see this," Kennedy said, shaking Wolf's from a deep sleep. "Put some clothes on. We're going to the roof."

L.A. at dawn most days was already its normal, tension-filled cacophony of cars, horns, and truck air brakes. This morning was different. The governor had made good on his threat. The Army National Guard's 143rd Military Police Battalion was in the streets to quell violence, and a week-long state of emergency was declared. Surface street traffic had dried up as MP checkpoints were at every major intersection, driving more traffic than ever onto already full freeways choked with commuters.

The media outrage was instantaneous and complete, vacillating between screaming for more protection from gang violence and outrage at the temporary means deployed to provide it.

Wolf cursed under his breath. The politicians at the state house did not have a clue about risk. You-cannot-fire-unless-fired- upon Rule of Engagement endangered the Guard MPs, and their deploy-ment had minimal effect on the cartels' destruction of each other. A lack of cartel ammunition would more likely slow the tempo of attacks better than any influence by the National Guard.

Over breakfast, Kennedy relayed negative findings from two of the three remaining sites. He outlined the plan to monitor the last site while getting the RC-12 in the air.

Kennedy said, "The kid is out at March AFB preparing the col-lection systems and tuning the RFID receiver. I expect he will do his job and listen in on us. He is going to fix Eliana's location and get us the data we need to make the call."

"Okay. I'll have Francisca ready to make the call," Wolf said.

Wolf put the surveillance teams to work correlating information on the police call-outs and reports of cartels fighting. His plan was to keep the fight going at a low level until it slowed down. They needed Eliana distracted, but not so much that she would focus on the fight over a new business opportunity.

The acetate-covered battle map hung on the wall. They used grease pencils to mark the cartel activity with a black "C" for Cortes and a red "T" for Tijuana to highlight the ebb and flow of the engagements. Wolf pointed to several of the larger fights, noting the advantage had gone to the Cortes element.

He grunted. "I find this interesting. While it seems she is winning, it is just the opposite. I see advantage Tijuana."

He was about to comment when Portes came in sporting a wicked-looking grin.

"Gentlemen, Benjamin Félix is dead. Sniper took him out in Mexico. The Tijuana police are reporting three shots from an eight hundred and forty meters. They found the brass."

Wolf and Kennedy said in unison, "The Tomador."

"The taker?" Portes said.

"Yeah, Tomador de Almas, the taker of souls. In a private moment with Joaquin Zapana, he told me their top assassin's name and he would kill us all," Wolf said.

"The same assassin that killed Colonel Gates and wounded Elle and Maya." K-man said.

Wolf called for Danner to join them and said, "We need to insert counter-sniper teams into our plan. If the Cortes top assassin is in the AO, we are all targets."

Danner smiled. "We already have two of the best. I'll ask them for some names. We have equipment for three more snipers."

"Good," he said. "The Tomador is high on my target list. We need him dead."

S hadow Tier comms room, Los Angeles, California
The sky was blue orange as the sun came over Sugarloaf Mountain. The Beechcraft RC-12X Guardrail aircraft gained altitude on the crisp morning air.

The pilot flew east into the sun over the mountain, then north toward Bear Lake. Kennedy imagined the Kid onboard testing his collection system one more time before they headed to the Redlands site.

"Hometown, Kestrel 2—r-radio check?" Wayne radioed.

Kennedy shook his head. "Kestrel 2, Hometown. Lima Charlie, Hotel Mike?" Loud and clear, how me?

"Copy Hometown, Lima Charlie. Kestrel 2, starting pattern." he turned to Wolf sitting next to him in the intel center.

"Guardrail is on station. Thirty minutes per site is the plan unless he finds an emitter he wants to focus on."

Wolf moved to a chair in front of the battle map. Where are you, Eliana? he wondered.

After forty minutes of listening to radio transmissions between Kennedy and the Kid, He left to make a sandwich and grab a Diet

Coke. He sat in the ops center eating and gaming the next moves for his teams when K-man stuck his head in the doorway.

"He's back," he said. Wolf looked at his watch, surprised it had only been three hours since the RC-12 had taken off. He followed Kennedy back to the intel cell for the debrief.

"Kid, glad you're here. What did you find for us?"

"Sir, a lot of emitters, all matching those the ground team identified. We believe she's at the Redlands site," he said.

"What makes you think that?"

"A concentration of cell emitters suggests a centralized command-and-control element. She is emulating her brother's mode of operation at the ranch."

"How do you know Alejandro's operation?"

"I gave him a six-hundred-page reading assignment last night."

"Okay, I'm impressed. Now that we know she is here, how do we get her cellphone number? I want to make a call versus an assault."

"Sir, cellphone surveillance is an area of personal interest to me. Gone is the advantage you had back in the old days when folks used landlines. The advantage now sits with the bad guys. Cell-phone and courier personnel for high-threat situations is the new way to do business."

"Kid, I appreciate you think I'm a dinosaur," Wolf said, "but you will find I am all about innovation. I'm as much tech as shooter. And, like I said, I want to make a call. Otherwise, I'd bomb her site to the ground."

"Sir, that's outstanding. Big Army isn't as nimble and open to change," he said.

"This is true. So, what is this new idea you have?"

"I want to put a cell tower in a van. If we can get her phone to connect, we can collect the IMSI and ESN." The looks on their faces prompted him to continue. "The international mobile subscriber number and electronic serial number."

Wolf thought for a second. "Once you have those, we can get the phone number and intercept her calls?"

Kennedy and the Kid were smiling ear to ear.

Wolf shouted down the hallway. "Danner! We need a van."

It took twenty-four hours to source all the gear and find a truck with suspension upgrades to handle the weight. L.A. water and power department stickers, traffic cones, and ladders to conceal the antennae finished the exterior. The Kid set up the equipment. Its first test would be on the safe house itself.

The collection team started the experiment five miles out, working their way in until the Shadow Tier team's cellphones and their IMSIs and ESNs appeared on the Apple PowerBook screen.

On the wall of the conference room, there was a hand-drawn map of the area around the safe house with concentric rings at equal spacing.

"What am I looking at?" Wolf said.

"Sensitivity map. How close we have to be to get a cellphone to respond," the kid said.

"That's good considering you just threw the system together."

Kennedy said, "We will need to be close. The cell tower she's hitting now is just down the block."

The headquarters team had packed the living room, and lively chatter stopped when Wolf appeared.

"Capn's on the bridge!" Danner called out. The others laughed and then settled down.

"Good to see morale is high," he said. "Let me introduce the kid, real last name Wayne, an Army type. He's a recent addition about to make a very positive impact on our operation. He's created a proto-type system to spoof a cell tower that will collect Eliana's and her crew's cellphone details."

The team filled the room with words of encouragement and admiration. The kid was red-faced, beaming with pride.

"So, tomorrow is the day, and the Redlands site is the primary target. We're coordinating a power outage with some follow-up fluctua-tions to give us cover for being in the area. SIGINT has their assign-ment. LeBlanc will put together a counter-sniper section and coordinate infiltration. We will divide the rest of you up to surveil the other sites in case she moves tonight. But before then, we need to amplify the cartel-on-cartel fight. Tonight, Danner and I will lead teams against locations of opportunity we have identified throughout the city. Danner's crew will hit Tijuana Cartel. My team will hit Cortes."

He looked around the room and saw only eager faces. "Meet back here at 2200 ready to gear up and get after it."

The assault teams rolled out just before midnight. Wolf was up first, hitting two locations run-and-gun style. he wasn't sure if the Cortes gunmen couldn't handle the tempo of activities or were just stupid, but the Shadow Tier squad eliminated the Cortes crew without opposition and drove away unscathed.

"Hawk Three, you're up," he radioed. Danner's response was crystal clear, if delayed by the encryption module. He adjusted his plate holder and checked and rechecked his M4 during the drive back to the safe house. Danner's situation report made up for the discomfort of waiting.

"Outlaw Six, Hawk Three. We are Condition One, I say again Condition One. Out." Danner said. The code phrase meant all teams were successful and returning to base.

The smile grew, Wolf nodding to himself. Sleep deprivation is a powerful tool, he thought. Let's see how well Eliana operates on little to no sleep. Pregnant.

Just as he suspected, the morning TV news reported on the outages and subsequent surges. An L.A. Water and Power spokesperson told viewers what they suspected had happened and that repair crews were on the way to investigate. The SIGINT team moved into position next to a pole on the southwest corner of the property. A borrowed bucket truck added to their cover.

The counter-sniper unit inserted in Pacific Bell repairmen uniforms. The six-story office building LeBlanc had selected provided a clear line of sight to the sniper position from a textbook-perfect overlook position.

Wolf, Kennedy, and Danner monitored the operation from the safe house ops center. The Kid sat in the back of the van and operated the system. A wave of data started flowing in as cellphones in the immediate area responded to the cell tower interrogation.

Twenty-six. Too many.

He turned down the antenna gain and focused the beam into the warehouse. He got nine responses.

"This may take a few hours," he radioed.

The system logs recorded a call starting at 1100. The Kid entered the IMSI and ESN into the system. The intercept was low grade, but understandable. He started a compact Nagra SNST tape recorder borrowed from the Secret Service.

"Sister, you are well?" a male said.

A female said, "Yes, Benjamin and Javier are on permanent vacation."

"Be careful. Ramon will want to renegotiate." she asked, "Eduardo and Luis?"

"They're elsewhere, but they will be located in due time. It's Ramon who wants a unique arrangement. His brother also supports this. Luis has already communicated that losing their brothers Benjamin and Javier is regrettable, but the cost of doing business."

"Okay, I will prepare" she said before the call dropped.

The kid stopped the tape, letting his cell tower prototype continue to collect. He keyed the mic. "Outlaw Six, Big Ears. Condition One. I say again, Condition One. Out here."

Wolf held back his excitement. He would have traded stacks of gold bars for the miniature recorder and its playback unit that now sat in front of the team. He, Kennedy, Danner, and Francisca leaned forward.

It had taken close to three hours to get the van back to the safe house area, before making the switch to a sedan that drove the kid to the brake shop. Kid rewound the tape and looked around the room, smug and smiling. Wolf gave him a "now is a good time" look, so he pushed the playback button.

Eliana's voice was unmistakable. His gaze turned icy cold, and adrenalin surged through his veins as he clenched his fists. The call dropped, and the kid stopped the recorder. He gave a three-by-five card to Kennedy, who handed it to Wolf.

Wolf's expression was hard, his voice devoid of emotion. "We know where she is, and now we have her cell number," he said, staring at the card.

Kennedy said, "Francisca, are you ready?" "Yes, let's get this witch!"

They scheduled the call for mid-afternoon.

A tech programmed a cellphone to emulate one that would seem to be calling from Cali, Colombia. The plan was for her to pretend she was Christina Santa Cruz London, an old friend of the Cortes family. Their fathers had been business partners until Romulo's death. They had spent time together as children in Mexico and Colombia, but life ensued, and Christina hadn't been in touch for years.

Kennedy and Wolf stood nearby while she made the call from a room at the back of the safe house, facing the highway. They cracked a window open to let in the sounds of the city. She dialed the number and Eliana picked up on the third ring.

"Brother?" she said.

Francisca said, "No, it is Christina Santa Cruz London. I am calling for my father."

She paused in surprise. "How do I know it is you?"

"Remember when you and Alejandro came to visit our ranch with your father?" she said.

"Yes."

"My father and yours met with El Padrino. We rode horses and Alejandro fell off, dislocating his shoulder. Remember?"

Eliana laughed with obvious relief. She could rely on so little these days. It was good to hear from an old friend.

"Christina! Are you okay? I heard about the kidnapping," she said. She could relate to that feeling of powerlessness.

"Being kidnapped was harder mentally than physically, but I am recovering, thank you. My father asked me to reach out and tell you he hopes to do business with you. He tried working with the Félix brothers, but they are not reliable." She cleared her throat. "Some of them are no longer taking any calls. We also see you taking back Los Angeles."

"Yes, I am pushing the cockroaches out of Los Angeles. Soon I will control from Monterey to the border," Eliana said.

"Impressive, mi amiga! We want you to be our partner to help grow our business in America. I will be in Malibu tomorrow. Shall I call you then?"

"I will look forward to it."

Francisca disconnected. Wolf smiled. "Where did you get that background?"

"It's an old El Padrino vendetta. I interviewed him in prison. He wants us to kill the Cortes for Romulo's part in his capture," Francisca said.

88

Eliana safe house, Los Angeles, California

She sat in her trailer, decaf coffee in hand, the other resting on her belly, counting her wins. Six of seven Félix brothers were out of play. Rafael was in prison. Benjamin and Javier were dead. Carlos had disappeared, believed absconded with a trunk of the brothers' drug money. Eduardo and Luis were running legit businesses. It left Ramon, the most dangerous.

What she knew about him was even scary to a woman who inspired fear in others. He was yet another crazy, violence-prone son of a drug lord. And her source had told her that Ramon was one hundred percent focused on finding and killing her.

Her phone rang. It was Christina.

"Meet me for dinner tonight at 25040 Pacific Coast Highway? I rent a home in Malibu for occasional use. You'll love the view of the ocean. We can discuss business and get caught up. I will be in bandages, so don't be alarmed," she said. "I surrendered to vanity and had my face done. Bit. I'll never be as beautiful as you, Eliana ..."

Eliana laughed. "Do you have security?" she asked.

"Yes, gracias. But no one cares about me here. Seven p.m.? I will look forward to seeing you then."

She didn't believe in luck. Hard work created opportunity. The praise she had received on her last update call to El Chapo confirmed her trajectory to a seat at his table. She did what Alejandro had not—could not. The exciting thought of replacing her domineering brother in the cartel hierarchy triggered a feeling of electricity through her body.

He would question a partnership at first. But its origination with Eliana would keep El Chapo safe from the remnants of the Medellin Cartel. The Cali Cartel was the new cocaine power, and she would bring them to him.

"Who is thinking now, brother?" She laughed. My fortunes have changed for the good.

89

B ody & Soul Cosmetic, Malibu, California

Wolf thought Francisca's plan was brilliant if complex. The clinic sat along the Pacific Coast Highway north of Malibu Bluffs.

It combined a skin-and-body-care spa with a reputation for discreet professional cosmetic upgrades among the stars of the film and TV industry. Oprah had profiled them on her show for their work with disfigured African children.

Briefed in on the objectives, the wealthy owner of the businesses, a former Air Force flight surgeon, was eager to help.

Francisca, posing as Christina London Santa Cruz, was on the schedule for a one p.m. appointment. Intake for thirty minutes, then the surgery, which would take two hours. They would hold her for observation for an additional hour in recovery.

Listed as reconstructive surgery to the right side of the face and forearm, the surgery would appear to take care of wounds received during the kidnapping. In an unorthodox change to procedure, this patient was bringing her own anesthesiologist and operating-room nurse. The doctor had worked with her before, and the staff, while miffed at the idea, enjoyed a cash bonus payment for their silence.

The procedure went as planned, and the record showed Ms. London tolerated the anesthesia well enough to leave after thirty minutes of observation. She was wheel-chaired to her a waiting car. Per standard operating procedure, they asked her to check in before five p.m. with a wellness check.

The team drove befitting a post-surgery passenger. The traffic was heavy, but no one paid attention. Bandaged patients were a common sight near the clinic.

Francisca and the team played the role until the front door of the safe house closed behind them. She stopped at an entryway mirror and laughed.

"I look like the Mummy's bride."

An hour later, Kennedy relayed Eliana had called the clinic to confirm that Ms. London's surgery had gone well. He theorized it was an additional security check before the meeting. She had confided to the clinic that she was going to visit Ms. London later and wanted to check to see if that was okay with her doc out of concern for her friend.

She had also made a call to Cali, Colombia, which the kid intercepted and re-routed to a busy signal. Kennedy had called an AT&T contact, and they programmed Eliana's number to call the kid's system anytime she dialed the Colombia country code.

Kennedy had a Spanish speaker with a native Colombian accent on standby if she called again, but Eliana would be familiar with routine telephone outages in Colombia and not getting through wasn't unusual.

AT THE APPOINTED TIME, the Malibu gate intercom squawked with a bodyguard's guttural croak. "Ms. Cortes."

Danner pressed the button to let them in, instructing them over the intercom to park under the portico. LeBlanc and Clinton met the car as Cali Cartel soldiers, their Uzis visible. LeBlanc stood on the left side of the car while Clinton stood by the door. Eliana's security lead scanned the area before letting her out. As Eliana approached the house, the front door opened, and Lizzy welcomed her inside.

"Ms. Cortes, please follow me. She is bandaged but awake and sitting up," Lizzy said.

They walked through the expansive living room, past the floor-to-ceiling windows to the master suite. Lizzy opened the door and let her in, blocking her security lead. Eliana signaled him to wait outside. Lizzy closed the door, standing next to Eliana's bodyguard. A professional, he stepped away, seeming to scan the area while giving himself room to maneuver.

She walked to the bedside and froze. He wondered if she had just realized her life was about to change. She turned to see his pistol in the high ready position as he walked out of the bathroom, and her face contorted in recognition.

"Lance Wolf," she hissed.

"Hello, Eliana. I've been looking forward to seeing you again."

90

Malibu & Goldstone Deep Space Communications Complex, Barstow, California

"Put your hands flat on the dresser," he ordered. "Don't bother calling out for your security. He isn't available."

He came from behind to take her pistol and reached around her to check for other weapons when his palm detected the contour of her belly.

"You're pregnant." he said.

"You think I don't know?"

He found her hidden dagger and was careful as he withdrew it before laying it on the bed. He finished frisking her legs, taking a holster and a Walther PPK pistol from her right ankle. Then he guided her to a chair. She sat, her left hand resting on her belly.

There she was, in the flesh, sitting across from him. After all this time—all the mayhem and murder and sleepless nights—he'd finally got her. And now he couldn't remember feeling this conflicted about anything in his life.

"The baby, it's yours and Joaquin's?" he asked.

Eliana's eyes burned with hate. "Yes. My child will have no father because of you."

"No, it's because of your brother. It was one of his gunmen who threw the grenade that killed Joaquin. He didn't suffer."

"You expect me to believe you?"

"I'm happy to give you the autopsy report. The grenade wounded one of the Mexican Army guys, too."

Eliana's face betrayed her thought.

"No, Eliana, I'm not going to kill you. Although, I admit to thinking about it every day since El Gran Pez. I would have used this." he held up Jose Torres's pistol.

"Jose's engraved pistol, I remember him waving it around in a meeting. Melodramatic, yes?" she asked.

"True. But instead of killing you and your baby, you will help me get Alejandro."

Eliana paused, "No. Turn me into law enforcement. You have no right to hold me."

"But I'm not holding you." he let that sink in for a three count. "You are being held by the Agency. Meet Targeting Officer Castro," he said, picking a name at random.

Francisca, rose from the bed, and stood beside her, squeezing her shoulder for effect.

"Eliana, you are not in the U.S. legally. You are not here at all, and neither are we," Francisca said. "We can do whatever we want with you, and that includes turning you over to Ramon Félix."

Wolf waited until her intensity drained. Her face grew softer as she accepted her new situation.

"Help me get Alejandro and we will put you in witness protection. A new identity and a safe place to raise your baby," he said.

She looked into Wolf's eyes, searching for the truth.

He turned to Francisca and said, "Give us a minute." She nodded and left the room. He pulled over a wingback chair and sat staring at Eliana.

"You know, we are more alike than not. We both have people we're fighting for, we both hate your brother, and we both want each other dead."

They sat sizing each other up.

"True enough." She pulled back the sleeve on her shirt, looking down at the pensar scar. "I hate my brother—with everything in my heart. But he is family. I would kill him, but I wouldn't give him up to you ..." She snorted. "... of all people."

He stared at the brand on her arm. He thought he could still turn her. "What if I help you take his place?" He stared into Eliana's eyes. "What if I—"

"Put me back in," Eliana interrupted. "Leave me and my child in peace and I will give you what your president wants...El Chapo."

Dumbfounded, he stared at her for a moment before uttering the one word capable of changing the entire trajectory of the drug war.

"Deal."

He wasn't sure what he was feeling, but he thought it was the right moment. He handed her a gold dog tag he'd taken from Joaquin. Her eyes brightened as she recognized it. She clutched it until her knuckles turned white.

The rest of the evening included Chinese takeout, body disposal, and site clean ups. It also gave Wolf time to call Kennedy and Danner to let them know what Eliana had said about El Chapo. It was 0100 before they headed out. The drive to the Malibu Sports Complex took five minutes. There were two contractor-piloted Black Hawks waiting for them. Crew chiefs were motioning them to board.

After a ninety-minute flight, the team landed at the Goldstone Deep Space Communications Complex, also known as Mars. It was a field of giant radio dishes whose primary mission was to communicate with NASA's interplanetary spacecraft.

One of three sites in the NASA Deep Space Network, its data network also served as a covert means of communications. The growing Agency activity went unnoticed by the NASA staff as the program continued to expand.

Wolf had briefed Kennedy and Danner on the site and its use at the start of Operation Thor's Hammer. Now the rest of the Shadow Tier team understood its importance. The building had one focus—extraordinary rendition.

Built to house and interrogate terrorists, the facility was also the perfect location for their operation. The facility's multilayer physical security was a technical advantage. With Eliana in a secure room and checked out by a doctor, Wolf worked the team through the checklist for the ultimate phase.

In the intel cell, there were several laptops and unmarked devices interconnected and surrounding Eliana's cellphone.

Wolf's inner tech nerd came alive at the sight. "What are you guys doing?"

A tech looked up and smiled.

"We call it digital forensics. We're getting her cell to give us its secrets. You'll have the number you want in another ten minutes. She has some foreign encryption we're working through."

He paced, waiting. Mission completion hinged on it. Then, without looking up, a tech raised his hand. In it, a piece of paper with a phone number. It started with the country code 52—for Mexico.

He grabbed Kennedy. They jumped into a Humvee and raced back toward Fort Irwin's main post before the cellphone registered a signal.

He continued to drive south until the phone registered three bars of signal power, then slid the Humvee to a stop. He took a deep breath, exhaled, and dialed the number. Someone answered on the second ring.

"Eliana, are you okay?" Alejandro said.

Wolf and Kennedy smiled. Yes, they thought. Everything is indeed okay.

91

G oldstone Deep Space Communications Complex, Barstow, California

"Alejandro, this is Lance Wolf, a voice from your past. Perhaps you don't remember me...I have Eliana."

Alejandro's howl reminded him of African lions fighting, then he laughed a high-pitched screech.

"Do you think I will ransom that worthless cow? You can keep my stupid sister! I sent her to Los Angeles so she wouldn't screw up my operations here."

Wolf held his hand over the mic and whispered. "I don't believe him." Kennedy nodded. He leaned back in his seat. "Okay, no problem. My next call is to El Chapo to tell him how you abandoned his rising star. I'll tell him how you are letting all of Eliana's hard work go back to the Félix brothers."

"He won't believe you."

"Are you betting your pathetic life on that?" he taunted as he hung up.

Kennedy smirked. "You are one evil and tricky son of a gun."

"Thank you, K-man. That's the nicest thing you've said to me in a while. A call to El Chapo is an option, in fact. But it comes with additional risk if he sends a team."

"True, but we can handle it. Our site gives us every potential advantage we can think of," he said.

"Yeah. I will lead the witness on our location. Not outright, but enough that even Alejandro or his Cuban intel officer should be able to figure it out."

Kennedy's eyes widened. "You aren't planning to disclose the location of a Special Access Program? That would put you in permanent residence at Leavenworth."

"No. I'm just going for a drive into Barstow, maybe Victorville. To your point, we need Alejandro to come to us. That way, we control the battle space."

Eliana's cellphone rang and Wolf put the call on the speaker. "Where are you?" the voice said in Spanish.

He looked at Kennedy and shrugged.

"This is Lance Wolf. I'm in Los Angeles."

A sensational wave of Spanish curse words directed at he and his mother followed.

"You should be ten times dead for the pain you have caused. What is it you want?" the voice said, switching to English.

He took a guess and said, "Ah—El Chapo, a pleasure to talk with you. It's very simple. I have Eliana Cortes. I want Alejandro."

"That's it? Alejandro?"

He sensed surprise in the response. "Yes. I would have killed them both. But unlike you, I don't kill pregnant women."

El Chapo laughed. "That's why America will not win. You're so weak, you can't take my kind of war."

"You are right. The politicians can't, but you know I can. I can disrupt your business for another two to five years. Somewhere during that time, your Colombian business partners will leave you or replace you. Or you can give Alejandro to me, and I will consider turning my attention elsewhere."

He sighed.

"I had great hopes for my cousin. He, Joaquin, and Martin helped us grow almost faster than we could handle, but he is pathetic. Likes to think he's smart and cunning. That means he is slow to adjust to new threats, like you. He has trouble deciding, unlike his sister. Call this number with the location, date, and time of the exchange." He read off a number with a 972-country code—Israel.

"You mean handoff. There is no exchange."

"I want Eliana or there is no deal," El Chapo said before he disconnected. Wolf's face creased in a subtle grin.

Everything was going to plan.

The team assembled in the chow hall, the only space large enough to hold both the shooters and support elements. The air was tense with the excitement for the last phase of the operation. Wolf stood in front of the map projection with Kennedy and Danner at his side.

"I want to start by letting you know how proud I am of you all. Your selfless focus on the mission inspires me. Tomorrow, we close on our ultimate target—the most dangerous phase of the operation yet. Our number-one task is to control the battle space. You have your tasking, so let's get it done."

Wolf dialed the 972 number, leaving the time and directions to the exchange site. The counter-sniper teams headed for their hides. Kennedy left for Edwards Air Force Base to meet the RC-12 crew and prep for the mission.

The location he had chosen was at the mouth of a wash, its banks providing additional cover from long-range fire. He paced as he thought, the variables eating at his confidence. It was a sure thing Alejandro would send the Tomador to kill Wolf. Ramon was the wild-card. Eliana had mentioned that Ramon was looking for her to avenge the deaths of his brothers.

AT 1940, the following day, Wolf and the team headed for the site. The sunlight faded and long shadows cast pockets of darkness across the terrain. The Shadow Tier vehicles stopped in a protective semi-circle, the armored black SUVs vanishing into the growing darkness. Wolf's team was in full combat gear with body armor, M4s, and night vision goggles. Wolf's radio came to life. It was Kennedy.

"Outlaw Actual, Romeo One. Two vehicles inbound from the south taking different routes. Tango One, bearing 303. Stopped at 400 meters. Tango Two, bearing 403. Inbound and closing. Copy?"

"Roger that," Wolf said before switching to the ops center frequency. "Nail Head, Outlaw Actual. Anything on GSR?"

"Negative, Actual. Getting some interference from the wind gusts."

The Agency had installed ground-surveillance radar at the site, and Wolf was seeing its limitations firsthand. On the positive side, the wind, steady at ten miles per hour, gusting to twelve, would make long-range shots difficult.

At a thousand yards, a .308-caliber sniper rifle shooting into a full-value ten-mile-per-hour crosswind required a point of aim more than eight feet aside of the target. Add a bullet drop of more than thirty-two feet, a real test for a sniper.

A teammate brought Eliana from a Shadow Tier vehicle and she stood in the harsh headlight glare, a gag tied across her mouth. If a gunfight broke out, the actual danger would be right in front of them. The moon was rising when the high beams from approaching vehicles illuminated the site.

Two Ford Excursions rolled to a stop side by side and facing Wolf's team. The doors opened and a bound-and-gagged Alejandro was dragged in front of the headlights.

He looked frightened and had blood trails running down his face. Another bound man stood next to him. An armed guy walked forward, disheveled but proud.

Wolf recognized him. But first things first.

92

Exchange site, Barstow, California

"Alejandro Cortes and Martin Amaro," Wolf said. "The dream team, welcome to the United States."

Shadow Tier operators rushed forward, M4s up and ready. They grabbed the two, hustling them into the darkness outside of the cones of light projected by the vehicles.

Then the third person, his hands extended from his sides, walked across the wash in backlit silhouette until stopping and extending his hand.

"Lance Bear Wolf. My man. Still in one piece, I see."

"Tim Nichols? Bro, what in the heck are you doing here?" he said. Nichols was rolled up in a sketchy off-the-books operation gone bad, not unlike some of Wolf's expeditionary adventures, and took his discharge in a plea deal that saved his retirement.

He had put his considerable training to work by forming his own security firm, but their operational circles hadn't crossed in many years.

"I haven't seen you since our teams worked that joint operation with the DEA and Colombian Army."

The men shook hands and hugged.

"I separated right after that mess," Nichols said, nodding with a knowing grin. "They were going to drop me two ranks for chasing that cocaine shipment across the border, so I got out and started my company. Got a couple of very sweet contracts in Mexico and Colombia. But we can catch up later. Cortez Limited has contracted me to make sure this exchange goes as planned."

"You're working for Senator Cortez? You know he's the cousin of the Sinaloa Cartel Cortes, right?" Wolf said.

Tim shook his head. "No. I just thought it was a common Hispanic name."

Wolf held his hand to his earpiece. "Are you expecting anyone else? My guy says we have two separate elements inbound that aren't ours."

"No, I'm not," Nichols said. His hands went to his AK-103. "Looks like we got us a fight."

"Are your Fords armored?"

He nodded. "But just battle rifle. Who's inbound?" Tim said.

"My guess is it's the Tijuana Cartel. We need to let our over watch know we're working together. Where is your guy?"

"Behind me." He said and tilted his head back toward the way he came in.

"Mine is on the dish tower."

Nichols moved the Excursions in front of the Suburban's, creating another layer of defense. His men dismounted and took defensive positions behind the trucks. Wolf adjusted his team to provide additional defense on their flanks.

"Romeo One, Outlaw Actual, status Blues Brothers?" Wolf said.

Kennedy said, "Outlaw Actual, one-five mikes. Your inbound vehicles stopped two-zero-zero meters bearing one six eight."

Just then someone shouted over the radio, "RPG!"

An operator pulled Eliana down and away as a rocket exploded on the far bank of the wash, another flashing by overhead. The second Ford exploded into the air, landing on its side and pinning one of Nichols's men underneath the burning wreck- age. He screamed for several minutes as spilled gasoline from the ruptured fuel tank flooded out and immolated him.

Well-placed heavy machine gun fire followed. Its report identified it as a 12.7mm DShK, the powerful Russian equivalent to the American M2 .50-cal.

Two shots from their left in rapid succession and another RPG skipped across the desert, exploding on a rock pile. LeBlanc's SR-25 sniper rifle barked twice in rapid succession.

"Outlaw Actual, two tangos down," he radioed.

Nichols yelled, "Contact left!" He turned and unloaded an AK-103 magazine on full auto.

Wolf and two teammates concentrated their fire on the six men trying to outflank them. As one gunman rose to throw a grenade, his chest caved inward from the impact of LeBlanc's sniper round that exited the gunman's spine. The grenade dropped at his feet and exploded, wounding two more, and then it was quiet.

They're reloading, Wolf thought. He executed a combat reload, placing his used magazine in his drop pouch and he heard a faint pop, then another. He sprinted towards the SUV, which provided shelter for the handcuffed Alejandro, Eliana, and Martin. The exchange would have to wait.

With an enormous boom, the trail Suburban disappeared in a massive explosion. Seconds later, another Ford SUV launched into the air before coming down onto its roof from the concussive blast. Its tires burned and adding black plumes of acrid smoke to the air.

"Mortar! Take cover!" Wolf yelled, angry that the sound had not registered.

"Romeo One—we need the Blues right now." "Inbound now," Kennedy said. "Two mikes."

"Outlaw Actual to all Outlaws—TOPHAT-TOPHAT, I say again, TOPHAT." Wolf shouted into the command net using the pre-defined code for fall back to the Agency facility.

For their safety, the three prisoners had their handcuffs removed. A Shadow Tier operator sat in the front passenger seat with an Army-issue 9mm M9 pistol pointed at the second row.

"Nothing cute from you three," he said, pointing the weapon.

As the Suburban sped away, it dove into a crater blown away by a mortar round. The front end thrown into the air as it climbed out of the hole. A rear door flew open, and a person jumped out and dashed into the gloom.

"All Outlaws keep going. I've got the squirter," Wolf radioed. "Romeo One, Outlaw Actual—stop that mortar!"

"Outlaw Actual, Romeo One. Roger that. Blues Brothers lined up and starting their run."

Wolf found Nichols and three team members taking cover against the bank of the wash. The light from burning vehicles flickered across the sandy, pockmarked scene.

"Tim, where are your guys? Do you have rear security?" "It's me and my sniper, and yes, two of your guys."

The DShK started firing again, first at the areas around the SUVs, then dirt fell from the bank top as it shifted. The sound of a heavy machine gun hid the bark of a mortar that sent 82mm rounds screaming toward the team.

"Keep your heads down! Air support is rolling in!" Wolf shouted, rising to one knee.

Nichols grabbed Wolf's arm. "Where are you going?" "After a squirter. I'll be right back."

Wolf was running past the burning hulks when the mortar round landed. He flew into the air and his world went black. His ears were ringing, and his vision was blurry when he came to. He didn't think he'd been out for more than a few seconds because he was kneeling, trying to focus, when he took two rounds to his back plate that slammed him face down into the dirt.

His attacker rolled him over and shot twice, hitting him in the chest plate at point-blank range, the gunpowder residue burning his chin. The armor plates had stopped the rounds, but Wolf found it hard to breathe.

His shadowy attacker hovered over him, and he acted on instinct. He exploded into action, grabbing the pistol and pulling it down and to the side, then getting one hand on his attacker's collar. He wrapped his legs around the enemy's neck and body, squeezing with every-thing he had.

He delivered two quick elbow strikes to the man's face and slid his thumb down the man's nose to his socket, pressing hard. The man screamed as his left eye popped out.

The gunman let go of the pistol as he raced to protect his eye. he picked up the discarded handgun and shot the man once in the shoulder. His attacker tried a weak punch with his right, but he pinned the arm on the dirt.

Flashes of light from the Air Force A-10 strafing run and the secondary explosions illuminated the area, revealing Amaro's dirty and bloody face.

"Well, hello, Martin. Not sure we can save your sight, but if you want to save your life, now is the time to talk," Wolf said.

"Why aren't you dead?" he croaked, gasping in agony.

Fireballs erupted in the darkness as the second A-10 made its run. The chain gun roared in anger, shredding the mortar team and the machine gun nest. Tracer illumination brought the grisly scene to life —sand, blood, and his eyeball dangling on his cheek.

Wolf pressed the pistol into Martin's neck. "If you want to live, tell me about the children in the drug factory compound."

"Please, please," he squealed. "It was all Joaquin and Jose Torres, I swear. He was the mastermind—"

He fired off a round next to his ear, erupting a chunk of the California desert. Martin screamed, the pain of his shattered eardrum overwhelming him. He went limp and sobbed.

"Okay, okay! It was my idea," he confessed. "Joaquin thought it was grotesque, but a Saudi construction company paid Alejandro a large sum to do some test runs and I kept it going. They were just product, the kids. Like the dope. It was business, it wasn't personal."

"It was damned personal to all those innocent children," he growled. He shoved the pistol barrel into Martin's mouth, chipping teeth, and paused two seconds for Martin to understand what was coming next. Then Wolf pulled the trigger once, splattering Martin's brain and skull fragments across the dark ground.

He heard a helicopter inbound and tried his radio, but it was non-op, so he pulled two yellow chem lights he cracked and shook. They lit up, and he clipped them to his vest. Across the way, he saw someone place infrared marker strobes to mark an evac LZ.

As he reached the line of wrecked vehicles, he yelled, "Outlaw Actual is coming in!"

Nichols met Wolf and remarked about the fresh blood on his neck and face. "Wow, you look like shit. Your squirter not coming with us?"

He looked him in the face. "No," was all he said. Turning to Danner, Wolf asked, "What's the count?"

Just then, Nichols flew backward, the sound of the large-caliber rifle shot following a split-second behind. Someone yelled, "Sniper!"

He dropped and Danner fell beside him.

Low crawling to his wounded friend, he pulled him back to the cover of a wrecked vehicle. He assessed and found a fist-size hole in Nichols's back. He grabbed Wolf's hand and squeezed it hard.

"Kill them all, brother," he whispered.

Wolf peered around the wreckage and heard two shots from two directions, then he heard an A-10 changing engine power to roll in for a gun run. The growl of the chain gun ended the event.

The helicopter whipped up the sand as it landed between strobing IR markers. The guys loaded four wounded on the bird.

"My comms are out. What's our status?" he asked.

"Two KIA, Clark and Carrier. Four WIA from our team. Nichols's crew have five KIA," Danner said.

"Bad guys?" he asked.

"Whole lot of body parts with Los Antrax tattoos, and a couple dead but identifiable eastern European types working the mortar. I suppose they're El Chapo's guys, right?" Danner said.

"Most likely," Wolf replied, his voice trailing off. El Chapo wanted them all dead? Why? he asked himself. Because he's crazy. It was the only answer he could think of. "I want the site processed for sensitive info and DNA."

Wolf had Clark's and Carrier's bodies placed in the bed of a

Humvee. He rode back to base with them. Clark's brother, a former Navy SEAL, worked for the Agency and he wanted to be the one to make that notification himself.

Back at the safe house compound, Hughes and the team surgeon met Wolf in bloody scrubs.

"Eliana was wounded, but she and the baby are okay," Army Major Lee Alan said. "She had a grazing bullet wound to her arm and abdomen, but neither were deep. There doesn't seem to have been excess shock to the fetus. She'll recover just fine."

Wolf's eyes widened. "What happened?"

"She took a round from your guy to her right arm when Amaro jumped ship," Hughes said.

"Where is Alejandro?"

"He's still out. The security guys put him to sleep when he tried to bail."

"Call me when he wakes up. I want some alone time with Alejandro," Wolf said.

93

Goldstone Deep Space Communications Complex, Barstow, California

The team gawked as he entered the Ops center Day Room. Bloody body armor scarred with hits he looked like Death had just walked in to borrow his phone. Nobody said a word and his look directed them to focus on their work.

He dialed a number from memory on an STE secure phone and waited for the encryption to handshake and authenticate.

Wolf gave Davidson an initial after-action report. The colonel paused on Martin Amaro's admission of responsibility for the sex trafficking of children.

"We need Alejandro and Amaro alive for interrogation," he said.

"Yes, sir. Alejandro and Eliana are safe and secure here. Amaro was killed in the firefight. We lost two, four wounded, and some civilian contractors working for California Senator Cortez won't be home for Thanksgiving this year. Did you know a former master sergeant named Tim Nichols?"

Davidson was silent for a moment. "Not personally."

"He was a good man. A good soldier."

"I'm sorry for your loss, Lance." There was silence on the call. Wolf didn't know what else to say.

"We'll talk tomorrow. Excellent job," Davidson said, ending the call.

Wolf walked into the chow hall, wanting to get the hot wash underway and then get a literal hot wash in a steamy shower. Kennedy joined him in the passageway and when they entered, it erupted in applause. Kennedy looked at him, getting a nod. The difference was striking. Covered in dried blood and gunpowder residue, Wolf looked a warrior. Kennedy looked dapper in his Patagonia hiker's kit.

"All right, all right, take your seats," he said. "Before we get started, let's have a moment of silence for the teammates who gave their lives that we could be here now."

He thanked the team in some detail for its extraordinary victory. He ordered them to take the rest of the day to get fed, take showers, and go to bed early. The full after-action would occur the next afternoon.

Wolf called Parker to check on her recovery, and to assure her he was still in one piece.

The Los Antrax firefight site exploitation had gone on all night under the lights. It uncovered one intact cellphone that the forensics team was working on. The other notable find was the late Ramon Félix himself, along with a sniper rifle nearby that they suspected had killed Nichols. The A-10s had taken care of Félix on that last strafing run.

Hughes knocked on Wolf's door frame. "He's awake."

Wolf's body flushed with adrenalin at the thought of being in the same room as Alejandro Cortes. He checked his pistol, secure in its holster at his hip. He took a deep breath to settle himself, then headed to sick bay.

Alejandro strained against his manacles as he entered the room. The hate was clear in his eyes. Wolf stood silent, knowing he was the alpha in this room.

Hughes exited, whispering, "I left some meds for you." he nodded and stepped up to the hospital bed.

"I've been looking forward to this day. It seems impossible to me you're here."

"Yes, I am sure you have. It is too bad that you were not man enough to come to me at the ranch. It took El Chapo to make it happen. You are a loser. You didn't save your parents or people you loved. All those dead bodies. Everywhere you are, people die."

Wolf's hand caressed his Randall knife. The thought of taking the man's life rushed before him. Steady. He smiled and changed gears.

"Let's talk about El Chapo. He sold you out. I caused so much trouble that he saw the exchange as an opportunity to get rid of you."

He opened a folder, laying photo after photo in Alejandro's lap. The remains of the Los Antrax team in graphic closeups of their destroyed bodies, tattoos cleaned up for identification.

"Los Antrax followed your delivery team and used heavy weapons against us. You are very lucky we planned for that."

Alejandro's head dipped. He sighed with acceptance of his limited options. "I want witness protection. You must protect me."

"No, I don't. I'm not here, and you're not in the custody of U.S. law enforcement," Wolf said and smiled. "You are a ghost."

Alejandro slumped, turning away and stared at the wall. Wolf could see his realization of defeat, but he expected the game to start. Little bits of information for a new life of relative freedom. There was no doubt he was going into hard core detention for life. Then Alejandro raised his head and there was a whisper of a smile. "I can get you a dirty California senator."

94

Goldstone Deep Space Communications Complex, Barstow, California

Wolf, Kennedy, and Danner sat by their secure phone in the SCIF. Colonel Davidson had scheduled Shadow Tier for a detailed mission brief for the chain of command up through the Secretary of Defense and Agency Director of Operations. Davidson had also passed back down the chain the message from SOCOM, the Joint Chiefs, and the president himself, complimenting the team on a job well done. Wolf made sure everyone got the message.

He smiled. Based on information provided by Eliana they were now requesting permission to enter Mexico to capture El Chapo. Wolf told the team the SOCOM Commander, JSMC Commander, and Joint Chiefs had approved the mission, but the final approval would come from the SECDEF.

When the phone line lit up at the scheduled time, he pushed the speaker button. Davidson spoke first, letting everyone know the call's participants. After more congratulations on the capture operation, the SECDEF asked for a mission brief.

"Sir, all the stakeholders on this call will have received the full briefing deck outlining assets and specific times, so I won't belabor them here. The BLUF: We have credible intel El Chapo will fly into a remote ranch west of Santa Isabel tomorrow night to meet with his West Coast distributors. We know the meeting location and time. We expect resistance from up to a dozen armed men. After we secure the HVI, we will exfil and return to base. Questions, comments, concerns?" Wolf said.

The SECDEF asked about time on target, comms, and extraction contingency plans. They answered his questions in detail.

"Shadow Tier," the SECDEF said, "excellent work. But I want JSMC personnel to lead the assault. Wolf, your team will support this time. The mission is a go. Good hunting Shadow Tier."

Colonel Davidson thanked everyone for their time and the call disconnected.

Wolf followed Kennedy into his admin office outside the intel center and perched on the edge of the desk. Kennedy laughed as he sat in his office chair and leaned back, feet on the desk and hands clasped behind his head. "I figure I should take this sitting down. What's on your mind?"

"I've been talking to Eliana about more than the location of El Chapo."

Wolf explained his plan and how it hinged on Eliana's commitment to saving herself and her baby. Ninety minutes prior to the El Chapo mission launch, Kennedy would take Eliana to the Victorville airport. She would board a cartel plane for Los Mochis, where she would take Alejandro's place in the cartel.

"I'm also betting she can use an 'exchange gone wrong' story to cover her escape and return," Wolf said.

"Why the sudden change? You wanted to end the Cortes bloodline, and you hate the idea of putting someone in place while the drugs still flow."

"The sweet taste of revenge turned bitter. I had a lot of time to think during my house arrest. You, Maya, and Elle reminded me who I am. I still want to win, but not at any cost. This crew is smarter and more agile than a drug cartel. With Eliana's help, we will win together."

Danner stuck his head in. "The SMU is inbound. It's only six of them but they were already in Arizona for training.

"What about the alert squadron?" Kennedy said.

"They're deployed, and the backup is on standby for tasking." Danner said.

"Ironic, isn't it? This is why they need Shadow Tier," Wolf said.

Wolf met the team leader and his five assaulters in the Ops center. They provided a quick target overview and then drove to the mockup of the objective. Built from Eliana's memory of the place, the ranch house sat inside a windowless sixty-thousand-square-foot building disguised as an aircraft maintenance hangar, complete with 1970s aircraft and a first-generation Bell UH-1 Huey slick outside.

They stopped at the sand table, discussing the route of flight in, assault and support teams' positions, and contingency plans. Over the next four hours, the SMU guys demonstrated their professionalism. They flowed through the mockup like water, with catlike awareness, and communicating without talking but for clear and jackpot when they had captured the high-value role player. Wolf nodded his approval.

"We leave for the airfield in ninety minutes. Now it's our turn to make sure El Chapo has a bad day. Capture or kill, either works."

95

Sonora, Mexico

The package of three 160th SOAR MH-60M Black Hawks were five minutes inside Mexico and fifteen minutes from the target when the Sierra One assault helicopter avionics panel lit up red, the warning speaker squawking a hydraulics failure alert. The grinding noise from a failing left engine signaled what the pilots knew Get the wounded bird on the ground before catastrophe strikes.

In the lead bird, Wolf heard the calm pilot describing his plan while his helicopter lost power. He switched to the command net and launched a precautionary medevac helicopter to their location. He switched back to the intercom and directed the team on Sierra Three to support the assaulters and pick up as many men as possible. He keyed the intercom.

"Sierra One is down. Echo is assisting. We are now the assault element. Our bird will be our blocking force until Echo arrives. You know your jobs. Let's get it done."

The MQ-1 Predator on over watch identified nine tangos. Wolf called an audible two minutes out, placing LeBlanc and another sniper in the open helicopter door to take out sentries while Shadow

Tier assaulters fast roped out the other. It would be a slower but a safer way to execute their forced entry.

As the helicopter settled and the ropes deployed, he was first on the ground, running past those killed by LeBlanc's suppressed SR-25 shots. He held at the corner of the sliding doors to the pool, waiting for the team to stack on him. He heard the racking of AKs and shouted orders. The element of surprise was gone.

They dropped the fast ropes and surged to house. He felt the squeeze on his shoulder and entered. All the lights were on as Wolf and the team cleared through the poolside living room and entered the kitchen.

Along the way, he noticed still-smoldering cigars and half-empty beer bottles, one of which lay sideways, knocked over in the rush to escape. Before leaving the kitchen, he yelled, "Clear!"

He was standing at the start of the hallway to the bedrooms when he saw movement at a door.

"Contact right!" he yelled. Then he fired three rounds into the wall beside the doorframe and a dead gunman slumped into a pile in the doorway.

Outside, more AK and M4 gunfights started and were quick to end.

Wolf moved down the hallway with purpose, stopping at the open doorway. He stepped over the dead body and into the room, clearing from the left to center. The men behind him secured the rest of the room.

"Clear," he yelled.

As they stacked for the next room entry, he heard Sierra Three inbound as the helicopter settled to a hover. Less than ten seconds later, it was off. Wolf and his guys cleared another bedroom. Danner yelled, "Clear!" They moved on to the door to the master bedroom. Instead of a squeeze indicating the stack was ready, he got a radio call.

"Bravo 1, Alpha 1, mind if we get in on the action?" the SMU team leader said. Wolf waved them by. They entered to immediate AK fire dominated by the sounds of the SMU team's suppressed M4s.

"Dry hole, I say again, dry hole," the leader radioed. "Break-break, Bravo 1. You need to see this."

Wolf joined him next to a walk-in closet.

"I sent two men down to check it out," he said, looking down a hatch leading to a tunnel. The tunnel was about four feet wide and five-and-a-half feet tall.

The muffled sounds of suppressed shots filled the quiet.

"Alpha 1, Otter 2, we're in a barn a hundred meters east your location. Two tango KIAs and HVI breakout in two gray SUVs."

Wolf radioed the Predator operators. "Razor, Razor—Bravo 1."

HVI, two SUVs headed south, do you have them?" "Roger, headed south," was the response.

Wolf raced out of the house. "Sierra 2, Bravo 1, LZ Hawk," he radioed as he ran for the landing zone. He ran onboard as Sierra Two touched down then surged back airborne. While he directed the pilot to overtake the vehicles racing south, LeBlanc clipped Wolf into his safety harness. He switched to the JSMC command net and heard the team leader's request.

"Havoc Actual, Alpha 1—Hotel Victor India breakout. Bravo 1 is in position to intercept. Do we have execute authority?"

The pilot of Sierra 2 raced in front of the convoy and slewed sideways to a hover across the road, slowing the vehicles down and giving Wolf and LeBlanc a clear shot at the lead vehicle before its occupants could bring their weapons to bear. He watched as the SUV slid to a stop and the doors opened. He unloaded a full magazine into the engine and driver's seat before yelling, "Reloading!" LeBlanc killed two gunmen on the left side of the vehicle.

Two gunmen on the right raised AKs at the helicopter, but Wolf put them down as the pilot worked to evade. He saw a third gunman armed with only a pistol run back to the second SUV.

El Chapo? He repositioned to take a shot.

"Alpha 1, Havoc Actual. Negative. You are not cleared to intercept. Say again, negative."

Wolf gritted his teeth and struggled with the order. Desire to avenge his parents, Gates, and Cárdenas coursed through veins like fire.

He leaned out of the helicopter, held only by his safety strap, and screamed a war cry. Wolf pulled back on the harness and slumped into the canvas seat.

"Roger that, Havoc Actual Copy," Wolf replied. He pulled his goggles from his face and shook his head.

Sierra Two surged back into the darkness and returned to the ranch.

The SMU leader came up and offered his hand. "Outstanding work. We couldn't have done it better."

"We stopped the SUVs and had a shot," Wolf said.

The team leader scowled. "The bastard got lucky today, but he'll slip up. We'll get him."

He nodded. Using his radio, he keyed his mic. "Outlaw Actual to all Sierra Tango teams, take everything you can for intel analysis and fall back to LZ Hawk. We depart in fifteen."

Wolf finished the headcount and was the last to board. As they flew north, he stared into the sky.

Next time, El Chapo.

96

Goldstone Deep Space Communications Complex, Barstow, California

The SMU leader praised the Shadow Tier teams during the hot wash, for adapting to the Murphy's Law section of the mission plan. It brought a round of laughs. The chow hall quieted when he held up a hand.

"I was 19th Group Colorado National Guard before selection. Shadow Tier makes me proud of my time as a weekend warrior. I'm very particular who we roll with because discretion has kept us alive. This mission made me a believer. I'd launch with you all anywhere, anytime."

The nods and looks of confident resolve underscored the pride and sense of accomplishment felt throughout the room, and everyone erupted into applause. Wolf back-slapped Kennedy.

"We made a team, brother."

Wolf, Kennedy, and Danner met in the SCIF. "Eliana?" Wolf asked.

"I have confirmation she's back at the ranch," Kennedy said.

"Got word this morning Rafael Félix is dead. Blown up in the car sent to pick him up from his prison release. Eliana has taken complete control. And El Chapo is still unaccounted for."

"When do the marshals pick up Alejandro?" he asked.

"At 2030 tonight," Danner said. "We need to get him to Bicycle Lake airfield."

"I called the Agency station chief in Peru and provided him details of the child-trafficking channel there. Amaro had known accomplices, and the pipeline is shut down," Kennedy said.

"There are still four open items. One, Senator Cortez. Two, the underground target. Three, the Tomador. And four, the Saudi construction company connection to sex trafficking of children," Kennedy said, writing on the white board.

"I bet there is an investigative reporter at the L.A. Times who would appreciate some intel on Senator Cortez. Check with Francisca. She has connections all over Los Angeles," Wolf said.

Kennedy laughed. "I like it."

"Any thoughts on that underground facility?" Danner asked.

"No, and its what bothers me."

"We know how you feel about the Tomador."

"Yeah, but he's a team target now," Wolf said.

"Shadow Tier has proven itself. The SECDEF didn't believe we could pull off a Tier 1 mission." Danner said.

"Unlikely one mission will change his mind, but we've started strong," Wolf said. "We need to build a selection process to create depth. By the end of the year, I want to support two simultaneous operations, and grow to four. You don't need an Agency briefing to see serious threats are proliferating."

Kennedy ticked off on his fingers. "Weapons of mass destruction. High-tech weapons proliferation. The Russians and Chinese harvesting of intellectual property and natural resources. Random scientists cooking up deadly bacteria in basement bio labs. It's just some of the stuff keeping me up."

Wolf crossed his arms and sighed. "You know I hate the drug cartels, but it's the rapid growth of Middle Eastern extremists keeping me up at night. There is something to this Saudi connection we uncovered. It could bring UBL into the mix."

Danner nodded. "We're going to be busy."

"Yeah, this isn't one and done. I'm sure we'll get other taskings now. It's a dangerous future we face."

Wolf walked to a window and stared at the dusky mountains submerging into the blue distance.

"We need to be ready."

THE END.

ACKNOWLEDGMENTS

Jerry Jenkins's Inner Circle encouraged, mentored, and offered honest feedback during my growth from storyteller to author.

My mother Joyce Stratton's provided the love, inspiration, and example that led me to who I am today.

Thanks to Chris Minchin, friend and former Army Intelligence specialist, who helped guide me during the development of this book, and for his selfless dedication to U.S. Special Forces in Afghanistan and Iraq.

Matt Kinard, Shel McClury, and Brad Seal reviewed chapters and the completed manuscript. Their feedback was invaluable. "Kat," for allowing me to base a character off her amazing career in counterintelligence.

Mark Elliot, for his reading of my writing and honest feedback about where I can improve, and to the writing community and all those who teach me something new every day.

Special thanks to the following authors kind enough to response to my questions and thoughts. If I missed you, know I value your support and encouragement.

Jeff Wilson, for guidance and support as I began my journey and that continues today. Jack Carr for pushing me to make my manuscript the best I can.

Eric Bishop, for his #NeverQuit attitude, beta reading, and feedback. Jack Stewart for your inspiration and writing feedback.

David Darling, a master of crime novels, for his permitting me to read his ARCs, hear his feedback, and learn from him in another of my favorite genres.

Brad Taylor and Mark Greaney, for all I learn about character development and scene setting when I read and listen to their terrific books.

Thank you to Rocky Mountain Fiction Writers, International Thriller Writers, and Career Authors for the various programs they offer that make us better.

CLEARED FOR RELEASE

ABOUT THE AUTHOR

Steve Stratton started his U.S. Army career at the White House Communications Agency, where his work took him around the world. The jump to the U.S. Secret Service was an easy transition, but after several years, Steve left for the commercial sector and joined the National Guard and its 20th Special Forces Group.

He was awarded his Green Beret in 1986. From the 1980s through 2000 he deployed with 20th SFGA on counter-drug and training missions in the SOUTHCOM region. His contractor work included supporting CENTCOM, SOCOM, and DIA. Today he is retired from developing cyber security products for the DOD and Intelligence Community.

When not writing or consulting, Steve splits his time between Aurora, Colorado and his cabin in the Tarryall mountain range west of Denver, You can find him on his dirt bike, mountain bike, or hiking, fishing and hunting.

Printed in Great Britain
by Amazon

59606150R00238